Praise for William Nicholson

'A subtle and addictive writer who deserves to be a household name ... with his remarkable eye for detail and for the weaknesses of human nature' *Observer*

'I absolutely adored *All The Hopeful Lovers*, gobbling it up in one (quite long) sitting ... full-blooded brilliance within: a series of interlinked love affairs over a period of seven days' Wendy Holden, *Daily Mail*

'An absolute winner ... amazingly perceptive, very moving, wholly absorbing. I was totally wrapped up in every person's daily anxieties and minded hugely about what happened to them. What a huge treat is waiting for those who have not yet read it!' Juliet Nicolson

'In territory normally covered by women writers it is fascinating to see the adultery-go-round from a male point of view. It's not so very different and Nicholson draws both genders with equal insight and sympathy' *The Times*

'Like a mature chick-lit, this novel is packed with people at different life stages ... Read it for a male perspective on attraction' *Psychologies*

'So incredibly accurate and true. Utterly captures the sense of quiet desperation of ordinary lives, the huge emotional vulnerability of having children and the ways in which life turns on a sixpence' Kate Mosse

William Nicholson grew up in Sussex and was educated at Downside School and Christ's College, Cambridge. His plays for television include *Shadowlands* and *Life Story*, both of which won the BAFTA Best Television Drama award of their year. His first play, an adaptation of *Shadowlands* for stage, was Evening Standard's Best Play of 1990. He was co-writer on the film *Gladiator*. *All the Hopeful Lovers* is the brilliant follow-up to his first novel, *The Secret Intensity of Everyday Life*. He is married with three children and lives in Sussex. Visit his website at www.williamnicholson.co.uk.

ALL THE HOPEFUL LOVERS

William Nicholson

Quercus

First published in Great Britain in 2010 by Quercus
This paperback edition first published in 2011 by

Quercus
21 Bloomsbury Square
London
WC1A 2NS

A CIP catalogue record for this book is available
from the British Library

ISBN 978 1 84916 390 3

10 9 8 7 6 5 4

Typeset by Ellipsis Books Limited, Glasgow
Printed and bound in Great Britain by Clays Ltd, St Ives plc

The story takes place over seven days
in December 2008

'Don't you find,' says Belinda, widening her blue eyes at Laura and wrinkling her pretty little nose, 'even though you're over fifty and married and da-de-da, don't you sometimes feel this overwhelming urge to, oh, you know – do it with someone else?'

Laura laughs and shakes her head, not disagreeing.

'Doesn't everyone?' she says.

They're sharing an early lunch, sitting at the end table of the restaurant called the Real Eating Company, by the glass doors onto the terrace, which is deserted on this cold December day. The nearest other diners are three tables away, but even so Laura keeps her voice down, hoping Belinda too will lower her voice.

'It's not like I'm dead yet,' says Belinda. 'I'm not so bad for my age.'

'You look fabulous, Belinda.' Laura is happy to offer the expected praise. 'You know you do.'

Impossible to be jealous of Belinda, she's so transparent in all her needs. Yes, she's pretty, with her chipmunk face and her limpid eyes and that bob of silky-soft blonde hair that you want to reach out and stroke. And she's kept her figure, slight as a girl, a boy almost. But with it all there's a generosity, a way of seeming to say, I'm pretty for you, it's my contribution, enjoy me. So when she calls and says she's having a crisis and let's do lunch, using those very words as if she's a New York businesswoman when as far as anyone knows she does nothing at all, Laura finds herself saying yes.

Belinda Redknapp is the least likely of all the school mothers from the old Underhill days to be her friend, but Laura has always had a sneaking admiration for her. In her Donna Karan jeans and her cashmere tops, shamelessly calling out for admiration, naively delighted by compliments, she's like a naked version of all of them: the school mothers who pretend not to care any more, who are too busy and too married and too grown-up to gaze at themselves in mirrors. When Laura's children Jack and Carrie were little Belinda was known as the 'yellow mummy' because of her blonde hair, and more than that, because of the glow of fine grooming that shone about her like a golden aureole. But who's laughing now? There's something courageous, even magnificent, in her refusal to surrender to the march of time.

Belinda's crisis turns out to be the imminent homecoming of her daughter Chloe.

'I adore Chloe,' she says, pouring herself a third glass of Pinot Grigio. 'But she's so like me when I was her age. Prettier really. It makes me feel like an aged crone. I never mind about my wrinkles until Chloe comes home. Then I want to die.'

Chloe is nineteen. Laura thinks of her own daughter Carrie, just seventeen and going through an awkward phase. Whatever you say to her she takes it the wrong way. Tell her she's pretty and she says, 'Just forget it, okay?'

'That's your crisis? Chloe coming home?'

'She has boys climbing all over her, Laura. How's that supposed to make me feel?'

'Happy. Proud.'

But even as she says the words Laura knows they're pomposities. Worse, falsehoods.

'I'm jealous!' cries Belinda. 'I can't help it! I want to be young again!'

Don't we all. But only Belinda says it aloud.

'I swear to you, Laura, I feel no different to when I was Chloe's age. I remember how I'd walk down the street and the men's heads would turn, and I'd feel their eyes on me, like, oh, you know, like I was Julia Roberts.'

'But you wouldn't want to be nineteen again.'

'I would! I would! I *loved* it!' She puts her fingers to her face and pulls at the skin to smooth out the wrinkles. 'Do you think I should get some work done?'

'What does Tom say?'

Tom her husband, a plastic surgeon.

'Oh, Tom. He just says I'm beautiful the way I am.'

'That's sweet of him.'

'It isn't sweet at all. He doesn't want to give up a paid job to do work on me for nothing.'

'Oh, come on, Belinda.'

'Oh, I suppose Tom would do it if I really wanted it. Actually he is very sweet. I wouldn't hurt him for the world.'

'Why should you hurt him?'

'Oh, you know.' She picks up the menu. 'I'm going to have a crème brûlée. Normally I'm careful about what I eat, but right now I feel what the hell.'

She waves to the young waiter, who has a ponytail and a tight waistcoat like a bullfighter. When he comes over she puts one hand on his arm as if to detain him, and gives him the full force of her beautiful eyes.

'Do you think it would be too evil of me to have a crème brûlée?'

'No problem,' says the waiter. 'I'll take these plates if you're finished with them.'

Laura watches with amusement. Pours herself the last of the wine. They're splitting the bill, she deserves her share.

Belinda pulls a face.

'Not a flicker,' she says. 'See what I mean?'

'He's probably gay.'

'Oh yes.' Belinda cheers up. 'I forgot about that.'

'So when does Chloe come home?'

'I'm supposed to meet her train just before five.'

'Supposed to?'

'Well, I will, of course.' She lets out a long sigh. 'What's so unfair is I'm so much better at sex than I was when I was young, and I have so much less of it.'

'Are you sure you want to tell me this?' says Laura. Belinda's a little drunk.

'Isn't it the same for you? Don't you have less sex now than when you were young? I thought it happened to everyone.'

'Yes. I suppose it does.'

'I was always up for it, but to be honest with you I didn't really get much out of it. You know how it was. You did it for them.'

Them. The boys. The men.

'It's different now.' She wrinkles her brow, puzzling over the poor arranging of it all. 'I really like it now. And all I've got is Tom.'

'Is it that bad?'

'No, not really. Tom's so sweet to me I'd never do anything to hurt him.'

'That's the second time you've said that.'

'Oh, God, is it?' She shoots Laura a quick fearful look as if she's been caught in the act. 'It's all Chloe's fault, coming home like this. You know I only say these things. I'd never actually do anything. Somehow it helps to say it. Do you think I'm a terrible slag?'

'No,' says Laura. 'You're not saying anything the rest of us aren't thinking.'

Grateful, Belinda takes Laura's hand in hers across the table. Like a child cadging for love.

'You're wonderful, Laura. Do you know that? And you're so beautiful.'

No higher praise coming from Belinda. But the compliment and the caress both have the same object. Look at me. Listen to me. Love me.

'It's a bugger, this getting older.'

Laura's about to agree, or to let her silence presume assent out of habitual politeness, when she realizes she doesn't share Belinda's regrets. This is a surprise.

'No, actually. No, I don't agree. I like being the age I am better. I don't want to be young again.'

'Really?' Belinda is astonished. 'How extraordinary.'

'I was always so anxious when I was young. I don't think I really enjoyed my youth at all.'

'Really?' says Belinda again, visibly struggling to credit what she hears. 'I wasn't anxious at all, not as far as I remember. Tom was anxious. I remember that.'

Her face creases into a smile.

'The first time Tom stayed the night with me I couldn't get him to believe I wanted it. He was so shy. I had to pretend to be cold. Come over here, Tom. Sit by me and keep me warm.' She laughs out loud at the memory. 'The wonder on his face as he crossed the room. Christ, that must be over twenty-five years ago now. And you know, I knew right away he'd be a good bet.'

Laura thinks about Henry. She could say the same thing. Funny how you just know. Maybe it's a matter of timing.

'How could you tell?' she says.

'God knows. I just knew. I remember thinking, He'll do.' She bursts into laughter. 'Christ, that sounds terrible. Like I'm trying on a cardigan.'

'No. I know what you mean.'

And Laura does know what Belinda means. It's all about the right fit. Hard to describe, but you know it when you see it.

'Tom used to be so funny,' Belinda says. 'He'd say these things in this really straight voice, talking about himself as if he was a clinical case. Like, he'd say, "The patient is not responding." Or, "Failure of motor coordination due to excess nervous stimulus." He was always suffering from excess nervous stimulus. It meant he'd got a hard-on.'

Belinda's crème brûlée arrives. She speaks as she eats, so as not to notice she's eating.

'I used to think I married Tom because it just seemed the obvious thing to do. You know, without actually being in love with him. But when I look back, it was love. Just not that dangerous on-edge sort of love. Just as well, really. You can't be on edge for twenty-four years.'

'No. I suppose not.'

Laura pictures Belinda's husband: a middling sort of

man, soft-faced, eager to please. Bald, of course, as they all seem to be these days.

'But the thing is,' says Belinda, 'soon it'll be too late.'

She's wriggling about in her seat.

'You have got it bad,' says Laura.

'I just can't stop thinking about it. That's all it is, a fantasy in my head. I'd never do anything. But it won't go away.'

Laura realizes that Belinda is wanting to make a kind of confession.

'Is this fantasy about someone in particular?'

'Well ...' Belinda bursts into laughter once more, and then actually blushes. 'There was this boy I had a crush on when I was seventeen. He was so gorgeous, and he liked me, you know? But I was going out with his best friend. Anyway, there was this one evening when I was round at Kenny's place and Dom wasn't there—'

'Hey! I'm lost already. Which is which?'

'Dom was my boyfriend. Kenny was this quiet lean gorgeous boy. Jimmy Kennaway. Everyone called him Kenny. We were just hanging out, talking, waiting for Dom, and then Dom called and said he couldn't make it, his car needed fixing. Dom was the one with the car. So Kenny said, Let's go and look at the sunset. That's all we did. Went out into the back garden and watched the sky. We stood on this little patio and watched the sky, and after a bit I held his hand. Then he turned and looked at me. Then we kissed.'

8

'Jesus, Belinda. I'm getting goose pimples.'

'That was all. We never spoke about it, not ever. Dom and me broke up a few months later, but Kenny was with someone else, and that was it. Except I've often wondered. Maybe Kenny was the one. Except he wasn't, of course.'

'What happened to him?'

'Oh, he's married. He's some kind of lawyer, lives in Wandsworth.' She blushes again. 'Henderson Road.'

'Belinda! Are you stalking him?'

'No. It's only a fantasy. I mean, one kiss. It's ridiculous. Only I have this feeling inside, it churns me up. Did you know all the surveys say women have their best sex in their forties and fifties? It something to do with oestrogen levels. You know the most common age for women to have affairs? Forty-five. That means I'm way overdue. I'm good now, Laura, I'm great, I'm never going to get any better. It's all downhill from here. And Tom – darling Tom – let's just say, Tom is past his peak. But I'd never actually *do* anything …'

She fades away, with a lift of her shoulders. But her eyes go on resting on Laura, waiting for a response. Laura wonders if she's asking for permission, or just for understanding. She thinks of how it's been for her and Henry.

'Things can change,' she says.

'Do you mean Tom could try Viagra?'

'Well, no, I wasn't thinking of that. But why not?'

'I don't know how to raise the subject. Men are sensitive about that sort of thing.'

9

'He'd probably be relieved if you did raise the subject. I expect it bothers him as much as it does you.'

'Yes. Maybe.' Belinda sounds unconvinced. 'He works so hard. He gets so tired. I don't want to make things harder for him. Oh, well. I'm sure I'll survive. I'll ask Chloe to keep the noise down.'

'What noise? Oh, that.'

'Is Henry still working with Aidan Massey?'

'Yes. They have a production company together.'

A wistful gaze from Belinda.

'I wouldn't say no if Aidan Massey wanted a quick poke.'

'From what Henry tells me, Aidan Massey likes them young.'

'Honestly. Men. When are they going to get it? Women get better as they grow older.'

Her eyes fall on the empty ramekin before her.

'Did I really eat a whole crème brûlée? I must be having a breakdown.'

They come out of the restaurant into the winter sunshine of Cliffe High Street.

'I remember when this was a garden shop,' says Laura, looking back into the restaurant.

'Oh, yes,' says Belinda. 'So it was. What was it called?'

'Elphicks.'

'I remember buying Christmas decorations there. Chloe was wearing that little powder-blue coat with the buttons. She must have been about four.'

The memory staggers her.

'She was simply adorable. I was so proud of her.'

'There you are, then,' says Laura. 'Not such a terrible crisis after all.'

'So have you got Jack home yet?'

A little late in the day Belinda has realized that she should show some interest in Laura's children.

'He's been home for ever. The Cambridge terms are so short.'

'How does he like it there?'

'It's fine, as far as I can tell. He has a sweet girlfriend.'

'Not pretty, then?'

'Oh, Belinda. I didn't say that. Hannah's lovely.'

'Not that it matters. Beauty isn't everything. Just as well, given the sneaky way it runs out on you when you're not looking.' She glances at her reflection in the side window of a parked car. 'But the party's not over yet. My clock's still ticking.'

The sound of piped carols drifts out onto the street as shoppers come and go through the glass doors of Woolworth's on the far side. Signs in the windows say BIGGEST EVER SALE.

'Isn't it terrible about Woolworth's?' says Belinda. 'Who'd have ever thought they'd go bust?'

2

Jack strides up the Downs, past the old landfill site, past the beeches with the low curving branches they call the swing trees. This was always the family walk in the days of his childhood. He wants to go back in time, to be a child again, to be anywhere but here, now.

He walks up on the high tussocky sides of the track, above the chalk-slime ruts. From here he can gaze down on the scoops of land, furrowed by sheep trails, empty of all human life, that are for him the shapes of history itself. In such a grand perspective, what does it matter that Hannah, his first love, his only love, has left him?

It's a steep pull up to the summit, and there's a cold wind coming off the sea that makes his eyes water. At least he never came up here with her.

He stops just above the swing trees, and as they always did when walking as a family he seeks out the roofs of their home. At this time of year the bare trees no longer screen the red tile-hung walls. As he looks he thinks he can just make out his mother's car coming down the lane to the house. His mother now drives a Smart car. Jack was appalled when he first saw it.

'What was wrong with the Volvo?'

'It was fifteen years old, Jack. And we can't just go on guzzling petrol any more. We have to think of the planet.'

'So why do we heat our home like a sauna?'

Jack doesn't want his parents to change their lifestyle to save the planet. Half his year may now be spent away at university, but this house remains his primary world. He wants his parents to continue in their comfortable profligate ways, and maintain the family home as it's always been.

Hannah came to stay at raspberry-picking time. They all loved her, of course. Even Carrie. When was that, last July? You have to pick raspberries slowly. Look under the leaves where the dark red ones hang, the sweet ones, the ones that drop off the branch at a touch. The fingers gripping so lightly it's almost not a grip, more a caress, so as not to bruise the fruit. Standing there close together, fingers probing among the leaves, learning a slower, kinder habit of touch. Then she puts one to his lips, pushes it into his mouth.

Then later, in his room in college, she told him it was over. Weeks ago now, right at the start of term, nothing to make a big deal out of any more.

'It's the last thing I want to do,' she said, 'but it's the only honest thing I can do.'

He turns and tramps on up the Downs. His denim jacket is not proof against the cold, which he welcomes. At least he minds the cold. It's the not-minding that's so wearing. The flat summit before him now, and the concrete column of the trig point that he used never to be able to climb alone; always his father had to lift him up. Then one day when he was eight years old he did it all on his own. Beyond, the bare land slopes down to the sea.

On this dull day the sky is the colour of the sea and there's barely a horizon. The sea all sky or the sky all sea. The shrill cries of the gulls from far off over Seaford. Only when they're close do you realize how big they are. And those cruel beaks.

The evening they agreed to part was not as he had feared. All the tension between them melted away, and they were close in a manner they hadn't been able to achieve for weeks. Hannah cried and said she loved him. That was how he knew for sure that it was over.

Then there came some days that his memory has blanked. No appetite, no desire. Alone in his room, wincing, trying to duck the waves of misery. But it passes. Everything passes. What remains is a low-level dullness of spirit. Carrie says, 'Why's Jack always grumpy?'

He walks fast along the broad summit track from Edenfield Hill to Firle Beacon. Below lies all England, laid out in pastoral tranquillity, a land for lovers, a land for families. Up here the wind cuts through clothes and there's a clear sight of the edge of the world and he knows the view is an illusion. Life does not go on in this orderly procession of meadows and woods, villages and farms, not for ever. There comes a time when it swoops up onto bald hills, and there reaches a brutal end.

People jump off cliffs when they can't take any more. Beachy Head not so far away to the east, the famous beauty spot waiting for the day the beauty dies.

Thank Christ I'm over it now, the pain. One day soon I'll be over thinking about how I'm over it.

There's a kind of fascination in it, similar to the close interest people show in their diseases. The ebb and flow of it, the shapes it makes in your life. You can watch it like a movie, you're the hero. In the beginning you get this savage beating and all of you hurts all the time, then just when you know you can't endure any more it stops, as if a switch has been thrown. Then for a short time, sometimes for as long as an hour, you're flooded with an extraordinary sensation of goodness. Not your own goodness: the goodness of things. The loyalty of the world. Gratitude to the ground, that it continues to support you, gratitude to the air that grants you breath. You're overwhelmed by stupid but beautiful thoughts, most of all that life has not ended just because your love has abandoned you. Then like the tick of a thermostat as the temperature rises above the set limit, the stream of warmth ceases, and cold dark returns.

But not for ever. It passes. Everything passes.

Not Hannah's fault. There's some consolation in knowing that. He had become too needy. He knew it, but it wasn't in his power to control it. Unable to believe she could really love him he had found grounds for fear everywhere he looked. When he saw her laughing with friends, he suffered. When he phoned and she didn't pick up, he suffered. Who wants a boyfriend whose default mode is silent reproach? It's no good loving someone too much. It makes you tiresome.

Her pictures long gone from his room, her pictures long deleted from his Facebook page. Only the occasional flash of memory. Sometimes she's flicking her hair out of her eyes, giving him that sideways look. Sometimes she's cross-legged on the floor, laughing, drunk. She got drunk so quickly, so inexpensively. 'One drink and I'm anybody's.'

He starts on the downward track, the long diagonal that clings to the steep side of Firle Beacon. Now the wind ceases, as the land wraps its protective arms round him. Below, the track turns into the valley, runs down to meet the coach road that will take him back into Edenfield.

There where the Downs path meets the rutted old road stands a solitary farm cottage, a square barn beside it, a garden round it, the whole enclosed by a low flint wall. The cottage has been empty ever since the family first came walking this way, which as far as Jack is concerned is all of his life. It has no services, no electricity or mains water or telephone. The garden has been left to run wild. Nettles and brambles grow right up to the front door. Carrie used to call it 'her' house, and talk of how she would buy it and live in it when she was grown up. This unjustified presumption of ownership always annoyed Jack, and he would explain to Carrie all the reasons why her plan was not feasible. The lack of electricity. The loneliness. Carrie said she didn't care and she'd have candles and wood fires, and her friends would visit her there.

The cottage is called America Cottage, because it once belonged to the farm just over the brow of the hill known as America Farm. As far as anyone knows it's still part of the Edenfield Estate, which was sold six years ago to a private equity consortium.

Now comes a small surprise: the cottage is occupied. Smoke rises from its single chimney. A blue car is parked on the rough ground by its garden gate. And there's a man in the garden, smashing things.

Jack makes his way down the descending track, watching the tiny figure gesticulating with jerky arm movements, hearing the sound of breaking crockery. As he comes nearer he makes out the details. The stranger is an old man with a mass of shaggy white hair and a thick white beard. He wears blue-checked cook's trousers and a navy blue Guernsey. He stands legs apart beside a garden table on which are stacked plates, bowls and mugs. One by one he's picking them up and hurling them at the flint garden wall. With each throw he lets out the same loud cry, which is a single repeated word.

'Die!'

Jack's path takes him past the cottage, past the ancient powder-blue Peugeot. The angry old man seems not to see him, nor does he cease in his hurling and smashing. At close quarters his rage is frightening. His face is bright red within its frame of white hair, and his eyes flash with a ferocious hatred.

'Die! Die!'

The smashed pieces of crockery pile up at the foot of the wall among the winter weeds. The destruction goes on. The old man shows stamina and dedication in his fury.

'Die! Die!'

Jack is impressed. He realizes for the first time that beneath his own disillusion and self-reproach there is anger. Better to rage at life than to suffer in silence. But if he were to cry out as the old man cries out, who would he want to die? Not Hannah. Not any of their mutual friends, whose intimacy with Hannah he used to watch with such jealousy and dread. The only possible candidate is himself. He would gladly smash the self that lost him his love. Not a suicidal impulse, he has no wish to die: just to be rid of this help-less needy creature who turns all his efforts at love into self-pity and desperation.

He passes on down the coach road and round the back of the big house. Not many cars parked in front of Edenfield Place, now operating as a hotel. Everyone in the village expects it to go bust because the long boom has ended. The rumour is the buyers spent five million converting the Victorian Gothic monstrosity. They started out asking £200 a night for the rooms. That made the local people laugh.

Turning off the Newhaven road to the lane that leads home, he feels his shoulders hunch and his face assume a wary defensive expression. As he pushes through the side gate and tramps over the gravel to the back door, Jack has the sensation of walking in water. All action has become effortful. For some reason he has never got round to telling his family that he and Hannah have split up, even though it's old news now and he stopped minding weeks ago.

To his irritation he finds his mother in the kitchen.

'Hello, darling. Been out for a walk?'

She looks up from the kitchen table where she's checking train times. Jack puts the kettle on for a cup of coffee.

'I have to go to London,' says his mother. 'Diana just called. She absolutely insists I go up to town right away. I'm meeting her at the Hayward to see this new exhibition.'

Jack is incredulous.

'Do you want to see it?'

'No, not really. But I expect it'll do me good. I'm hopeless about modern art. I really should make more effort.'

'I don't understand why you always give in to Diana,' says Jack. 'She snaps her fingers and you come running.'

'Well, to tell you the truth, I think she may be having some kind of little crisis.'

'About modern art?'

'It was something in her voice. After all, she is my only sister.'

The kettle boils. Jack shuffles about fetching a mug and the jar of Gold Blend.

'There's someone living at America Cottage,' he says.

'Is there? Who?'

'A crazy old man. He was smashing plates.'

'Did you get yourself some lunch, darling? You were still asleep when I went out.'

'I'm not hungry.'

She looks at him with anxious eyes, which only annoys him more. He just wants her to leave him alone. He knows he's behaving badly, staying in his room for hours, doing the chores he can't avoid with a poor grace. But that's just how it is.

'I just had lunch with Belinda Redknapp,' says his mother, pulling on her outdoor coat. She's using her bright voice to show she's not thinking about what's getting Jack down. 'She's in a great state because Chloe's coming home today. She says whenever she sees Chloe she feels old. Belinda really is amazing. She actually told me she was jealous of Chloe's love life.'

'Does Chloe have such a great love life?'

'I don't know about great. Apparently it's plentiful.' She searches round for her handbag. 'If I hurry I should make the two-sixteen.'

Jack takes his mug of instant coffee upstairs to his room. This information about Chloe Redknapp interests him. He remembers meeting her in Lewes at the end of the summer. They stood on School Hill outside Strutt and Parker and chatted for five minutes. All the time she was talking to him she kept her eyes fixed on his and smiled, moving her body slightly from side to side. She was wearing a low-necked shirt and he had to take care not to stare at her amazing tits, though he must have looked a little because he can see them now. They talked about nothing, about half-forgotten friends from Underhill, about university life to come; but it had seemed to him that her soft laughing voice carried beneath its commonplace words a secret message: do you find me desirable? Do you want me? Only flirting, of course. The habitual exercise of power by a pretty girl who knows how to tease. The actual delivery not available to the likes of him.

In matters of the heart, as in everything else, there is a hierarchy. There are those who make the phone call and those who wait to receive it. Jack is a waiter by the phone. He's incapable of making a move until he's sure the move is welcome; which means he's never the one who makes the first move. He has found a language to justify this hesitancy: he calls it respect. But it's only fear.

'You're such a sweet boy,' Hannah said.

But she still left.

Jack drinks his coffee alone in his bedroom and contemplates

Chloe's plentiful love life. Nice to have something to think about other than not thinking about Hannah. Chloe, so blonde, so blue-eyed, so smiling, has opened a window into his imagination and let in a shaft of bright sunlight.

Easy to imagine kissing Chloe. Easy to imagine that soft pliant body pressing against his own. And if she has amassed plentiful boyfriends, why not one more? Somehow the fact of her promiscuity makes him less afraid. This is not a simple matter. It's not some notion that she's 'easy' and so he's in with a chance. It's all to do with his own fragile self-belief. There would be very little shame in making a move on Chloe and getting rejected. He hardly knows her. It would all be casual and superficial. No investment, no risk of loss.

In this way Jack Broad conceives a plan for the Christmas vacation. He will re-make contact with Chloe Redknapp. Beyond that, who knows? At the very least he will gain, for a while, the return of hope.

He looks Chloe up on Facebook and is entranced. Everything about her is laughing, irreverent, bursting with life. There's a picture of her in a bikini taken in the summer in Greece, her body so tanned and gorgeous, her head thrown back – the abandonment of it, the unselfconsciousness, the sheer sexual power leaves Jack giddy with longing.

He could leave a message on her wall, but what's he to say? No, what he needs is a casual encounter, like last time, something that appears spontaneous. Shame that it's winter now and she'll be all covered up.

One step at a time.

When he comes downstairs later he finds his sister Carrie alone in the kitchen.

'Where's Mum?' she says.

'She went to London.'

'That's a bit sudden, isn't it?'

'She's allowed a life, Carrie.'

'So? Did I ever say she wasn't?'

You can't win with Carrie. Which is odd when you consider what a loser she is. Everything about her droops. Presumably she's unhappy about something or other but Jack doesn't know what and doesn't ask. If Carrie wants sympathy she should stop getting at him all the time.

'When's she coming back?'

'No idea.'

'She must have said something.'

'She's gone to some exhibition. That's all I know.'

'Well, I'm not cooking dinner.'

'Nobody asked you.'

'What's your problem, Jack? Why do you have to be such a boring creep all the time?'

Jack says nothing to this. Carrie makes him so angry he doesn't trust himself to speak.

Maybe I should go out into the garden and smash plates.

'Your house has an old man living in it,' he says.

'What are you talking about?'

'Your house on the swing tree walk.'

This has the desired effect.

'My house? But that's my house! No one lives there. What old man?'

'I don't know. I saw him in the garden smashing plates and stuff.'

'Oh, no!'

To Jack's surprise Carrie is genuinely dismayed. Her face crumples.

'That was going to be my retreat,' she says. 'As soon as I've got money of my own I'm going to buy it and do it up.'

'Yes, but only in your imagination.'

'What do you mean, only in my imagination?'

There are the beginnings of tears in her eyes. Her brown hair falls over her squirrel's face. She pushes it away with an impatient gesture.

'I hate him,' she says. 'I hope he dies.'

Now she's actually crying. Mortified, she leaves the kitchen. He hears her running up the stairs to her room.

Jack now realizes he's come down to the kitchen because he's hungry. He forages in the fridge for something to eat and finds a bowl of left-over apple crumble covered in cling film. He takes it up to his room. There, as he eats the chilled crumble, he taps search-words into his laptop. In this way he learns that Exeter University's term ends on Friday, 12 December. Which is today.

So Chloe will be coming home any day now.

3

Belinda checks her watch as she drives back home to Plumpton. Just gone two. The post will have come by now, it gets later every day. Maybe some emails. No phone messages on the answerphone, no one does that any more.

That makes her think of Alex, her son, who she hasn't seen for weeks. He's living his own life in London, a life of which she knows nothing because he tells her nothing. Why should he? And yet this is the same longed-for baby she nearly died giving birth to, the same darling boy she held in her arms and kissed until she was half-drunk with ecstasy.

You want intensity, there it is. Nothing beats a first-born. Oh, Alex. Just ring me, you ungrateful little shit.

She swings the Range Rover into the yard beside the house. It's a tight corner but she's done it a million times. She goes in by the back door, through the boot room to the kitchen. Funny about front doors, no one uses them any more either.

I talked too much at lunch. Laura must think I'm an airhead. Why on earth did I tell her about Kenny?

As always, after she's been talking about herself Belinda feels an afterwash of self-disgust. At the time the words just come pouring out, she can't stop them, all it takes is a smile, a nod, any sign that her listener is sympathetic. Belinda knows her friends laugh at her. They say, 'God, Belinda, you're outrageous! You can't say things like that!' And she does, and they drink it in with sparkling eyes, and she comes home and feels like she wants to be sick.

I'm a party girl, that's God's own truth. I don't do noble solitude.

The mail is all Christmas cards. The coming festivities fill her with panic and dread. Let's not have Christmas this year. A crashing stock market, all those job losses, who's feeling jolly? Give it a miss for once. Cut to January, and let's get on with the long slow plod towards spring.

She turns on the radio and there's Patti Smith belting out 'Because the Night'. She moves about the kitchen half-dancing, mouthing the words, enjoying the feel of her body in motion. No one to see. Why not? Then because she's dancing she has a sudden longing for a cigarette.

Christ I could murder a fag.

She gave up almost ten years ago now; hardest thing I ever did, they should hand out medals. But it screws with your complexion. Tom knows all about that. Smoking reduces the blood flow to the skin, dries it out. Plus all that puckering to inhale gives you mouth wrinkles. Mouth wrinkles!

Chloe smokes. Not much, but you can smell it on her hair. No mouth wrinkles yet but she better watch out.

Did Jackie remember to turn on the radiator in Chloe's room?

Belinda goes up the back stairs to Chloe's room and sure enough it's like an ice-box in there. She turns on the radiator and lingers, looking round. The room hasn't changed much over the years. All those mornings waking Chloe from indignant sleep to get her up in time for school. The daylight throwing a bright beam over the bed where the curtains never did quite meet. The way she slept, as if tossed onto the bed, her limbs all over the place. Her perfect skin.

Always grumpy in the mornings.

'Are you awake, darling? Promise me you won't go back to sleep.'

A grunt if I'm lucky. The cat curled up by her feet. Possum loved Chloe best, slept on her bed every night, until she got too old to make it up the stairs.

Chloe sitting beside me on the school run prattling away about nothing. God knows how many times I drove down that godawful road. But I miss it now. It was our time together.

The phone rings, making an echoey chime as the different extensions sound from bedroom, drawing room, kitchen, study. Belinda goes back down the stairs and takes it on the kitchen cordless.

'Hello?'

It's Michelle, Tom's secretary. Tom's going to be late home. After seven, half past at the latest.

'Oh, honestly!' exclaims Belinda. 'He knows Chloe's coming home today.'

In Chloe's honour she's got some fillet steaks for dinner, and plans to make a clafoutis using their own plums, picked, stoned and frozen in October. You'd never think it to look at her but Chloe eats like a horse. Always scrounging in the fridge, ice cream, soft-bake cookies, her diet is appalling. She can eat an entire tube of Pringles, sitting there tapping away at Facebook, one after another, until they're all gone. Remarkable, in its way.

A car pulls into the yard. Belinda looks out of the kitchen window and recognises Lisa's bright yellow Fiat 500, a car like a toy. Lisa gets out and reaches back into the car for a file. She holds the file hugged in her arms like a baby. Some of Tom's medical records, presumably, for him to work on at home.

Belinda lets Lisa in the back door, closing it again quickly against the cold air. She finds she's pleased to have company, which comes as a surprise. She's never thought of herself as a lonely person, and even if she was, sad Lisa, single thirty-something Lisa, is hardly the companion she would choose.

'Sorry to bother you,' says Lisa, standing by the door, her body sagging as if she lacks even the will to resist gravity. 'I was going to leave it in the garage. Then I saw you were in.'

She holds out the file, as if it confers on her a legitimacy that she herself lacks. Clinical photographs processed and filed by Lisa herself, one of the three women Tom calls 'my crew'. They fuss round him like hens. Nice to be a man.

'How about a cup of tea now you're here?' says Belinda.

'That would be lovely,' says Lisa.

She puts the file down on the kitchen table. Belinda fills the kettle and switches it on.

'Michelle just called,' she said. 'Tom's coming back late.'

'He works too hard,' says Lisa.

'His choice. He'd better not be too late. Chloe's coming home today.'

'That'll be nice. She's a lovely girl.'

As she gets out the tea bags and the mugs Belinda feels Lisa's sad eyes following her every move. She turns to look at her and catches a strange expression on her face: expectant, fearful.

'What?' she says.

'Nothing,' says Lisa.

It crosses Belinda's mind then that it's odd of Lisa to drive all the way here in the middle of the afternoon with a medical file. Why not give it to Tom in the office? If he needs to work on it at home he can always bring it back himself. But they spoil him, these women. Tom the dominant male figure in all their lives. A sort of office harem. They probably all get their periods at the same time.

She makes the mugs of tea in silence, waiting for Lisa to speak. She's getting this feeling that there's something Lisa wants to tell her.

'Tom stays late a lot these days,' Lisa says.

Her slightly protuberant eyes have a pitiful shine to them. Maybe she's in love with Tom. Five years of devoted service and her faithful heart is breaking.

'Yes,' says Belinda. 'Usually this is a quiet time. The run-up to Christmas.'

People don't want surgery before Christmas because they don't want to be in bandages for the Christmas parties. The busy time starts again in the new year.

She gives Lisa her mug of tea and Lisa holds it cupped in both hands as if she needs its warmth.

'I shouldn't be bothering you,' she says.

'Oh, I don't mind. I've got nothing on till it's time to pick Chloe up from the station.'

'Karen said I shouldn't come.'

Karen the office manager. The hen mother.

'But you escaped anyway?'

'Karen's not in today. It's Billy's Christmas play this afternoon. He's a three king. One of the three kings, I mean. Karen made his costume.'

She starts to cry.

'Lisa! What is it?'

'It's not fair,' she says, snuffling. 'It's not fair.'

'What's not fair?'

She blows her nose and dabs at her eyes, turning her face away.

'Sorry. I'm being stupid.'

Now Belinda's sure of it. One word from her and Lisa will pour out her unreciprocated love. She feels a flash of irritation. Tom never notices Lisa from one month to the next. Probably can't even remember her name. Trots in, picks up the file of pictures she's prepared so perfectly — it's a highly-skilled job in its way, but everyone needs the human touch, the sense they're appreciated — and trots out again without a word.

'He can be a selfish bastard, I know,' she says.

'Do you?' says Lisa. 'Do you really?'

Again that look. She wants something to happen, but she's afraid to make it happen.

'Well, he's a man, isn't he?' says Belinda.

'Oh, yes. He's a man all right.'

Please. Tom must have groped Lisa or something. It's all a bit sad.

'I suppose you know,' Lisa says.

'Know what?'

Now for the first time Belinda feels a sudden sinking feeling in her stomach.

What do I know?

'Karen said of course you knew and it's none of our business, but I said, what if she doesn't? It's not fair, us knowing and you not, it's not right.' The words tumbling out now, evidently they've been backing up in her throat, pushing at her mouth. 'I mean, why should he be able to do as he likes? I don't care what anyone says, it's not fair, he shouldn't do that to you, it's not right.'

Now Belinda doesn't want to know. Maybe she's been not wanting to know for a long time. But it's too late. Lisa wants her to know. She wants someone to share the suffering.

Lisa holds out her mug.

'Do you have any sugar?' she says.

Belinda gives her the sugar bowl and a teaspoon. Lisa sweetens her tea and stirs it and sips it, and somehow during this interlude Belinda realises they have moved beyond the point at which she can pretend not to know. She has entered Lisa's world. It's not fair. It's not right.

'Who is it?' she says.

'One of the office staff. He thinks no one knows.'

'At the hospital?'

'Someone in marketing. I don't know who she is. I've never even seen her. She started in September. Works in the Portakabins.'

Someone in marketing in a Portakabin. None of it seems real to Belinda. She drinks her tea. She feels numb.

'Was I wrong to tell you?'

'No.' What else can she say? Once you know, you know for ever. Lisa wants her to cry, but she can't cry.

Lisa says, 'Don't say anything to Karen, will you? She says it's none of our business.'

'No. I won't say anything to Karen.'

Alone again in the kitchen Belinda sits at the table looking out of the window at the bare branches of the willow by the pond. The bark is patched with yellow lichen, to make up for the lost leaves.

High piles of clouds are moving slowly across the sky, but you never see them move, you'd swear they were fixed, static, like the curve of the Downs on the horizon. Then your attention shifts and when you look again the clouds have changed their shape.

She feels cold. She pretended to be cold once, many years ago. Come over here, Tom. Sit by me and keep me warm. And we laughed, didn't we, Tom?

Don't think about that.

The sound of cars whining past on the Ditchling road. The hum of the freezer.

Almost three hours before it's time to go to the station to meet Chloe. Things to do, but they can wait. Everything can wait.

Life on hold.

4

On the train to London to meet her sister Diana, Laura
Broad allows herself the luxury of idle thought. Somehow
at home there's always something waiting to be done. This
short hour of the train journey she can give to herself.

Except she doesn't think of herself, she thinks of her
children. Both Jack and Carrie are unhappy, and she doesn't
know why. You think when your children get big that
caring for them will be easier, but instead it gets much
harder. When they're little and in distress they come crying
to you, they tell you about their bad dreams and their broken
friendships. It's easy then to take them in your arms and
love them, giving them with kisses and caresses the comfort
they need. What is a mother if she can't comfort her children? The impulse is so primitive, so overwhelming. But
neither Jack nor Carrie seek her comfort now. When she
tries to find out what's making them unhappy they get

34

angry with her and ask to be left alone. So she leaves them alone. But that doesn't lessen the ache in her.

I'd rather be unhappy myself.

Not some self-dramatizing pose: simply the truth. If she could save her children from unhappiness by taking their pain onto herself she would gladly do it. When you're hurt yourself you can do things to mitigate the pain. When your children are hurt, all you can do is suffer.

Laura thinks then of Diana's children, who've grown up to be such self-possessed young Londoners. Isla, now twenty-two, making money as a model, without of course taking it seriously as a career. Max at Oxford, but already interning at one of the big international banks, Credit Suisse, is it? Jack and Carrie so clumsy and provincial by comparison. Lonely, surly, struggling to find their place in the world. But so gallant, both of them. So precious and so beautiful.

Live your own lives, my darlings. I won't burden you with the need to be happy for my sake. But when the clouds lift, I'll be here waiting for you.

Diana is already in the Hayward lobby, impatiently glancing from the exhibition programme in her hands to the people drifting in and out of the gallery. Laura sees her before she is seen: her older sister, her lifelong companion, the person with the power to annoy her most in the world. You'd think when you both pass the age of fifty some kind of truce could be declared, some plateau of maturity achieved. But as soon as she sets eyes on Diana Laura is six years old again, and Diana is nine, and Diana holds all the cards.

'Where have you been, Laura? I've been here for ever.'

Laura compliments Diana on her coat, clearly a new acquisition: purple wool, fitted to the waist, then flared. It looks chic on Diana's bird-like frame. But her face has grown thinner. Laura can feel her unhappiness like a shiver in the air.

'Prada,' Diana says. 'Bicester Village, forty per cent off.' She offers no comment on Laura's own appearance. 'Come along, then. Let's do the rooms.'

She nods to a passing couple, murmuring to Laura, 'You must know him, he owns the Wolseley.' Laura knows nobody. Diana is in her element as metropolitan guide to her country sister. Presumably this is why Laura has been summoned to meet her in an art gallery. Diana appreciates the avant-garde much more in the company of one who is, artistically speaking, bringing up the rear.

The show is called BREAK OUT, and features installations by three artists. The first installation is a complete recreated prison cell, built out of real concrete blocks with real iron doors and real bars in the window. The front wall has been ripped open, leaving a big jagged hole. Through this hole can be seen a realistic corpse hanging by a twist of sheet from the window bars. It's called *Break Out*.

Diana casts a rapid eye over the scene.

'Interesting,' she says.

Laura stares at the artwork and feels her usual sense of bewilderment. How does one judge something like this? It's disturbing to look at, which is presumably part of the point. The hole in the wall should have offered the prisoner a way out, but instead he has hanged himself. Is that interesting?

But already Diana is moving on.

The second room contains a sculpture in plastic of a life-size pregnant woman. Through the translucent skin of her distended belly can be seen a grotesque foetus, an armoured creature with long clawed fingers. The claws pierce the plastic skin, causing a dribble of water to come seeping out. The work is called *Break Water*.

'Interesting,' says Diana.

Laura hates it. It's ugly and frightening.

'I don't get it,' she says.

'Male violence,' explains Diana curtly. 'Maternal complicity.'

'It's horrible,' says Laura.

'It's meant to be.'

What can you say to that?

They move on briskly to the third artist. To Laura's relief there is no horror here. A wooden table raised on a plinth has been laid with blue-striped china, a milk bottle, and all the other elements of what seems to be a 1960s breakfast. A box of Kellogg's Cornflakes stands beside a rack of toast and a jar of Robinson's Golden Shred. The work is called *Break Fast*.

'Interesting,' says Diana.

'But it's just a breakfast table,' says Laura.

'Nostalgic. Iconic.'

As before, she shows no desire to linger. This has always been Diana's way in art galleries. Register, categorize, move on. She views art like a general inspecting troops: the essence of the response is contained in the act of being present. Her sharp mind moves rapidly, she's easily bored. But she does not tire.

'Time for a cup of tea. There's a café outside.'

As they head for the café Diana chides Laura for her naive responses.

'Really, Laura, you must expose yourself to the modern world a bit more. You never would have come if I hadn't made you, would you?'

'No,' says Laura. 'I don't get it. Why does it have to be so nasty?'

'What do you want art to be? Hay-wains and views of the Grand Canal?'

As they cross the lobby they're accosted by a young woman with a microphone. She smiles at Laura as if she knows her.

'Could you spare a minute?'

Laura becomes aware that behind the young woman hovers a man with a large video camera on his shoulder.

The young woman is slim, intelligent-looking, forceful in a quiet way.

'We're making a film about Joe Nola,' she says. 'What did you make of his work?'

'Which one was Joe Nola?' says Laura.

'The breakfast table.'

'Oh, yes.' Laura can think of nothing to say. She can feel Diana fretting beside her. 'I don't think I understood it.'

'Laura, honestly,' says Diana. The camera moves to her. She addresses the lens directly. 'It made me aware of all we've lost,' she says fluently. 'The innocence of childhood. The structured family. Shared mealtimes.'

The young woman has not moved the microphone away from Laura.

'Don't do that, Jim,' she murmurs.

The camera returns.

'So you didn't understand it,' she says. 'But what did it make you feel?'

'Golly,' says Laura. 'Nothing, really. I mean, how is that art? It's just a breakfast table. Can anything be art?'

'What do you think?'

'Look, this isn't my thing, really. I only came because my sister insisted. I've never understood modern art. Ask Diana. She understands it.'

The young woman is undeterred.

'Actually, Joe Nola is interested in reaching people just

like you,' she says. 'His work isn't a puzzle to be decrypted. It's simply a process of pointing. He's saying, Look at something ordinary, and see it as something extraordinary. So your response is always the right response. There is no wrong response.'

'Right,' says Laura.

'So all you have to do is say what thoughts went through your mind when you looked at it.'

What thoughts did go through my mind? Feelings of inadequacy. Embarrassment.

Then she remembers something else.

'I think I thought about Golden Shred. I used to collect the golliwogs. Then they stopped doing them because they were racist. But all I thought was how sweet they were. And I wanted the golliwog badge, of course.'

'Perfect.' The director smiles. She looks genuinely pleased. 'Joe will love that. Thank you very much. Okay, Jim. That's it for today.'

Diana and Laura go on into the café.

'Golliwogs!' says Diana. 'What drivel you talk, Laura.'

'I didn't know what else to say.'

'She was looking for a mug to say something moronic and you obliged. That's what they do on TV today. Make fools of people.'

Laura doesn't disagree aloud, but inside herself she thinks Diana is wrong. In the past she would have said so and they would have bickered, perhaps even fought. But Diana is muted, her scornful dismissal of Laura's point of view has no animus to it. She speaks out of long habit, almost unaware of what she's saying.

Diana gets an espresso, Laura an Earl Grey. They sit by the window looking out onto the concrete walkway and the blank back of the Queen Elizabeth Hall.

'I'm worried about Roddy,' says Diana.

So now at last they have come to it, the real purpose of their meeting. Diana has never in all her life directly asked Laura for help, or admitted that she needs it. But there have been times when she's thrown out a casual remark at some inappropriate moment, using words that can be disowned later when the crisis is past.

The little crisis is about her husband Roddy.

'I think he's depressed,' she says. 'Does Henry get depressed?'

'Yes, sometimes.'

'Does he stop talking?'

'Sometimes.'

'What do you do when he does that?'

'Nothing, really. I don't mind if he needs time alone.'

'Not alone. Just not talking.'

'You mean, like, at dinner?'

'At dinner. At night. Over breakfast. All the time.'

Diana takes care not to meet her eyes. Laura is shocked.

'Roddy's not talking all the time?'

'Well, he says the odd word. But that's about it.'

41

'Why? Have you asked him?'

'Of course I've asked him. He doesn't answer.'

'What, he just sits there?'

'Well, he might laugh, or give the odd grunt.'

Laura wants to laugh. The image is so comical, Roddy gazing back at Diana and parrying her every spoken thrust with silence. But Diana's eyes reveal real panic. She's blinking rapidly, pressing her lips tight together. Nothing to laugh at here.

'How long's this been going on?'

'Almost a week now. I don't really know what to do. I'm sure it's something to do with what's happening at his work. It's an absolute nightmare, this crash. All the banks have lost fortunes. I suppose he's having some sort of breakdown. I've asked him to see a doctor, but he ... Well, he won't talk about it.'

'Is he like this with everyone?'

'He must talk at work. But at home he won't even answer the phone. The thing is, Laura, he doesn't look unhappy. I mean, he eats and sleeps and everything, just like before. And he has this little smile on his face, like – oh God, it's a horrible smile. I hate it.'

'Like he's gone somewhere else in his head?'

'Yes.' Diana looks at Laura in surprise. 'How did you know that?'

'I didn't.'

'The thing is, he might talk to you.'

'Me?'

'Roddy's always had a soft spot for you.' The words are coming out faster now. 'I wondered if you'd come up one evening and talk to him, try to find out what's going on. He just might tell you. I can't help worrying that he's been sacked and hasn't dared to tell me. You know, sitting with his briefcase in the park all day. But why wouldn't he tell me? I always thought we were rather good as a team. It's not as if all I care about is the money.'

Diana has never come as close as this to admitting weakness. Laura is touched.

'Of course I'll come. I expect I'll be no use, but I'll give it a try.'

'Not on a special visit to talk to Roddy, of course. He'd smell a rat at once. But you and Henry could come to dinner. Then after dinner I'll work it so you have some time with Roddy alone.'

'Yes, all right. If the dates work for Henry.'

'It's got to be tomorrow night, really.'

'Tomorrow? That may be a problem.'

Diana reaches out one hand and clasps Laura's wrist.

'Please,' she says. 'We're having the Lymans to dinner. Come too. You must. I can't go on like this.'

'I'll talk to Henry.'

'If Henry can't come, come alone. Just come.'

What can she say? This is a cry from the heart.

'All right.'

43

Only then does Diana let her go. And at once, Laura's agreement secured, she reverts to type. The window that opened briefly onto her inner panic has closed again.

'That TV crew,' she says. 'They never got you to sign a release form. They can't use what you said without your permission.'

'I don't mind,' says Laura.

'Golliwogs! Honestly.'

'You can't talk. You got the golliwog badge. We only collected enough golliwogs for one badge and you said you had to have it even though you never ate any of the marmalade.'

'Nor did you.'

'You made Mummy buy a jar we didn't even need.'

'So I deserved the badge.'

'Mummy said we were to share it but you never gave me my share.'

'I was going to, but Anne Duncan stole it.'

'You gave it to Anne Duncan. You swapped our golliwog for a tube of Refreshers.'

'My God, don't you ever forget anything?'

Diana gazes at Laura with a blend of irritation and wonder. Laura herself is amazed at the way the long-distant past has returned. She remembers Diana's betrayal as if it was yesterday. So typical of Diana: she never really wanted the golliwog badge for herself, she just wanted her sister not to have it. And that's how she is, Laura thinks. It's not personal. In her own way she's as loyal and loving as she knows how to be.

'You will come tomorrow, won't you?'

'Yes. I'll come.'

'I'm doing slow-cooked shoulder of lamb.' Then, with barely a pause, 'You don't think Roddy could be having an affair, do you?'

'I shouldn't think so. Not Roddy.'

'I know that's what men do. But if he was having an affair, why stop talking to me?'

'Exactly.'

'No,' says Diana, comforting herself. 'I think it must be a breakdown.'

5

For a simple job the pipe work is quite tricky. The problem is getting the fall for the drain so that it flows freely to the external soil pipe. Everything would be so much easier if the toilet could be placed against the back wall, but the clients want the bath under the window. The tub is to be raised on a 300 millimeter stand so that when you lie in the bath you can see out of the window, over the railway lines and the water meadows to the Downs.

It's a nice idea, and it presents the plumber, Matt Early, with a nice little challenge, which he appreciates.

'If it's impossible,' Liz says, 'we'll do it another way.'

Liz Dickinson is an understanding client. She has a partner called Alan Strachan, and two children, one a Dickinson and one a Strachan. That's how families are these days.

'Nothing's impossible,' Matt replies. 'There's always a way.'

The room in which the new bathroom is to be built is

46

a top back bedroom, with a chimney breast and a small working fireplace. Liz and Alan say they want to keep the fireplace, even though they won't use it. The door is in the wall that faces the fireplace. This leaves only the inside wall for the wash basin and the toilet, which means a three metre pipe run to the drains.

Matt has been pondering the problem in silence. He's a big man, just entering his fortieth year; a man of few words. When he meets a client with a view to taking on a job he lets them do the talking, nodding from time to time to show he's listening, his eyes fixed on the ground. A gentle giant, people say, because people know nothing. They think because you don't say much you go about your life like a dumb animal, a horse, maybe, content with your lot. Who knows what goes on inside horses? Rage, perhaps, that they have to haul carts heavy with goods not their own. A passion for liberty, thwarted by the barred gates and the electric fences that hem them round. Why should animals be presumed to be humble?

Matt listens when others talk, and offers no contribution, because he does not regard his view of things as having any status. He does not have the habit of opinions. But he is not humble. He nurses a deep and steady contempt for shoddy workmanship and processed food, for television game shows and politicians who tell people what they want to hear and newspapers that tell lies and credit cards that enable you to buy what you can't afford and computers and the Internet. 'I don't bother with all that,' he says.

To be sure of providing a decent flow he needs to steal at least fifty millimetres at one end or the other. He can raise the toilet bowl, but this will leave a ridge in the floor in the middle of the room. Therefore the soil pipe must drop fifty millimetres lower at the outer end, which means it will cut through the ceiling of the room below. This is the boy's bedroom.

Matt pads down the stairs to the floor below, which is the second floor. He makes as little noise as possible, even though he's alone in the house. In the nature of his work he's often alone in people's houses. They give him a key, tell him to let himself in, lock up when he leaves. Everyone works such long hours these days. Alan in London for a meeting on his film script. Liz in Folkestone working on an article about Saga cruises. Matt knows these things because he has heard them speaking to each other. He has no wish to eavesdrop but they forget you're there, or maybe they think you don't understand, like a household pet. Down the years he has overheard quarrels and anger, bitterness and tears. Very little joy, very little love. You wonder why people stay together when you hear the ways they set out to hurt each other.

Alan and Liz aren't so bad. They have a six-year-old boy who Liz spoils because she's out at work so much. There's a girl too, who's away at university. When Alan accuses Liz, saying, 'Cas loves you best because you always give in to him,' Liz replies, 'Well, Alice loves you best, so we're evens.' It's only a kind of joke between them, except that jokes are real.

He enters the second-floor back bedroom and studies the section of the ceiling which will have to be cut away for the soil pipe. It will get in the way of nothing, of course, but the sloping box will look ugly and intrusive. Matt's aesthetic sense is driven by a strong view on what is fitting. In a corner, between wall and ceiling, a box section would be fitting. In the middle of the ceiling it would be a bodge. And yet it can go nowhere else.

The trick, thinks Matt, is to make a box section in just that position be as necessary to the little boy's bedroom as it is to the bathroom above. Suppose he evens out the boxing to make it run parallel to the ceiling, and takes it right across from wall to wall: it would then look as if it was a central beam, a part of the structure of the ceiling. But it isn't a beam. This offends another of Matt's instinctive rules. You don't make things pretend to be something they're not.

I could drop the whole ceiling by fifty millimetres, he thinks. But what do you do with the void? Mice will nest there and eat the plastic coating off the electric cables, and there'll be the devil's own job to get back in there and sort it out. You have to think about access. You have to think about the poor sod who gets called out ten years from now to fix a leaking pipe or a fused circuit. It's a matter of pride; and Matt Early is a proud man.

No point in rushing it. This next stage requires thought. So he goes all the way down to the basement kitchen to make himself a cup of coffee. When he started the job he brought his own Thermos, but Alan said, 'Use the kitchen.' Then Alan would hear him going downstairs and would emerge from his study to join him, welcoming a little company while the kettle boiled. A lonely job, sitting all day in front of a computer screen.

One day Alan asked him about his work. Matt thought at first he was wanting a progress report on the new bathroom.

'No, I mean, does your work interest you?' Alan said. 'Does it really interest you?'

No one had ever asked such a question before. Plumbing's nothing much, Matt knows that. What he usually says is that it suits him. Everyone has to make a living somehow.

'But would you do it if you weren't paid to do it?' says Alan.

There's a question. A well-made joint in a copper pipe's a thing of rightness. You can be satisfied by that. A well-designed central heating system with its pumps and its valves, its intersecting runs of pipes and its thermo-switches, is a perfect thing in its way, almost a living creature. The veins, the arteries, the beating heart of a home.

'I shouldn't think so,' he says. 'But money isn't everything.'

Matt hates quoting a price for a job. How can you tell

how long it will take to solve the hundreds of problems that each new location throws up? It has to be done right. Cut corners and you'll be found out. Water finds you out. Any weakness in the system, the water will worry at it until it gives way. Water always wins in the end. The job is not to hold the flow back, but to guide it. Persuade it to go the way you want it to go. You can't say any of that to the clients. So Matt always ends up under-quoting for the job.

'You're a fool, Matthew,' his mother says. 'You always were. They don't thank you for it.'

No, they don't thank him for it. They don't even know. But he can't explain to his mother. And she wouldn't listen. She's only repeating her lifelong complaint against his father: You let people take advantage of you.

Alan persists.

'What would you rather be doing, then? If you could.'

There is an answer to this question, but Matt rarely gives it. People never quite know how to respond. It doesn't fit the role they've allotted to him. But Alan is unusually curious.

'What do you do when you stop work?'

'This and that,' says Matt. 'Go down the shed.'

'Down the shed?'

'I've got a shed at the bottom of the garden.'

'And what happens there?'

Matt stares at his feet. Mumbles his answer.

'Violins.'

'What?'

'I work with my violins.'

Alan is astonished. They always are. They think his mind must be too coarse, his hands too callused, to play a violin.

'You play the violin?'

'A little.'

'But that's wonderful!'

His face expresses genuine delight. That's when Matt realizes this conversation hasn't been about him at all. So easy to forget: when people ask you a question about yourself, they're really asking it of themselves.

Alan is asking himself about his own work. About how much it interests him. About what he would rather be doing.

'Play the violin! All by yourself! Just for the joy of it!'

'Yes.'

'Oh, how glorious!'

An odd little conversation, that. Because Matt isn't much of a talker he doesn't tell Alan about the rest of his work with violins. Alan is sufficiently gratified already.

'A plumber who plays the violin! I'll have to put you in a play.'

A horse that talks. A savage who recites Shakespeare. You could get angry over this sort of thing but what's the point? He means well. At least he asks.

But I'm not a plumber who plays the violin. I'm a man living my life as best as I can. I love music. I care for a sick mother. I feel trapped. I have long moments of pure joy.

I'm lonely. I worry that my eyes aren't as good as they were. I'm too easily enraged by little things. I'm growing older. I miss my dad.

Alone in the kitchen of someone else's house Matt drinks his mug of coffee, putting it to his lips while the bitter liquid is still so hot he can only sip. He feels the caffeine buzz in his body. All round the kitchen walls there are drawings done by Caspar, put up by Liz, his proud mother. Drawings of monsters and spiky figures wielding weapons. He'll be back from school in a little while. Alan hasn't yet returned, but he promised he'd be home before Cas gets back.

The doorbell rings.

At first Matt does nothing, on the grounds that the caller won't have come for him. Then he remembers that the caller has come for him. Alan's sister needs a plumber. Alan arranged for her to drop by this afternoon.

Matt climbs the stairs to the ground floor and opens the front door. A youngish woman is standing outside, caught in the moment of turning to leave. Straight brown hair cut just above the shoulder. A plain bare face. Greenish eyes.

She turns back in some confusion.

'Oh, you are here,' she says. 'I thought maybe I'd missed you.'

'No,' says Matt. 'Come on in.'

As she comes past him into the hall he glances at her again. She's wearing a dark grey suit that gives her a business-like air, she moves with brisk economy, but the way she casts her eyes down, that he recognizes. She's nervous.

'I don't like to interrupt your work.'

'No, that's okay. Alan said you'd be coming round.'

They go into the living room, each aware of the incongruity, as if Matt is the host and she his guest.

'I'm Meg,' she says.

'Right.'

Now that they have reached a destination of sorts, neither sits down. Nor do they look at each other. Unlikely though it seems, Meg is clearly shy in his presence. She is the employer, he the employee. The servant, almost. But she seems not to believe she has the right to command his time.

'I expect you're too busy,' she says.

'That depends.'

Matt too has his eyes on the floor.

'It's the shower,' she says. 'It was never much good. Now it doesn't work at all.'

'Where is this?'

'Uckfield. I expect it's out of your area.'

'I don't exactly have an area.'

'It's just so hard to find anyone to take on the small jobs. Which I do understand. It can't really be worth your while. But Alan was telling me how good you are. So I just thought, well, I can ask.'

Matt listens to her low hesitant voice with a growing sensation that is not familiar to him. He looks up and catches a glimpse of uncertainty in her eyes just as she's looking at him. Both look down again at once, but not before Matt has registered the cause of his confusion.

Meg is beautiful.

Her beauty is not obvious. Not the current style at all, very understated, almost withdrawn. Hers is a severe face, solemn as a saint in a picture. It's the tremor behind the severity, the modesty you could call it, that makes her beautiful.

'I'll be on this job till Christmas,' he says. 'Then I've got a boiler to put in. When would you be wanting the work done?'

'Oh, any time, really. No hurry.'

'Well, then.'

He looks up at her again. She meets his gaze with that uncertain smile. She's biting her lower lip.

'I'd best come and take a look,' he says.

'Oh, would you? I'd be so grateful.'

She takes out a pen and a business card and writes her home address on the back, and her phone number. He watches the way she frowns as she writes.

'When do you think you could come?'

'I could look in tomorrow, end of the morning.' Tomorrow is Saturday. 'Twelvish.'

'Are you sure? That would be perfect.'

She gives him the card, and she goes.

That's all that happens.

Matt turns the card over. *Meg Strachan, Assistant Marketing Manager, Hartfield Surgical Centre*.

He washes up his coffee mug, then climbs the stairs once more to the top of the house. There he resumes work building the steading for the bath. As he works, he pictures Meg's face.

You can tell a lot from a face. Her face is a real face. When she looked at me she saw me.

Matt works away steadily, forming a frame of two-by-fours, cutting the joins to fit neatly even though the structure will be concealed behind plywood panels.

A new shower shouldn't take too long to install. Alan won't mind if he takes a day out to squeeze it in some time next week.

6

From where he sits in the basement conference room Alan Strachan can see the feet and ankles of the people passing by on the street outside. Before him on the black glass table is spread an array of pastries and muffins, two jugs of coffee, one of which is decaffeinated, and a teapot filled with hot water. Jane Langridge, his producer, drinks only hot water. She sits on his right hand side, simultaneously attentive to a copy of his screenplay, a thick wad of notes, and her BlackBerry. This is a script meeting and etiquette prevents her from sending out messages on her BlackBerry; but she feels it's acceptable to receive.

'The dog is brilliant, Alan,' she says. 'We all adore the dog.'

Jane smiles as she speaks. She's beginning the meeting as is traditional with a garnish of praise. She opens her eyes very wide and leans towards Alan, as if to imply that her enthusiasm borders on sexual desire. She's a slender woman in her late forties, still very beautiful, but hollowed out by a combination of insincerity and dieting. Her close-cropped shiny black hair guards her like a helmet.

'The dog is the star,' echoes Ben Nokes. He sits facing Alan with a laptop open before him. Alan likes Ben Nokes, he's intelligent and self-effacing. Unfortunately he's entirely powerless in the process.

'Is the business of brainwashing the dog true?' says Jane. 'I mean, does it really happen?'

'Yes, it happens,' says Alan. 'A friend of mine had it done to stop her dog chasing sheep.'

'They put the dog in a pen with a sheep?'

'With a nursing ewe. The ewe will go for any dog, however big, to protect her lamb.'

'Isn't nature wonderful?' says Jane, reading a message on her BlackBerry.

'A sheepdog that's frightened of sheep,' says Ben Nokes. He chuckles encouragingly and taps a note into his laptop.

On the fourth side of the table sits a very young, very pretty girl called Flora, writing rapidly in profound silence. At the end of the meeting Flora will type up this record of the meeting twice, in full form and in a brief digest. Both versions will be circulated to all concerned, none of whom will read a word. Beside her is a stack of screenplays, each with the same title written in black marker pen on the edge: SHEPHERD. The letters are formed on the paper-ends. If the screenplay were to be unclipped and the sheets separated, the title would fragment and cease to exist; a process that Alan feels is already taking place before his helpless gaze.

'This time round you've really dealt with Hector's passivity,' says Jane. Hector is the hero of *Shepherd*. Jane has worried over Hector's passivity through two earlier drafts. Alan can't help feeling that this is a criticism of his own passivity. 'You've transformed him.'

'Firing on all barrels,' says Ben Nokes.

'My only question is …' Jane wrinkles up her white face as if searching for the right words. Alan can see her glancing over the studio notes, where the right words are to be found. 'My only question is – have we lost some of our sympathy for Hector? Do we *like* Hector?'

'He is very angry,' says Ben Nokes.

Alan's heart sinks.

'I thought maybe the anger energized him,' he says. 'You did say he lacked energy.'

'Just a question,' says Jane, pouring herself a cup of hot water. 'Just something to throw into the mix as we move forward.'

Alan watches the shoes click by on the pavement outside and wants it all to be over. The only good page in the third draft is the outpouring of rage he put into his hero's mouth. There was something from the heart. But who needs the writer's heart?

He first pitched the idea for *Shepherd* over a year ago,

when high-fliers in the City were making obscene amounts of money. A simple story of an investment banker who gives up his millions to become a shepherd on the South Downs. He had meant it to be an exploration of the roots of happiness. In his first bittersweet draft, the draft that delivers his original idea, the banker's experiment fails and he's forced by financial need to return to the City. There his colleagues tease him with baa-ing noises, which he takes with good grace. He has emerged with a new hard-won equilibrium. Every weekend he goes back to the quiet of the Downs.

This first draft, received with ecstasy, was considered a little too dark for a mainstream audience. In the second draft the hero leaves the City as before, and makes a success of being a shepherd. This was said to lack conflict in the third act. To resolve this, and to meet a perceived lack of lighter moments, in the third draft the hero gets a sheepdog who is afraid of sheep. Now, as Alan faces work on a fourth draft, the context of his story has changed. Banks are failing. Bankers have become villains.

Does any of this matter? Is any of it real? Somewhere round the third draft Alan lost all grip on the sense of the story he was writing. Now he responds to production notes and banks the cheques.

What was that Jane Langridge just said? 'The mix as we move forward.' There's a phrase worth deconstructing. *The mix*: my work of imaginative fiction reduced to ingredients that can be changed as thought necessary. *We*: the work is communal, no one to blame, no one to praise, no one's individual voice. *Move forward*: the distant echo of revolutionary rhetoric is not accidental, bringing to mind as it does the virility of an armed uprising. Kick off the shackles of the past. Take no prisoners. There's a new dawn breaking.

Oh, hell. Can I bear it all over again?

'Okay.' Jane Langridge puts down her cup of hot water and squares the notes on the table before her. Now action is to be taken. 'We love this project, Alan. We're all passionate about it here.'

'Passionate,' echoes Ben Nokes.

'We love the concept. We love the topicality. We love the humanity. We love the dog.'

Alan runs his hands through his unruly hair and sighs. He feels like one of the followers of Kerensky who found their zeal for reform upstaged by Lenin. However profound his commitment, however dazzling his talent, the game has moved on.

'But is it time to take a fresh look at our approach?'

Apparently it is.

'Obviously,' says Alan, not wanting to appear pointlessly defensive, 'times have changed.'

Jane turns to Ben Nokes.

'Why don't you try Alan with your idea, Ben.'

'Sure thing,' says Ben. 'I was just kicking it around to see what came loose. This is the bad version.'

This is the bad version. A widely-used opening by production executives. Partly it's a disclaimer: don't judge me on this, I'm not a writer. Partly it's an expression of respect: you're the writer, you'll do this so much better than me. And partly it's the sugar on the pill: let's all pretend we're buddies sharing crazy ideas, but actually, pal, this is an order.

'What we started with is Hector as a banker deciding to throw it all away for the simple life. He becomes a shepherd. Okay. Now we have bankers losing their jobs in their thousands, it doesn't look noble any more. It looks like plain old failure.'

'Double failure,' says Jane. 'He fails as a banker. Then he becomes a shepherd.'

'Right. But we all love the shepherd idea.'

Oh no, thinks Alan. Don't let this go the way I think it's going.

He tries to recall the terms of his contract. There's three more payments to come, good-sized payments: for the delivery of the first draft, and for commencement and delivery of the second draft. The last three drafts he has handed in have all been stages in the evolution of the first contractual draft. Everyone in London agrees that the screenplay should not be shown to the studio in Los Angeles until it's in its best possible form, thus generating 'momentum'. And until the studio receives a contractual draft, the next payment is not triggered.

'So here's my wild idea,' says Ben Nokes. 'How about

we reverse the shift? We keep every single element, we keep the central concept, we just flip it.'

'I did try this on Nancy,' says Jane. 'She loves it.'

Nancy is the one person who has to love it. Nancy is in LA. So there's a message.

'Flip it?' says Alan.

'Right. We start with a shepherd. He becomes a banker. He turns out to be brilliant.'

'All the shepherding skills translate into the world of the City,' says Jane. 'Maybe he even brings his dog with him.'

'And,' says Ben Nokes, patting Alan on the arm as if to imply that this is the bit that will please him most, '*and* we keep the whole dog brainwashing sequence you created. Which we all love.'

'Great work there, Alan,' says Jane.

Alan says nothing. What is there to say? He's caught in a trap of his own making. This is how the film business works, and he has chosen to offer his talents to the film business. No one ever pretended to him that they wanted his distinctive vision as a writer. They're paying for a reservoir of ideas into which they can dip their little tin cups. When the reservoir runs dry there are others waiting, proffering their taps.

'Can I think about that one?' he says. 'It's a big change.'

'Not as big as it seems at first glance,' says Jane.

'You think we should try this before Nancy sees anything?'

'Absolutely,' says Jane.

So we're still working on the first draft.

Alan watches the shoes go by on the street. I have to get out of this business, he thinks. This can't go on. I'd rather go back to teaching. Except that for this one screenplay they will one day pay him a sum that would take him five years of teaching to earn.

Maybe none of it matters. Reality is not as straightforward as it seems. The plumber currently at work putting a new bathroom in their house has a shed at the bottom of his garden where he plays the violin. The *Guardian* has a story this morning about a teacher sacked for telling her class Santa Claus doesn't exist. The head teacher reassures the nation: 'The children are unscathed and back on the right track thanks to the professionalism of our resident staff and the lovely snow we experienced last week.'

A shepherd goes to work in Canary Wharf. Super-modern high-rise glass-walled testosterone-fuelled trading floor. And a sheepdog.

Is that hilarious? Is it insane? Can I tell the difference any more?

7

They sit facing him, side by side, husband and wife; he a leathery little man in his fifties, she at least ten years younger, hair dyed, face heavily made up. They are called Lazarus, a name that casts the consultation in a surreal light. The surgeon, neat in pinstripe suit and humorous tie, a design of flying toasters, gives them his full attention.

They sit facing him, side by side, husband and wife; he a leathery little man in his fifties, she at least ten years younger, hair dyed, face heavily made up. They are called Lazarus, a name that casts the consultation in a surreal light. The surgeon, neat in pinstripe suit and humorous tie, a design of flying toasters, gives them his full attention.

The wife does the talking.

'My husband is a saint, Mr Redknapp. He should be in heaven with the angels. He works like a dog all day. You can't imagine the trouble I had to get him to come here. And he worries about me so. He's a saint and a darling.'

She throws her husband a fond smile. The saint sits silently studying his shoes.

'He says it's a waste of money and I'll probably die under the knife.' She laughs merrily at this notion. 'He's such a joker. But it is your money, darling' – this to the husband – 'and I do so want you to be happy about this too.'

The surgeon does not intervene. His job at this early stage is to listen.

'Harry thinks I don't need any work done,' says Mrs Lazarus, 'but I tell him, You don't come shopping with me, darling. You try finding clothes that fit top and bottom. And if you can do something about it, well, why not? We'd all like to stay a little younger a little longer.'

Tom Redknapp nods and smiles. He's not humouring Mrs Lazarus, his agreement is genuine. Just because she's willing to subject herself to unnecessary surgical procedures to satisfy her vanity, the surgeon will not judge her. He has seen so many cases of this sort, and knows how subtle are the threads that link vanity and generosity, appearance and confidence, self-belief and self-love. For all he knows this is the way Mrs Lazarus seeks to show her husband how much she values him, and looks forward, beyond the transforming touch of the scalpel, to the renewed blessing of his love.

'So what do you have in mind?'

'Well, a little more here would be nice.' Her hands move in the air before her breasts. 'And I said to Harry, in for a penny, in for a pound.' She pats her cheeks, her chin, her neck. 'Why not go for this too?'

The surgeon nods, writing swift notes in a flowing longhand.

'I've looked in your brochure,' says Mrs Lazarus. 'I believe it's called Facial Rejuvenation Package. Breast Augmentation.' She raises her voice, a little nervous at naming these

66

professional terms. 'And I've shown Harry what it costs.'

The saint nods silent assent.

'Guess what he said? He said, I don't care about the money. I just don't want you to be hurt. He never thinks of himself. But you do know, darling' – she touches his knee – 'I'm doing this for both of us.' She turns back to the surgeon. 'It's our Christmas present to each other.'

A gift. An act of love. Tom Redknapp thinks how little outsiders know of the profound emotions with which he engages daily. Sometimes at dinner parties he comes up against the old distaste for cosmetic surgery, offered up by decent people who are not stupid but have never thought seriously about the matter. Most times he smiles and lets it go, accepting that they see him as a mercenary, a traitor to the caring ethos of medicine, who disfigures helpless women for his gain. Sometimes he teases out the discussion a little further. Do you believe that you must accept the body you were born with, and do nothing to improve it? Would you operate on a face scarred by disfiguring burns? Do you allow the use of make-up? of hair dye? Do you diet and exercise to stay slim? Ah, so it is acceptable to want to manage our body shape so that we look our best. The only area of debate is where we draw the line, and why.

Over the years he has learned humility. He respects his patients even when he thinks he understands their motives better than they do themselves. The relationship between body image and self-esteem is so profound. He'll give Mrs Lazarus bigger breasts. She'll feel more sexually confident. Mr Lazarus will be surprised and grateful. She'll be proud and happy.

We all long to be objects of desire.

No, none of this causes the surgeon a moment's doubt. And yet all is not well. In recent weeks questions of quite a different order have begun to torment him. Absurd to be kept awake at night by what amount to philosophical imponderables, but certain concerns have lodged in his brain and will not be dismissed.

What is it that his clients want? Deliverance from shame? The restoration of normality? But he knows there is no normality. So many examinations over the years, so many women standing, trembling, exposed, naked in his office: he more than anyone knows the commonplace oddity of the human body. If only they could see what he sees, the shame would evaporate. But instead they see this fantasy called beauty: a fantasy because no single individual believes they have it, but all believe others have it. Beauty is a state that is always just out of reach. Or you could say there's no such thing as beauty. We define it so variously that it doesn't exist. What does exist, what remains constant, is our feelings about beauty: what we seek is a certain feeling about ourselves which is stimulated by the perceptions of others. The entire process actually happens in the mind, in our own minds and in the minds of the people round us. Beauty turns out to be a group delusion. So much is obvious. The plastic surgeon operates on the minds of his patients.

So why stop there? What else is illusion? My value as an individual? The meaning of my existence?

The consultation proceeds. The surgeon understands that his client has already made up her mind. After all, it takes courage to come into the office of a stranger and speak openly of your body and its limitations, let alone show that body. She will have scoured the Internet, studied brochures, talked to friends. Now she is fired up and ready to go. Nevertheless, he must take her through the risks: infection, allergic reaction, pulmonary embolism, everything up to and including death.

'But they're rare, aren't they?' she says. 'I mean, I'm more at risk driving my car, right?'

She laughs and touches her husband's knee, to reassure him.

'That's true,' says the surgeon. 'But it's important that you're fully informed.'

He hears the nervousness in her laugh, and feels as always a wave of protective tenderness. Beneath the make-up, behind the quick bobbing glances at her husband, there lies such bravery. All these women were once girls in school, dreading the weekly swimming lesson where they would have to expose their awkward bodies to the cold blue light.

'Now,' he says, 'I think the next step is the examination.'

Mr Lazarus stands up.

'You're very welcome to stay, Mr Lazarus. It's entirely as you and Mrs Lazarus wish.'

Mr Lazarus looks to his wife.

'Stay, darling,' says Mrs Lazarus. 'It's not like you're going to get any surprises.'

Her husband sits down again.

'He's the one gets the surprises,' she says, nodding at Tom Redknapp.

The surgeon smiles.

'Not any more,' he says. 'In my business you get to see what people really look like, thank God, not the touched-up fake version.'

'So hey-ho,' says Mrs Lazarus, her voice bright. 'I suppose this is where I take my top off.'

When he first saw Meg naked she covered her breasts with her hands, out of shame.

'Don't you wish they were bigger?' she said.

'I don't want any part of you different to the way you are,' Tom replied.

Does that make me a better man than Mr Lazarus? Not at all. We both act in obedience to our desires.

Here lies the terrible possibility: that my existence only becomes meaningful in the short highly-charged interval between the birth of a desire and its satisfaction. That this is what the struggle of my days is directed towards. That this is all there is.

After the consultation he catches up on his paperwork. Then

he calls Meg's office and learns she's out for the rest of the day. He tries her mobile and reaches her in her car.

'I was thinking of looking in about six-thirty. If you're going to be in.'

'Of course I'll be in.'

'I'll only have half an hour or so.'

'All right. See you then.'

He attends a management meeting of the hospital board. The planned extension from twenty-five to fifty beds is proceeding on schedule, with the new floor expected to be ready by February. However, bookings are down.

'December's always a slow month,' says Vernon, the finance manager. 'But we have to assume current financial conditions will affect business going forward. We may not experience the usual mid-January pick-up.'

Tom Redknapp plays very little part in the discussion. His mind is on the mystery of desire.

I desire because I am desired.

A man can have a fine opinion of himself bred in him by a loving family and all the privileges of his class; he can go to a fine university and build an enviable career; he can do all these things and never for one moment believe himself to be desirable.

We're talking about sex, of course. But does that make it any less significant? There's nothing shallow about sex, nothing superficial. Marriage, if you like, you can call that

71

superficial: a social arrangement, a bargain struck at a certain moment in time. But sexual desire goes to the very core.

Looking back over his life he realizes that he has always believed in his own desire but never in theirs. Not the desire of the women. He always suspected in them, more than suspected, assumed in them an ulterior motive. The man wants sex and baits it with the chance of commitment. The woman wants commitment and baits it with the chance of sex. So far, so obvious. Except that there are casualties here that lie unremarked on the field of combat: the death of female desire; the loss of men as sexually desirable beings.

We collude. I collude. So frantic in my twenties in the pursuit of sex by any means I fed the hope of something more. Why else would she oblige me? Then the parting, the accusation of betrayal, the guilt. You lied to me! You didn't love me! After a while the act of lying itself comes to be sexually charged, or at least the intensity of the sexual excitement seems to be contingent on the level of the moral transgression. We collude in the lie that sex is an early way station on the road to love. Even our bodies collude in the lie, because always after the sex comes the revulsion, the sense of worthlessness, the self-accusation: was it for that that I lied?

No, not for that. Not for the short shudder of bliss. For the gathering storm that preceded it, for the rolling thunder that begins low and far away and comes ever closer until it fills the sky and drowns the world. For desire.

'You're very quiet, Tom,' says Vernon.

'Why aren't we talking about low-season discounts?' says Richard Graves.

'We can't advertise discounts,' says Vernon. 'That's an inducement, and inducements are illegal.'

'Bloody stupid if you ask me,' says Richard Graves. 'So how are we going to pay the bills when we've doubled in size and halved our bookings?'

'Maybe,' says Tom, who hasn't been listening and so says what they've all been thinking, 'maybe we shouldn't go ahead with the expansion.'

'But we've built it!'

'So? We don't have to equip it, staff it, heat it.'

'That is a legitimate option,' says Vernon cautiously, looking round the table.

'So what do we do with it?'

'I don't know. Put it to sleep. Wait for better times.'

This precipitates an explosion of disagreement. Tom withdraws once more into his own thoughts. He's indifferent to the outcome one way or the other. What's the worst that can happen? The hospital goes bust. He's a shareholder, he loses his stake. So what? He has a marketable skill. Life goes on.

So I have no ambition any more?

In some strange way he feels as if he's started his life over again. This time round there's no drive to achieve, no deferring of pleasure in the interests of later gain. This time, the pleasure.

73

Yes, she said. Of course I'll be in.

The other day she asked for a picture of him when he was young. He showed her the photograph his friend Olly took of him dancing at his twenty-first. He's always liked it because he looks happy though in fact he wasn't.

'Oh, you're so gorgeous!' Meg said when she saw it.

Looking through her eyes he saw a sweet-faced boy with shaggy hair, a lithe body. It was as if he was looking at a stranger. His own memory is of physical awkwardness, sticky-out ears, narrow chest, freckles, eyes that plead and look away. The musty odour of desperation.

Now, of course, thirty years later, three stone heavier, balding, cheeks sagging, eyes bagging, he can no longer be called gorgeous. But it's now that he's desired.

The meeting comes to a conclusion. The hospital expansion will proceed. A new marketing drive will aim to lift patient numbers. Vernon undertakes to brief the marketing team and Pegasus, the retained PR company.

As they leave Richard Graves murmurs to Tom, 'I should have thought you'd have more to say, with your new-found interest in marketing.'

Meg is in marketing.

'I leave that to you youngsters,' says Tom. Richard Graves is at most ten years his junior. 'In my day only the charlatans advertised.'

'Oh, the charlatans are advertising, all right,' says Richard. 'Any quack can offer cosmetic surgery these days. That's why we have to get out there, make our case, save the suckers from their own stupidity.'

Tom has now been made aware that his attentions to Meg have not gone unnoticed. What do you expect in a place this size? A staff of a hundred and twenty or so, everyone knows everything. They'll be joking about it, maybe expressing surprise, Meg isn't an obvious candidate for seduction in her sober business suit and her sober business face. Not exactly a beauty, they'll be saying. Nothing to write home about. And there's the wonder of it. Beauty turns out not to create desire after all. Desire creates beauty.

These things take you by surprise. He has almost no memory of Meg in the first weeks after her arrival. Once she stopped him on the corridor to tell him that she needed case histories to feed to journalists, how rhinoplasty saved my life and so forth. But he paid her no attention until the BAAPS conference in London.

They found themselves in a lift together, in the Waldorf Hilton. It was the end of the last session, they were both tired. He noticed that her hands were shaking. They made polite conversation. Then she closed her eyes. No more than the kind of thing you do if your eyes are hurting at the end of the day. She was telling him how much she was learning, her lips moving, her eyes closed, and he studied her face, and there were her hands, shaking. Then she opened her eyes and met his gaze without her defences in place, and he saw it as naked as a kiss: she desires me.

The lift doors opened. They went their separate ways. But from that moment on he looked at her differently. She changed under his eyes. She became beautiful.

So in a little while, in about an hour and a quarter, he'll pull in to one of the parking spaces reserved for residents of the Victorian mansion called Ridgewood Grange. There, in a two-bedroom flat with views of the communally-maintained park, Meg will be waiting.

Chloe has to run, dragging her wheeled suitcase with the
worn wheels that bang like a machine-gun, and only just
gets onto the train before the doors close for departure. She
left masses of time to get from Paddington to Victoria but
of course no Circle line train came for ever. Now she feels
hot and cross and the train is full.

She jerks her suitcase down the aisle through four carriages
to get into the half that will go on to Lewes after the train
divides at Haywards Heath. The only empty seat is a foursome occupied by a fat young mother and two fat young
children. The children are sprawled on the seats in such a
way that there's no room for a fourth.

Chloe stands her suitcase in the aisle beside them and
says as sweetly as she can, 'Any chance of a seat?'

'Move, Wayne,' says the mother. 'Out of the way, Jordan.'

The children don't move.

Chloe waits, smiling, wanting to smack their fat bored faces. Their mother goes red, raises one hand, and screams.

'*Move* or I belt you one!'

The children move, slowly, sulkily. Chloe sits down. The small fat boy starts to whine.

'Mu-um. I'm hungry.'

'No you're not. You had chips.'

'But I'm hungry.'

'Me too,' says the girl. 'I'm hungry.'

'Not now,' says their mother. 'Later.'

'But I'm *hungry*,' says the boy. 'My tummy hurts.'

'And mine,' says the girl. 'My tummy hurts.'

'Will you be *quiet*!' shrieks the mother. 'I said *no*!'

Both children begin to cry. 'Jesus God!' says the mother.

She stares at the children as if she hates them. Undeterred they maintain their steady snivelling. Chloe hates them too. She puts her iPod earpieces into her ears but she can hear the children crying over the beat of the music. People on trains complain when iPods have their volume turned up too high. How about children with their volume turned up too high?

Outside the train window darkness has fallen, and it's not yet half past four. Short days, long nights. Chloe hates winter. She sees herself reflected in the carriage window, and unthinkingly adjusts her lips to a slight pout, a *moue* her mother calls it, and passes a hand through her blonde hair. She's wearing her hair partly pinned at the back to make it fluff out on top, the bed-head look. She's an extremely pretty girl, in a style that's no longer fashionable, pink cheeks and blue eyes, petite and curvy, reassuringly feminine. Not looking her best right now, she needs at least forty-eight hours sleep, the end of term has been murder. To her expert eye her skin lacks lustre, her hair is drooping. Also she's just started her period. She wants to be home where she can shut herself in her room and have no one bother her.

The fat mother cracks. She pulls out a bag of Celebrations and lays it on the table between the fat children. The children stop whining and fall to an absorbed concentration of the choice before them. Mini-Mars Bars, mini-Snickers, mini-Bounties, mini-Milky Ways. Then they begin to eat. Steadily, crackling the wrappers, they suck and chew their way through Celebration after Celebration. The fat mother produces a bag of smoky bacon crinkle-cut crisps for herself. Chloe is no stranger to junk food herself, but this is a horror show. This mother is murdering her children.

Her phone pings. A text from Hal.

Sorry sorry sorry

Now he's sorry. What happened to 'You fucking slut I hope you die'? It's not as if she didn't tell him. It's not as if she didn't feel bad. He's the one chose to turn it into the biggest betrayal in history. Everyone cheats from time to time, boys most of all. What matters is what you do afterwards. So she had a fling with Robbie, these things happen, it didn't mean anything, and she told Hal right away. He was cool about it, she cried as she was telling him, he held her in his arms, he said, 'Hey, no big deal.' And then that same evening, that very same evening, he goes crazy. Talk about Jekyll and Hyde. You fucking slut, you make me sick, I hope you die, and all the rest.

Robbie is a bit of a twat to be honest, one tab of E and he thinks he can fuck for England. 'You want more? You want more?' No more, thank you, Robbie. If I start moaning now will you get the fuck on with it and come so I can get some sleep? Oh-Oh-Oh! No one's made me come like that before! You're the one! Whoop-de-doo.

Now Robbie's following me round like a sodding puppy. What is it with boys? You go for them because they're mean and dangerous and next thing they're all over you like a wet duvet. The fun all happens at the beginning, when they're not sure if they want you, and you say to yourself, I'm going to make that boy crazy about me. But then it happens and you're screwed. Like every way. Who wants a boyfriend for life when you're nineteen? Can't I just have one for Christmas? That way I can throw him away on Boxing Day when I'm bored with him.

Chloe giggles to herself. I'm such a cow. But why not? Why does everyone get so stressy like I've married them or something? It wasn't my idea to break up with Hal. I didn't have to tell him about Robbie. It's not like I did it to hurt him. What difference does it make anyway? Seriously.

I'm not Hal's wife. He doesn't own me. It's not like Robbie's stolen something from him. It's only sex, for fuck's sake.

So he dumped me and now he's sorry and what am I supposed to do?

She texts back: *Me too. Call later.*

Hal's sweet really. She remembers how crazy she was about him in the first week of term, with his long curly hair and his bobble hat and his acoustic guitar. Back then she felt almost shy with him because she had rich parents and had been to private school and he was out of this ultra-hard estate in Cardiff. She was soft and southern and blue-eyed and blonde and he was dark and wild. He laughed at her accent and called her Babe and pretended she was too delicate to go out in the rain, and she said, 'Yeah, right, I'm delicate,' and put her hand down his jeans. That was a good time.

The refreshments trolley approaches, rattling and clinking its cargo of drinks. The fat children look up, their lips and fingers smeared with chocolate, and set up a new whine.

'Want a Coke, Mum!'

'Thirsty, Mum!'

'You want me to belt you one?' offers the fat mother.

'But Mu-u-um!'

'I'm warning you, Wayne!'

'But I'm thirsty!'

So she gets them both Cokes, and they drink eagerly, sucking on their straws with long pulls. Then they return to the Celebrations.

The train is coming in to East Croydon. People are getting up, leaving their seats. Chloe gets up too. She drags her suitcase through to the next carriage, pushing her way past the people who are preparing to get off.

There she finds an empty window seat with just one other person on the other side, and she's sat down and pulled her suitcase in beside her before she realizes it's someone she knows.

'Alice?'

'Chloe?'

It's Alice Dickinson. She's hardly seen her since they were at prep school together over five years ago. Now she's all tall and thin, her face a little too long for her features, and more interesting than she used to be. Chloe runs a rapid check and decides it's the eyes. There's something appealing about those big brown eyes.

'Home for Christmas?'

'Yes,' says Alice. 'Term just ended.'

Her voice is soft and musical. Chloe remembers Alice as a silent child. People change.

'Me too. I'm at Exeter. I've been on trains for bloody hours.'

'I'm at UCL.'

'How's it going?'

'Okay. Still settling in, really.'

'My first term's been a total disaster,' says Chloe cheerfully. Already in such a brief exchange she has satisfied herself that Alice remains one of life's losers. She can tell from her tone of voice, and from the way she looks at her. The combination of timidity and envy gives Chloe a familiar sensation of power.

'Why? What happened?' says Alice.

'Oh, I got this boyfriend called Hal, and then I had a thing with a guy called Robbie, and Hal went nuts and dumped me, and Robbie turned out to be a pain in the bum, and I had a row with the girls in my house, I thought this girl had such a great personality but really she's so insecure, and I feel like I've not slept for a whole term, so all I'm going to do over Christmas is sleep.'

'Wow.'

'How about you?'

'I'm pretty tired, actually. The work's been pretty relentless.'

They talk about their work and their teachers and never having enough money, with Chloe doing most of the talking, but little by little Alice opens up. By the time they get to Gatwick Chloe feels able to move on to more personal topics.

'So what's the story with boyfriends?' she asks.

'Not much of a story at all,' says Alice.

'No boyfriends?'

'I'm not like you, Chloe.'

'So what? I should hope not. But you look great, Alice. Why shouldn't you have boyfriends?'

'Oh, I expect I will. I'm just not very good at it, I suppose. I'm not sure I know how to play the game.'

This interests Chloe.

'You're right,' she says. 'It is a game. If I fancy a boy I tell a friend, like, hey, I really like Hal, but don't tell him. So the friend tells him. Then Hal comes on to me, and I play hard to get. Even though I'm the one started it.'

Alice listens and a smile forms on her thin face. When she smiles she's almost beautiful. Chloe senses her admiration, and it makes her like her.

'I could never do that,' says Alice.

'It's all a bit juvenile. I expect I'll grow up one day.'

'No, I think it's great. I wish I could do it. But I just can't.'

'Why not?'

'I don't know. I suppose I don't really believe it would ever work.'

'Why not? Don't you think boys fancy you?'

'No. Not really.'

'Well, you're wrong. Believe in yourself. Think sexy and you become sexy.'

Alice laughs. 'You, maybe,' she says.

'I'm serious. It's not hard. Boys want girls. You just have to show you're interested, without being too easy. You have to make them work for it a bit.'

'But I don't know how.'

She gazes at Chloe with such a puzzled yearning that

Chloe is enchanted. This is a new role for her: teacher of the art of love. Back in the Underhill days Alice had always been cleverer than her. She probably still is. There's something delicious about this reversal of roles.

'You want me to help you?'

'Help me how?'

'Get you fixed up. Over Christmas.'

Alice blushes a deep red.

'Who with?'

'I don't know. Who do you fancy? There must be some boy you know who you like.'

'No, not really.'

'How about Jack Broad?'

Jack Broad comes to mind because Chloe met him on the street in Lewes a week or so before term started, and they stopped and talked for a few minutes. He was friendly, a little nervous, they gossiped about school friends, exchanged numbers so they could link up in the Christmas holidays, maybe get some others together from the old Underhill crowd. Jack isn't Chloe's type at all, to her eyes he seems too young, barely fifteen, though presumably he's eighteen or nineteen like all the rest of their year.

'I haven't seen Jack for ages,' says Alice.

'He got into Cambridge.'

'Good for him.'

'So he'd do, wouldn't he?'

Alice laughs, blushing still.

'Honestly, Chloe.'

'I promise you, it's easier than you think. It's all about putting ideas into people's heads. I'll meet up with Jack, tell him about you, how you blush when I talk about him, da-de-da, he can look you up on Facebook – you are on Facebook?'

'Yes.'

'Got some pictures of you looking gorgeous?'

'Well …'

'Sure you have. We all have. So I give him your number or I give you his or whatever. Then you meet up. And you're away.'

'Or not.'

'This is Christmas. People are up for it. All you have to do is look like you want it.'

'How do I do that?'

'Like this.'

Chloe puts her elbows on the table and her chin in her hands, and gazes at Alice with her eyes lifted up in the pose made famous by Princess Diana.

'You look at him like there's nothing in the world but him, and you're all his.'

She doesn't add that it helps to put your hand down his jeans. Alice is a learner. One step at a time.

'Isn't that too obvious?'

'You can't be too obvious. There's no such thing as too obvious. The best method of all would be to say, Hey, big boy, want a fuck? But we're too ladylike for that. Just.'

Alice laughs, covering her mouth with her hand.

Chloe's phone chirps. A text from Baz.

When RU back?

'Oh, God. Barry Unwin. Did you ever meet him? Boy with red hair, hangs out at the Snowdrop, thinks he's going to be a rock star.'

'No.'

'I went out with him a couple of times. Big mistake. But I'll tell you what, he's got a big one. And doesn't he know it. It's like no one ever told him size isn't everything.'

Alice covers her face with her hands.

'You okay, Alice?'

She looks out from between her hands, and she's smiling.

'How many boys have you slept with, Chloe?'

'Christ, I don't know.'

'You must know.'

'Well, it's over ten, because the last time I counted it was ten. Twelve, maybe. No, thirteen. That's over four years. Does that seem to you like too many?'

'I'm awestruck. I'm still at zero.'

'Well, we're going to put that right.'

The train goes into the tunnel before Lewes station, and all at once they're scrambling, getting their bags and cases, pulling on their coats against the December cold.

They part in the car park, Alice has only a short way to

walk to her house, and Chloe's mother is waiting in the Range Rover, engine running and headlights blazing.

'I'll call you. I will! I'm going to do it!'

Chloe heaves her bag into the boot, slides into the passenger seat, leans across to kiss her mother.

'Jesus, Mum, you look awful.'

Her mother pulls down the visor mirror and frowns into it, patting her cheeks.

'I'm fifty-two years old,' she says. 'I look like I'm a hundred.'

Chloe feels a wave of exhaustion wash over her. Talking to Alice has kept it at bay. Now she can hardly force her eyes open.

'I'm just about dead,' she says.

They drive out and up Station Street, past the War Memorial, on to the Offham road. Lewes looks small and safe and familiar in the glow of the streetlights.

'So have you had a good first term?'

'Horrendous,' says Chloe. 'What's for dinner?'

'I got some fillet steak. Only I'm not sure when we're going to eat. Everything is a bit up in the air.'

She's using her suffering voice.

'Don't do this to me, Mum. Okay? I've completely had it. All I want is a long hot bath, and dinner, and sleep. I can't deal with any more hassle.'

Her mother says nothing in reply. Chloe feels faintly guilty, but it's all true, no point in pretending. She's come home for peace and quiet and no demands. So it's Christmas and Christmas always stresses everyone, but it's not for two weeks.

I'm allowed a couple of days to get myself together, aren't I?

9

Lovelorn Christina drives south down the M23 dreaming
of breakfast tables set for young families in suburban semis,
of blue-striped china, the red-and-green cockerel on the
Kellogg's Cornflakes packet, the amber glow of a jar of
Golden Shred. Joe Nola's visions of domesticity invade her
mind and enchant her heart, even as the Puck-like image
of the artist himself dances backwards before her, forever
seductive, forever out of reach.

Before her tired eyes a river of car headlights streams
north from Gatwick. The day ends too soon, the night lasts
too long.

Oh, Joe. I love your dancer's body, your tactile grace. I
love your laughing celebration of this disappointing world.
But I mustn't fall in love with you, Joe, because you are
the star of my show. Not appropriate for the filmmaker to
fall in love with her subject. That way lies conflict of interest,
not to mention heartbreak.

Everyone loves you, Joe. Allow me to take my place in line, concealing my adoration beneath a veneer of professionalism and an easy teasing manner. Though as I have taken care to let slip, I am currently, possibly briefly, available. There is a window of opportunity. I am also currently thirty-one years old and not by any means desperate, not in this age of mature pregnancies.

Her mobile rings as she's passing Pease Pottage and the blue road signs are giving way to green. She shouldn't answer while driving but she does. It's Paul, her series editor.

'Where the fuck are you?'

'I'm on my way to meet Anthony Armitage. I want to bring him up to the gallery and catch his reactions to the Joe Nola show.'

'Who the fuck is Anthony Armitage?'

She can hear him Googling the name even as he asks.

'He taught Joe way back, in some art school somewhere. He was Joe's mentor.'

Clickety-click. Tappety-tap.

'Fuck! He's eighty!'

'He hates all modern art. Including Joe's.'

'Is that a fact?' She can almost hear Paul's brain working, clicking its way to the conclusion she herself reached at lunchtime, which is when Joe told her about the old man.

'So has he agreed to do it?'

'Paul, this is a man at war with the modern world. He

has no phone, no mobile, no agent, no gallery, no dealer, and no known relations.'

Paul ponders through the digital ether.

'Better and better.' He's still on Google. 'He's got two of his portraits in the NPG and one in the Royal Collection.'

'Sure. He's good. He's just way past his sell-by date. Like fifty years past.'

'And he hates Joe's work.'

'So Joe says.'

'Good girl. Drive on.'

Joe at lunch surrounded by the white-tiled proletarian chic of Livebait in Waterloo, eating high-priced fish and chips, pointing his fork at her, tomato ketchup on his lips, telling her about Anthony Armitage.

'Ran into him at the RA a few years back. He poked my chest with one finger – jab! jab! – and hissed, "Cancer! Cancer!"'

What do you make of me, Joe? Of course I know you take the trouble to charm me because I'm the best boost your career has had to date, or so you hope. I must be made to love you so that the show applauds you. But what happens after transmission? The screen goes black, the credits roll, and then? We've been together so much these last weeks. We've had fun, haven't we? What you don't know is that in my private life I'm shy. I'm only this brazen and self-assured because my job requires it. Take away the film camera and I shrink into the wallpaper. I am the wallpaper.

Here's the big question, Joe. Are you gay?

The general assumption is, Come on, guys, what you see is what you get. Is the Pope a Catholic? As it happens Joe's a Catholic, or at least he was raised in that mother-ridden faith. But there is such a thing as strategic gayness, a calculated addition to the image. Consider the blithely ruthless way he dropped the final consonant of his name: Joe Nola was once Joseph Xavier Nolan from one of the rougher quarters of Dublin. And Lottie, the unit gossip, claims to know two women Joe has slept with, one of whom she swears lived with him for over a year.

Oh shit! Nearly missed the slip road onto the Brighton bypass.

Christina checks the printout showing her route. Past Lewes, take a right at the Edenfield roundabout. Through the village, take a left.

Edenfield is where Henry Broad lives, her one-time boss. Her first job in television, and her first crush.

Christ, I was such a child. What can he have thought of me?

What do you think of me, Joe? Are we mates? You're not in a relationship right now, gay or straight, not as far as I know, and I know everything about you, so there's nothing to stop us loving each other except that old hump in the road. Between friendship and love the road rises, and the hump can feel insurmountable. What we need is a burst of speed. Move on to the more volatile emotions. I'm talking about the show, Joe. I want to see you caught off guard. Hurt, angry, open to surprise.

'He'll never do it,' Joe says about Anthony Armitage. 'He despises television even more than he despises me.'

But it's worth a shot. For a whole lot of reasons.

Driving through Edenfield now. One of those houses might be where Henry lives. And his wife, and his children, and his dog and his cat and his slippers.

Easy now. No need to be bitchy.

Turn left past the Edenfield Place Hotel. It's a road for about a hundred metres then it turns into an assault course. Her little Fiat, built for town, lurches like a beer can in a mill race. No human habitation in sight. Can one doubt the all-knowing Google? If so, in what can we trust? All is mere opinion and rumour.

A soft gleam in a window ahead. Christina pulls the trembling Fiat to a stop by a wall: beyond, the black bulk of the house draped in night. One window shines a private shine.

Lamplight. Or candlelight. Six o'clock on a Friday evening but here it's midnight in the Middle Ages.

She has to knock many times before there comes an answering growl through the closed door.

'I'm not here.'

'Mr Armitage? I'm a friend of Joe Nola's.'

She shouts in case he's deaf as well as blockaded behind a locked door.

'Who?'

'Joe Nola.'

'Never heard of him.'

'I've come down from London to see you.'

No answer.

'Can I please tell you why?'

No answer.

'I'm a television journalist. I work for Sky Arts.' She pauses. The magic of television not working its spell. 'I might even be young and gorgeous.'

The door opens. Men are simple creatures at heart, even in old age.

He stands in the doorway, the light such as it is behind him, presenting a semi-silhouette of some disarray. His white hair sticks out in odd clumps. He wears a thick-knit jersey from beneath which protrudes the tails of a shirt. He's staring at Christina with an expression of irritable disappointment.

'You're not gorgeous at all,' he says. 'You're not even young.'

'Oh, come on. I'm not bad.'

He's eighty, for Christ's sake. Who does he hang out with? Kate Moss?

'Joe Nola is a fraud,' he says, still standing like a sentry in the doorway. 'His real name is Joe Nolan.'

'I know.'

'He's a circus act. But then, so are they all.'

'I'm cold. I'm freezing my tits off out here.'

He looks surprised.

'A potty-mouth,' he says. 'And a liar. Lucky for you I was brought up to respect the fair sex.'

He stands back and indicates that she should go into the room to the right of the front door, the room in which the only lamp is lit. There's a wood fire burning in the small grate.

'You don't respect women at all,' says Christina. 'You exploit them. Look at *Ariadne, Sleeping*.' This is one of Armitage's paintings. 'She's not sleeping at all. She's lying naked on a chaise longue like Manet's Olympia, peeping out from between her eyelids thinking, A hard man is good to find.'

'The Manet reference is deliberate.'

'Just like Manet ripped off Velasquez.'

After this he's putty in her hands. It's a technique she's used many times before: flirtatious, obscene, flatteringly well-informed. Men of middle years and more are bewitched. All's fair in love and journalism.

'Sit down, now that you're here. Sit where you get the warmth of the fire. Tell me your name.'

'Christina Tennant.'

She gives him her card, heavy with professional integrity. He doesn't look at it. He looks at her. At a guess she reckons he's revising his judgement that she's not gorgeous at all. She's maybe a little bit gorgeous. Seen in three-quarter profile so her nose doesn't spoil the effect, and in this extremely flattering lamplight.

All round the wall and stacked on the floor are canvases; there must be over a hundred of them. Most of them seem to be figures: group studies, portraits. Also bottles. This man drinks.

'So what do you want from me?' he says.

'I'm making a television film about Joe. You know his work is part of the new exhibition at the Hayward?'

'Yes. I do know.'

'He thinks of you as his mentor.'

'He's a presumptuous fool.'

'So I want you to come up and take a look at his work.'

'You must be insane.'

'I'd be fascinated to see, and film, what you make of it.'

He's breathing heavily now. Sitting in the other armchair before the fire, hands folded over his stomach, legs stretched out.

'Well, I'll tell you now what I'll make of it, Miss Potty-Mouth. I'll make trash of it. I'll reduce his trashy work to much smaller pieces of trash. I'll bring a hammer with me and I'll smash it into tiny little pieces and sweep it up into black bin-bags and then his adoring public can come and admire it, because they won't be able to tell the difference.'

'That would be wonderful,' says Christina.

'Oh, it would, would it? I doubt if that cocky little Irish prick would agree with you on that.'

'I wouldn't tell him.'

The old man stares at her.

'You mean you'd let me loose in the Hayward with a hammer and turn a blind eye?'

'But not a blind camera.'

'Of course. Slow of me. You want a scandal.'

'Just because I'm gorgeous doesn't mean I'm stupid.'

His first smile.

'Well, well. I'll be the judge of that.' He reaches behind his chair and produces a bottle of Scotch and a glass. He fills the glass and proceeds to drink it. 'Here's a question for you,' he says. 'If you answer it correctly I will consider your proposition. What is your opinion of Joe as an artist?'

'I think he's magnificent.'

'Wrong answer. You have failed the test.'

'Ah, but have I? A moderately attentive three-year-old could work out that you don't rate Joe's work. So why didn't I tell you what you wanted to hear?'

'Because you flatter yourself that you have integrity.'

'Integrity is for the young. I'm over thirty.'

'Over thirty! My, oh my!'

But he's enjoying this. The Scotch is mellowing him.

'You asked me my opinion of Joe as an artist. You didn't ask me for my definition of artist. You yourself called him a circus act. A high-wire artist. A trapeze artist. A human cannonball. Joe performs magnificently in the three-ring big top that is the art world today.'

Anthony Armitage gazes at Christina for a long silent minute.

'Not bad,' he says at last. 'Nifty footwork. Fancy a snout?'

He holds out his glass. She declines with a gesture of one hand.

'So you'll do it?'

'Smash Joe's art on camera? I'd be locked up.'

'Better and better. Middle England would gather in candlelit vigil outside the prison gates.'

'You are a witch. You are a temptress.'

'I would deny all knowledge, of course.'

The old man looks into the fire. The flicker of the flames reflects on the lenses of his glasses.

'My God!' he says. 'I could do it.' He falls silent, brooding. Then: 'When did you have in mind?'

'The show closes in five days. How about Monday? That's always a quiet day for visitors.'

'Would Joe be there to see?'

'If you want him to be.'

'No. Better not. He'd stop me.'

He rises slowly from his chair and raises his glass in a toast.

'A blow for truth!' he cries. 'A blow for sanity! Pinoncelli *redivivus*!'

'Pinoncelli?'

'The man who urinated in Marcel Duchamp's *Fountain*, which is, as you know, the *fons et origo* of ready-made art, and an actual urinal. Then he attacked it with a hammer.'

'I've never heard of him.'

'You disappoint me. His act was dismissed as a bid for self-publicity. And naturally the making of art has no truck with any attempts at self-publicity. Oh, the bastards! Oh, the tawdry little hypocrites! What lies they tell. What smug little lies. And the poor deluded public, frightened out of their wits, bullied and bewildered, obedient as sheep. Anything not to be called bourgeois, anything not to be called philistine, off they troop, nodding and grinning, through the halls of shame and nonsense. Oh, madness, madness!'

He clutches at his hair with his free hand and groans aloud. Then he comes to a stop and shoots Christina a sharp interrogative look.

'Is there money in it?'

'We can't exactly pay you to smash Joe's installation.'

'How about expenses? Travel, hammer, etc.'

'Yes, we'd pay your expenses.'

He glowers at her.

'I'm not greedy. I'm broke. Look at this place. I'm not living here for the view. The roof leaks and there's no electricity. This crap lamp isn't for period detail. I'm penniless. Skint. Not funny when you're eighty, let me tell you.'

'I'm sorry.'

'I don't want pity. I want cash.'

Christina reaches into her bag.

'How about an advance on expenses?'

She holds out five twenty-pound notes. He takes them.

'This doesn't mean you've bought me.'

'I know. You cost more than that.'

He grunts in approval.

'Monday, then,' she says. 'I'll send a car to pick you up at ten.'

'Too early.'

'No, it isn't. You're on the payroll now. Office hours.'

He smiles at her, a wistful smile.

'Why didn't you come knocking on my door fifty years ago?' he says. 'I was beautiful as a god then, and I had the world at my feet. The man you see before you now is no more than a ghost. I have nothing left to offer the world.'

'You have your truth,' says Christina. 'And you have your anger.'

10

By the time Meg Strachan gets home it's almost six in the evening, and most of the residents' parking bays are occupied. A man is unloading his car, bag after bag bulging with groceries from Sainsbury's. He straightens under his load, gives Meg a friendly nod. He's called Malcolm, and he occupies the flat below. Meg nods back. She's still in her office clothes, charcoal grey skirt and jacket from M&S, white blouse, black tights, comfortable black shoes. You'd think it was a uniform, but she chose it all herself, aiming to project an air of quiet competence. There are other signals here too: that she understands her modest place in the ranks of professionals, that her behaviour will be predictable, that she neither asks nor expects to be noticed as an individual.

Malcolm goes ahead of her to the side door. He makes a brief show of holding the door for her, burdened as he is.

'Don't bother,' Meg calls. 'I'll be fine.'

Ridiculous, but she feels responsible for the weight of the shopping bags on his arms. Meg's day-to-day life is driven by a battery of minor fears. She hates to be thought of as being in the way; she's fearful of doing the wrong thing, of not being wanted. Given the option she would like best to be invisible, and if she is noticed, if she does enter the consciousness of a fellow human being, she wants above all to be helpful.

The side door has closed after Malcolm and locked itself. Meg has her key ready. Inside, the light on the stairwell, set to switch off automatically after just less time than it takes to climb the stairs, illuminates what was once the servants' entrance. There are no windows onto this narrow stairway. When you emerge onto the second floor, where her flat is, there's a tall window at the far end of the passage through which, in day-time, you can see past mature beeches to the East Sussex National Golf Club beyond the main road. There was a similar view from the landing window of the house she grew up in, and sometimes she thinks she bought the flat for this momentary echo of home.

Not that I was ever really happy there, she reflects. But familiarity isn't the same thing as happiness.

The flat has lost value since she bought it at the height of the property bubble. But at the same time interest rates have come down, cutting almost one third off her monthly mortgage repayments, so she's better off, really, given that she has no plans to move. The flat is a conversion, two bedrooms, kitchen-living room and a bathroom, squeezed into what was originally the nursery suite. The conversion looked very smart when she bought the flat, with its granite-topped kitchen units and its sea-grass carpets and its down-lighters. She has discovered since that the work was poorly done. The doors stick, there are far too few power points, and the shower has never worked. Despite all this, Meg loves her flat. This is where her most intense life is lived. Here, at this kitchen table. On this sofa. On this bed.

Just time for a bath if she's quick. While the bath runs she turns on the television to people the room. *The Weakest Link* is coming to an end, not a programme she likes, but the news will follow shortly. She pours herself half a glass of wine and thinks as she drinks it how surprised her mother would be to see her, her mother who never touched alcohol, who never smiled, who never said she loved her.

I've got a lover now, Mum. Bet you never expected that.

Naked in the bath she relaxes, not looking but sensing the outlines of her own body. The not-looking is habitual, like the clothes she wears that are designed to deflect attention. Meg is no beauty, her mother used to say, but she's such a help. Her reputation in the family as the one who can do anything. Not, of course, the grand achievements like writing plays, that's for her brother Alan. Meg's skills lie in fixing domestic appliances, finding lost spectacles, ordering tickets on the Internet. Now, because she has a lover, she finds she has a body. Not the approved brand of the day, her breasts too small, her hips too wide, but still a body that inspires desire. This is the wonder of her life: that he desires her. And desired, she becomes beautiful.

Out of the bath, she dries herself and puts on clean new underwear. Special pretty underwear, for which she undertook a special shopping trip to Brighton, where she would not be recognized. This is her love offering. The first time she wore the skimpy lacy garments she undressed quickly, turning away from him, dreading being ridiculous. But he saw and approved. He made her lie down beside him with her underclothes still on. He wanted to look at her.

She shivers as she remembers. The feeling is so strong. It frightens her sometimes, the enormity of her debt. This gift of desire which he makes her with every visit has changed her life. There is literally nothing she would not do for him.

She puts on a bathrobe on top of her underwear, and goes through to the bedroom. She folds the bed cover back, smoothes the pillows.

This is where I'll lie with him in my arms.

Already her body, tingling and alive, is anticipating the caresses to come. The moment when he pulls her towards him. The touch of his lips on her nipples. The weight of his body on her body.

She lights the candle on the bedside table and waits for the flame to steady. Then she turns out the lamps.

Candlelight is so gentle, so sexy. He loves to look at her naked by candlelight.

No talk of love, no talk of the future. Only now, and the life-changing discovery of sexual desire. His desire creates hers. Oh yes, she wants him all right. She wants him in her arms and in her body.

The phone rings. Her brother Alan wanting to know about the plumber.

'He's coming tomorrow. He's going to take a look at the shower tomorrow.'

'He'll fix it. There's nothing Matt can't fix.'

'How was the meeting?'

He was in London today for one of his glamorous film meetings.

'No grimmer than usual.'

Meg admires Alan: four years older, the family favourite, the one who bears the full weight of their parents' hopes. His life has become unimaginable to her. He meets film stars. He flies to Hollywood.

For a few short perfect years she and Alan shared a bedroom. Then when he was nine years old he announced he wanted a bedroom of his own. Meg, aged five, remained in the room they had shared, weeping herself to sleep every night. She never blamed Alan. How could she? He was so much more worthy than her. Why should he be burdened by her love? But from that day on she had known she was alone in the world.

'Let me know how it works out,' he says on the phone. 'Everything else okay? Job still okay?'

'Yes. I'm just about staying on top of it.'

He still feels responsible for her, at least far enough to want to be told there's nothing he need do for her. So the short phone call ends and Meg is released to her waiting.

She hasn't told her brother about her lover. What happens between them is outside place and time, it has nothing to do with the rest of her life. Nor with his marriage, his home, his family. It's a secret and a dream. A few short hours that give meaning to her entire existence.

The television has moved on to the news. The pound has dropped to a new record low against the euro. Four Marines have been killed in Afghanistan. Carol Vorderman has left *Countdown* after twenty-six years.

Odd how comforting the news is. For all its tales of death and despair it manages to be reassuring. Maybe it's because most of the misery is inflicted on others. Or because for all the changes of name and location, essentially the same things keep on happening, and the world doesn't come to an end. As if every news item functions as a talismanic prayer that wards off the unnamed evil and keeps us safe from harm.

Parisians are flocking to London to spend their euros in Marks & Spencer and Top Shop. Meg finds this mildly offensive. What has Paris to do with supermarket bargains? Paris is where she and Tom have talked of going for the weekend, if ever his professional and family commitments allow. At least, he said it once, asked her if she would like that, and she said yes she would.

Actually anywhere would do. The magic would be that they could go about as a couple. Stroll down a shopping street. Eat in a café. Go to a film. All the things couples do together that become meaningful because they are shared. Once you're in a couple the film can be bad and the evening is still memorable. As for walking down the street side by side: the gaze of every passer-by is as binding as the voice of a priest in a wedding church. The sacrament of the boulevard.

Did he mean it? He's never spoken about it since.

Carol Vorderman wept as she left the show.

A car driving up outside. Meg goes to the kitchen window which overlooks the residents' car park and sees him pulling up, getting out of his car, glancing back as he presses the remote lock to see the answering flash of orange lights.

She turns off the television, checks herself in the mirror in the living room, pulls the belt of her bathrobe tight around her waist, runs a hand through her hair. Not what you'd call a beauty, but she'll do.

Hyper-receptive to every detail of his coming, she hears the outer door open and close two floors below. He uses the key she had cut for him, the key that he keeps openly, unquestioned, on his key ring, the way into her private space that lies warm in his pocket.

Now his footsteps up the stairs: utterly recognizable, though impossible to say what it is that singles him out. His soft confident tap on the door. He knows she's there, waiting, listening.

And all at once she's in his arms.

'Oh, Meg.'

His sigh of happiness. He kisses her. She whispers in his ear the words he has taught her, the words he longs to hear.

'I want you to fuck me, Tom. I want to be fucked.'

Afterwards, lying in bed by candlelight, they slip into a half-sleep. Only five minutes or so, but Meg treasures the sweet shared moments of peace.

Then he stirs, and sits up.

'Is the shower fixed yet?'

'No, not yet.'

'No time for a bath. Never mind.'

He must go home to his wife. Meg feels no guilt. This is nothing to do with his marriage. She has no claim on him, does not presume to regard herself as a rival. He has a wife, family, home, job, and from the fullness of his full life he shares with her this infinitesimally small part of himself. It's the part that only exists with her, and so it rightfully belongs to her. Small for him; for her, all the world.

'I expect I'll be playing a round of golf tomorrow.'

This is code. He comes to her after golf.

'What sort of time?'

'Twelvish?'

'Yes, okay. Oh, no. I've got the plumber coming round then. I'll call him and put him off.'

'Don't do that. The shower needs fixing.'

She can't say: I'd rather see you once, for half an hour between a game of golf and family lunch, than ever have a shower again in all the rest of my life. So instead, compliant as ever, she says, 'Maybe later tomorrow?'

'Maybe. I'll call.'

And I'll be waiting, says Meg silently. Not aloud, because she doesn't want him to know how much he means to her.

11

'But you live in London,' says Caspar, puzzled, twisting his fingers through Alice's hair. 'And Guy lives in London.'

'London's huge, Cas. Absolutely huge.'

'I'm going to London to see Guy.'

'All right. But he's a very busy man. He may be out.'

'Out where?'

'At a meeting. Or a lunch. Or seeing someone.'

Caspar wrinkles his brow, trying to imagine this far-away life.

'Dad doesn't go out,' he says. Then remembering his father went to London today he adds: 'Mostly.'

'Alan works from home.'

'Doesn't Guy work from home?'

'No. He has an office.'

Alice smiles as she watches Caspar's thoughts come and go on his open face. Six years old and he's as precious to her as the day he was born. Her little half-brother.

'What's all this about Guy anyway? Why do you want to see him?'

Guy, her own father, hasn't so much as called her the entire term, her first term in London, even though she's been living in a hall on Maple Street, five minutes from his office.

'I just do.'

'Well, then, I'll tell you what. Why don't you phone him?'

A big smile lights up Caspar's face.

'Yes! I could phone him!'

Alice gets out Guy's number and Caspar presses the phone buttons for himself. To her amusement, Guy evidently answers in person.

'Hello? Are you Guy? I'm Caspar. I want to see you.'

She watches him as he listens intently, nodding.

'Yes,' he says. 'She came home today.' Then, after listening some more, 'All right.'

He puts down the phone.

'He's coming to see me.'

'What! Here?'

'Yes. Tomorrow afternoon.'

'Blimey.'

'What does blimey mean?'

'It means I'm surprised.'

Alan now emerges from his study where he retreated to deal with his emails as soon as he got home. It turns out he travelled on the same train from London as Alice, which is a bit spooky.

'Dad,' says Caspar, 'have you stopped using your computer?'

'For now.'

'Can I go on it?'

'Okay. But just for half an hour.'

Caspar hurtles away to Alan's study.

'Bloody computer games,' sighs Alan.

'How was the meeting?' says Alice.

'Oh, you know. The usual. Pretty damnable, actually. I have to start again from scratch, more or less.'

'Oh, Alan.' She's had this conversation with him so many times before. 'You shouldn't be doing film work. You should go back to writing plays.'

He smiles and shrugs. He looks so defeated she wants to hug him.

'How was your term?'

'Okay,' she says. 'I'm glad it's over.'

'No better than that?'

'I like my course. I've made some friends.'

'But no one special.'

'Not yet.'

'You will. There aren't many out there like you, but there are some.'

He takes her in his arms and they have a hug.

'You're my special friend,' says Alice. 'You and Mum.'

'I'm your stepfather. You're supposed to hate me.'

'I don't hate you. I love you.'

So easy in his arms. Why aren't there boys her age like Alan?

'Guess who I met on the train?'

'Who?'

'Chloe Redknapp.'

'Chloe Redknapp!' Alan was their teacher, all those years ago. 'The blonde bombshell.'

'She's exactly the same, only now she plays her games on boys.'

'She was a monster. She used to bully you.'

'The funny thing is she seems to have no memory of all that. She was really quite friendly.'

'I'm all in favour of Chloe Redknapp. You and I bonded over her. That's why you fixed me up with your mother. For which I'll be eternally grateful.'

'Oh, Alan. I just wish you were doing the writing you like. You look so miserable.'

'What have I got to be miserable about? I'm lucky to be in work.'

'Does Mum know?'

'Oh, I'm always moaning to her.'

She takes his hands, looks solemnly into his eyes.

'You're to say to her, I'm packing in the films, I'm going to write a new play. We'll have less money, but we'll be fine, and I'll be so much happier.'

He says nothing for a long moment.

'Like I said,' he says at last. 'There aren't many out there like you.'

Alice goes to her room and unpacks her suitcase, slowly re-establishing her presence in the familiar space. She hasn't said so to Alan, and she won't say so to her mother, but she hates her hall of residence in London. Her room there is small and anonymous, and London makes her feel lonely. It came as a shock to find in her first few days that she was homesick, just at the time she was supposed to be having the most exciting week of her life. She forced herself to go to the freshers' events, but every night that week, alone in her narrow and unfamiliar bed, she cried herself to sleep.

This is not something to share with anyone. Alice is ashamed of her own social failure. She's ashamed that she's never had a real boyfriend. The hurt of it goes so deep and has been in her for so long that it's got out of proportion with reality. So as well as confiding in no one, she does not confide in herself. When she catches herself brooding on her failure she reprimands herself sharply, often aloud, saying, 'That's enough of that! Snap out of it!' She has learned to cope by expecting nothing to change, by shutting the doors on that part of her imaginings, and walking away. But all the time it's there, waiting, the unvisited house with its empty rooms where she had once dreamed of finding love.

She pulls out her laptop and plugs it in to charge.

Her phone beeps. A text from Chloe.

Operation Jack under way.

Alice sits down on her bed and closes her eyes. Why is Chloe doing this? Her first instinct is to text her back and tell her to leave her alone, get out of her life. But she does not text Chloe back.

Do I really want this to happen?

She tries to understand her own chaos of intense feelings. There's longing there, a heartbreaking cry that says, 'Oh, if only it could work out.' There's gratitude, even to Chloe Redknapp, for taking action, for compelling her to leave her lonely room. And there's fear, because surely nothing will come of it but failure and humiliation.

Of course she knows Jack Broad. She hasn't kept up with him, but they've met from time to time. She saw him only last summer in Bill's Café, they talked for a few minutes. He was clutching a book by W. G. Sebald, which he recommended to her, but she hasn't read it. He was friendly and rather thoughtful. His hair was long, she remembered, not in a cool way, more in a way that showed he didn't really know what to do with it. She liked him for that.

She opens up her laptop and logs onto Facebook. She goes to Jack's page. There are several pictures of him at Cambridge: on a bicycle by the river; with two friends, both male, at a party; in his room, surrounded by books, holding an imaginary gun to his head. No evidence of a girlfriend.

He has a sweet face, still boyish. He seems to be always wearing the same clothes, jeans, check shirt, black jacket. Sometimes a stripy scarf wound round his neck. His Facebook status reads: *Jack is working too hard and his brain hurts.*

She can feel it starting, growing unbidden within her, the secret hope that looks so plausible but is really no more than a fantasy. Why do I do this to myself? When will I learn? But this time it's different, because there's a third party. Chloe's intervention gives the absurd little dream some dressing of reality.

I'm not just making this up. Chloe is doing it too.

How ridiculous to invest so much authority in a person she barely knows, and neither likes nor respects. Alice wants to say that Chloe is an empty-headed fool. That she'd be ashamed to be like her, chasing boys and jumping from bed to bed. And it's true, she doesn't want Chloe's life. But for all this, she bows down before Chloe and acknowledges her superiority: because she's pretty, because boys want her, because all other pursuits and achievements in life seem worthless without this one elusive essential, love.

Why should I care so much? Why do I mind so much about not being pretty? Why can't I see that having a boyfriend is only one among many ways of leading a rich and fulfilled life?

Her mother says to her, 'Why do you say you're not pretty? You're beautiful.' But when Alice looks in a mirror and sees that sad long face peering uncertainly back at her she knows her mother is lying. 'Don't lie to me,' she says. 'I look like a donkey.' Then her mother gets annoyed and says she's not lying, it's true, she is beautiful. So apparently it's true for her. That's how it goes. To your mother you're beautiful, to everyone else, not. So what does that tell you about beauty?

Her mother enlists Alan on her side.

'Of course she's beautiful,' he says. 'She's worth more than the lot of them put together.'

Alice knows that she's clever, and hard-working, and maybe more: maybe she's original, maybe she's creative. Secretly she's begun to do some serious writing of her own, just a short story, just dipping a toe in the water. With a mother a journalist and a stepfather a playwright it would be odd if she didn't try out her own abilities. But she would rather die than show either Liz or Alan her work in progress.

Her story has no title as yet, and it certainly isn't autobiographical. People say, 'Write what you know.' Alice chooses to do the opposite. She is writing about someone as unlike herself as it's possible to be. Her central character is a boy, quite a young boy, who doesn't yet know that it's impolite to speak openly of the unhappiness of others. He can see quite clearly how miserable everyone is, but he doesn't understand why they're so miserable. He asks them awkward and insightful questions, which make everyone embarrassed. In a way he's like one of Dostoevsky's holy fools, only he's young, still a child. Then one day something happens that hurts him terribly, and after that he understands, and the questions stop. So it's a story of first unhappiness. The inverse of all the stories of first love.

Alice finds writing her story both very difficult and very exciting. In her head it's all real and true, but as it emerges onto the laptop screen it reads as false and unconvincing. But still she persists. If only the words would start to come out right, there's something there, just ahead, almost within reach, that is more intense and satisfying than anything in existence. That something gives worth and meaning to her life even if she has nothing else. It shines on her like the sun, it seduces her like a dream of paradise. What to call it? Pure consciousness, perhaps. Enlightenment. Or the simplest strongest name of all: truth.

So what price love? Truth trumps love every time.

But love is so insidious. It slithers into so many of the corners of life. Love is company, and conversation, and someone to go to see a film with and talk about the plot with afterwards. Love is not eating alone. Love is touch and kiss and hold tight. Love is joy in nakedness. Love is sex. Love is babies, and family, and a shared home, and not growing old alone.

And all this mighty lifelong edifice begins with the stupid frightening unmanageable game of getting a boyfriend. So easy for Chloe Redknapp, so hard for Alice.

Operation Jack under way.

She hears the slam of the front door two floors below. Her mother is home. She leaps up and bounds down the stairs.

'Mum!'

Liz Dickinson wraps Alice in her arms, kisses her warm face with her cold face.

'Darling. I got home as soon as I could.'

They look at each other, smiling, hunting out the little changes. Alice knows her mother almost as well as she knows herself.

'You've had a bad day.'

'Yes.' Liz sighs, unbuttons her coat. 'Not one of my best.'

'You need a drink.'

'Coming up.' This is Alan from the kitchen, bottle in hand. 'One unit of alcohol for the lady.'

They join him in the kitchen. Liz keeps hold of Alice's hand.

'I've missed you so much, darling. You have no idea.'

'Oh, Mum. You've got Alan, and Cas.'

'But you're my little girl. There'll never be anyone like you for me.'

Alice bursts into tears. She smiles as she cries, feeling foolish, but both Liz and Alan are looking at her as if they understand. Liz takes her in her arms again, and whispers their secret.

'Love you, Addle.'

'Love you, Mum. Love you the most and the longest.'

'The most and the longest.'

After that she dries her eyes and they all have a drink to celebrate Alice's homecoming. Alice talks about her term, making herself be light and cheerful, turning it into a joke, because she can see how tired Liz is. Caspar appears to ask for more time, just five minutes, maybe ten, so he can make it to the next level of his game, and Liz says yes. Alice sees the way her mother's eyes avoid Alan's as she grants this permission.

'No point in being too rigid,' she says.

Alice remembers Caspar's phone call.

'I think Guy may be coming tomorrow.'

'Here? Why?'

'Cas called him. He wants to see him.'

'Why on earth does Cas want to see Guy?'

'I don't really know.'

'I have to work tomorrow, I think. I wish I didn't.'

Tomorrow is Saturday. Alice is long used to her mother's irregular hours. Liz turns her attention to Alan.

'How's it been for you, love? How was your meeting?'

'Triumphant. They like my work so much they want me to do it all again.'

'Oh, no.'

Alice says, 'I've been telling him to stop doing film work. I'm right, aren't I, Mum? He hates it.'

'Yes, of course. Let's all stop. I'm so sick of doing stupid interviews with stupid people. I was kept waiting for two and a half hours yesterday before being granted the unique privilege of fifteen minutes with guess who? Alexandra Burke. And she's not even allowed to say anything bitchy about Simon Cowell.'

'Who is Alexandra Burke?' says Alan.

'Oh, Alan,' says Alice. 'Even I know that. She's the one who sings "Hallelujah" on *The X-Factor*.'

Alan gives a shrug. It all means nothing to him.

'Anyway,' says Liz, 'I expect I won't have to suffer much longer. Everyone at work is expecting the knife to fall. They're talking about cutting four hundred jobs.'

'Might you lose your job, Mum?'

'Of course. None of us is irreplaceable.'

'But you've been there for ever! And you're so good!'

'Well, we don't care, do we?' says Alan. 'If they don't want her, we don't want them. I've got money coming in. We won't starve.'

'But Alan—'

He flashes Alice a look and she says no more.

'The thing about film work,' says Alan, 'is it's a pain in the bum, but it is quite sociable. And all those drafts they make you do are like a master class in craft. I'd never want to give it up altogether.'

Alice says nothing and Liz doesn't seem to notice. She's starting to forage in the fridge for something for their supper.

'Stop that,' says Alan. 'Supper's all sorted. I made a lasagne before I left, and I've just taken it out of the fridge and put it in the oven.'

'Oh, you angel.'

He is too, thinks Alice. He's a good man. He just notices things, and then quietly gets on and does what has to be done, as if it's the most natural thing in the world. And he loves Mum, anyone can see that. So it's possible. Good men do exist. Unless he's the only one.

She runs her mind over the boys she's met in the last year or so. None of them comes close. Without exception they are dull and immature. Not stupid, some can talk very cleverly, on subjects she can't even begin to understand. But they are all unaware, somehow enclosed, their senses dimmed, so that they have no idea what to say when she's with them, how to behave. They don't really perceive her at all. It's like she's on the other side of soundproof glass, and most of the time they're not even looking. How on earth do people ever get together? We flounder about in the fog, crash into each other, cling on for a while, and so are presumed by others to be a couple. But no actual personal connection has been made at all.

So why do I care so much? If it's all a fraud and a delusion, who wants it? Better to let ten years pass, and we can all grow up, and then try again when we're capable of knowing each other. Liz was thirty when she met Alan.

No, thirty-one. When she was Alice's age she went out with Guy, and look what a disaster that was. So give it ten years. Let herself off. It's not as if the boys are forming an orderly line.

But no harm in meeting up with Jack.

12

Belinda is the kitchen making the clafoutis for pudding because that's what she planned and she can't think what else to do. Chloe is upstairs on the phone, she can hear her voice shrilling away, the high notes of her exclamations, but not the words. The red cabbage is simmering on the slow plate. The potatoes are in the oven. The steaks won't go on until the last minute. There's the table to lay before Tom gets back.

She pours herself another glass of wine and takes a big gulp. Getting drunk. The stage of numb paralysis has passed, and Belinda finds herself in an unfamiliar world where nothing is what she supposed it to be. Has she been blind for years? Does everyone know but her?

She keeps switching between panic and disbelief. She tells herself Lisa made it all up to hurt her, to break up her marriage, to get Tom for herself. Tom can't be having an affair. They have a good marriage. So it's not perfect, but it works, doesn't it?

She argues with him in her head as she mixes the eggs and cornflour and sugar and cream and halved plums. You're not having an affair, Tom. Don't give me that crap. You're not the type. If anyone round here is going to have an affair it's me. Except I'm not, because I'd never do anything to hurt you.

Tell me you would never do anything to hurt me, either. Just say it. Say you wouldn't fall for a younger woman and leave me alone and ashamed and a whole lot poorer. You wouldn't do that, would you, Tom? Because that would be shit, shit, shit.

She sprinkles sugar onto the inside of a buttered dish and scoops the sticky batter into it from the mixing bowl. Tom loves puddings, wishes I made them more often. So here's a pudding for you.

Shit, shit, shit. Of course he's having an affair.

He'll be back any minute. No, in half an hour or so. She's timing dinner for eight-thirty, the cabbage and the potatoes will be done by then, and she needs a moment to freshen up.

When do I tell him I know? Not in front of Chloe. Chloe doesn't have to know. Belinda realizes with a shock that she's ashamed before her daughter. This is a kind of failure as a woman, she doesn't want Chloe's pity. Or Chloe's pain.

What's going on, Tom? Why are you pissing on all our lives? If you are.

Oh, Christ, I was going to do baked tomatoes.

Might as well get the clafoutis in. That way it can sit for an hour after it's cooked. You don't want to eat it hot.

She gets two big beef tomatoes from the fridge and cuts them in half, and there's only three of them for dinner, unless you'd like to invite your floozy, would you, Tom? Your tart to share the tart. Out with the mezzaluna to fine-chop the garlic and thyme and the oregano. Grate the Parmesan in the Magimix. A drizzle of olive oil. How many times have I done this in my life? How many times have you done it with her? If you have. Which I doubt, because half the time you can't even rise to the occasion, can you?

Is that why? Oh, God. Why did I never think of that?

The panic terror pushes up her throat from somewhere deep in her belly, and she has to press her hands onto the island unit and let her head hang down. She feels giddy with fear, her mouth's dry, her heart pounding.

Don't make me be one of them. I don't want to be a left woman. Haven't I been a good wife?

The giddiness passes. She drains her glass of wine.

A door bangs in a bedroom above. The rattle of Chloe's trainers on the stairs. The flash of her blonde head in the hall doorway.

'I'm going out, Mum. Won't be long.'

'Hey! What about dinner?'

'I'll be back.'

'Eight-thirty. We're eating at eight-thirty!'

'Okay!'

The front door slams.

Belinda sprinkles the herbs onto the halved tomatoes, then the parmesan, then the olive oil. Maybe there'll be no dinner at eight-thirty. Maybe by then it'll all be over. But what can you do? You just carry on as if nothing's ever going to change.

She lifts the pan lid on the cabbage. It's been cooking for an hour, slowly absorbing the red wine vinegar and the grated orange rind and the cloves. Let it stew: the longer the better. So that's it until it's time to do the steaks. She checks the time. Twenty past seven. He'll be home any minute.

Suddenly, seized with a sense of urgency, she runs upstairs to their bedroom. She pulls off her jersey, puts on a pale green silk top that she knows looks good on her. A little remedial work on her face. Brush her hair. A touch of scent, not too much. She doesn't usually tart herself up for Tom's homecoming. It happens every day, for God's sake.

As she comes down the stairs again she feels a sudden urge to phone someone and tell them all about it. She needs advice, a sympathetic ear, a second opinion. But who? And what's she to say? 'Guess what? Tom's been caught diddling someone in marketing in a Portakabin.' Except he hasn't.

Nothing is certain. If she tells a friend it will become real, and it isn't real yet. It may be a lot of fuss about nothing.

Tears sting Belinda's eyes. Hold me in your arms, Tom. Tell me it's not true. Tell me I'm your girl. So many nights my body twined in yours, I can't count how many. Don't make me spend my nights alone.

Now she's crying actual tears. She dabs them away with a drying-up cloth warm from the Aga rail. She presses it lightly to her cheeks, grateful for its comfort.

What an idiot! I forgot to set the timer for the clafoutis! How long has it been in the oven? Can't be more than five minutes. Give it twenty more.

Red plums, red tomato, red cabbage, red meat. This is a red meal. How did that happen? Every meal needs visual variety. I'm losing my touch.

She laughs at that. What touch? You have to admit this is a ridiculous situation. If we were both young and gorgeous it might be tragic. But he's fifty-five years old, with a thirty-seven-inch waist and a bald head, and I'm as wrinkly as a prune. We're old enough to be grandparents, if only Alex would start to get serious about his life.

Don't make me tell Alex. Don't make me tell Chloe. Don't make me tell myself.

The shudder of gravel. His car in the drive. You have to give it to him, he's always punctual. If he says he'll be home by seven-thirty, he's home by seven-thirty.

She makes her decision in the few short moments

between the sound of the car door closing and the opening of the front door. She'll say nothing. There'll be time enough later, after dinner, after Chloe's gone back up to her room. This is supposed to be a celebration dinner to welcome Chloe home.

He bustles in the same as ever.

'Hi, darling. Sorry I'm late. Did you get my message?'

'Yes. Michelle called.'

'Is Chloe back?'

'She's gone out.'

'What, already?'

'She'll be back for dinner.'

'I'm going to grab a quick shower, okay?'

And off he goes, up the stairs. No sign that anything is different. There's a rush and an energy to him that she hasn't remarked before, it's nothing new, but he brings with him a breeze of activity that fills the house. Tom's always been a man who never has enough time, he doesn't loiter. She likes that about him. She likes many things about him.

Christ, the not knowing is going to kill me. I have to know.

She abandons the wait-till-later approach. There are no tell-tale signs. There is no easing into knowledge, no dab of anaesthetic before the knife cuts. You know or you don't know. The only question is how to open the box.

I've been hearing rumours, Tom. Probably just stupid gossip. But you would tell me, wouldn't you?

She starts laying the table for dinner. These automatic tasks bring their own form of comfort. Surely if I lay down the knives and forks in their due places my life will go on in its familiar way? These patterns form our life. They shape us and bind us. Surely he feels that too.

She hears him singing upstairs. He has a good singing voice. He's singing a Christmas carol, 'Once in Royal David's City'. Someone's happy.

He comes downstairs and into the kitchen pink and clean as a baby, wearing jeans and a blue polo shirt, still humming his carol.

'Smells good,' he says. 'I'm starving. How's your day been?'

Belinda takes the lid from the heavy pan, grasps the pan handle with the oven gloves, and throws the red cabbage at him. She had no idea she was going to do it. He just looked so pleased with himself.

'You fucker!' she screams. 'You fucking fucker!'

He's turning aside towards the fridge to get himself a glass of wine as she throws the slushy contents of the pan, and her aim is poor, and the soft cabbage doesn't throw very far. It splatters onto the floor and over part of the dresser, but none of it hits him.

'What – what – what—'

Shock makes him stammer.

'I'm going to kill you!' she screams. 'How could you do it? You fucking little fucker!'

Now he's pawing the air with his palms, like someone trying to calm a horse.

'Please – Belinda, please – what is this? What have I done?'

'You know what you've done!' She rages at him, entirely out of control, hearing herself with horror. She sounds like a witch. 'Don't give me that! You know what you've done!'

Somewhere below the level of rage there's a cautionary instinct at work. She won't name the crime. Let him confess. Or let him tell her there is no crime. Let him swear it's all untrue.

'I've done nothing! Where's all this coming from? What am I supposed to have done?'

As suddenly as it flared up her rage subsides. Not because she believes him: quite the opposite. She can see it in his face and hear it in his voice. Of course it's true. Why did she even bother to doubt it? An overwhelming weariness possesses her.

'Oh, Tom. How could you?'

She sits down at the kitchen table and covers her face with her hands. He says nothing. No denial, then.

She waits in the merciless silence. So is this how it ends? Twenty-four years, two children, a home, a world. Can it all vanish in a puff of breath?

'Please. Don't cry. It's nothing.'

She didn't know she was crying again but it turns out she is. Sobbing softly into her hands.

'I don't know what you've been told but it's nothing. I promise you. It means nothing. It's just – oh, Christ, these things happen. Just a fling.'

A fling. Such an odd word. Like something you throw away, in a light-hearted manner. Only she's the one he's throwing away.

She hides her face in her hands, her voice muffled.

'Everyone knows.'

She doesn't want to look at him. Not yet.

He comes closer.

'Belinda. Darling. I mean it. It's nothing.'

Oh, let it be nothing. Let it never have happened. But this is a nothing that hurts her and frightens her so much.

'Why?' she says. 'I don't understand why.'

'I don't know why,' he says. 'Because it was there.'

Because it was there. *It* is another woman. *There* is in his arms. Do I want details? No. Yes. No. What does she give you that I don't? How have I failed? Don't ask. There's no good answer to that.

'It's over,' he says. 'It won't happen again. I swear.'

'Over when?'

'Now. From tonight.'

If she hadn't found out he'd have carried on. He has no shame. He has no decency. He'd have gone on poking his, poking his—

'You fucking fucker!'

She lashes out, catches him across one shoulder. Not

133

looking to see where her blows land she hits and hits, feeling him flinch and cower before her rage. But he doesn't retreat. Instead he advances. She feels his arms around her, partly restraining, partly embracing. She presses herself against him, sobbing.

'Don't leave me. Don't leave me.'

'No one's leaving. It's all nothing. It's all over.'

He strokes her back, holding her, placating her.

'How could you do it, Tom?'

'It's over now. I promise.'

'I don't understand. I don't understand.'

'Hush, now. I've been stupid, that's all. I'm very sorry. I won't do it again. Here, let's dry your eyes before Chloe gets back.'

The timer pings.

'I have to get something out of the oven. I made a pudding.'

They part. She goes to the oven. She still hasn't looked at him. She dare not look. She knows she'll see the guilt in his eyes. She doesn't know what to do with the anger and the hurt. The betrayal goes so deep, but he has no idea, he says it's nothing, it's over. It's not nothing. It's not over. It's only just beginning.

Why am I taking the clafoutis out of the oven, when the cabbage is all over the floor? What do we do now? Have dinner like nothing's happened?

How do you go on after the world's ended?

13

Jack keeps being asked what he wants for Christmas. When he says 'Nothing' they don't believe him, Carrie most of all.

'That's stupid,' she says. 'All that does is make it harder for us.'

'I don't really want any presents. How is that harder?'

'So now we have to guess what you want and get it wrong and waste our money.'

'Why? I've told you. I don't want anything.'

'All right, darling,' says their mother, just back from London, hurriedly putting on a pan for pasta. 'Don't worry about it. I'll come up with something.'

'See,' says Carrie. 'Now Mum has to do all the work. Now you're the centre of attention. Oh dear, what can we get Jack? Let's all talk about Jack for the rest of our lives. How can we make Jack happy?'

'For God's sake!' Their mother tired by a busy day. 'Just stop getting at each other. I can't stand it.'

'I'm not getting at anyone,' says Jack. 'All I said was I didn't want Christmas presents. I never said anything about not being happy. Carrie just made that up.'

His father appears and his mother says they have to go to dinner in London tomorrow night. His father groans.

'Must we?'

'Diana's got a crisis. Tell you later.'

Jack starts laying the table without even being asked, which is something his mother is always asking them to do. Actually he's hungry and wants to eat as soon as possible. The others start talking about when to get the Christmas tree. The family tradition is that the tree is fetched, erected and decorated by all four of them. A decision is made to drive to the garden centre after lunch tomorrow.

'Okay with you, Jack?' says his father.

Jack has other plans for tomorrow afternoon. He wants to borrow his mother's car and drive into Lewes. It's a small town and there's a fair chance he'll meet someone he knows. For example, Chloe Redknapp. The one with the plentiful love life.

'Not sure,' he says, mumbling his words because the thoughts behind them are unclear to him.

'You have to come,' says Carrie, indignant. 'It's what we do.'

Jack shrugs. His lack of loyalty to family tradition enrages Carrie.

'So you don't want presents and you don't want a Christmas tree. What do you want?'

I want Chloe Redknapp. Only he doesn't say it aloud.

His phone rings. He pulls it out and checks the screen and can't believe what he sees. It's Chloe Redknapp calling. Like a magic trick. Think of a card, here it is. From desire to reality in one easy bound. Big surprise.

He goes upstairs to the privacy of his room to take the call. His family probably think it's Hannah. Let them.

It's Chloe, miraculously making the first move.

'Hey, Jack. You busy?'

'Not exactly.'

'Any chance we could meet up? There's something I want to ask you.'

'Sure. Why not?'

'You drive, right?'

'Yes.'

'Any chance you could come over to Plumpton? I've still not passed my test.'

'When?'

'Now.'

With these few words Chloe turns Jack's life around. By some mysterious mechanism his own longings have generated this phone call. He has willed Chloe into his life.

'I suppose I could,' he says, faking reluctance.

'Meet me at the pub. You know the Half Moon?'

'Sure.'

'See you there in what? Twenty minutes?'

Jack goes back downstairs in a daze of excitement.

'Mum, can I take the car?'

'Take it where? What about supper?'

A wave of irrational but violent anger surges through him.

'I don't want any supper. Stop trying to run my life.'

'But you have to eat, darling.'

'I won't die. Just leave it alone, okay?'

He sees the hurt in his mother's eyes and hates himself because he knows she only wants what's best for him. But she doesn't know and he's not telling and that's how it is.

'What's the matter with you, Jack?' His father gets in on the act, defending his mother. 'It's impossible saying anything to you these days. You're not the only one having a hard time, you know.'

'Yes, okay. I'm sorry. Can I take the car?'

You want me to lighten up, give me the fucking car. Chloe is waiting for me.

'What for?'

'To meet a friend. So I have a life. Or is one of you going to drive me?'

All those years of being driven to friends' houses to play. Nothing changes.

'Well, I suppose so, darling.' This is his mother. 'Will you be back late?'

'I don't know. Why does it matter?'

She sighs and gives in, as he always knew she would. It's both comforting and scary, knowing your parents can be bent to your will. No time to chew on that one.

He takes the despised Smart car which actually is excitingly nippy once you're in the driving seat. A new stretch of road has been built that swoops over the railway line, past the dog kennels, to the Lewes roundabout. In the orange light of Cuilfail tunnel he puzzles over what Chloe Redknapp can want from him. Whatever it is, there are others she could have turned to. Why him?

Everyone's heard the stories about Chloe. How she lost her virginity on her fifteenth birthday for a bet. How she performed a striptease at a charity fundraiser with the bids rising as her clothes came off.

You don't call someone you hardly know and ask them to come on over now unless you want to make something happen.

Maybe she picks boys up on impulse. Maybe she just likes the idea of having fun with a virtual stranger. She can play with me if she likes. I'm not proud.

Up the silent High Street and out past the hospital. On the main road the Chalk Pit Inn is a blaze of lights between the leafless winter trees. Just past the garage the left turn into the narrow winding road to Plumpton.

The car park of the Half Moon is surprisingly full. Inside, the bar is crowded. No sign of Chloe. He got here faster than he thought he would. Girls always come late, they hate to sit in pubs alone.

He gets himself a beer and settles down at a table beside the Christmas tree. It's quite a big tree, generously draped with gold and silver tinsel. A large party of staff from the agricultural college are laughing loudly nearby, taking pictures of each other on their phones and passing them round.

Jack realizes how hungry he is. He's about to get up and buy a packet of crisps from the bar when Chloe appears. She's wearing a heavy-knit navy blue jumper that comes almost to her knees, and a bright red scarf right up to her nose. Her eyes are smiling at him.

'Christ it's cold!' she says, unwinding the scarf. Golden hair spills out like tinsel. 'You're looking good, Jack. Hey, look at your hair. Very retro.'

He pushes his fingers through his hair, blushing.

'I never know what to do with it.'

'So how's Cambridge? Is everyone there really brainy, like you?'

The rush of speech leaves Jack a little breathless. But then Chloe reaches out and puts her hand on his arm.

'Good place for nerd-spotting, right?' she says, touching

him, giving him a radiant smile. Suddenly he feels that whatever he says will be right.

'Oh, definitely. We all wear spectacles and our trousers are too short and we sit in libraries all day.'

Chloe laughs.

'Ri-i-ight! So really you're hopped up and fucking your mighty brains out.'

'If only. Is that how it is down your way?'

'Exeter is Dullsville Central. Nobody has any brains to fuck out. Myself included.'

Enchanted, he gets her a drink at the bar. Vodka and Coke. They sit by the Christmas tree grinning at each other.

'So what's the story on the girlfriend front?' Chloe says.

'Not great. I was with someone in the summer, but we broke up a while back.'

He says it with an easy smile, as if the decision was mutual. Painless.

'So you're available. That's perfect.' Not exactly Jack's experience: but it's refreshing to have it presented in this way. Chloe's eyes have never left him for one second. He feels intoxicated. If it wasn't so totally unlikely he'd say Chloe is flirting with him.

'Do you ever meet up with the old crowd from Underhill?' she says.

'Not really.'

'I met Alice Dickinson on the train down. Do you remember Alice?'

'Just about. Her mum married Mr Strachan, didn't she?'

'She remembers you.'

Jack can think of nothing to say to this. He's not interested in Alice Dickinson. He's interested in Chloe.

'So how about you?' he offers. 'How's your love life?'

'Oh, insane as usual. I met this boy called Hal and I decided he was the love of my life but now I think maybe he's a bit of a tit.'

'Sounds like you're available, too.'

'That's me. Always available. Why not? I'm only nineteen. I'm not about to settle down, for fuck's sake. So if I'm not settling down I'm available, right? Not exactly rocket science. But certain people don't seem to get the message. It's not as if I'm asking them to be saints in shining armour. Why can't everyone just lighten up?'

Jack smiles and nods, struck by the obvious wisdom of this attitude. We're young. Live for the moment. Just lighten up. As uttered by Chloe, wriggling on a barstool before him in a way that makes him acutely aware of her body, it has the force of revelation.

'You should meet up with Alice,' says Chloe. 'You'd like her.'

'Alice?'

'Yes, Alice. Remember? We were talking about her. Oh, maybe ten or twelve seconds ago.'

'Then we were talking about you.'

'Oh, you don't want to talk about me.'

'Why not? You are sitting here, in front of me.'

'I'm not your type at all. I'm far too empty-headed.'

'Oh, sure. I bet you secretly believe you know what's going on better than anyone.'

'Well, yes.' She opens her blue eyes very wide. 'How did you guess? Can you read my mind?'

'Everyone secretly believes that.'

Her pretty lips curl into a slow smile.

'Aren't you the clever one.'

She finishes her vodka and Coke, still smiling at him.

'You want another drink?' he says.

'No, I'm supposed to be getting back for dinner. My first day home.'

'God, I've been home for days.'

'So you've got plenty of time on your hands.'

'You could say that.'

'Why don't we meet up in Lewes for lunch sometime?'

Jack is astonished all over again, but he's careful not to show it.

'Sure. I'd like that.'

'I'm meeting Alice on Sunday. Harvey's at one o'clock. You could join us.'

So it's not quite the hot date it looked like for one shining moment, but it's a start.

'Seems like you and Alice have turned into best friends.'

'She's really interesting, you know? You'll see when you meet her.'

She looks round and catches sight of the clock over the bar.

'Shit! I have to go.'

She jumps up and starts muffling herself up with her scarf.

'So Sunday, okay?'

'Okay.'

'Thanks for driving over. If I ever pass my test I'll do the same for you.'

'No sweat.'

She gives him a peck on the cheek, her face warm against his.

'I really have to run.'

Jack drives home more slowly than he came, absorbing the implications of their brief meeting. Chloe asked him if he was single. She made sure he knew she herself was available. She fixed for them to meet again. All that points one way, doesn't it?

So where does Alice Dickinson come in?

Suppose Chloe's got the idea that she might like him, but isn't quite sure. It would make sense for her to make a date for lunchtime, to check him out, and to bring along a friend. That's what girls do.

This explanation fits all the facts but one. Why should

Chloe show this sudden interest in him? Such a thing has never happened to Jack before. He just isn't the sort that girls go after, not like this. With Hannah it took weeks. Even then he found it hard to believe she wanted more than friendship.

But Chloe plays a different game. She just wants to have fun.

Jack feels it then, like the approach of a warm wind. What if it could really happen? Teasing and smiling, touching and kissing, no talk about for ever, Chloe in his arms.

Oh yes, I'd like that. I'd go for that. Nothing grand, nothing serious, just fooling around till the real thing comes along. Or returns. Secretly he hasn't given up on that possibility. Maybe Chloe is just what he needs, to win Hannah back. If some of Chloe's casual way of love rubs off on him it would take the pressure off and then Hannah could love him again. Cruel that people only love you if you don't love them too much. Loving too much makes you needy. You become passive. You look for ways to please her, you want to do what she wants, you stop caring about your own desires because you have only the one desire, for her to stay with you. So she goes. Your love is selfless, sacrificial, perfect. So she goes.

Was I too passive with Chloe? He reruns their meeting in the pub and it seems to him he let her make all the moves. Apart from when I did my mind-reading thing. She liked that. She's not the airhead she likes to make out she is. Maybe I was too ready to agree to everything. I could have said I wasn't available Sunday lunchtime, except I am. I could have told her not to bring Alice, except what right do I have to tell her what to do?

Face it, I'm not the forceful type. I'm not her type at all. But she called me. She asked me to drive all the way to Plumpton. For what? A bit of Christmas cheer? Christ knows I could do with that.

When he gets home he finds the rest of the family are eating supper. He's still starving.

'We didn't wait,' says his mother. 'You said you didn't want supper.'

'No problem,' says Jack. 'I'll get myself some bread or something.'

'Don't be silly.'

So he gets himself a plate and there's plenty of pasta left. It smells wonderful.

'Where have you been?' says Carrie.

'Checking in with a friend.'

He starts eating.

'Not really good enough, Jack,' says his father. He's using his disappointed voice. 'No one's forcing you to eat with us, but you can't just come and go as you please.'

'Right,' says Jack.

His mother watches him eating.

'Are you all right, darling?'

'I'm fine,' says Jack. 'Me and Hannah split up.'

'When?'

'Weeks ago.'

They all stare at him. So that's it: now they know. It doesn't seem such a big deal any more. He's seeing Chloe again on Sunday.

'I'm sorry,' says his mother. 'I liked Hannah.'

'Why?' says Carrie accusingly, as if once again Jack has failed to respect the family tradition.

'I'm only nineteen, for God's sake,' says Jack. 'I'm not about to settle down. Just lighten up.'

14

Tom pours another glass of red wine for Belinda, and one for himself. Chloe is back, upstairs in her room, but she'll be down any minute. By an unspoken accord they're both concealing what has happened from Chloe. Belinda has repaired the damage to her face so Chloe won't know she's been crying. Tom has cleared up the red cabbage, or at least, he tried to. Apparently he was doing it wrong because Belinda took over, pushing him angrily out of the way.

'Not like that!' she said. 'You can't pick it up with a wooden spoon!'

Now she's banging a bag of frozen peas on the work surface to loosen them up. She's not looking at him but she's not crying any more.

What am I supposed to do now?

Tom feels aggrieved even though he's the guilty party. He's not stupid, he knows that's illegitimate, even

148

outrageous, but it's how he feels. He's confessed his crime, he's promised restitution. He's promised his little fling is over, which by the way is something of a wrench, but he's not allowed to present that in mitigation. Now what does he have to do?

The truth is he's frightened. He doesn't want his marriage to be over. He wants to say, 'I still love you', but he feels as if he no longer has that right.

Chloe comes bouncing in. She comes to him for a kiss.

'Dad! I've hardly had a chance to say hello.'

He hugs her. He admires her.

'So how's your term been, darling? Are you a star?'

'Not exactly. I don't think I'm much good at drama. But apparently we're developing our presentational skills, and they'll help us in our careers.'

'Of course they will. Got to have presentational skills.'

'Not that there are going to be any jobs when I graduate. Will you go on supporting me, Dad?'

'For how long?'

'Till you die and leave me all your money.'

'And Alex.'

'Forget Alex. You love me much more than him.'

'No, I don't. I love you both just the same.'

But it's not true. Alex is unreachable. You can't love someone who's never there. But this is treacherous ground. He can see Belinda watching him.

She's just put the steaks on the griddle pan. The smells

and sounds of frying fill the room. Chloe goes over to the stove.

'I am so hungry,' she says.

'Well, I couldn't put them on until I knew you were back, could I? And the red cabbage got ruined so we're having frozen peas, but at least that means it won't be an all-red meal.'

'All right, chill out, Mum, I'm not complaining.'

Belinda starts to cry. Tom braces himself. Here it comes.

'What is it?' says Chloe. 'Is it me?'

'Just everything,' Belinda says. 'Sometimes it's all too much.'

'Oh, Mum.' Chloe takes her mother in her arms. 'I shouldn't have gone out. I was ever so quick, wasn't I? We're not really late, are we? We're going to have some lovely steak and some wine and you'll feel much better. Say you'll feel better.'

'Yes. I expect so.'

'I hate it when you cry.'

'I'd better turn the steaks.'

She dries her eyes. Chloe fetches her half-drunk glass of wine and makes her drink some more. So the moment passes.

Over dinner Chloe does most of the talking, telling them silly stories about her life in Exeter. She's decided she's responsible for the family's morale. Then she tells them about meeting Alice Dickinson on the train.

'I'm going to fix her up with Jack Broad,' she says. 'My Christmas present.'

Tom says, 'Does she want to be fixed up with Jack Broad?'

'Definitely. I get to play Cupid.'

Belinda looks down, bites her lip. Tom closes his eyes for a moment. This is heavy pulling. When he opens his eyes Chloe is gazing at him across the dinner table.

'You look tired, Dad.'

'I am tired. Early night tonight.'

Chloe helps him with the clearing away and the washing up. For a brief moment he thinks she must know what has happened. But when she starts to chat again it's clear she knows nothing.

'Don't you think I'd make a great Cupid?' she says.

'Yes, darling.'

Belinda is at the other end of the room by the fire.

'He makes people love each other. Don't you think that would be a great job to have? I mean, if you got people together, and they ended up married and having kids and all the rest, you'd feel pretty good, wouldn't you?'

'I expect you would.'

Chloe is scrubbing the tin the tomatoes were baked in, which is the kind of dirty job she usually evades.

'Do you think I'm an entirely worthless person, Dad?'

'Of course I don't. You're my pride and joy.'

'I've decided to be a better person. I'm going to start thinking of others from now on.'

Belinda lets out a sudden cry. Tom turns to her with nervous dread.

'I made a pudding!' she says. 'I forgot all about it.'

The table is cleared. The moment has passed.

'We'll have it tomorrow, Mum,' says Chloe. 'It'll be even more delicious tomorrow.'

It's a big bed, so wide that they can lie in it side by side and not touch, as they are now doing. Impossible for Tom to know what's going on inside Belinda except that it's not good. He can tell that because she's crying again.

She lies half curled on her side, face in the pillow, and makes this pitiful whimpering sound. Once he reaches out and puts a hand on her shoulder but she shakes him off and twists her head even further away. So he's not welcome. No surprise there.

He's dizzy with tiredness and can't sleep. Unwillingly awake in the darkness he tries to work out what he should do. What he should say to Belinda in the morning. He'll say anything, he'll say whatever she wants him to say. But she won't accept that. Words won't do it. She'll want feelings. She'll want to know how he could do something that hurts her so much and he won't be able to explain.

Here's the question, which he can't speak aloud because it's unacceptable: how bad have I been? How unforgivable has my conduct been?

It's Tom's nature to respond to any given crisis in an entirely practical way. Analyse the problem, identify a solution, act. Don't flinch from the harshest reality. Is the marriage over? If so, what will that be like? Not good. Let it not be over.

Let this be about me for a few moments, while I'm alone with myself in the night.

What do I need for my happiness?

To his surprise the answer is work. Only when he's in the moment of doing what he's been trained to do, fully focused on the precise and delicate task in hand, cutting through tissue, suturing blood vessels, slowly and with infinite patience stitching a wound he himself has made, is he fully himself. People think a surgeon's work must be stressful but it isn't. It's his time of tranquillity.

By contrast all the rest of life is a mess. Tom hates being in a situation where he doesn't know what he's supposed to do. Like now.

Tell me what I'm to do. Tell me what price I'm to pay. If I'm to be punished, let me be punished. And then can we forgive and forget?

Unacceptable, of course. And yet, and yet – his crime is so very small, he's done no more than all men do, and if they don't it's only for lack of opportunity. If you only knew – he addresses Belinda in his mind – it changes nothing between you and me. I still love you as much as before. I still want to be married to you. I still want to come home to you. Why do you have to be so hurt, when I never meant to hurt you?

You want to know the simple truth? It's different for men. For us sex is something that happens outside our bodies. It's something that has no consequences. For you, for women, it's an act that takes trust and surrender, it has lifelong consequences. So don't grant my actions the emotions that would accompany them if they were yours.

He hears her snuffling on the other side of the bed. He feels the urge to shake her into full wakefulness. Don't just lie there and suffer. Let's sort this out. But he knows he must let her come to him in her own time. This is a grieving process, it can't be rushed. She's grieving over me.

Every hour that passes in the dark bedroom leaves him more exhausted. Guilt, of course, but also other emotions that are not appropriate but nevertheless drain away his energy. Frustration, that the problems can't be thrashed out and resolved. Self-pity, because however this thing works out he's going to suffer. And anger, secret anger, impermissible anger, that his life should be ruined by such a minor offence.

At last, maddened by sleeplessness, he gets up and pads softly out of the bedroom. Once the bedroom door is closed behind him he feels for the landing light switch, but then decides not to turn on the light, not wanting the shock of brightness. The landing window looms above the stairs, a rectangular grey blur in the surrounding blackness. Somewhere out there is a full moon, more than a full moon. He read about it in the paper, the moon's orbit is an ellipse, every fifteen years it reaches its closest point to earth, and so appears bigger and brighter. Except that right now clouds cover the sky, and the rare phenomenon is of course invisible.

He feels for the banister rail and descends the stairs like a blind man, by touch and memory. He likes doing this, it makes him feel he's coping with his difficulties. So feeling his way he crosses the hall below and enters the kitchen.

Here to his surprise he finds an array of tiny lights, as if fairies have taken up residence while the family sleeps. They are the pilot lights of the many electrical appliances the kitchen holds, far more than he ever knew. The amber light on the fridge-freezer, with its illuminated temperature display. The red charging light on the cordless phone. The green light on the dishwasher that says its cycle is completed. The white numerals on the cooker's digital timer. The red standby light on the TV. There's no need to turn on the main room lights. The fairy lights show him all he needs to see.

He sits at the kitchen table and considers whether he wants a drink of some kind. Brandy, perhaps, or hot chocolate. But he makes no further move. Slowly, as his eyes adjust to the darkness, he makes out the faint forms of the two tall kitchen windows, and the night garden outside. The roof of the stable block against the sky. The thin bare branches of the willow tree. The curving line of the Downs.

How long have we lived here? Chloe was seven when we came, she went straight into Year Three at Underhill, that makes it twelve years. Bad time to sell the house, of course. Probably worth as much as two million at the peak, whenever that was, a year or so ago. Now it has to be down thirty, forty per cent. That's a loss of £800,000. Except it's not a loss because he never had the two million and paid way less than that back in '96, not much more than half a million, though they've spent a fortune since.

It's all an illusion. The things we talk about as if they govern our lives, money, youth, beauty, none of them matter. They're all just accidents. He wants to say this to Belinda but he knows it will sound as if he's trying to excuse himself. Maybe he is. But it doesn't feel that way to him, it feels as if it's the other way round entirely. These deeply disturbing thoughts came first, about the randomness of all our values. And out of their disintegration he reached for something simple and strong, or rather, as it seems now to him when he looks back, the simple strong impulse reached out to him, and it was desire.

That moment, which in the past would have been called the moment he gave in to temptation, the moment he fell, the fulcrum of sin, can only be understood as an accumulation of a million moments: a million impulses, from puberty to today, so much longing, so little expectation of joy. You get so that it seems to be the natural order of things, that you want something with all your being, a touch, a kiss, a generosity of the body, but it never comes, you don't deserve it, such bliss is for others. But knowing this does nothing to diminish the longing. Instead, every moment of the day is made just a little more burdensome by the sadness, the gap between the aching need and the reality of life. From every street hoarding, from every magazine cover, desirable women smile and beckon, a taunting chorus, until you truly believe you alone are alone, that all round you this same insistent desire is being actively explored, that all the world but you is making joyous love – and why shouldn't it be so, since you'd do it yourself if you could?

But you're married, she says. If you want sex, you've got me. You've got a wife, a bedroom, a king size double bed. What more do you want?

I want to be desired.

Think about it, Belinda. Think about how it happens between us, the wordless negotiation that ends in lovemaking. Always the same pattern. An overture from me, God knows modest enough, a tone of voice, a touch. Never ambiguous, we know each other well. Often welcome, not always. Your response minimal but unmistakable, the momentary pause, the slow exhalation. Sometimes there's a weary reluctance. Why not? You're tired. A few words, 'Not tonight, do you mind?' Of course I don't mind.

Sometimes no words, only a reaching embrace. But on every single occasion, for me at least, the moment of uncertainty: is my desire welcome? And why should it be otherwise? You're not a toy, maintained for my pleasure.

But can you understand this? Because if you can't, I have no case. I have no defence. I have longed all my life for the response that matches my desire. For the woman who wants me for sex just as much as I want her for sex. I've wanted to be used so that I can use, without all the intervening layers of guilt and lies. I've wanted to make up for the ten million moments when I've been alone with my desire. So when it comes – unlooked for, like grace from above – how can I resist? Why should I resist? This is the confirmation I have never had: that I am desirable. And being desired, the desire breaks within me like a storm.

You, my beloved wife, have given me your loyalty and your love. But you've never whispered down the phone to me: 'I want you to fuck me now. I'm waiting for you. Come home and fuck me.'

Yes, I know, I should have asked you to say it. If that's what I want, why can't I say so? Because, because. We men are so full of shame. These simple desires, these primitive desires, they have low status in civilized society, they represent an immature stage of human relationships. Which is bullshit. These simple desires are all the glory we'll ever know on earth.

So that's all it is. Call it making up for lost time. Or

grabbing my chance of one last dance before the music stops. One first dance. But don't call it sad. I'm not trying to prove anything. I'm just a man who has stumbled upon his heart's desire and said yes.

How can I tell you any of this?

No, I must speak another language. How I've cheated you, how I've demeaned you, how I've hurt you. We'll tell of all that has been taken from you and none of what has been added to me, because I shouldn't have wanted any more. My crime is greed, because wasn't I well enough fed already? I must be tried and found guilty and sentenced, and must be punished, and if I accept the punishment with true contrition I will in time be rehabilitated. And so the charade must be played out to the end because that's what everyone deems right and proper. Everyone being all the women, who have no idea what goes on in men, and all the men, who know perfectly well what goes on but who lie, as they have lied for centuries.

You don't agree? You, my imaginary male listener? So tell me: does your wife know you'd gladly, joyfully, pick up a hooker in a hotel lobby and take her up to your hotel room and fuck her and pay her and never ask her name? Does your wife know the only reasons you don't do so are you're afraid of being seen, afraid of it getting back to her, afraid of diseases? Nothing about how it would deprive her of your love, because it wouldn't. Men are different. You know it, I know it, but we lie, don't we? Oh no, we say, the prostitutes and the pornography, that's for the sad old men and the sailors. Oh, and millionaire footballers and rock stars. Oh, and businessmen abroad. Oh, and politicians caught in sex scandals. Oh, and young men who get drunk on holiday when the sun shines. But not us, not the normal guys with wives, we're too sophisticated and too mature and too complex to want something so elementary as a mindless fuck.

So we lie about what we want. And sometimes, if God relents and we get to do what we want, we lie about what we do. And then we get caught, and everyone's life gets ruined.

How stupid is that?

The kitchen is cold. He realizes he's shivering, has been shivering for some time. Better get back to bed.

All this ranting in his head has calmed him. He thinks he'll be able to sleep now. But as he treads softly into the bedroom, back to his side of the bed, as he folds back the duvet, Belinda speaks.

'Where did you go?'

'Kitchen.'

'Why?'

'Can't sleep.'

He eases himself back into bed. The sheets have gone cold on his side. He must have been downstairs for some time.

'Me neither.'

So they lie there, side by side, not sleeping. He could slip into sleep, he's pretty sure of it, but now it would be a desertion. He can feel her unhappiness welling over.

'I suppose it's my fault,' she says at last.

'No,' he says. 'It's not your fault at all. It's me who's done it. I'm the only one to blame here.'

Which is nothing but the simple truth. So why does it sound like a line in some pre-rehearsed script?

Nothing for a few moments. Then:

'So why did you do it?'

Her voice in the darkness so small, so bewildered, so hurt. The question that can't be answered.

'It was nothing. Really. Not any kind of a big deal at all.'

'So why do it?'

'Oh, God, I don't know. Because I got a chance. Because I could, I suppose. Don't you ever give way to temptation?'

'Tom, this isn't like having another chocolate or something. This is about me, too.'

'Yes. I know that.'

'So why did you do it?'

'I suppose I thought you'd never know.'

'You can't have thought that. All the girls in the office know.'

So that's how she knows. Until this moment he hasn't asked himself who told her. It could have been so many. Everyone at the clinic seems to know.

'Was it Karen?'

'No. It was Lisa. She felt sorry for me.'

Lisa who's always so sorry for herself. Kind, conscientious, lonely Lisa. Why would she want to hurt me?

'You didn't feel sorry for me,' says Belinda. 'You didn't think about me at all.'

No, I didn't think about you. Must I think about you all the time? Have I no life of my own? If you want to know the truth, Belinda, even if I had thought about you, it was too strong for me to resist. I knew I was being a fool but I still wanted it. I still do. Life is so short. Don't grudge me this.

'I don't understand. What do you get from her you don't get from me?'

Dangerous territory. Don't go there.

'Nothing.'

'So why do it? I've been over it and over it and I just can't make any sense of it.'

He sighs. This is to signal that he's cornered. That he's going to admit the real truth.

'I don't know. Maybe I felt I still have something to prove.'

There. That's what she thinks is going on. I'm fifty-five years old, I'm trying to prove I'm still young again. What I can't say is I was never young. I'm young now, with Meg.

'What do you have to prove? That you're still attractive to women?'

'I suppose so.'

'Can't you do that without screwing them?'

'Well, up to a point.'

Silence. Here it comes.

'Is it about virility?'

She doesn't say it but he hears it: sometimes you can't get it up with me. More than sometimes. Men are supposed to be keen on the mechanics. Fine. Go with that.

'Could be.'

'So does it work with her?'

Yes, it works with her. Every time.

'More or less.'

That hurts. What was I supposed to say?

'What does she look like?'

'Just kind of ordinary.'

'Ordinary? What does that mean?'

'I don't know how to describe someone.'

'Is she pretty? Is she young? Is she sexy?'

'Nothing special. I think she's round thirty. Not especially pretty, no.'

'God!'

Now Belinda's crying again.

'What do you want me to say?'

'I just want to understand.' She's speaking through her tears. 'It doesn't make any sense.'

'I don't know what else to tell you.'

'Why did you do it? Why did you do it? Did you think

of me for one second? Did you say to yourself, ever, this will break Belinda's heart?'

'No.'

'Why not?'

Goaded, he risks a little truth.

'Because it was nothing to do with you and me. Any more than playing a round of golf.'

'Playing a round of golf!'

'It's just something I like doing that doesn't involve you.'

'What!'

She starts flailing at him with one hand, but feebly. She's very tired.

'I'm sorry. I've said I'm sorry.'

'Well, it's not fucking enough! You think you can screw your staff and say sorry and we just go on like we were before?'

No, Tom doesn't think this. But oh, if only.

'No.'

'So what are you going to do about it?'

Grovel. Be punished. Show remorse. Oh, Christ.

'What do you want me to do?'

'Tell me why you did it!'

Round we go. How can I tell her? Sex is what we share. Sex made our children. How can sex be a pleasure, like a round of golf? That did not go down well.

She's crying more and more. Oh, God, I don't want to

hurt you. Truly truly truly. Let me be the one who's hurt. Sweetheart. Belinda.

'It's because I'm too old, isn't it?' No more shouting. This is a whisper between the sobs. 'I'm all wrinkly now. That's why you don't want me any more.'

'No, no, no.' He reaches out an arm to touch her, and she rolls towards him, lets him hug her. 'That's not it at all. Not at all. You're my gorgeous wife. Of course I still want you.'

'I can't bear it, Tom. Can't bear it. I do what I can. What I can. I try to stay pretty for you. For you.'

Sobbing out her heartbreak. Now he's crying too.

'I'm the luckiest man in the world. Everyone says so. They envy me my gorgeous wife. You know I fell in love with you the first day I set eyes on you. I've never stopped loving you.'

'Then why – why – why—'

'It's all over now. All over. Let's not talk any more. We're too tired, we're not making any sense, it's four in the morning. Plenty of time to talk tomorrow, and the next day, and all the rest of our lives.'

'I don't understand …'

Her voice muffled now, blurring into sleep.

'There, now. Dry your eyes. We'll come through this, I promise.'

'Don't leave me, Tom. Don't leave.'

'I'll never leave. Promise.'

'Even if I get old and ugly?'

'I'll be old and ugly too.'

'Oh, yes. So you will.'

'Sleep now, darling.'

And so exhaustion brings respite. He thinks he won't sleep that night, but within minutes he's asleep. The body more merciful than the mind.

15

Anthony Armitage has been planning his final show since he took possession of America Cottage. It's to be a retrospective. Much of his work is in private hands but there's still plenty left, unframed canvases that represent between them sixty-five years of his evolution as a painter. For several days now he has been going through them, picking out the best, and hanging them on the bare walls of the empty barn. He has a list of people he means to invite to the private view: past patrons, gallery owners, arts journalists, friends from long ago, enemies. Who knows how many of them will come? Perhaps none of them. Joe Nola is on the list. Now he adds Christina.

In a nod to the modern style, his show will also be what is called an 'installation'. It will be a surprise; perhaps even, to use the word appropriated for another show many years ago, a sensation.

He can recall, as he handles each canvas, exactly what he

was trying to achieve when he painted it. He can see the ambition and the excitement caught for ever in the brush strokes, but bolder than both he can see the disappointment. He stands holding a small canvas in his hands, gazing at the face of a now dead friend. He had been reaching for a certain quality of regret, he had glimpsed it and almost caught it, but in the end it had eluded him. This is his art, to make dabs of paint portray fugitive emotions. Human beings are so defended, so fragile, so heartbreakingly vulnerable. Titian saw it, and Velasquez: painting as a triumph of humanity. But who cares any more? Even the few who still deign to hold a brush care nothing for the truth of their subjects. Bacon, Freud, all they have to offer is their own inner pain. Can no one use their eyes any more? An entire tradition stretching back hundreds of years now lost. Worse than lost, despised.

Grunting with the effort, he stands on a chair to hang a work he began in 1965, and has returned to many times over the years. It's a painting of his first wife Nell sitting on the little terrace of their house in Houlgate in Normandy. The glass in the windows behind her reflects the bright sea at which she gazes. She looks as if she wishes she could sail away over the sea. Nell hated the picture, she said it made her look old, but really she hated it because it made her look unhappy. That's how people mostly are: unhappy, disappointed, sick, dying.

He climbs down off the chair and stands back to look at the painting.

It's good. It's alive. I could do it then.

When they came back from Normandy everything had changed. His work embarrassed people. Nell left, taking her unhappiness with her. You wait for the wheel of fashion to turn, you'd think forty years would be time enough, but instead the madness becomes institutionalized. The lunatics have taken over the asylum. The plump and cosseted middle classes long to be abused, to expiate their guilt. The old hunger for penance. The preachers in the pulpits won't tell them they're sinners any more, so art must do the job. Art must be hard and hurtful, and mysterious and unfathomable.

Oh, the villains. They have murdered beauty. They have taught the people not to see. Oh, the villains.

But I am old now, and usually drunk. For me the war is over.

He looks at Nell hanging on the barn wall and wonders if he ever loved her.

'What a cunt you were, Nell,' he says aloud.

A sudden imperious pressure in his bladder. Here we go again. No wonder old people stink of pee.

He goes out of the barn, moving slowly, in pain. Any kind of movement hurts these days. He takes painkillers but all they do is dull the sharper edges. The pain is deep within him, in the very marrow of his bones, in his back and his hips and his knees. They talk of treatment as if it were a malfunctioning of his body, but he knows the truth. His body has begun to die from the extremities. He is dragging an arthritic corpse after him wherever he goes. Which isn't very far these days.

What is to be done? When he sits still the pain eases, but he can't sit still for ever. There's a subject for you: old man marooned in armchair. Still life. Or as the French call it, *nature morte*.

Standing between the elder trees, screened by the crumbling garden wall, he releases a thin but blessed stream into the winter nettles. Who'd have thought the old man had so much piss in him? One of the few pleasures not yet taken from him by the cruel years.

Then as he fumbles his flies into closure he sees a face staring at him through the branches. The face is pale, intense, accusatory: a teenage girl. As she sees him register her presence she turns away.

'Wait!' he calls. 'Don't go!'

Such a face! The face of a child who is also a woman, caught at that moment when the mask has not yet formed. Full of fear, free of concealment.

'Please help me,' he calls after her.

An unpremeditated cry, all he means is that he wants to have the use of her face, perhaps to paint her; but it sounds in the morning chill like a cry from the heart. And perhaps it is.

She stops and turns. A teenage girl in jeans and hoodie, her trainers caked in mud. She looks at him, unsure what he wants. Maybe he's a crazy old paedophile.

'I'm an artist,' he says. 'I paint pictures.'

Still she says nothing. Artists can be rapists too.

'I paint pictures of people.'

'Okay,' she says. Giving nothing away.

'Do you live near here?'

She nods her head towards the track. 'In the village.'

'I moved in here last month. I don't know anybody.'

She nods, and takes a step nearer to her side of the wall. She gestures at the cottage.

'Did you buy it?' she says.

'Oh, no. Only renting. Just for a couple of months.'

That seems to please her.

'That's okay, then.'

'Do you want to see my paintings?' he says.

She stares at him, suspicious again. Once that kind of offer might have held danger, or promise.

'I'm eighty-two years old,' he says. 'I have severe osteoarthritis. I can't see a thing without my glasses. I get out of breath if I climb stairs. You're perfectly safe.'

A slow smile.

'Okay,' she says.

She comes in to the garden, closing the gate behind her. At first she stands in the barn doorway, reluctant to enter. He goes ahead of her.

'See. My paintings.'

He offers the canvases for her inspection. She looks in

silence, solemn as a critic. Her attention lingers longest over the portrait of Nell in Normandy.

'You're good,' she says.

'Yes, I am good. I'm very good. Or I was once.'

'So what are you doing here?'

Fair question. Would a successful artist choose to live out his old age in a hovel under the Downs? Or even a failed artist?

'It gives me all I want. Which isn't much.'

He wants to paint her. The impulse which left him years ago has returned, like the final flicker of a dying fire.

'What's your name?' he says.

'Carrie.'

'My name is Anthony Armitage.'

She goes on looking at his portraits.

'You paint people that really look like people,' she says.

'Yes, I do. Sorry.'

'Why sorry?'

'That's supposed to be the job of photography nowadays. Artists who paint people who look like people are called historicists.'

'What's that?'

'It means we're stuck in the past.'

She frowns, trying to understand.

'Don't worry about it,' he says. 'They're all wankers.'

She blushes, then smiles. Such an awkward child, but beneath the clumsy surface there is an angry grace. The artist in him has awoken and is issuing the old dictatorial commands.

'I'd like to paint you,' he says.

'Really?' She's surprised. 'Why?'

'Because you have a beautiful face.'

'Do I?'

Now she's astonished, but also pleased. Such a simple line, but it never fails. And he never says it unless it's true. That's how artists change the world. They see the beauty that is overlooked by the fashion of the day. Then others come to their shows and see in their turn, and so the truth of beauty is preserved. Except they don't come, and the truth is lost.

'Would you let me?' he says.

He wants to start now, at once, before the impulse leaves him.

She agrees, without further discussion. Some simple decision takes place within her, and she delivers herself into his hands. He feels a surge of gratitude.

He sits her down in the front room of the cottage where the cool light from the window falls across her cheek, and sets up a hurried easel. She can't stay too long, she says, her parents will worry. No more than half an hour. Her brother won't worry, he wouldn't know if she was dead or alive. She knows some people would be happier if she was dead, but who cares about them? Really who cares about people anyway? All they think about is themselves. You have to be able to cope with being alone, because that's how you are in the end. You can have one million friends on Facebook but it's all just a joke because not one of them would lift a finger for you if you needed them.

He lets her talk on, his hand moving rapidly, making an initial sketch in charcoal.

'I'm not really beautiful, you know,' she says.

'Yes, you are.' He studies her with the impersonal precision of a surgeon. 'You have a clear high brow. Strong cheekbones. Your eyes are intensely expressive. Your mouth has a curve that echoes your brow. And you should never cover that neck of yours. Your neck is perfect.'

'Oh,' she says. She's gone pink.

'A remarkable face.'

'But I'm not – I mean, really I'm not – I'm not anything.'

'Yes, you are,' he says, his charcoal flying. 'You're a pure form.'

'Oh.'

She stays for an hour, long enough for the initial sketch to be laid down. She promises she'll return. As she leaves she says, without looking at him, 'Do you smash crockery?'

'Yes,' he says.

'Why?'

He goes and retrieves the newspaper from the bin, and shows her the article about the work of Joe Nola. She looks at the picture of the recreated breakfast table. The coffee mugs. The cereal bowls.

'That's art?'

'So they tell us.'

'Why?'

'Don't ask me.'

'No, I mean why did you smash the crockery?'

'I was angry. You have to do something.'

'Yes,' she said. 'I suppose you do.'

16

Meg arrives for the rehearsal at the church hall. John Cartwright is there, trying to light the portable gas heater. The hall is bitterly cold. Four other members of the choir are there, still in their coats and gloves. Fanny Waller is jumping up and down as if on an invisible pogo stick to keep warm. Gill Cartwright appears from the kitchenette at the back to say she has a kettle on for tea. The Richardsons arrive, four members of the same family, all very alike, even the husband and wife, with their grey faces and sad eyes. Ben Costa, their tenor soloist, gets out his music and starts to do vocal exercises. A car pulls up right outside the church hall with its stereo system playing urban rap at top volume. Peter Tindall catches Meg's eye and pulls a face at the racket. Meg smiles. Encouraged, Peter Tindall crosses the hall to her side, following a curving path as if to show he has only reached her by accident.

'I don't call that music,' he says. 'Abba, now, I can take. Did you hear that Putin is an Abba fan?'

Meg has not taken off her brown quilted winter coat, even though she knows it makes her look middle-aged. That and her woolly hat pulled down over her ears. Peter Tindall is unmarried, middle-aged, lonely; the kind of person she would once have avoided, too near to his own condition to endure the timid overtures. But her secret liaison has changed everything.

'I love Abba,' she says. 'I love "Mamma Mia".'

The gas fire blazes to life at last and they all gather round its arc of heat. The tea appears, in big white mugs. John Cartwright opens the piano and runs his fingers over the keys.

'Dear God,' he exclaims. 'Don't listen, George Frederick. Stop your ears with clay.'

They are here to rehearse Handel's oratorio *Alexander's Feast* for a performance on New Year's Day. Meg has a good singing voice and she loves to sing. As a recent recruit to the choir she is part of the chorus, but John Cartwright has already noted her ability, and says he'll give her a solo part in the next production.

The choir is twenty-two strong, but this Saturday morning they are four short. This is their first time rehearsing in the church hall and it seems some choir members have got lost. John Cartwright, annoyed, says he'll wait ten minutes but no more.

'Everyone else has managed to come on time. Why can't they?'

Meg has always belonged to choirs, wherever she has lived. Joined with others in song she has felt, for as long as the music lasts, part of the world. People say amateur choirs are excellent meeting places for lonely hearts, but that has never been Meg's motive. She has always been lonely, but not a lonely heart. That implies one who is looking for romance. Meg is in another place entirely, a place that is somehow not in the world. She passes through the world without being a part of it, like the deer that sometimes run out across the road as she's driving to work. The deer live among the housing estates and golf courses, there's not much woodland left, their lives and the lives of people intersect all the time, and yet they might as well be on different planets. Meg too feels as if that other race, the bright and the powerful, only ever sees her as a flicker in their headlights. But when she sings, her voice harmonizing with other voices, she comes in from the cold and knows the sweetness of fellowship.

The tea is hot and strong and revivifying. The cry goes up for biscuits. Gill Cartwright has biscuits, she holds up a packet of Hobnobs, but they are for the break, not now. Choirs have to be firmly handled, like schoolchildren. Both Cartwrights are teachers.

So the rehearsal begins at last.

'Happy, happy, happy pair,' sings the chorus. 'None but the brave deserves the fair.'

In usual Handel style these few words are repeated over and over so that they are drained of all sense and become notes of sound, their voices instruments as innocent as violins. Meg sings merrily, filled with the peculiar bonhomie ascribed to the angels at the Nativity, 'goodwill to all men'. Her secret affair has transformed her perception of the world. Strange that so illicit a liaison, carried out in conscious furtiveness, should make her feel like a latter-day Virgin Mary welcomed by angelic hosts. But so it is. She glows with secret knowledge. This same dowdy figure in a shapeless brown windcheater poses for her lover in sexy lingerie. This new version of herself is present, almost as if she wears the skimpy bra and panties beneath her sober business suit, as she goes about her unremarkable day; and the world, sensing the secret, gives her the privileges of membership she has never had.

> *Happy, happy, happy pair*
> *None but the brave deserves the fair.*

It's a quarter to twelve by the time she gets back to her flat, and the plumber is coming at twelve. There's a message on her answerphone from Tom saying don't call him, he'll call again. He didn't need to say that. She never calls him. This is how their affair has defined itself from the beginning: he is the one who desires, she is the object of his desire. His is the call, hers the response.

Just time to clean the bathroom, which is ridiculous, because the plumber won't care, and it's not as if it's dirty. But she can't help herself. So few people come into her flat, she wants it to be at its best. Also the bathroom will then smell as if it's been cleaned, which is almost more important.

She pulls on yellow rubber gloves and squirts cream cleaner over bath and surrounding tiles, and runs the tap. Then passing the bath brush from white enamel to running water and back, she scrubs the surfaces clean. The lights in the bathroom are bright and there's satisfaction in the gleam of the perfect surfaces as the water runs away. Meg never used to be a tidy person. It really only began when she had a place of her own. But now she likes it all, the wiping and sweeping and hoovering.

The phone rings. She picks it up still wearing rubber gloves. It's Tom.

'Oh, hi,' she says. Their phone conversations are always about arrangements, nothing more. But this time his voice is different.

'I've got a problem,' he says.

'Oh?'

'Belinda knows.'

'How?'

The question comes out instinctively, like a hand reaching up to avert a blow. What does it matter how?

'One of the girls who works for me. People pick this sort of thing up.'

This sort of thing.

She's standing in the doorway between the bathroom and the living room. The central heating is full on. She feels cold.

'It's all pretty nightmarish, to be honest.'

'Oh. I'm sorry.'

The words are inadequate, but it's hard to know what to say. They have a language of intimacy with their bodies, but not with words. He has taught her to say 'Fuck me.' Not what to say when his wife finds out about their affair.

'I've told her it's over,' he says.

'Yes, of course.'

She doesn't know as she speaks if she's agreeing that it's over, or just that this is what he's told her. She feels numb.

'It's not what I want,' he says. 'But I have no choice.'

'So what does that mean for us?'

She's being stupid, but she's not following this. What has happened? What does it mean?

'I can't come to you any more, Meg. I'm sorry. I just can't.'

'Yes. I see.'

She sees nothing. She understands nothing. He seems to be saying their affair is over, but that's impossible.

'We knew it couldn't go on for ever. I just thought we'd get a bit more time than this.'

Meg makes an immense effort of will. She drags herself out of the fog of passivity that holds her in its grip.

'We have to talk.'

'It's not easy,' he says.

'Come over. Any time. You can find an excuse.'

'That's just it. I can't.'

'But I have to see you. At least once more. This can't be it.'

'You don't understand,' he says. 'Things are bad here. I've promised Belinda it's over. I had to. You do see that?'

'Yes,' she says.

'We both knew this day would come. I've never pretended with you, have I?'

'No. You've never pretended.'

'I'm really sorry, Meg. I suppose I should never have started it. But I'm not sorry I did. You've been so wonderful. I'll never forget you.'

Meg can't answer. Her neck and face are flushing and she feels herself choking up. Abruptly she presses the End Call button on her phone. She wants to cut off their conversation before it's ended. That way it hasn't ended. That way he'll have to call again.

She peels off the yellow rubber gloves.

She switches off the phone and the answering machine. So long as she's not in contact with him it's not over. Tomorrow, maybe.

She sits down in one of her white armchairs. Only now does she realize she's shaking, heaving, palpitating. Her body is beyond her control. The shaking turns into sobbing. She feels tears on her cheeks. She starts to cry aloud. The cry becomes a wail, a howl. She's keening like a bereaved peasant, rocking back and forth in the armchair, making this sound like the world is ending.

No no no no no no no no—

The doorbell rings.

Oh fuck! The plumber.

The word *fuck* belongs to him. As she thinks it she feels a stab of pure pain.

She jumps up, hurries to the bathroom, splashes water on her face, dabs at her eyes. She looks like hell. Only a plumber for God's sake.

When she opens the flat door he's standing there with his shoes in one hand and his tool bag in the other.

'Don't like to mess up your carpets,' he says.

She hadn't really noticed him before. What she sees now is a big man with a bearded face. He speaks quietly. He gets in one proper look at her, and she knows in that look that he sees she's been crying. After that he keeps his eyes down, waiting to be told which way to go.

'It's good of you to come,' she says. 'It's the shower. In here.'

He follows her to the bathroom and stands looking round, working out the flow of the system. He tries the shower, sees for himself that only a trickle comes out.

'Looks like the pump,' he says.

He opens up his tool bag.

'Okay if I turn off the water for a couple of minutes?'

Meg goes back into the living room and sits down again. She feels weak. She thinks: I should offer to make him a cup of tea or something. But the effort is too great. All she wants to do is creep away into a hole and hide.

The mocking phrases of Handel's music echo through her brain.

Happy, happy, happy pair …

She closes her eyes. When she opens them he's standing before her, and tears are streaming down her cheeks.

No point in pretending now.

'Sorry,' she says. 'I had a bit of bad news. Just before you came.'

'That's a pity,' he says.

She can tell at once from the tone of his voice that although he has just used the word pity he doesn't pity her. He respects her unhappiness. He regards it as a normal part of life. All this she hears in his soft voice.

Then he says, 'My granddad always told me, however hard it gets, it's worse in Russia.'

She can't help smiling at that.

'Russia? Why?'

'He'd got it in his head that everyone in Russia starved and froze to death. So if you weren't starving and freezing you could count yourself lucky.'

'Yes, I suppose he's right.'

'I don't know that he is right. At least with starving and freezing after a bit you die and it's over.'

'Yes.'

What an odd conversation to be having with the plumber.

'Anyway. It's the pump is the problem. I've taken the details. I can pick up a new one on Monday, it's a standard model.'

'Look, would you like a cup of tea or something?'

'No, no. You've got enough to deal with. I'll be off. I'll call you when I've got a price on the pump, quote for the whole job. Shouldn't be too much.'

'Thank you.'

She feels confused. There's more, isn't there?

'Look, I'm really sorry. I've forgotten your name.'

'Matt. Matt Early.'

'Yes, of course.'

'I'll call you with the price Monday morning.'

She sees him out. He keeps his shoes in his hands all the way down the stairs.

Back in the flat she feels such a desolation of loneliness she wants to run out after the plumber and call him back. Instead she sits in the armchair again and clasps her hands in her lap and closes her eyes. She wants not to be here if Tom is never coming again. She wants not to be her if Tom is never coming again.

But of course it's impossible. Life can't end like this. The very fact that she's breathing means, guarantees, promises that she will see Tom again. And if they meet, what has ended? Not love. Love lives on. So this is not something that's in the past, whatever he says. It's in the present. It goes on.

No doubt there'll be changes. Tom will have to be very careful. But he won't leave her. Why should he? She asks for so little.

She wants to go to Tom's wife and beg her, plead with her. Half an hour a week, that's all I want. You don't need him every minute of the day. You have so much. Spare me a crumb.

He said on the phone, I've promised Belinda it's over. Not: I want it to be over. But then he said, I'll never forget you. That was so horrible. You shouldn't have to say something like that. A husband doesn't say to his wife, 'I'll never forget you.' Not unless he is leaving and planning on forgetting her.

So he's going to leave me and forget me.

How is that possible?

17

It's past midday when Chloe finally makes it downstairs. There's no one in the kitchen. She can hear her mother talking on the phone in the drawing room. Her father's out somewhere as usual. Probably playing golf.

Chloe feels restless and irritable, despite having slept for over twelve hours. You go without sleep, you get so you're sick for sleep, then you get one good night and wake up with a head stuffed full of old socks. It's a bummer. Bodies should be more grateful.

She wonders if she dares sneak a cigarette but decides instead that what she wants is breakfast cereal. There's Sugar Puffs and there's Weetabix, both where she left them weeks ago, no one else eats them. There are five Weetabixes left in the box. She puts two in a bowl, then adds a third. Ladles on the caster sugar. Fills the bowl with milk.

She eats fast, greedily, wanting each mouthful to be

part-crunchy, part-soggy. As soon as the bowl is empty she takes out the last two Weetabixes and repeats the process. Finding she's still hungry she pours out a mound of Sugar Puffs and eats that too.

Her mother comes in and finds her spooning in the sweet cereal.

'Don't eat too much or you won't want your lunch.'

'I don't want my lunch,' says Chloe.

'Why didn't you tell me? I've got a chicken roasting.'

'Because I didn't know.'

Chloe knows she sounds peevish but it all seems perfectly reasonable to her. What's she supposed to do? See into the future?

'I got it specially for you. Who's going to eat it now?'

'I don't know, Mum.'

'This isn't a hotel, Chloe. You can't just come and go as you want.'

'So what is it? A prison?'

'A prison?' Her mother sits down on one of the kitchen chairs. Her face has gone blank. 'No. It's not a prison.'

Chloe's phone shudders. She looks to see who it is. Hal.

'Got to take this.'

She goes out into the hall to talk.

'Hi, Hal. How's things?'

'I'm going crazy, that's how things are. Why didn't you call me?'

Wrong move. Chloe feels her defences rising.

'I just got home, Hal. Take it easy, for fuck's sake. One day. It's not the end of the world.'

'You know I've been trying to reach you. You know we need to talk.'

Everyone always has to do all this talking. Talk talk talk. Why can't people just go with the flow? Live your life, Hal.

'You're the one said you never wanted to see me again.'

'Oh, Chloe. Baby. You know I didn't mean it. Oh, fuck. Tell me you know it. What do I have to do? Come on, baby. I'm going crazy here.'

'Okay. Fine. You didn't mean it. I believe you.'

'So are we cool? Are we good?'

'Sure.'

'You're sure?'

This is what happens. If you're not hyperventilating with excitement over them they start to sulk. Someone should tell them: don't beg for it. Begging turns the heart to stone. She can feel her heart turning to stone and she hates that.

'Listen to me, Hal. You're in Cardiff, I'm in Sussex. It's Christmas and everyone gets stressed out. Let's just all give ourselves some time off, and then it'll be the new term and we can take it from there.'

'But are we still good?'

'Yes. We're still good.'

'And it's okay if I call you?'

'Course it's okay.'

'Send me a picture of you. Try to look as if you're missing me.'

'I am missing you.'

'I love you, babe.'

'Me too.'

By the end the plaintive note has gone out of his voice and she's able to sound friendly enough for him to end the call, but it's an effort. What is it that happens to them? They start out so strong and end up so weak.

She goes back into the kitchen and there's her mother sitting where she left her, the same dead look on her face.

Something not right.

'What is it, Mum?'

Her mother turns and stares at her as if she doesn't know her. This is not good at all.

Chloe sits down facing her.

'Tell me.'

Her mother says nothing. She presses her lips together as if to stop herself from speaking, and when she lets them go for a moment they're white. She looks at her hands. Out of the window.

'Mum. Tell me. Please.'

'I don't want to talk about it. I don't want to worry you.'

'Okay,' says Chloe. 'So now I'm worried.'

Her mother turns her gaze back from the window and meets her daughter's eyes with a look of utter helplessness.

'Your father's having an affair,' she says.

'What?'

For some reason Chloe finds herself totally unprepared for this. So much so that at first she can't take it in. Dad having an affair?

'He can't be.'

'I know. But he is.'

'Why?'

'I don't know. Ask him.'

Now Chloe's beginning to register the enormity of the news. She feels as if something unknown and frightening has come into the house. Their home.

'He can't. He mustn't.'

'Tell him that.'

'Oh, God, Mum. This is horrible. Can't we stop him?'

'He says it's over.'

Chloe catches a tiny fragment of what her mother must be feeling, and at once, grateful for the chance, she transfers the turbulent emotions inside herself to concern for her mother.

'How can he do that to you? What does he think he's doing? I can't believe this. Mum, this is not on. Seriously, he can't do this.' Then, still catching up with the reality of what's happening, 'Who is it?'

'Some woman at his hospital.'

'Has it been going on long?'

'I don't think so. I don't really know. Oh, Chloe, I feel so sick of it all. I just want it to go away.'

'Where is he now?'

'He's in his study.'

'Right. I'm going to talk to him.'

Her mother says nothing. She goes back to looking out of the window. Chloe gets up. The house phone rings. Chloe gets it. It's her brother Alex.

'Hi, Alex. You coming home for Christmas or what?'

They talk briefly. He's planning to come home next Thursday.

'Is Jess coming with you?'

'No,' he says. 'She'll be in Yorkshire. Is Mum there?'

Chloe hands the phone to her mother.

'It's Alex. He's coming home on Thursday.'

She leaves them talking.

Her father's study is at the far end of the house, deliberately chosen for its privacy and quietness. These days the house is always quiet, and he rarely goes there. She finds him sitting at the big leather-inlaid desk, looking at nothing at all. He acknowledges her appearance with a turn of his head towards her. He looks terrible, his skin blotchy, his eyes puffy.

'What's going on, Dad?'

He frowns. He seems to be having trouble collecting his thoughts.

'You can't do this to Mum. You know that? It's not on. She doesn't deserve it.' As she speaks the anger rises. 'I never had you down for a pig, I thought you were one of

the good guys. So how come all of a sudden you turn into
a pig? Don't you care what you're doing to Mum? Don't
you give a fuck about her? How can you do this to her?'

'Chloe, darling—'

'Is it over? She says it's over.'

'Yes. It's over.'

'So you're not walking out on Mum?'

And me, Dad. You're not walking out on me.

'No. I'd never do that.'

'And you're sorry?'

'Yes. I'm sorry.'

He looks so tired. So beaten. Don't do this to us, Dad.
Be loving for ever, but be strong. Hold me in your arms
and tell me you'll never leave. Tell me I'm too little to
understand. Tell me I don't need to worry, there's nothing
to be afraid of, it's only noises in the night.

'Then come into the kitchen and be with Mum. Don't
hide out here.'

'Chloe, sweetheart. It's not what you think.'

'I don't think anything, okay? You say it's over, so it's
over. I don't want to hear any details. I really don't want
to know.'

'I'm saying sorry to you, too.'

'Yes, okay. So you're sorry. Great. Meanwhile Mum's
dying in there.'

She knows he wants her forgiveness but she can't do it.
It won't come. Too much anger.

Why do they always have to fuck everything up and then turn round and ask for pity? I hate pity. If you want to fuck the nurses then for fuck's sake enjoy it.

Don't do this to me, Dad. Don't leave me. Don't go and leave behind this sad old fart who wants to be forgiven. I've got issues of my own. It's Christmas. I came home for a rest.

He stands up.

'You're right,' he says. 'It'll be lunch soon.'

There's a chicken roasting in the oven. Family lunch. Whoop-de-doo.

18

Alice tries to tell him but Cas won't listen. Stubbornly he sits by the front window looking out onto the street, expecting to see Guy come walking up from the station at any moment.

'He may not be able to make it, Cas.'

'Yes, he will. He said he'd come.'

Alice is appalled by her little brother's unshakeable faith. She does her best to instil doubts in him by pointing out all the reasonable and honourable accidents that may arise: pressure of work, a minor illness, a breakdown of his car. Caspar merely shakes his head and goes on staring out of the window. What more can she do? Impossible to give him the real information that lies beneath her lack of faith in Guy, that he's an entirely selfish person driven by the whim of the moment. Cas has chosen Guy as his imaginary friend. How else can you describe it? He knows nothing about Guy and has only ever met him twice. It's all very strange.

'I don't understand why you've got so keen on Guy all of a sudden.'

'He's my half-father,' says Cas.

'Your half-father? No, he's not.'

'Yes, he is. You're my half-sister, and he's your father.'

Liz and Alan are both out. They have the house to themselves. Alice has had various plans for today, she thought she might sort out the mess of her room, maybe do some more on her story. But she has done nothing. She made lunch for Cas and herself, it was supposed to be cheese omelettes but Cas wanted baked beans, so she made baked beans on toast; the toast being her nod to cooking. Then she tried to get Cas to come out Christmas shopping with her but he said, 'No, Guy's coming.' He's been waiting since he got up.

Alice too is waiting, though she does her best not to think about it. Chloe's text was ambiguous: *All fixed up for Sunday.* What has she fixed? Alice can't stop herself from investing that one word, *fixed*, with a little freight of hope. Chloe is active where she herself is passive. Chloe makes things happen.

'There he is!'

A shrill cry of triumph from Caspar. He races for the front door, hauls it open before Alice can stop him.

But he's right. Against all the odds, there's Guy standing on the doorstep, smiling his usual irrepressible smile.

'Guy! Guy! You came!' cries Cas, bouncing up and down.

'Stroke of luck, eh?' he says. And to Alice in the hallway behind, 'I had to come down to Brighton anyway.'

'Good to see you, Guy.' She never calls him Dad.

A peck on the cheek as he comes in. He's carrying a box in a carrier bag. He lets Caspar take him by the hand and lead him into the front room.

'You know how you live in London?' says Cas.

'Yes.'

'I'm going to come and visit you.'

'Great. When are you coming?'

'It's to be a surprise.'

Alice looks on: the little boy so unaware, the man so unthinking. He seems to her never to have changed, always handsome, always worthless. She wants to call out to Cas, He'll let you down. It's what he does.

'You want some coffee or something, Guy?'

'That would be great.'

She goes into the kitchen to put on a kettle. Instant will do, he doesn't deserve better. Probably can't tell the difference. She thinks as she does every time she sees him how odd it is that he doesn't seem to age. His floppy shiny hair still abundant, his face unlined, his smile youthful. And yet he's over forty now.

Why has he come? He hasn't asked after Liz. He hasn't shown much interest in her, his own daughter. What is this thing with Cas?

When she takes the coffee into the front room she finds he's bought Cas a Christmas present and allowed him to open it right away. It's a robot.

'Jesus! That is so ugly!'

'Isn't he just?' says Guy.

The robot is the size of a small dog and looks like a grotesque parody of maleness: bulging chest and arms, tiny head. It's made of black and white plastic and has red illuminated eyes. Caspar is gazing at it in a trance of admiration.

'Shall I put him through his paces for you?' Guy says to Cas.

'Yes please!'

Guy picks up a remote control that looks as complicated as a computer keyboard and starts pressing buttons. The robot lurches forward, red eyes flashing. Then it does a little dance. It isn't pretty, but it is fascinating. Then Guy makes it hold out its gripper for Cas to shake, and the robot speaks in a gruff grunting voice.

'What did he say?' cries Cas.

'He's talking Caveman,' says Guy. 'And listen to this.'

He presses more buttons. The robot emits a long fart. Cas convulses with laughter.

'Honestly, Guy,' says Alice. 'How old are you?'

'About six,' says Guy.

'What's his name?' says Cas.

'Well, he's called Robosapien V1. But I think you should give him a name of his own.'

'I will,' says Cas, nodding and frowning. He takes the task seriously.

Guy starts showing him how to work the robot, lying down on the floor by Cas's side and at his level. He makes the robot kick and punch, and do a lumbering run across the room. Alice watches without taking part. This is boy stuff.

She feels angry at Guy and ashamed of her anger. She is his real daughter and he's never bought her a gift of such magnificence, or laid himself down on the floor to play with her.

'How much did that thing cost, Guy?' she says. 'It must have cost a fortune.'

'Not at all,' he says. 'I didn't pay a penny. It came in as a promotional gift. But they're not that pricey, to be honest. You can find them on the Internet for £25.'

Cas isn't listening, he's too absorbed in the robot. But somehow Guy can get away with this sort of thing, telling you his present was a freebie, and you still feel honoured to receive it.

The doorbell rings. Alice goes to answer it. It's Chloe.

'Bad time?'

'No. Come on in.'

Chloe comes in, looking round curiously.

'I'm supposed to be shopping. I hate Christmas.'

She seems subdued. Through the open door to the living room she sees the robot's flashing red eyes.

'Fuck! What's that thing?' Then, seeing Cas, 'Sorry.'

Guy is amused by the fuck. His eyes linger on Chloe. Alice introduces them.

'Guy, my dad. This is Chloe.'

'Hi,' says Chloe.

'My robot says hi,' says Cas.

He presses a button and the robot makes a growling noise.

'Kick me out if I'm in the way,' says Guy.

'No,' says Alice, 'you go on playing with Cas. Me and Chloe will go up to my room, if that's okay.'

Guy gives a regal wave.

'Off you go.'

Upstairs in Alice's room the two girls sit on the bed and Chloe is silent, so Alice has to prompt her.

'Well?'

'Well.'

Another silence. Then Chloe comes out with, 'So that's your dad?'

'Yes.'

'He looks too young to be your dad.'

'He's forty-one.'

'And he lives in London?'

'Yes. Actually, Chloe, he's a useless dad and I hardly ever see him so I'm not really all that interested in talking about him.'

'Okay.'

'So what's your news?'

'My news?' She looks startled. 'Why should I have news?'

Blushing slightly, Alice says, 'You talked to Jack.'

'Oh, yes. Right. Jack.'

All this is odd and disappointing. Yesterday on the train Chloe had been so positive, Alice had let herself start to believe in her power to make things happen. Now she seems distracted. So why come round?

'How did he sound?'

'Fine.' Then she seems to remember why she's here. She sits up straighter, becomes more animated. 'We talked a lot about you. He remembers you really well.'

'We were at school together for nine years.'

'You know what I mean. Anyway, it's all fixed. You're meeting him for lunch at Harvey's, one o'clock tomorrow.'

'He agreed to that?'

'Sure. Why wouldn't he?'

'Did you tell him I wanted to see him?'

'Don't worry, I kept it all very casual. I said you'd love to get together, talk about the old days, blah-de-blah. I said if I could make it I'd join you. But I won't, of course.'

'So it's just meeting up and chatting?'

'That's all. You don't have to put on clean knickers.'

Alice gives a nervous laugh.

'You have no idea how this kind of thing scares me.'

'What's there to be scared of? If it doesn't work out, what have you lost? Nothing.'

Just another little flicker of hope, thinks Alice. Every tiny failure adds to the burden that I drag behind me, that keeps me earthbound. One day I'll stop trying. Just sit down on the ground and go nowhere ever again.

'It's easy for you,' she says. 'You know what to do.'

'There's nothing to do. Just be friendly. Then, if it looks like it's going well' – she leans over to Alice and lays one hand on her thigh – 'touch him.'

'I can't do that!'

'Why not? I'm not saying feel him up. Just a friendly touch, like this.'

'Honestly, I could never do that.'

'Couldn't you?' Chloe gazes at her thoughtfully. 'It really speeds things up, touching.'

'But how do I know if he wants it?'

'Oh, boys just do.'

'With you, maybe.'

'See here, Alice. I'm not going to let you screw this up.' All at once Chloe has become engaged. 'You can make this happen. He's only a stupid boy. We're so much smarter than them. All you have to do is take charge and you can switch them on and off like a Hoover.'

'Like a Hoover?'

'Well, I was trying to think of something that makes a noise and then just fizzles out.'

They both started laughing.

'You don't sound as if you think much of boys,' says Alice.

'I don't. Or men.'

'So why do we bother?'

'Oh, you know,' says Chloe. 'It's biology. Or evolution. Or something. Why do you bother?'

'I think I've read too many stories,' says Alice, 'seen too many films. I can see through it with my brain but somewhere deep down I've bought the whole romantic couple thing. I want a soulmate. Someone I can love body and soul, who loves me the same way. It's pathetic really.'

'Same,' says Chloe.

'You've at least got a chance. Thirteen and counting.'

'Yes, but I've got no staying power.'

'What do you mean?'

'Well, I'm always falling in love, but somehow when it all starts to work out, I get bored. I don't know why. I wish I did, actually. Maybe I'm just a natural born slut.'

They start laughing again.

'We should team up,' says Alice. 'You can get them started. Then I'll move in and take over for the long haul. Like breaking in wild horses.'

'Wild horses! If only.'

Alice watches Chloe laughing and thinks how pretty she is, how if she was a boy she'd want to love her. Maybe that's all it is after all, a quirk of the genes, a nose like this and not like that, and you get love or you don't. The mind revolts against such a conclusion, it's too brutal, too impersonal, but why should nature care about our feelings?

'Look, I'm going to get back to my shopping. You meet Jack for lunch tomorrow and just keep telling yourself, I'm doing this saddo a favour. Okay?'

'Okay.'

They go back downstairs. Guy hears them coming and gets up off the floor.

'See this kid go!' he says.

Cas works the remote control, tongue protruding between his lips. The robot marches, turns, picks up a Lego man from the floor, throws him aside. Then Cas makes him roar, and roars himself.

'He's a monster,' says Alice.

'He's wicked,' says Cas. 'He's blinding.'

'My God,' says Chloe. 'I feel so old.'

Guy catches sight of the time. 'Christ! I have to motor.'

'Are you going, Guy?' For a moment Cas's little face is bereft.

This is what he does, half-brother. He comes, he makes you feel life can be magical and bright, then he goes.

'Yep. I'm off.' Not a hint of remorse. 'But the roboguy stays with you.'

Roboguy. Please. How much of a giveaway is that? But Cas is innocent and willing to take the trade.

'Okay. Roboguy says goodbye.'

He makes the robot wave a claw.

'Love to Liz, yes?'

Guy's on his way out. Chloe gives Alice a kiss.

'Kill 'em dead, sister.'

Then she too is gone.

Alice turns back to watch Cas at play with the pin-headed monster.

'The batteries'll run out,' she says.

'I don't care.'

'Is that why you wanted to see Guy? So he'd give you a present?'

'No.'

'He didn't give me a present.'

'You're a grown-up.'

'Yes. I suppose I am.'

Cas makes the robot speak a whole string of growls and grunts.

'He says, I'm Roboguy and I rule the world.'

Alice bends down and topples the robot onto his back.

'Hey! What did you do that for?'

He rights the robot, handling him with respectful care.

'He's so ugly,' says Alice. 'He's got bosoms. His head's too small.'

Cas isn't listening. He's back working the buttons of the remote, murmuring to himself in his own version of a growly voice.

'Nobody messes with Roboguy.'

19

Matt Early is working in his shed, absorbed, locked in silent concentration, when the bell rings. This is the bell he rigged up himself when he first built the shed, so that his mother could call him if ever there was an emergency. There never has been an emergency, but still she calls him, sometimes several times an evening.

Matt sighs, but he obeys. He turns out the lights in the windowless shed and locks the door behind him. He alone has the key. He strides down the concrete path to the back door of the house, a path he laid himself, a distance of some ten metres: to him as wide as an ocean, a journey from the new world back to the old.

His mother is sitting in the lounge with the television on, watching *Close Encounters of the Third Kind* on Channel 4. Except she's not watching: her head and upper body are twisted round towards the back entry, looking out for him. She's wearing an orange shawl draped over her thin shoulders to demonstrate that she suffers from the cold, even though the house is heated to a temperature of twenty-two degrees.

Every time he sees her again, even after a short interval, he's surprised by how small she is. She paints her eyebrows with a thin line of brown eyebrow pencil, so she always looks disapproving. Her hair is dyed a colour she calls chestnut, more red than brown, entirely unconvincing. She wears tan-coloured slacks and carpet slippers made of tartan cloth. Round her neck hangs the button he gave her, a wireless bell-push designed for front doors that communicates by radio waves with the bell in his shed.

'Yes?' he says. 'What is it?'

He can see at a glance that nothing is wrong. His mother claims to be disabled.

'I'm sorry, Matthew, but it's not easy for me, you know. You try sitting in a chair for three hours all by yourself. It makes you want to scream. I would scream, only what's the point? Who'd hear me?'

'If you don't like sitting in the chair you can always get up.'

Matt speaks softly, as ever, but there's a dull note in his voice. They've been here before.

'But I can't, can I?'

She presses her hands on the chair's arms, and pretends to try to rise.

'You try getting to your feet when your joints are in spasm. Do you have the slightest idea what it feels like?

No, not the slightest. Well, I'll tell you. It's like being stabbed by knives. It's unbearable, Matthew.'

'You've managed before, Mum.'

'Sometimes I think you just don't care.'

It's true: Matt doesn't care. All his capacity to care is used up doing the mundane tasks she requires of him. He has no surplus energy left for actual sympathy.

'You should move about more, Mum. I keep telling you. If you just sit and watch telly you stiffen up.'

'Stiffen up! What do you know? Do you have arthritis? Are you the expert? Come over here and help me.'

He goes to her side and offers his arm. With many a groan, pulling faces that would be comical if they didn't irritate him so much, she pulls herself to her feet.

'Mother of God have mercy on me!'

They walk from the lounge to the kitchen, Mrs Early leaning heavily on her son and dragging one leg.

'You were walking fine earlier,' he says.

'I was not. I just kept quiet about the pain.'

'Come on, now. You don't need me.'

Matt stopped believing in his mother's pain long ago. She's perfectly healthy, and sixty-six isn't old. The only pain she suffers is that she's a lonely woman living a mean- ingless life.

'So now you want to get away too? Is that it?'

Yes, Matt wants to get away. His mother has never forgiven his father for what she calls 'getting away':

slithering out of his responsibilities by staging a fatal heart attack.

'I'm here, aren't I?'

'Not that anyone would know it. I never see you. What do you get up to in that disgusting shed of yours?'

'It's not disgusting.'

'Well, I've never cleaned it. Have you ever cleaned it?'

'Yes.'

'That's a lie. Now put the kettle on. I want a cup of tea.'

'You can do it for yourself, Mum. You're not a cripple. If you stop doing things for yourself you'll end up a cripple.'

'Not a cripple? What do you know? You never did have any imagination, Matthew. Just like your father.'

'There. Make your own tea. You can do it.'

He parks her by the sink.

'Where are you going?'

'I'm going back outside.'

'What about me?'

'You'll be all right, Mum.'

'How am I supposed to get back to the lounge?'

'Walk.'

'I told you. I can't walk.'

Her gaze holds him, never letting go, accusing, needing. The anger breaks within him.

'Then crawl,' he says.

'Oh, if your father were alive to hear you!'

'He's fine. He got away. I wish I could.'

'So go away! I don't care. Leave me. You're no use to me. You never help me. You're never here. You might as well just go.'

'Right. I'll be off in the morning.'

Always the same exchange, always the same conclusion. He can't leave, and she knows he can't leave.

'If I wasn't here to help you, you'd be walking all by yourself soon enough.'

'Oh, yes,' she says. 'I'm just pretending. I can walk.'

She takes a step away from the sink. For a brief moment she stands unsupported. Then as her legs start to give way she turns back, hands scrabbling for the sink's edge. Heaving with exertion and stress, she pushes herself upright again.

Then she turns to Matt with a look that says, I told you.

But in that moment Matt sees something else. He sees his mother standing by the sink thirty or more years ago, turning round to smile down at him, happy to be interrupted in her chores. That unfailing welcome that you take for granted as a child. The simple profound conviction that this all-powerful being will love and protect you for ever. How do you ever repay that?

'I wish you'd try harder, Mum. One day I'll be gone. Then you'll have to manage by yourself.'

'Gone? Where have you got to go?'

'I'll get married. I'll have my own house.'

'Married! Who'd have you? What are you now? Forty?

It's a bit late to expect the girls to come knocking on your door.'

'If you say so.'

This is where they always end: he just starts agreeing with everything she says. He does it because he doesn't want to argue with her any more. But still they argue.

'Why, have you got somebody?'

'I wouldn't tell you if I had.'

'So you haven't.'

'If you say so.'

'I do say so. You're like your father. He'd never have married me if it'd been left to him. Had to do it all myself.'

This too is an old refrain. Nothing hurts Matt more deeply than her contempt for his father.

'There you are, then. You know it all. I'm going to go outside.'

'Get my cup of tea first. And help me back into the lounge. Look at you, dithering in the doorway. Just like your father. I never knew whether he was coming in or going out.'

Matt stands there in the doorway, his powerful body caught between conflicting forces, one of which is his desire to escape, the other the lifelong pull of this bitter, lonely woman, his mother. Just as his father was caught.

'Rosemary from next door says it's pornography. She says that's what all men have in their sheds. But I told her. He goes out there to play his violin. "Oh, it's violins, is it?" she said, like we were talking about paedophiles. You're not a paedophile, are you, Matt? You're not locking little girls up in your shed, are you?'

'No, I'm not.'

'It's just violins, isn't it?'

'Yes, Mum. Just violins.'

'I don't know why you can't play it in the house.'

Because you put your fingers in your ears when I play, and make a face like it hurts. Because you told me from the start I was no good. Because you want to destroy anything I love that isn't you. Because you love me too much.

'I'm going back out now, Mum.'

'Help me through first.'

She's made herself a cup of tea. He helps her through, as she knew he would. Her weight so slight on his arm. And this the body that brought him into the world.

'You only go out there to annoy me,' she says.

'That's right, Mum. I sit there all by myself thinking how much I'm annoying you.'

'With your little violin.'

He settles her back into the armchair.

'There you are. Watch the telly. I'm going out.'

'I don't understand this film at all.'

'There's nothing to understand. Aliens are coming to earth, and all these people want to meet them, and then they meet.'

'Why?'

'I don't know why.'

'So why is he making a mountain out of clay?'

'You'll see. I'm going now.'

'Matt—'

'I'll be another hour or so. No more.'

She reaches up her hand and he takes it. She squeezes his hand with hers, the slight familiar pressure that says, You know I'll always love you. This strong hand that has held him all his life.

He returns the pressure, and lets her hand go. He leaves the room without saying anything more. It's the only way to get away.

Matt does more in his shed than play the violin. He builds violins. He buys old and broken violins in junk shops or at car boot sales. Sometimes they're undamaged but undistinguished instruments no longer wanted by owners who've found out how many hours of practice it takes to make an acceptable sound; but mostly they're in a bad way, the belly cracked, the strings gone, the bridge broken. The Collin-Mezin, his best find, was in pieces when he chanced upon it. But there was the signature in pencil, dated 1889. He paid £10 for the bag of fragments. When restored he'll get maybe £7,000 for it.

He's never told his mother. She'd say it was all a waste of money.

His tools line one wall. Violins in various stages of renovation line another. His workbench is brightly illuminated by two powerful daylight lamps. A bandsaw the size of a fridge-freezer fills one corner. A tailor-made rack houses his prized possessions, a collection of bronze Lie-Nielsen planes. Whenever he sells a violin he pours the proceeds back into the buying of tools. This shed must house several thousand pounds' worth of instruments and materials. So it's not about making money. It's about peace of mind.

He takes up the bridge blank he's been working on, and a small carving knife, and continues the slow careful process of fitting the bridge to the belly of the violin. The violin is a Jesse Dennis, bought in Brighton for £40 cash. The bridge is French maple, made by Aubert. The carving of its feet alone will take him hours. The fit must be perfect. But once in his workshop time ceases to exist for Matt. He has passed into eternity.

He works away steadily, his knife shaving the bridge in microscopic slices, and so slips into a concentration so absolute that his mind is free to roam where it will. His mind chooses to think about Meg Strachan, her face in her hands, weeping. No surprise that this has had a strong effect on him. It's natural when you see a woman in tears to want to help. But it goes deeper than that. It's as if this single sight, her face raised up to him, her eyes shining, her cheeks running with her tears, has penetrated to his innermost soul and taken possession of him.

A bit late to expect the girls to come knocking on my door.

'Meg,' he says aloud as he works.

The sound of her name brings her into the shed with him.

'You're the one for me, Meg.'

There it is: the ridiculous truth. But there's no one here to laugh. Matt has never known a conviction like it in all his life. He looks on it with awe. It's come from nowhere, for no reason, and so he trusts it. This must be what it's like to be greeted by an angel. The angel appears and dazzles you, and whatever the message you accept it, because of the way it's delivered. Follow that star, the angel says. Fine, you follow it. You don't know why, or where you're going. You just do what the angel says.

She lives alone. That much he knows.

Matt is observant in his way. A bathroom tells more than you might think. Just the one toothbrush. A modest array of make-up materials. A lavatory seat that won't stay up unless you hold it. Strange how many builders don't know how to fit a lavatory seat. You have to turn the off-centre hinges so that the base of the hinge is thrown forward, not back. Then the seat will lean against the cistern. Get it wrong and it won't stay up without your hand holding it, which is awkward to say the least. Matt always carries a small adjustable spanner with him, so that he can refit wrongly-fitted lavatory seats. It only takes a couple of minutes. It just bothers him too much, to think of the house owners enduring the faulty fitting for month after month, as if it were some kind of natural hazard.

Most people are so helpless. It's odd, he never thinks of himself as better than others, but why do they tolerate poor workmanship? Why don't they make their gates close properly, and their tables not wobble? Why live with low-level irritation when you can do something about it? It's not hard. He's no genius, God knows. All it takes is a little care, a little close looking, a little time. You get a reputation for being handy, for being able to fix things, and people throw jobs your way, even jobs you know nothing about. But you get into the habit of having a go, and you find most things aren't really so difficult. Even violins.

People see a violin in pieces and they think that's it, it's over. But violins never die. You could run over a violin with a truck and still put it together again. If you take your time with it no one will ever see the joins, and the sound will be as good as ever.

I had a bit of bad news, she said.

Crying her eyes out. Why? Maybe one day I'll be able to ask her. Maybe one day I'll be able to make things better for her.

By being hurt, Meg has placed herself within his reach. His mother says, who'd want you? Matt does not disagree. He has as low an opinion of his powers of attraction as his mother could wish. But in other ways, and at the same time, he's a proud man.

Who is there who knows me? Who is my superior? Who can judge me? No man I ever met.

The way she looked at me. Such pitiful eyes, not daring to believe I'd understand her. After all, what am I? Just the plumber come to fix the shower.

Maybe I'll get hurt. Time I got hurt. Better to be hurt than go on the way I am.

All the time working away, shaving whispers of wood from the maple feet.

He has a clear visual memory of her face. Very pale clear skin. Those startled green-brown eyes, beneath dark eyebrows. Her hesitant look, checking to see how she's being received.

On Monday he'll pick up the replacement shower pump. Sometime on Tuesday he'll go round to her flat and do the work. Then some words will be spoken. He has no idea what. Then his life will change for ever. Or it won't.

20

The anger in Belinda hasn't gone away. It's grown.

Tom sits in his usual chair in front of the fire reading the papers, an early evening glass of wine by his side, as if nothing has changed. Belinda moves back and forth between the kitchen and the living room the way she always does when cooking dinner, except she's not cooking dinner. There is no dinner.

Tom doesn't know this yet. He thinks everything's gone back to normal.

That's how they think. They have a little fling, they say they're sorry, life goes on. They say, 'It's nothing,' and it's all forgotten. Like hell it is.

The anger has been growing in Belinda all day. The initial shock has passed, and some of the panic fear that came with it. Now all she can see is the stupendous self-ishness of what Tom has done. The careless cruelty. What he has done isn't nothing, it's a physical act with physical consequences. Like rape, when you think about it. Rape is when a man uses a woman's body against a woman's will for his own pleasure. Well, he's used a woman's body, hers, against a woman's will, mine, for his own pleasure. This is a three-person sex crime. There's an act of selfish lust, and there's an injury. So why isn't he being punished? Why is he sitting reading the paper as if nothing has changed?

She pours herself another glass of wine, her fourth, but does not offer to refill his glass. He gets up, puts more wood on the fire, resumes his seat and his newspaper. He must know she's standing in the doorway watching him. Why doesn't he say something? What does he imagine she's feeling?

Pound slips below euro on Britain's high streets. Brown moves out of Blair's shadow. Arkansas woman gives birth to eighteenth child.

Even the newspaper's playing his game, acting as if life goes on and we all still care about the financial crisis and the war in Afghanistan.

Husband shits on family home for fun. Leading surgeon lies and cheats and expects to be forgiven. That's the news.

He looks round, lifts his spectacles.

'Anything I can do?'

'I don't know,' says Belinda. 'You tell me.'

'I mean about dinner.'

'What dinner?'

There, that's stumped him. He likes his food.

'Don't you want dinner?' he says.

'Since when did you care what I want?'

'For Christ's sake!'

It comes out like a shout of pain. Well, good. Time he shared some of the grief round here. But he's choking it back. Mr Reasonable returns.

'We've been through all that.'

'Have we? Where did we end up?'

'I just don't know what more you want me to do. I've said sorry. I've said it's over. What else am I supposed to do?'

You're supposed to be punished. You're supposed to hurt. But she doesn't say it.

'You're such a fucker,' she says.

'All right. *All right!* But if we're going to try to make a go of this—'

'If!'

'I want to. I've said so. It's what I want. But you have to want it too. I can't do this all by myself.'

'You did the other bit all by yourself.'

'Jesus, Belinda! Can't we – can't we – just move on?'

'Pretend it never happened.'

'No. Just … give it a rest.'

'No. We can't. It's not that easy, Tom.'

He throws the newspaper onto the floor. What's this? A tantrum. Are we throwing our toys out of the pram?

She goes into the kitchen. These twitches of distress

almost hurt more than the other coping mechanisms, the let's-be-grown-up shit. Don't cope, Tom. Join the party. Crack up.

She's too proud to pity herself and too angry to pity him but there's a load of pity going for the asking here.

He follows her.

'Look,' he says, his voice gruff and angry. 'You may not want to eat but I do. I'm going to go into Lewes and get a takeaway pizza.'

'If that's what you want,' she says.

As if the problem is dinner. As if fetching takeaway pizzas solves anything. How about some takeaway sex while you're at it, Tom? But off he goes, pulls on his coat, picks up his car keys, happy to be in motion, making something happen. Maybe he thinks if he goes and gets the dinner then everything'll be all right again.

She hears his car reversing onto the lane.

Incredible. Piss away your marriage, take away a pizza.

Belinda doesn't know what to do with her anger. In some distant part of herself she's aware that it's not constructive, that it's in danger of making a bad situation worse. But she can do nothing about that. The anger possesses her. She prowls about the house looking for something to smash. She wants her own hurt to be reflected in the world around her. The handsome rooms of the expensive house seem to mock her. All this good taste, representing so many hours poring over colour charts and fabric swatches, all that furniture shopping that had once absorbed her – every item has its history, the lampshades she found in the little shop in Wells-next-the-Sea, the Turk's head pot from Sicily, the Wilton carpet that was such an amazing deal because the line had been discontinued – what does any of it matter now? With one stroke he's destroyed the value of their shared home, which is – she never knew this before – the outward form of their marriage, their family. What has been a source of comfort and reassurance is now become a hollow mockery. There is no marriage. There is no family. Only four separate individuals following their own impulses, whose paths cross from time to time under this roof.

Very well, says Belinda to herself. If that's the game I can play it as well as any of you. Why should I sit at home being mother while Tom and Chloe and Alex do what the hell they like?

She goes into the little room she calls her study, though no studies ever take place there. Here she has her computer, used for emails and Internet shopping. She opens Entourage and taps in an email address she obtained over a year ago now, after bumping into a friend from way back. Then she starts typing in a message.

Hi Kenny. I bet you don't remember me but I met Mark Pugh the other day and we bored on about the old days and he said he was still in touch with you and that got me remembering. Funny how little things stay in the mind. Like that evening we watched the sunset, bet you've forgotten. Anyway how's things? I'm an old married lady now but inside I feel I'm still 17, actually I wish I was, I'd do a lot of things differently believe me. It's Saturday evening and I'm bored and you don't have to reply. Belinda.

She clicks Send without rereading it, not wanting to give herself the chance to have second thoughts. The computer makes a whooshing sound and she pictures her message flying like an arrow from Plumpton to Wandsworth.

On an impulse she opens Google Earth and types in Henderson Road, Wandsworth. There before her on her screen appears a bird's-eye view of a street surrounded by parkland. The satellite took the picture late one afternoon in autumn, the trees are brown and throw long shadows. The houses seen from above seem unlike London houses, the roofs longer and flatter. There are cars parked on both sides of the road before every house. One of them is Kenny's car. Why not? The picture was taken, it says, in 2006. He was living there then.

What sort of life has he had? Is he happy? Does he have affairs? At the time that she knew him he was rumoured to have an unusually big dick, but no one she ever spoke to had actually seen it.

Which house is his house? She has no way of knowing, so she chooses a house at random, the third house down, the one with the largest back garden. She clicks on the Zoom Out button and makes the streets recede until they look like furrows scored in green fields. Then she zooms in once more, journeying to Kenny's house, drawing him ever closer to her.

Stupid game. What am I trying to prove?

Ping! An email back.

So I'm at my screen searching for Xmas junk and I get this smack in the face. Do I remember you? You're the one that got away. Beautiful Belinda, don't talk to me about the sunset. How about THE KISS? I can feel it still. You think I'm joking? My God I don't even want to know how long ago that was, I say it was the day before yesterday. So I want to see you again. When? Where? Kenny.

Belinda sits staring at the screen. How can it be so fast? So easy? She feels ridiculously excited, tells herself to behave, fails to listen. At least it's better than wanting to smash things. Or just another way of smashing things. Actually she doesn't give a damn what it is. She's on the road again.

She pecks out her reply.

I can't believe it's you after all these years. Both of us married with kids, both of us growing old. It would be good to meet up and talk over the old days. I don't expect you're ever down in Sussex but I come up to London most weeks. I'm planning a Christmas shopping trip on Tuesday but you'll be working I'm sure or we could meet for lunch. Or some time in the new year. Yes I remember the kiss it was so odd wasn't it the way we had that and nothing ever again. That's life I guess. B.

She sends it. This time she does nothing. Sits and waits. The reply comes within a minute.

Tuesday's good but I'll be at Gatwick all day how about you stop off on your way back maybe 5pm ask for me at the Hilton South Terminal I'll leave a message for you. As for that's life well it's not over yet and if you're half the girl I remember you're not one to go quietly either. Don't know about you but some things haven't worked out the way I hoped hey I'm not complaining win some lose some. I remember you so well girl you were sunshine and honey just the most adorable creature I ever set eyes on. Why I didn't grab you while I could I'll never know one of the great if-onlys of life. So tell me you're good for Tuesday because now I'm all excited and you're not to let me down. One kiss is not enough. K.

She trembles as she reads. She remembers him with extraordinary vividness, the flop of dark hair, the high cheekbones, the look in his eyes, all cocky and amused, just before he kissed her. The kiss itself she recalls less clearly, only that she shouldn't, and what would Dom say if he found out, which he never did.

What would Tom say if he found out?

Found out what? That she's planning to meet up with a boy she kissed when she was seventeen? Not exactly on a par with poking someone in marketing. And to tell you the truth, Tom, I don't give a toss what you say. You went your own sweet way so I'll go mine.

I expect I can make that work though I may not be able to stay long and the kiss will have to be a peck on the cheek from an old lady. Gatwick Hilton at 5 on Tuesday. See you then. B.

Keep it simple, keep it clean. But she does appreciate being sunshine and honey. Not the sort of thing Tom ever says to her.

She catches herself referring in her thoughts to old-model Tom, the one who's unimaginative but reliable. This has been superseded. New-model Tom is a cheating fucker. Who knows, he probably tells someone in marketing that she's sunshine and honey.

Kenny is back. This is turning into a conversation.

Sod the peck on the cheek, I've been on to Mark Pugh and he says you're still gorgeous and don't look a day

over 30. We knew each other before we were married so
the way I see it is we go back to that time and pick up
where we left off. Are you up for this, beautiful? You'll
make an old man very happy. Not so old, actually, I keep
myself fit, nothing's dropped off yet. So let's pretend that
the sun's still setting and we've just kissed and there's
no reason in the world why we shouldn't move on from
there – Gotta go, gorgeous. I hear the witch parking her
broomstick.

Belinda sits very still and allows the glow of satisfaction
to spread all through her body. It does a girl good to be
complimented once in a while, even if it's just flattery. Still
gorgeous and don't look a day over thirty. If only. But I
could pass for forty by candlelight. Do they have candles
in the Gatwick Hilton?

She goes through the little chain of emails one by one,
rereading them, feeling as she felt on Google Earth that
she's zooming towards Kenny. Then she closes the emails.
Should she delete them? Why? She has nothing to hide.
Tom's the one with secrets. If he wants to go snooping
among her emails, let him.

She wonders if she'll tell him about her date with Kenny,
regarding her own future behaviour as unpredictable. Well,
I never guessed I'd throw the cabbage at him. You don't
know what you'll do until it happens.

This sensation pleases her. She feels out of control. That

means she's in a state of diminished responsibility. Tom started it, he can't talk.

She fills up her glass once more and takes it and sits by the fire and thinks of Kenny. Is it really that big? You don't get that sort of a reputation for no reason.

When Tom comes back carrying boxes of pizza he finds her there, silent before a dying fire. He seems to have calmed down.

'I didn't know what to get you,' he says. 'I had a dim idea that you like Cappriciosa.'

'Fine,' she says.

'I'll put them out on the kitchen table. Shall I open another bottle of wine?'

'Might as well.'

He goes and clatters about in the kitchen. Then he calls her. 'All ready to go.'

The pizzas are immense and she's not all that hungry. She manages about half of hers. He eats all of his.

'So is it a truce?' he says.

'I don't know what it is, Tom,' she says. 'I'm just taking it a day at a time.'

21

Diana's house feels cold. At first Laura assumes this is her response to the minimalist décor Diana favours: pale grey walls, blond wood floors, white leather sofas so low and backless they could almost be beds. Small spotlights pick out unassertive works of art, a white-on-white Ben Nicholson, an Anthony Gormley maquette. The tall Islington windows have no curtains.

However, Diana reveals that the chill of the room has another explanation.

'We really feel we have to do something about our carbon footprint. I know you like to heat your house like a sauna, Laura. I'm sorry. You'll just have to keep your coat on.'

The Lymans are already here, irretrievably sunk on the low sofas, adding a splash of much-needed colour. Neil Lyman, a genial book agent, is a startlingly ugly man who has turned himself by sheer will-power into a dandy. He's wearing a mustard-yellow needlecord suit over a white T-shirt that carries the red mouth and lolling tongue of the old Rolling Stones logo. Lynne Lyman, a cookery writer, has abandoned all attempts to control her weight and now aims at grandeur. She is arrayed in what looks like a gold brocade tent.

She laughs merrily at Diana's new approach to central heating.

'I carry my own insulation,' she says.

Roddy gives Laura a kiss and asks her and Henry what they want to drink. So the not-talking that so disturbs Diana is not universal.

'Brandy,' says Henry.

'We'll have red wine,' says Laura, smacking him lightly so that the others can see he's only joking.

Roddy is in jersey and jeans and slippers, looking rumpled and homely. He seems to Laura to be much the same as ever. He always did have the air of someone who has forgotten why he came into the room.

Diana brings the Broads up to date with the Lymans' news. Their daughter Polly has joined Plane Stupid, and was part of the group that shut down Stansted airport a few days ago.

'There was a picture of her in the *Telegraph*!'

Neil and Lynne exhibit pride muted by irony.

'Poor Polly was mortified,' says Neil. 'She was so hoping to be arrested.'

'Fifty-two flights cancelled,' says Diana. 'You have to hand it to them.'

'I'm glad I wasn't flying out of Stansted on Monday,' says Henry.

'Well, why would you?' says Diana. 'It's all Ryanair at Stansted. Surely you don't fly Ryanair?'

'Can you believe it?' says Lynne. 'Plane Stupid gives their members training on how to handle their parents.'

'What are they supposed to do?' asks Laura, interested.

'We don't know. Polly told them we were cool about her protesting. So I suppose we've done something right.'

'It's not as if it's a mystery,' says Neil. 'We get it. We're taking action. We're on board. It's going to hurt a bit, but we'll survive.'

'We've talked so much about this, haven't we, Roddy?' Diana throws an anxious look at her husband, who's sitting on a low stool smiling to himself. 'Turning down the central heating is the first step. Then of course there's food miles. We're buying as local as we can.'

'That's a tricky one,' says Lynne. 'Moroccan tomatoes consume less carbon than English tomatoes, even allowing for the flights. It's because of the oil burned to heat the polytunnels.'

'And of course buying from developing countries boosts their economies,' says Neil.

'We've downsized our car,' says Laura. 'From a Volvo to a Smart. I'm getting over sixty miles to the gallon.'

'We thought of trading in our car,' says Neil. 'But when

you account for the carbon costs of building a new car, you're probably better off staying as you are.'

'And anyway,' says Henry, 'it makes no real difference what any of us do. Once all the Chinese start driving cars, the planet's screwed.'

'Oh, Henry,' says Diana. 'You're such a contrarian.'

'Every little helps,' says Lynne. 'Neil and I felt we needed to make a statement. Everyone talks so much. We wanted to do something.'

'Roddy and I have talked about going vegetarian,' says Diana. She directs this at Roddy, but he does not respond. 'Apparently this thing about cows farting isn't a joke at all.'

Even so everyone laughs.

'Polly's a vegan,' says Lynne. 'I'm so in awe.'

'Sheep are less of an issue,' says Diana, who has cooked lamb for dinner tonight. 'I don't think sheep fart.'

Laura is put out that her own gesture over the car has gained her no merit. 'So what is this statement you're making, Lynne?' she says.

Neil and Lynne's eyes meet as if to say, Will you tell or shall I?

'Well,' says Neil. 'This is very new. You're the first to hear it. But the die is cast.' He allows a brief dramatic pause. 'We're selling the Aga.'

'No!' exclaims Diana. 'You love your Aga!'

'I shall go into mourning,' says Lynne. 'It's a sacrifice, I admit. But you know what they say. If it isn't hurting, it isn't working.'

'How much do you expect to get for it?' says Henry.

'Zip,' says Neil. 'That beast cost over ten grand, admittedly fifteen years ago. Now it's worth nothing. We may even have to pay to have it taken away.'

'Good Lord!' says Laura. 'We've got an Aga.'

'Valueless.'

'I've always preferred to cook on gas,' says Diana. 'I've always thought the Aga thing was a bit of a cult.'

'I adore my Aga,' says Lynne. 'It'll be like losing a member of the family.'

'And a source of much-needed warmth,' says Neil. 'We're having to put in two extra radiators to compensate for the heat loss in the kitchen.'

Roddy utters a sudden snort.

'What's that, Roddy?' says Diana.

But Roddy just shakes his head, and gazes into his empty wine glass.

'So there it is,' says Neil. 'Each of us has to do our bit.'

After dinner the Lymans announce that they have to leave.

'No coffee, Neil?'

'Bless you, Diana, no. I don't drink coffee any more.'

Laura suspects that this early departure has been concerted in advance, but if so it's convincingly done. Roddy has said barely a word all evening. Round the dinner table his silence

233

has not been obtrusive. He nods and smiles and gives the occasional chuckle as he moves about filling glasses with wine, and so plays his part well enough. Once or twice Laura finds his eyes on hers. Then comes a small lift of his eyebrows that says, I know you know.

As soon as the Lymans are out of the door Diana takes Henry by the arm and propels him into the kitchen.

'Come on, Henry. I need some help.'

Laura is left alone in the bleak living room with Roddy. She has been preparing herself for this moment, and has resolved to be direct.

'All right, Roddy,' she says. 'What's going on?'

He gives a slow shrug and seems about to answer, but in the end he says nothing.

'Have you taken a vow of silence or something?'

He shoots Laura a keen look.

'Not exactly,' he says.

So at least he's willing to talk.

'Well, could you please stop. It's scaring Diana.'

'I'm not ready quite yet.'

He speaks slowly and carefully, as if each word has to be precisely weighed.

'What do you mean, not ready?'

'I need more time.'

'For God's sake, Roddy. Think of Diana.'

'I am thinking of Diana. That's exactly what I'm doing.'

'Then why don't you tell her what's going on?'

'Because.' He hesitates. 'Things are in flux, you might say. If I speak now, it'll only confuse matters.'

'Roddy, please tell me. Are you having an affair?'

'No. Certainly not.'

'Are things okay between you and Diana?'

Another long hesitation.

'I wouldn't go that far, no.'

'Then you have to tell her. Whatever it is you think Diana's done or not done, she can't deal with it if she doesn't know.'

'She hasn't done anything. She's just gone on being Diana.'

'But something's wrong.'

'As I say, things are in flux. Something has changed. You pretend it isn't happening for as long as you can. Then the day comes when you can't pretend any more.'

'It does sound awfully like an affair. You're sure there isn't someone else?'

'Quite sure. Look, Laura, I'm sorry to be so cryptic. It's just all rather personal, you see. I can't go into it with Diana quite yet. On the other hand, I find going on the same old way quite impossible. So I prefer to remain silent.'

'You can't.' Laura has no idea what's going on, but she holds fast to this one conviction. 'You can't stay silent.'

'What we cannot talk about we must pass over in silence. That's Wittgenstein, of course. For some reason the quotation is far better known in the more pompous rendering.

"Whereof one cannot speak, thereof one must be silent."
People do so love to inflate things.'

'If you can't tell Diana, then tell me.'

'So that you can tell her?'

'Yes.'

He starts to circle the room. His earlier sleepy calm has
vanished. He seems excited.

'That would rather defeat the point of the exercise,
wouldn't it?'

'I don't know what the point of the exercise is.'

'Not to cause unnecessary damage.'

'You've caused damage already, Roddy. She doesn't show
it, but she's really upset.'

'Is she? Is she?'

He circles the coffee table, now frowning, pushing one
hand through the sparse hair on the back of his head.

'Diana is a wonderful wife in so many ways,' he says.
'She can be sharp, but she's loyal to me, and utterly devoted
to the children. I'm an odd sort of bod, it's good of her to
put up with me. So you see, I'm trying to manage the situation as best as I can.'

'Roddy, you're talking like a man who wants to leave
his wife.'

'Well, that's it, really. In a way, I have left.'

He comes to a stop in front of her, gazing down at her,
looking for understanding. And for forgiveness, perhaps.

Laura is in shock.

'Diana's devoted to you. She'd be devastated if you left.'

'But I'm not leaving. I have considered it. But I know my duty.'

'You're staying only because it's your duty?'

'Not a word much used any more, I know. But I made a vow when we got married, and I regard myself as bound by that vow. I know that's no longer a widely held view. I think the general idea is you do what makes you feel happy, and when you don't like it so much any more you abandon it. Well, here's another old-fashioned idea. Being happy isn't what matters most.'

Laura stares at him. A piece of the puzzle is dropping into place.

'Roddy,' she says, 'have you gone and got religion?'

He responds with a funny little smile. That smile that Diana spoke about, that he seems to be smiling from somewhere far away.

'You could put it that way.'

'Oh my God.'

'Quite.'

Laura, like Diana, has no religious belief. Diana goes further. She regards religious belief as a form of backwardness, evidence of congenital ignorance.

'What sort of religion?'

'That's what I'm still working out.'

'You haven't joined some cult, have you?'

'No. I'm doing this all on my own.'

'Oh, Roddy.'

Diana will not take kindly to this. She'll see it as an attack on her world view, possibly on herself. And she may not be wrong. Roddy turning to God is Roddy turning away from her.

'What did you mean when you said you'd left?'

'I mean that I'm a stranger and a pilgrim on the earth.'

'Oh, God.'

'That's another quotation, by the way.'

'Diana won't understand.'

'I know. That's why I have to work out my own position before I talk to her. Diana's not the pilgrim sort.'

'You can say that again.'

'One of the by-products of all this,' he says, now moving away again, 'is that one becomes more aware. Take this house. Why are we living like this? The works of art. What are they for? Our conversation at dinner this evening. So many opinions – for what? Isn't it all a rather sad parade of ego and self-righteousness? Isn't it all vanity and hypocrisy? I include myself, of course. I too am part of this – what? – this waste of breath – this illusion.'

'Except you didn't take part.'

'I accept guilt by association. But Laura' – his eyes gleam at her, and his voice drops to an intense whisper – 'I mean to change my life. I must. Once you see it, there's no turning back.'

'Oh, Roddy.'

In a way she can't help admiring him. He looks so absurd in his baggy jersey and his slippers, his ungainly features all puffy with excitement: this sixty-year-old rediscovering the passions of adolescence. Of course Diana will put a stop to it. She won't like being told her life is all vanity and hypocrisy. No wonder he's kept silent about it so far.

'Look, Roddy, I have to say something to Diana. I'll keep it as vague as I can. But she'll want the full version from you.'

'Yes, I know.'

All his excitement now drains away. He senses that his brief bid for freedom will soon be over.

'And really, Henry and I have to go.' She looks at the time. 'We'll miss our last train.'

'Thank you for listening, Laura.'

'Thank you for speaking, Roddy.'

It's all rather touching in its way.

She goes to the kitchen door. She's hardly turned the handle when Henry comes bursting out, looking a little crazed, as he always does when left alone with Diana for too long.

'We're going to miss our bloody train,' he says, reaching for his coat.

Diana follows, her eyes on Roddy. She sees at once that some kind of meaningful exchange has taken place.

'You're better off getting a cab,' she says. 'The Northern line can take for ever this late in the evening.'

'What if there aren't any cabs?'

Henry is panicking.

'There'll be cabs on Upper Street. Come on, I'll come with you.'

Out into the London night, walking fast up Duncan Street, Laura gives Diana her edited version of Roddy's state.

'He's having a sort of philosophical crisis,' she says. 'He's questioning a lot of very basic stuff.'

'But he's not having an affair?'

'No. Definitely not.'

'Well, that's something.'

Only then, hearing Diana's soft expulsion of breath, does Laura realize how much her sister has feared this.

'He's still working out what he thinks about things. That's why he doesn't feel like talking.'

'Well, he's bloody well going to have to feel like it. It sounds like some sort of a breakdown to me, Laura. Did he seem odd to you?'

'A bit, yes. But Roddy's always been odd.'

'Did he say anything about things at the bank?'

'No. Nothing at all.'

'Well, if he's not having an affair and he's not been sacked, then I expect we'll manage.'

As they reach the glow of Upper Street a cab sails into view, its amber light shining. Diana gives Laura a quick hug.

'Thanks,' she says. 'Big help.'

In the cab Laura tells Henry about Roddy's turn towards religion. Henry is fascinated.

'What on earth will Diana say?'

'She'll die of shame,' says Laura.

'Christ, it was cold in that bloody house.'

'How did you get on in the kitchen?'

'I dried up. I mean, with a tea towel. Diana scrubbed away in the sink and I rubbed away beside her like we were cleansing the sins of the world.'

'What's wrong with the dishwasher?'

'Not green, apparently.'

'Oh, Henry. What are we going to do?' She recalls Roddy's outburst. 'It's all vanity, isn't it? Vanity and hypocrisy.'

'Probably,' says Henry.

He doesn't sound at all troubled. Tired now, Laura leans her head on his shoulder and closes her eyes. Am I wrong to want a quiet life? she thinks. To love my family and my home and not to think all that much of others? Yes, I'm wrong. I mustn't let myself become so narrow that I only really care for Henry and Jack and Carrie. But caring for all the world is so difficult. Once you start, where do you stop?

Should I not be using the dishwasher, then?

22

The strange power of the passing of time. Some forty hours ago Jack met Chloe in the Half Moon and they had a drink together, talked about this and that. Nothing happened, no intimacies took place. Since then they have had no contact. And yet, like a seed planted in warm soil, that short half-hour they spent together has sent down branching roots, and pushed up eager shoots, and assumed a vigorous life all of its own. Shortly Jack will drive into Lewes to meet Chloe again, and it feels to him that this will be a reunion of lovers. Apart so long, the emotions so overwhelming, they'll fly into each other's arms, he'll cry with joy, she'll—

It's embarrassing. Jack knows very well that he's made it all up, but he can't help himself. Somehow the hours he's spent thinking about Chloe have played the part of an actual relationship with her, as if she's been party to his secret roller-coaster of hopes and fears. Impossible to meet again as common friends. And anyway, what about all the resolutions he's been making? This time, he tells himself, he'll behave differently. No more passivity. This time he takes control.

He comes down to a late Sunday breakfast to find his father still at the kitchen table, reading about the collapse of sterling.

'More horror with the toast,' his father says.

'What now?'

'Oh, just the financial crisis getting worse.'

'Serves them right,' says Jack.

His father has no means of knowing this, but Jack's stern moral stance has more to do with his new non-passivity than with any clear grasp of what's going on.

'Serves who right?'

'The bankers. They deserve everything they get.'

'What about the rest of us? We're suffering too. Do we deserve it?'

'It's our greed that's screwing up the planet.'

Jack hadn't quite meant to follow this line but he has to defend himself somehow. He can't just say, Oh, sorry, I was talking without thinking. So now he's got himself into an argument that actually doesn't interest him at all.

'That's a bit of a sweeping statement, Jack.'

'I don't see why. If we go on the way we're going, Planet Earth will be uninhabitable in fifty years.'

'You don't seriously believe that.'

Actually Jack doesn't seriously believe it, but he can't back down now.

'Why wouldn't I believe it? All the scientists say the same thing. Just because it's scary, or inconvenient, doesn't mean it isn't true.'

And only a couple of weeks ago in his college room he'd argued with passion that feeling guilty about something doesn't mean you're doing something wrong. Look at all the Victorians who were racked with guilt over masturbation, and really they needn't have bothered.

'Jack,' says his father. 'I'm a historian. History tells me that every generation thinks they're living in the end time. When I was young we all believed we'd be wiped out by a nuclear war. It's a kind of mass vanity. Every generation convinces itself it's facing the apocalypse.'

'So history says don't bother? History says it'll all come out fine in the end?'

'Pretty much.'

'Then history's part of the problem. You're using history as a comfort blanket, Dad.'

Jack is bemused to hear himself. Why is he being so aggressive to his father? Somehow a chain of cause and effect has led him from shame at his passivity with girls to contempt for his father's use of history. And this even though he knows very well it's a sensitive area. His father's job is making television programmes about history. He once said, 'Watch out for those last two syllables, Jack. History is mostly story. Heavily simplified accounts of the past give people the illusion that everything works out in the end.'

Now over the breakfast table Henry Broad breaks the unintended deadlock with his disarming lopsided grin.

'Oh, it's far worse than that,' he says. 'I'm using history as a way to make a living. At least until the commissions dry up.'

For two years now he and his partner Aidan Massey have been at work on a major series tracing forms of social organization, from the hunter-gatherer tribes of the Stone Age to the multinational corporations of today. It's called *The Power of Society*.

'You've always got work,' Jack says. 'More than you want.'

'ITV's stopped commissioning. Channel 4's broke. That leaves the BBC as the only act in town.' Again that rueful grin. 'People are scared. I've never known it like this.'

'Is Aidan scared?'

'He doesn't show it, but he is. He doesn't fancy living on his academic salary alone. But at least he's got that.'

'So how bad could it get, Dad?'

Both on the same side now, the way it should be.

'Oh, we won't starve. We've got Laura's money. Though that's not what it was, of course. And if I don't pick up another job when this one ends, I'll be able to get on with my own work, won't I?'

The history book he's always wanted to write, but never had the time. Jack feels a pang of love.

'The new series will be a huge hit, Dad. They won't let you go yet.'

His mother comes into the kitchen.

'Are you in for lunch, Jack?'

'No, I'm going out. Can I borrow your car?'

He picks a table in the saloon bar at Harvey's that looks towards the door so that he can see when Chloe comes in. He gets himself a drink but leaves the food until she comes. The fantasy is back and now out of control. It broke out of its cage as he left home, and is become a monster. He has wild notions of Chloe greeting him with a kiss, holding his hand in hers, whispering words of love. Then more: half-glimpsed images of her naked body, half-felt impressions of her embrace. His reason is powerless in the face of this onslaught of longing. He mocks himself, he predicts humiliation, all in vain. It's not that he seriously expects any of his dreams to come true; but on the other hand this is no longer pure fantasy. Chloe is real and near and about to walk through the door.

Only of course it's Alice Dickinson who shows up first.

She looks round, finds him, gives an awkward little wave. She's taller than he remembers, probably taller than him. A long thin face that reminds him of someone. Her eyes wear that tentative look he knows so well, because it's his own default mode, the expression that says: Do you want my company? If not I'll go away again.

'Hi,' she says.

He jumps up to greet her. A boy with manners.

'What do you want to drink?'

'Oh, anything,' she says. 'White wine.'

He goes to the bar and gets her a drink, glancing all the time towards the door. When he returns to the table Alice has got her coat off and is sitting there smiling at him.

'Thanks,' she says.

'So how's things?'

'Oh, not too bad. How about you?'

'Good. Yes, good.'

He looks towards the door, and sees Alice catch his look. No point in hiding it.

'So you still keep up with Chloe,' he says.

'Not really,' says Alice. 'I met her on the train on Friday, coming home. We got talking. Before that ... well, I don't know that I've seen her since Underhill.'

'Do you see any of the others from Underhill?'

'No. Not really. Do you?'

'I meet up with Angus Critchell now and then. He lives in our village.'

'I remember Angus. His hair always stuck up.'

'Still does.'

'The funny thing is when I think of Underhill I go all nostalgic, but actually I was miserable there.'

'Were you?' says Jack. 'Why?'

'I didn't fit in, somehow. I think I didn't have much in

247

the way of social skills as a child.' She gives a quick shy smile. 'Still don't.'

'I was just an idiot,' says Jack. 'It embarrasses me to think about it. Do you remember Toby Clore?'

'Of course.'

'I was obsessed with Toby Clore. I wanted to be Toby Clore. I wonder what's happened to him? He'll be doing something glamorous but dodgy.'

'And you wanted to be like him? Glamorous but dodgy?'

'God, yes. Instead I'm decent but dull. I'm learning to live with it.'

She laughs, not nervously this time.

'I know that one,' she says. 'That's a pre-emptive defence.'

'A what?'

'You name the thing you don't want to be, to make it not happen. Like when you get asked about some exam and you say, I'll probably make a mess of it. You're not planning on making a mess of it, but you think if you say it aloud you'll earn the pity of the gods or something.'

'That's so exactly what I do.'

Another glance at the door. He checks his watch.

'I don't know what's happened to Chloe.'

'I don't think she's coming,' says Alice.

'Why not? She's the one fixed this up.'

'I know,' says Alice. She looks away. 'But she can't make it.'

'Did she tell you?'

'Yes.'

'She never called me.'

Even as he says it Jack knows he's being stupid. Of course Chloe was never going to come. Miracles don't happen. It's all just been a game.

Suddenly the situation has turned embarrassing. There's a silence he can't break.

'Okay,' says Alice. 'This is all a really bad idea. I should never have let Chloe talk me into it.' She's pushing a beer mat round the shiny tabletop with one finger. 'She thought she was doing me a favour.'

Jack can't speak. He feels angry with himself for letting himself hope so much. And beyond the anger, the sinking feeling, the start of school term feeling. The long empty hallway waiting to take him back, the cheap light of a low-powered bulb, the walls a faded institutional grey: the place where you pass the long days before your real life begins.

Alice says, 'How about we just cut our losses and go?'

Her game effort at being bright and easy penetrates Jack's self-pity. What can this be costing her? He can't just get up and walk away. And anyway, where's he going to go where it'll be any better?

'What about lunch?' he says.

'I'm not sure I want any lunch.'

'Aren't you hungry?'

Of course she isn't hungry, any more than he is. But you

always revert to the conventions in times of stress. Never underestimate the usefulness of the superficial.

'It's not that,' she says. 'But you came here to be with Chloe, and I'm not Chloe.'

A simple statement of truth. To his own surprise Jack is released by this.

'What the hell,' he says. 'We might as well eat.'

So they order food from the bar. Alice has a cheese toastie, Jack has a hamburger, and everything changes. Their lunch ceases to be a date, whether intended or not, and because Jack has failed to get anywhere with Chloe, and Alice has failed to get anywhere with Jack, they fall into a rueful mode of mutual sympathy.

Alice tells Jack about how she met Chloe on the train.

'It was like she had too many boys after her and I had too few, so she more or less offered to donate one of hers.'

She's half-laughing as she speaks but she's also dying of embarrassment.

'God, what a loser I am,' she says.

'Try being me,' says Jack. 'I thought just because she asked me to have lunch with her that she was interested in me.'

'Why wouldn't you? I think you've been cheated. If I were you I'd ask for my money back.'

'Still, no harm done.'

'Really?'

'How about you?'

'Harm done,' she says.

Their eyes meet. A moment of silence. Alice smiles, then shrugs.

'Oh, God,' says Jack. 'Why does it have to be so hard?'

'My stepfather says the big mistake we make is expecting things to work out. Once you get it that the natural order is for things not to work out, everything makes much more sense.'

'But it's not exactly cheering, is it?'

'It is in a way. I mean, take Chloe. She's so pretty, I could easily think everything works out for her, but it doesn't. So I don't need to envy her. Except I do.' She pulls a comical face at her own absurdity. 'That's how stupid I am.'

'But you wouldn't rather be Chloe than you.'

'Yes, I would. Any day. Like you wanting to be Toby Clore.'

'I don't want to be Toby Clore. I just want his confidence. Actually what I want is his selfishness. He just does what he wants. Or he did.'

'And you're all sensitive to the needs of others.'

'Yes,' says Jack. 'Unfortunately.'

'What's unfortunate about that?'

'Well, it doesn't get me what I want, for a start.'

His eyes on her as she listens. He catches a sudden glimpse

of how you can see a person in a face. Nothing to do with how good-looking they are.

'Actually it's not me being unselfish at all. It's me being timid. The thing about Toby is he was fearless.'

'And Chloe.'

'Or here's another possibility. Maybe they're both just thick.'

Alice laughs. 'Yes, I like that. Chloe the dim bimbo. I have to salvage my dignity somehow. I'm the one in the corner of the library with the spectacles who's going to discover a cure for cancer.'

'Are you a scientist?'

'No, Jack. And I don't wear spectacles. I'm doing English. Not much scope for saving the world there.'

'I'm doing English too,' Jack says.

'Yes, I know.' Facebook tells all. Then she blushes and covers her tracks. 'Alan keeps up with his old class. My stepfather.'

'So how are you finding it?'

'I love it. The reading, I mean. *Paradise Lost* turns out to be amazing.'

'We're still on *Gawain and the Green Knight*.'

'No *Beowulf*?'

'No, thank God.'

'Lucky you,' says Alice. 'And you're in a proper university town. London's not a university town. All I have to do is go out into the street to feel irrelevant.'

'You think being at Cambridge makes everyone feel relevant?'

'I should think you feel like one of the rulers of the world.'

'Well, I don't. I feel like a fraud. I feel like I'm the one who was let in by mistake.'

Suddenly he realizes who she reminds him of.

'You look a bit like Virginia Woolf.'

'Thanks. Now do I go and drown myself?'

'Good writer.'

'I've never read her.'

'I've only read *To the Lighthouse*.' He grins. Somehow by starting off with Alice on such a footing of honesty everything they say is made easier. 'Do you have secret books you love?' he says. 'Books you don't admit you read?'

'Yes. Do you?'

'Yes.'

'I'll tell if you tell.'

'Go on, then,' he says. 'You first.'

'*Little House on the Prairie*. All eight books. I still cry when Mary goes blind.'

'I've never read them.'

'Works of genius.'

'*Tintin*,' says Jack. 'I still read my old *Tintin*s.'

'We never had *Tintin*.'

'Works of genius.'

By now they've just about finished their lunch.

'You want another drink?' says Jack.

'Sure, why not? My round.'

She gets a glass of wine for herself, another beer for Jack. Her way of making it clear she expects no more than friendship.

'Do you read Jane Austen?' she says.

'Of course.'

'You realize Chloe's been doing an Emma on us?'

'Oh, God! That makes me the ghastly vicar. What was his name?'

'Mr Elton. And I'm dim little Harriet Smith.'

'Didn't Mr Elton convince himself Emma was interested in him when she wasn't at all?'

'Yes. She was trying to set him up with Harriet Smith.'

'This is appalling.'

'The difference is, Chloe could easily be interested in you.'

'I don't think so.'

'Why wouldn't she be?'

'She just doesn't think of me that way, that's all.'

'She might. People change.'

Jack thinks about that. Maybe he should take a longer view.

'She's bound to ask me about you,' says Alice. 'She'll want to know what happened today.'

'What will you tell her?'

'What do you want me to tell her?'

'I don't see that it really matters,' says Jack. 'I can't think of anything you could tell Chloe about me that would get her interested.'

'I could tell her you dragged me onto the railway land and ravished me and it was the most thrilling sex I've ever had in my life.'

'Do you think she'd believe you?'

'No. Not really.'

'You could tell her I'm dark and brooding and moody.'

'Are you?'

'Well, I brood a lot.'

'I know what,' says Alice. 'I'll tell her you've got a girl-friend at Cambridge. I think she'd get off on the idea of stealing you from another girl.'

'I haven't got a girlfriend at Cambridge. Or I did, but we broke up. I told Chloe I was available.'

'I could say you lied. You have girlfriends all over the place. You pretend to be available because you're so promis-cuous.'

'Serious fantasy time.' Jack's impressed. 'Why not? Make up anything you like.'

'You drive a Porsche.'

'I'm renting one tomorrow.'

They grin at each other again. This is how I should be with all girls, Jack thinks. Light and easy. This is how I should be with Chloe. But he knows he can only be funny with Alice because he doesn't fancy her. It's a cruel game played by fate or evolution or something. When you really love someone you turn into a wally.

23

Carrie sits as still as she can in the chair by the window, and talks as the old man paints. She hasn't decided yet whether he's a weirdo or a saddo but when you think about it, what does it matter? It's different. She's never been painted before.

'What will you do with the picture when it's finished?'

'I don't really know,' he says. He never stops painting when he talks. His eyes keep on moving back and forth between her and the canvas. This has a freeing effect on Carrie, as if whatever she says to him will have no consequences. 'Maybe I'll put it in my show. I don't know. When you paint a picture you don't think about what will happen to it. You think about painting it.'

'What show?'

'I'm having a show in the barn here. The Thursday before Christmas.'

'That's this Thursday.'

'Is it? Then I'd better buck up.'

But he keeps on working in the same careful way, mixing little squeezes of paint, stabbing at the canvas, bright eyes behind the gleam of spectacles jumping back and forth.

'Can I come to your show?'

'No.'

'Oh.'

She didn't expect that. Probably he thinks she's too young, or too stupid.

'Come the day before. I'll give you a private view.'

'You don't have to.'

'No, you must. I'd like you to.'

She feels restless.

'Do you have a toilet?'

'Only a thunderbox out in the yard.'

'A thunderbox?'

'No flush. No sewer.'

'What! So where does everything go?'

'Into a hole in the ground.'

She pulls a face, decides she can wait till she's home. But she doesn't want to go home yet.

'Really when you think about it,' he says, 'everything goes into a hole in the ground. Including us.'

This strikes Carrie as both true and important.

'Right,' she says. 'I mean, why do anything?'

'There's a question.'

Carrie warms to the theme.

'I mean, what's the point? You're supposed to work hard and do well and stuff, but what difference does it make? So what if you get good A-levels? So what if you go to uni? They try to tell you you've got all this choice but really everyone ends up just the same. It's like at school, they make this big deal over uniform, you get to the sixth form and you're allowed to wear trousers, and you know what makes me laugh? People really care about it. They do that to you. They make you feel like you're more impor- tant because you can wear trousers.'

'Don't you like school?'

'It's okay. It's the same as everywhere else.'

He pauses in his painting, points his brush at her over his easel.

'You sound like a very disappointed young woman.'

'Maybe I am. What's to get excited about?'

'Aren't you a bit young to be disappointed by life?'

'Why? Does it get better?'

He laughs at that.

'No,' he says. 'It gets worse.'

'There you are, then.'

She realizes she likes him. No adult has ever admitted it to her before. It gets worse. There's an odd consolation in that. It's the fake passion she can't stand. People squealing with joy like game show hosts and everyone throwing their arms round each other and saying 'Omigod!'

'I'm the emperor of disappointment,' he says. 'I've been

disappointed since 1966. That's over forty years of disappointment.'

'But at least you've got a talent,' she says. 'You can paint people who look like people.'

'The greater the talent, the greater the disappointment.'

'So why not pack it in?'

'Why not? I'll tell you why not. Because underneath this almighty shit heap of disappointment that is my life there hides a tiny seed of hope. That's what keeps prodding me on, making me think maybe my luck will change, maybe they'll wake up from their trance and say, How foolish! What can we have been thinking? We've been worshipping trash! But of course, they never do. So that little seed of hope is really my worst tormentor. If it wasn't for that, who knows? Maybe I could have lived a contented life as a taxi driver.'

Carrie understands only part of this, but the part she understands she agrees with strongly.

'It's no good thinking it'll get better,' she says. 'It gets worse.'

'It gets worse,' he agrees.

'You know how they tell you to keep on trying, try, try and try again, all those stories of people who never gave up and ended up these big successes? Well, I say, give up now. Fuck everything. Sorry. I didn't mean to say that.'

'With you all the way,' he says. 'Fuck everything.'

'At least that way nothing can ever let you down again. I mean, if you've already given up, you can't fail, can you?

Tell that to your dad and he doesn't get it. He has all these expectations of you, and I'm like, Please, Dad, just get off my back. And Mum's worse, always giving me these little boosty chats that are supposed to encourage me, like, Darling you look so pretty in your blue dress, why not wear that? But who says I want to look pretty anyway? What if I look like a cow? So what?'

The older man is entirely undisturbed by all this, and keeps painting away. His attention to her is both total and indifferent. Talking like this puts Carrie in an excellent mood.

'It's different when you say I'm beautiful,' she says. 'You don't make it sound like it's some kind of competition.'

'No,' he says. 'It's not a competition. It's a gift, like talent. I'm not beautiful, but I have talent. And for that reason I've never been happy and I never will.'

'Me too,' says Carrie contentedly.

She looks round the little room in which she's sitting. There's a deep old fireplace, but the fire hasn't been lit so far today. Canvases stand in stacks, face to the walls. Newspaper on the floor, maybe to catch drips of paint, maybe because the old man is just too lazy to pick it up. A table covered in books, plates that have been eaten off, glasses that have held beer or whisky. Candles in saucers of melted wax.

'You could make this room really pretty if you tried,' she says.

'I'm not staying long.'

'You know something? I used to call this my house. We'd come on walks, and everyone would say, There it is. There's Carrie's house. It was all falling down and stuff, and I had this dream that I'd buy it really cheaply and do it up and live here.'

'You still could.'

'Oh, it was only a game. I never came inside. I imagined how it would be, and where I'd have my bedroom, and where I'd put the kitchen, and how I'd make the garden have a place with a swing seat under the trees, and how I'd paint the front door this blue colour, do you know the flowers called morning glories? I was going to paint the front door morning glory blue.'

Suddenly she wants to cry. How stupid is that?

'Hold that! Don't move!'

He's painting at furious speed. She gazes at him, tears pricking at her eyes, thinking: he's amazing. He doesn't want to make me into anything. He just wants me to be the way I am.

This has never happened to Carrie before. People want you to be something you aren't, so you pretend. Wear these clothes, put on this make-up, smile this smile, talk in this voice. This old man doesn't want her to be anything, and he says she's beautiful.

Now she's crying. She's crying because she wants so much to be beautiful.

He stops work when the light starts to fail. She wants to see what he's painted so far but he says no, wait till he's finished. She can't tell if he's pleased with his picture or not but now she knows she wants him to be pleased.

He asks her to help him move an armchair. He wants to drag it out of the house and into the barn where he's hanging his pictures for his show. It turns out to be quite a struggle, because the doorways are narrow and he's not strong at all. Carrie does most of the pulling and heaving herself.

'Why do you want an armchair in your show? Won't it get in the way?'

'It's part of the show.'

'What, for people to sit on and look at the pictures?'

'Something like that.'

By the time Carrie leaves it's dusk in the sunken lane. She turns and looks back at the cottage and sees the glow of a candle in one window.

That's okay, she says to herself. You can live in my house for now.

24

The noble Henry Willis organ is sighing and murmuring, its reverberant notes floating out into the great space of the chapel; rising past the rose window of trumpeting angels to the high carved roof. A student at the keyboard, perhaps. Someone too respectful to unleash the mighty roar that so offended the preacher Charles Spurgeon. 'The only sound of praise God cares to hear is the human voice,' Spurgeon thundered in his much-admired human voice, and was hissed by the congregation for his pains. That must have been a famous day.

Roddy Dalgliesh sits at the end of a pew at the back of the Union Chapel, which is just a few streets from his home. He's taken to dropping in here, not for the services or the concerts, but for the quietness. He needs space to think, and the Union Chapel is a grand space.

For prayer too, perhaps. Roddy is reluctant to call what passes through his mind by the name of prayer because he has no clear notion of a recipient of his prayer. He has left unbelief behind, but has not yet arrived at belief. This is what is so hard to explain to others. He is embarked on a great adventure.

Keep thyself as a stranger and a pilgrim upon the earth.

Roddy finds these words profoundly moving. They move him emotionally, but also physically, too. They make him want to move. They make him want to disburden himself and pass as lightly as a bird or a cloud over the landscape. He wants to cut all ties, to shed all responsibilities, to float free. Impossible, of course. But when the longing struck him, when he stopped, literally, in his tracks – he was walking down Ludgate Hill at the time, heading for the tube station – he knew that something he had been resisting for most of his life could be resisted no more. This life is not all there is. This world is not all there is.

Not an intellectual capitulation. There's no theory to it. Just a sudden acceptance. His response, standing there on Ludgate Hill as the home-going crowds brushed past his motionless figure, was to say to himself: Of course. Once he had let go of his petty insistence that there be answers, which is after all no more than one of the many forms of vanity – for why should he, or anyone, understand such immense mysteries? – once he had humbled himself, it became easy to surrender. The act of surrender an act of trust, like falling into water. Like falling in love.

Just stop fighting. Just release the controls. Just let go.

From that moment on, everything changed for Roddy. Everything is still changing. Here in the Union Chapel where Dr Henry Allon preached to Gladstone and Asquith, in this great octagonal space designed so that 'every person could see and hear the preacher without conscious effort', as Dr Allon demanded of the architect, here Roddy can let his eager mind roam free, chasing the chords of the mighty organ.

So much now looks so different. The injustices of the world, great and small; the apparent futility of human activity; the anxieties that grate on us and make us fretful even in the midst of security and plenty; all can now take their place in an utterly changed landscape. Down in the valley the mist seems to have no end, but from the mountaintop it's no more than a puddle in the land. There is more, more, so much more. Maybe heaven. Maybe eternity. Maybe God.

These are all human approximations, attempts with the limited tools at our command to name and categorize what can't be named and categorized. So why argue about it? Every culture finds its own forms, its own rituals, with which to grasp what is beyond our grasp and imagine what is beyond our imagining. All that matters in the end is humility of the intellect. Do not presume to know.

Once you know that you don't know, everything changes. The absurdity of so much of our lives ceases to be a puzzle. Of course we're ridiculous. Of course we make fools of ourselves. Why wouldn't we? We are fools. We know so little. But not any the less loveable for all that.

Roddy is filled with a joyful compassion. Once this would have been called the milk of human kindness; now only a term used for comic effect. How can he speak of this to Diana? She'll think he's turned into a simpleton. The tone of speech of the modern educated person is narrow in its range: critical, ironical, not to be deceived. No room for wonder. Little room for joy. All the thoughts that are now sweeping through him have a low status in Diana's world. They're fables for peasants and children. The opium of the masses. She has no language with which to take seriously the presence of God.

Soon now he will have to leave this place and return home, where Diana waits for his much-delayed explanation. She supposes he is currently out for a reflective walk. He has not told her of his habit of dropping in to the Union Chapel.

One of the stained-glass windows features Dr Henry Allon himself, who was minister here for forty-eight years, to the day of his death. Did Dr Henry Allon ever come to a stop on Ludgate Hill and feel himself lifted up as if by the wings of angels?

Angels, now. I have gone simple-minded.

By two wings a man is lifted up from things earthly, namely by Simplicity and Purity.

That's Thomas à Kempis, one of the devotional writers

Roddy has begun to read. But he keeps the book hidden at home.

'We're going to have this out now, Roddy,' says Diana. 'It's gone on long enough. If you're having a breakdown I need to know.'

They're sitting facing each other in the kitchen of their Islington house, later that evening. Roddy reaches across and takes her hand in his. This is how he's resolved to proceed. First, make true contact.

Diana, not understanding this, is merely irritated.

'Stop pawing me. What did you say to Laura? She says you're having a philosophical crisis. I've no idea what that means.'

Roddy has planned his next step, too. He won't tell Diana the way he told Laura, inching his way bit by bit towards the awkward truth. He's not been talking to Diana because he knows talking will be no use. He still thinks so. Therefore his task is not to explain but to inform. No lead-in is possible, no softening up. Just tell it as it is.

'I'm looking for God,' he says.

She stares at him.

'Don't be ridiculous, Roddy.'

'I'm looking for God.'

He's ready to go on saying it as often as necessary, until she hears him.

'You can't be.'

'I'm looking for God.'

'Yes, yes, you've said that already. But it doesn't mean anything, Roddy. How can you look for God? Where do you think he is? In a cave in Palestine?'

'No. I don't think God's in a cave in Palestine. Though it's possible, I suppose. I won't rule it out.'

'You're having a breakdown, aren't you? Is it because of work?'

'No.'

'Is it me?'

'No.'

'Then what is it?'

'I'm not having a breakdown, Diana. I'm looking for God.'

Diana pulls a face Roddy knows well: impatient, disappointed, a little hurt. 'I think that is so unfair of you. What am I supposed to do while you're looking for God? Stay home and cook your dinner?'

'You can come too.'

'I will not! You may be off your rocker, but I'm not. How many people know about this?'

'Laura. That's all.'

'She'll have told Henry. Oh, Lord. Look here, Roddy. You're to keep quiet about this. You're to start talking again, like a normal human being, and you're not to let it get in the way of your work. Do you understand me? I'm serious about this. If you must go looking for God, then

269

do it somewhere where no one can see. Why are you grinning at me like an ape?'

'Sorry.'

'It's not a joke, Roddy. I think I'm being amazingly reasonable under the circumstances. Most other wives would have you straight off to the funny farm.'

'Thank you. I'm grateful for your forbearance.'

She stares at him suspiciously. A new thought has struck her. 'What happens if you find God?'

'I've no idea.'

'You're not going to become a vicar, are you? Because if you are, I want a divorce. I will not be a vicar's wife.'

'No. I'm not going to become a vicar.'

'Well, then. Just try to keep it under control.'

After this Roddy does his best to talk in the old way, but it's not the same. It's as if both of them are playing a part. He knows Diana feels betrayed, but what can he do? Things have changed.

He thinks from time to time of Laura, and the way she looked at him the other evening, just before she had to hurry away to catch her train. He's sure that Laura understands, in a way that Diana never will. Diana has always said he has a soft spot for Laura.

If I was married to Laura, how different it would all be. She might even come with me on my journey. That would be true companionship. But it's not to be.

Keep thyself as a stranger and a pilgrim upon the earth.

25

It's just gone eight-thirty on Monday morning. The patient, already fully anaesthetized, is moved with a pat slide from bed to operating table. Fergus, the anaesthetist, checks the patient's position, adjusts the height and tilt of the table. Harriet, the theatre nurse, preps the patient, exposing the operating site, cleaning the skin with Betadine solution.

Now in what is so fittingly called a theatre the surgeon makes his entrance. Tom Redknapp, costumed in scrub suit and gown, takes the stage, ready for a performance he has given many times before. No curtain to rise, no audience to applaud, but there is a spotlight on his rubber-clad hands, and in due course there'll be gratitude to spare from the principal beneficiary of his skills. Her name is Lyn Goodall, thirty-two years old, an actress. The augmentation of her breasts is designed to augment her career.

'They don't say it, not right out,' she explained, 'but for

a lot of parts it's no cleavage, no thanks. I go up for the wench parts, and wenches have to show tit.'

An attractive woman, with a humorous view of her dilemma that hides something more, something sadder. She stood in Tom's office, naked to the waist, her hands pushing up beneath her breasts.

'See? Uplift does nothing if there's nothing to lift up.'

No cleavages in Shakespeare's day, not real ones at least, all the parts were played by boys. Nowadays it's expected, a bonus for the male patrons of classic theatre, a flash of culturally-approved flesh. Like all those ballets in the nineteenth century designed to let men stare at women's legs. And all those artistically painted nudes on academy walls. The world fuelled by male desire, but when we talk of it we can only tut or snigger.

The sterile towels are clipped into place round the operating site.

'Happy your end?' says the surgeon.

'Good to go,' says Fergus.

Tom takes a fine paintbrush, dips it in methylene blue dye, and with a steady hand draws the incision marks beneath both breasts. He will cut just above the crease line, an opening of six centimetres.

'How was your weekend, Harriet?'

'Very quiet. Simon's got himself a new tractor. Well, I say new.'

'You're a tractor widow, Harriet.'

'It gives him something to do.'

Fergus fiddles with his iPod, which is plugged into the theatre's speakers. The mellow sound of Miles Davis fills the sterilized air.

'Right. Knife, please.'

So long as he works his mind is clear and he's at peace. The intense focus of the operating theatre frees him from himself and the complications of his life. Here is something he can do well – or rather, taking away the value judgement, the implied praise, something he can do as it should be done. There's a rightness about certain procedures that is demonstrated by the outcome: the freedom from infection, the almost-invisible scar. Tom makes no great claims for what he does, he sees himself as akin to Harriet's husband who restores vintage tractors. The work brings a satisfaction in the doing of it that has no relation to the value of the end product. Simon sells the tractors on when they're working again, shiny with new paintwork, but the price he gets doesn't begin to cover the hours he's devoted to the restoration.

Tom has no idea what his own work is worth. For this operation, one hour in the theatre, his patient is paying £4,000, but that money buys not only his services. There's Fergus and Harriet, and the running costs of the theatre, and the hospital bed, and the after-care, and the wider over-heads of the clinic: receptionists, nurses, cleaners, accountants, marketing team.

Meg has asked to see him.

He dreads the meeting and is ashamed of himself for dreading it. So many fears. Suddenly his life is beset by fears. Belinda seems to have more or less stopped speaking to him.

Clearly he's to blame. And yet, in the privileged sanctuary of his own thoughts, he feels himself to be innocent. Innocent both in the sense that he has not committed a crime, and in the other sense, that he is without evil intent.

One man can love more than one woman. That's how men are made. Why turn it into a crime? Why assume that what's given to one must be taken from another? Why this obsession with all-or-nothing? Whose big idea was it that the act of copulation is the closing of a lock, that once joined two lovers become bound together in a legal union that can't be undone? The fuck itself, the fuck alone, has become the declaration of fidelity. What's that all about? There are a million levels of intimacy, and here they are, reduced to two: you're friends, or you're lovers. If you don't fuck, you're friends. If you do fuck, you're lovers. And lovers get to have rights over each other. You get the right to be outraged, wounded, betrayed if your lover fucks anyone else.

But there are fucks and fucks, right? There's the spur-of-the-moment fuck that means nothing, except that the opportunity came up and you both thought it might be fun. There's the nameless fuck, with a call girl in a hotel room. There's the holiday fuck, which neither of you wants to bring home.

Or am I missing something fundamental here? Is the act of sex for a woman simply too intimate and vulnerable ever to be spur-of-the-moment or nameless? Is it always and of its nature possessive? Like a ticket-operated turnstile, you can go in but you can't come out. Sex as a one-way street. If that's the way it is, God help us all. Us all being men, that is.

Belinda crying in bed. No, I never wanted to hurt her.

A flash of memory. They're side by side on the sofa in the living room of her flat by Battersea Bridge. They're kissing, his hands moving over her body, not undressing her but wanting to be closer. Then she's leaning away from him, crossing her arms over her head, pulling up her blouse, slipping off her bra, so that he can see and touch her beautiful breasts. With the excitement comes a surge of gratitude for this gift of nakedness. He remembers how he kissed her breasts.

There it is. Gratitude. Of her own free will she gives; he, grateful, receives. The obligation is on his side. The repayment comes in fidelity, and now he has broken the bargain. How can he ever say to her how much he has longed for a reciprocal gratitude?

He wants to be wanted.

Meg wants me.

Is she pretty? Is she young? Is she sexy?

Don't ask about her, ask about me. Am I pretty? Am I young? Am I sexy?

Yes, I know, the very idea is comical. There you have it. But I never meant to hurt you, Belinda. I love you. I don't want you to leave me. I'm sorry. I should have been more grateful. But it's done now.

Later. He calls Meg in her office, suggests she comes over to his consulting room. He tells Michelle he doesn't want to be disturbed, without offering any explanation because none is necessary. Meg will sit where his patients sit when they have consultations on surgery. Not the most appropriate setting for the words that must be exchanged between them, but where else are they to go? All public places expose them to the view of colleagues. Meg's flat, the arena of their private life, would be a cruel setting for this last encounter.

What demeanour is proper to these circumstances? Tom finds himself so bewildered by his role as bad boy that he hardly knows which way to turn. Should he be sad and calm? Should he be distressed and incoherent? Should he be passionate? People say, as if it were obvious, just be yourself. But he has many selves.

As he sits at his desk waiting for Meg to come, failing to work on his backlog of case reports, he asks himself a simple question: what do I want?

I want to keep my wife and my home and my family.

Therefore Meg and I have to stop seeing each other. At the same time I want to go on seeing Meg. So knowing what you want achieves precisely nothing.

Meg comes. Closes the door behind her.

'Is it all right me coming here?'

'Yes, it's all right,' he says. 'It's somewhere where we can talk.'

She looks white, defeated. She sits in the chair facing him and hangs her head. Her physical presence shocks him. He wants to reach out and touch her, hold her in his arms. He wants her to be so close to him that no words are necessary. But she sits on the far side of his desk, and he finds it hard to look at her.

'I suppose we should never have got into this in the first place,' he says.

As he speaks he realizes he's saying, I didn't do this on my own. You're responsible too. Is that unfair? They share the guilt but somehow she gets a bigger slice of the pain.

'No,' she says. 'I suppose not.'

Her voice dull and far away.

'Belinda's in quite a state. I'm sorry about telling you over the phone. I just felt I had no choice.'

'No.'

'It's not what I want, Meg. But there's no point in me saying that.'

'Yes. There is.' She looks up at him now, and he sees in her eyes that she doesn't understand how he's taking all this, and wants to understand. 'I want you to say all of it.'

'I've got no secrets from you, Meg.'

'No. But we've never really talked.'

'I suppose we haven't.'

'It didn't matter before. But I need to know now.'

For a long moment he doesn't speak. He's feeling a panic impulse to shut this conversation down. Again, he feels shock. *What am I so afraid of?*

'Look,' he says. 'I don't see that there's any point in agonizing over it. We have to stop seeing each other. I don't want that, you don't want that, but that's how it is. What else is there to say?'

'It would help me,' she says. She speaks humbly, not making demands, appealing to his pity, which makes him restless.

'We've always known it couldn't go on for ever,' he says.

Back into the first person plural. *We did this as consenting adults.*

'Yes,' she says. 'I know it has to stop now. But there's something I have to ask you. I'm not trying to get anything out of you, Tom. I just need to know for my own sake. When you came to me in my flat, who were you coming to see?'

Tom allows himself to look puzzled. He's not puzzled, he's in flight. Running scared. He understands at once what she's asking him, but he has no idea how to answer.

'Well, you,' he says. 'Who else?'

'So it was me?'

'Yes,' he says, acting as if this is self-evident. 'Of course it was you.'

'Sometimes,' she says, 'I think it could have been anyone. Anyone who was willing to give you what you wanted.'

His heart pounding. Always the same. The man wants, the woman grants. Not you too, Meg,

'I thought you wanted it too,' he says.

'Yes. I did. I do.'

'Then why are you saying all this?'

'I just need to know it was me you came for. That it couldn't have been just anyone.'

'It was you, Meg.'

She gazes at him, imploring him.

'Can you say more?'

'What more is there to say?'

Run. Get away. What more can he offer her? Love? This thing that women distinguish from sex, the sticky residue that's left over when you take sex out of the equation. The thing that lasts, where everyone knows sex is fleeting. But love and sex can't be separated like this, they're both somewhere in the seething mess along with vanity and habit and dread and self-doubt. Even on its own no one knows what love is. Is it the flush of infatuation? Is it the confession of desperate need? Or a heightened form of friendship? Take away sex and love is either an anxious longing or a deep-rooted familiarity. Add sex and it's much the same, with the occasional spasm of intimacy. Whatever it is, for all the propaganda for the coupled state, it's a private affair. None of us really knows what it means to be loved. We know only that we do deals with others to mitigate our loneliness. You act like my existence has some value, and I'll do the same for you. Let's live in a state of mutual deception.

Meg says, Was it me? Could it have been anyone? What can I say? Yes, it could have been anyone, but it wasn't anyone. It was you. Hold on to that. It was the real you I came to in your flat, not some figment of my imagination. Please don't ask for any more meaning than that. Who we meet, who we love, it's all accident. But once the accident has happened it becomes individual. Don't read life backwards, keep going forwards. I could have been anyone too, Meg. But I turned out to be me.

'I don't know what I want you to say, really,' says Meg. 'I feel so miserable. I know that's not fair. We never made any promises. It had to stop one day. I do know all that. But when I think I may never see you again, at least not in that way, I get this frightening feeling that we never really knew each other at all. Like we've been strangers all along.'

'How can you say that?' says Tom.

'Don't you feel it?'

'Not at all. I've felt closer to you than almost anyone in my life.'

'Really?'

'Why do you doubt it?'

'Isn't that just sex?'

'Yes,' he says. 'It's just sex. Which is just the intensest way I know how to live.'

'But you can have sex with anybody.'

'Then why do I do it with you?'

'That's what I'm asking you, Tom. Why me?'

Because I thought you wanted to have sex with me. But this is the one answer he can't give.

'I can't analyse it, Meg. What is it people say? We clicked. Didn't you feel it?'

'Yes. I did. But if you ask me why, I can tell you. Because of your smile. Because you have beautiful hands. Because you're the best at what you do. Because you wear funny ties. Because of the way you look at me. Because of the way you touch me.'

'I could say all of that back to you. Except the bit about the funny ties.'

'Then say it.'

He starts to speak, and breaks off. Some inhibition closes his throat. What's so hard about repeating a few words as an act of kindness? But some inner censor cuts him off each time he begins to speak.

He gets up, walks to the window, hoping that with his back to her the words will come, but they don't.

'I know it's over,' she says. 'I'm just asking you to leave

me in a better place than you found me.' Close to tears now. 'Don't send me back to where I was before, Tom. Please.'

Tom has no idea what demon has possession of him. But the more pitifully she asks for loving words the less he is able to utter them. Some instinct of self-preservation has him in its powerful grip. Nothing to do with Belinda and loyalty to his marriage. This is about fear of being needed. Fear of responsibility for the happiness of another.

'Well, I'll tell you this,' he says at last. 'I've had the best sex of my whole life with you.'

She gives a small muffly laugh.

'Have you, Tom? So have I.'

'That's something, isn't it?'

'Yes. More than something.'

'You're a wonderful lover, Meg.'

'Am I? I want to be.'

'You are.'

He's not giving her what she asks for, but it's something. He's not choking on his words any more.

'You're a natural,' he says. 'You understand instinctively what a man wants.'

'That's because you told me. And I wanted it to be good for you.'

'And for you.'

'Yes. For me too.'

But Tom can't deceive himself any longer. He had believed

that with Meg he had found a mutuality of desire, but it was only wishful thinking. For Meg, sex was a means to another end.

'You never thought I'd leave my wife or something, did you?'

'No. Never.'

'I never said anything to make you think that.'

'No. Never.'

'It was our secret other life, wasn't it? Our stolen pleasures.'

His phone buzzes. Michelle.

'I know you said not to disturb you, but Mrs Lazarus is waiting.'

'Oh, God, is that the time? Tell her two minutes.'

Meg is already on her feet.

'Meg. I'm sorry.'

She gives him an odd look, almost as if she pities him.

'I'm sorry too.'

'I'm no good at this sort of thing. I don't know what to say. I feel terrible. I've just made a mess of everything, haven't I?'

'Not just a mess,' she says. 'Not just something to be sorry for.'

'No, you're right. I'm not sorry, really. It's been so special. Can't we hold onto that?'

'Yes.'

He opens his arms, inviting her for a last kiss. She comes

to him and leans against him. He holds her in his arms, kisses her cheek. She's crying.

'Now, now. None of that.'

'It's been more than special, Tom.' She takes out a tissue and dries her eyes. 'You've changed my life.'

'Have I?'

'But you have no idea, do you?'

One last hurt smile and she leaves his consulting room, walking fast. No goodbyes.

And now comes the pang of loss. Now he can say all the words she longs to hear. I need you, Meg. I love you. I think about you all the time. Now that she's walking so briskly out of his life.

You changed my life too, Meg. Only I don't yet know how.

26

Chloe climbs the stairs from the tube station and comes out onto the crowded pavement at Oxford Circus. The Christmas illuminations hang unlit overhead. People are moving slowly, forcing their way doggedly through the throng. Red buses line up at the traffic lights like islands round which flow the eddies of Christmas shoppers. A dull cloud-shuttered day which makes the shop windows bright, enticing.

Her phone wakes up after its underground hibernation and bip-bips as texts come through. Pippa, one of her Exeter housemates. Baz, still hoping. A passing man stares at her, apparently unaware that if he can see her she can see him. She knows that look, the sullen and insolent gape of desire from a man who does not expect to be desired in return. You're on the money there, pal. You'd think men like that would have some shame. Fifty at least, overweight, in a ski jacket and jeans. He doesn't care what I think. About Dad's age.

Did Dad stare like that?

She's been not thinking about her father all the way up from Sussex on the train. Really she's been not thinking about him since she learned about his affair. It sits there, just out of her vision, like a dark mass. Not offensive, just embarrassing. Him wanting her forgiveness.

She shudders, and looks into the glowing windows of Top Shop. Not that she can afford to buy anything. What is it about money? Her dad gives her £500 a month on top of her rent, it's much more than most of her friends, but it never lasts to the end of the month. Coming up on the train today, that's nearly twenty for a start. At least she'll get a free lunch.

Jesus, Oxford Street goes on for ever. Who are all these people? Isn't there supposed to be a recession? The free-newspaper pushers try to make eye contact. What do you make in a job like that? Has to be rubbish money or they'd have better-looking people. How hard is it to give something away for free? The picture on the front page is Bush in Iraq ducking a flying shoe. Apparently a shoe is seriously insulting. Who knew?

A smile from a pretty boy loping towards her in a cute Pete Doherty hat. She smiles back. He raises one hand and shoots her with a thumb and extended finger, and goes on by. So many boys, so many missed chances. He could have been the one. How are you supposed to know? Except they all turn into boring creeps in the end. Not even in the end, after a week. If you're lucky. She looks back but he's disappeared into the crowd.

Dad having sex, that is so sick. There should be a law, you reproduce and that's it. No more porking. You've had your day, now show some self-respect and act your age. Apparently old age pensioners still do it. We're supposed to go Aah! That's so romantic, but it's not, it's just gross. There should be a word for it, like paedophilia or bestiality. Wrinklefuck. Please.

Off Oxford Street at last, round by the umpteenth branch of Prêt à Manger into Radcliffe Place. The restaurant's up here, she Googled it before leaving home. In Charlotte Street.

Turns out there's nothing but restaurants, both sides of the street. It's called Passione: small, Italian, smart. Chloe approves. She checks her watch, she's not as late as she'd hoped, but when she looks in through the window she can see him inside, at a table. He's reading a magazine, drinking a glass of wine. He looks like he's in his own home.

Why am I here? Because he asked me. Why not?

She goes in to the warmth, feels her face turn pink. Guy Caulder looks up from his magazine.

'How about that?' he says. 'I bet myself a fiver you wouldn't come.'

'I said I'd come,' says Chloe, shrugging off her coat. A nice waiter takes it from behind her.

Guy subjects her to a critical examination. Chloe doesn't

mind, she's taken trouble with her clothes. Mostly boys never notice.

'You look stunning,' he says.

'Well, it is Christmas.'

She sits down, feeling suddenly unsure of herself. Guy's never taken his eyes off her.

'No shopping?'

'What?'

'You said you were coming up to town to do some shopping.'

'Oh, yes. Later.'

'Have a drink.'

He pours her a glass of wine from the bottle standing in a cooler.

'I never shop,' he says. 'I'm too mean to give Christmas presents.'

'I love giving Christmas presents,' says Chloe. 'I just never have enough money.'

'You're wearing Chanel. Coco. Not exactly broke.'

'Mum gave it to me last birthday.'

She's awestruck that he can tell her perfume.

'So what do you fancy?'

He picks up the menu.

'I expect you're not all that hungry. How about skipping the starters and the mains, and going for a pasta? I'm having the pasta with broccoli and provola.'

'Who says I'm not hungry?'

'Are you?'

'No. Not very.'

So he orders the *maloreddus con broccoli e provola* for both of them. Chloe feels dizzy.

'Tell me about yourself,' he says. 'I don't really know anything about you.'

'What's to tell?' she says. 'I live in Sussex, in a village called Plumpton. My dad's a surgeon, he does boob jobs and stuff like that. I've just started uni at Exeter. I'm doing drama.'

'Do you want to be an actress?'

'I thought so once. I'm not so sure any more.'

'Why's that?'

His interest in her is focused, almost fierce. His eyes never leave her.

'I don't think I'm good enough,' she says.

'Just as well,' he says. 'Acting is a pitiful existence.'

'That's a bit strong.'

'I work in advertising. We use actors all the time. They line up for auditions like tarts in a Bangkok brothel. I'm Susi, buy me.'

'Is that what tarts say in Bangkok brothels?'

'I wouldn't know,' he says with a smile.

'These days everyone has to sell themselves,' she says.

'Who told you that?'

'I don't know. It's what you hear. Present yourself in the best light. Give yourself the best chance. Da-de-da.'

She pushes stray hair from her face. Presenting herself in the best light.

'I don't agree,' he says.

'Oh.' She's not used to flat contradiction. 'Okay.'

'The way I see it, in any deal, in any transaction, there's a master and there's a servant. The master wants whatever it is he wants. The servant wants to please the master. All of us can be either masters or servants. We switch back and forth, depending on the deal.'

'Okay …'

'I believe that if you think and act like a master, you force the other person into the role of the servant.'

Chloe listens, fascinated. Not just by what he's saying: by the feeling that he's taking her seriously.

'And the way to act like a master,' he says, 'is to go into any deal, any transaction, with a clear picture of what you want out of it. Which is exactly what most people don't do. They think they have to sell themselves, like you said. They come into the room thinking, How can I please this person? How can I make him like me? And there you are. Before you've even opened your mouth, you're the servant.'

It seems to Chloe that he's obviously and undeniably right. She wonders that she never thought it before.

'Only,' she says, 'I don't see what you can do about it. I mean, you're talking about confidence. Some people just don't have it.'

'So fake it,' he says. 'You'd be surprised. It works just as well.'

'Okay,' she says. 'I'll try.'

He's looking at her over the top of his glass of wine. 'Now tell me why you're here.'

'Oh, I'll go anywhere for a free lunch.' He says nothing. 'You did offer.'

'I did.'

'So here I am.'

'And here I am.'

It's not what he says, it's how he says it. As if they're having two conversations at the same time, one very ordinary and one that's shockingly intimate. Chloe is entirely out of her depth. A new sensation.

'I think I should make it clear to you,' he says, 'that I'm not here for the shopping or the lunch. I'm here for you.'

'That's nice.'

What kind of answer is that? That's nice. I'm being the servant here.

'I wanted to see you again.'

'Sure,' she says. 'Me too.'

'Because you're a very attractive young woman. As I'm sure you know.'

'Oh, well. Not really.'

'Don't do that.'

'What?'

'Say things you don't mean. I'm not a very good man,

291

in a whole lot of ways, but I say what I mean. If we're going to be friends, let's agree, right from the start, no bull-shit. No lies.'

'Okay.'

He's so sure of himself. Chloe realizes she wants to please him even if that does make her the servant, only she doesn't know how.

'What has Alice told you about me?'

'Nothing, really.'

'I'm a lousy father. But then, it was never my idea in the first place. To be a good father you need to be reliable. Responsible. Faithful. I'm none of these things.'

'You're quite reliable. I mean, you showed up here.'

'That's because I wanted to. I'm very reliable about doing things I want to do.'

Chloe drinks more wine. Feels it working its magic.

'I think you're not nearly as bad as you like to make out.'

'Why would I want to pretend to be bad?'

'Oh, because it's more – you know – glamorous and stuff.'

'If you want to know what I really think, I don't think I'm bad at all. I don't deceive people. I pay my way. I'd be no good as a husband, but hey, I'm not married.'

'My dad's having an affair.'

Chloe has no idea why she says this, it catches her by surprise. She stops, full of confusion.

'And your mum's pissed off about that?'

'Very.'

'There you go. He broke the deal.'

'I'm kind of pissed about it as well.'

'I can understand that. But think about it. Just because he's your dad, he doesn't stop being a man. Men like sex with lots of different women. It's how we're wired. There's nothing freakish about married men having affairs. The freaks are the ones who don't.'

'That's a bit hard.'

'Maybe freaks is wrong. The exceptions.'

'Do you really think so?'

'Look at the boys you go out with. Are they monogamous?'

'No. Not at all.'

'So why should they morph into some kind of different creature when they get married?'

'Well, that's the whole idea, isn't it? You settle down. You're faithful.'

'Sure. That's the deal. Just don't think it's easy. What your dad's done may not be so very terrible.'

'Actually, I don't want to think about it.'

Their pasta arrives. Annoyingly Chloe finds she can't persuade herself to eat. Her stomach is shivering. She finds Guy's company unsettling.

Guy himself has no trouble eating.

'So are you planning on settling down and being faithful, Chloe?'

'Maybe one day.'

'You have a steady boyfriend?'

'There's a boy who thinks he's my boyfriend.'

'But you're not so sure.'

'Well, I'm only nineteen. I mean, it's not like he's asking me to marry him or anything. So we both know there'll be other relationships coming along sooner or later. Or sooner, in my case. So who are we kidding?'

'Sounds pretty normal to me.'

'Tell that to Hal.'

'You like to keep your options open. Have fun. Life's an adventure.'

'Right.'

'I'm the same.'

'Are you?'

'I have a feeling you and I understand each other, Chloe.'

Chloe is absurdly flattered. She's stopped even pretending to eat. 'Maybe we do,' she says.

'If you weren't young enough to be my daughter ...' he says.

'What's that got to do with anything?'

'Don't flirt with me unless you mean it.'

She blushes. He reaches out one hand and strokes her cheek.

'Don't tease me, Chloe. I told you. I go into any transaction knowing what I want. I want you.'

'Do you?'

She's mesmerized. She wants him to want her. Those

steady blue eyes that have never left her. That possessive touch.

'I want you to come with me to a place just round the corner. It's a flat owned by a friend of mine. I want to take you into the bedroom there and lie you down on the bed. And I want to make love to you.'

'Do you?'

'Looks like you've had enough pasta.'

'Yes. Sorry.'

'Never apologize. You're too gorgeous. You don't need to.'

He calls the waiter and asks for the bill. No, no dessert, no coffee. Just the bill.

So I've said yes, thinks Chloe. I've said I'll make love with him. And I didn't have to say a word. He did it all.

Take me into the bedroom. Lie me on the bed.

Don't ask me to make any decisions. I'm not in control any more. This is what I came for. As if I didn't know, from the moment outside Alice's house when he said, 'Do you ever come up to London?'

Now he's paid, and the waiter's getting her coat.

I don't have to do anything. Not a fucking thing.

27

Christina paces up and down the drab walkway. To one side, the grey back of the Queen Elizabeth Hall; to the other the low concrete and glass block of the Hayward Gallery. Between the two the curving concrete walls of a stairwell rise up like a defensive pillbox, a pillbox painted a startling cherry-red. How did that happen? Did it dawn one day on the keepers of this dismal domain that they had overdone the grey? If so, why stop at the stairwell?

London buses rumble by over Waterloo Bridge, pulses of red between the concrete and the sky. Above, a flat layer of dull grey cloud. A hint of rain in the chill air.

Through the windows of the gallery café, which is defiantly called Concrete, she can see her crew waiting for her, drinking coffee. On the wall above, the title of the current show is spelled out in big neon letters: BREAK OUT. Visitors are drifting in and out of the Hayward lobby, muffled against the cold, speaking in low voices. Not exactly a crowd-puller.

Her phone buzzes. The driver of the car she sent to Sussex. He has Anthony Armitage on board, he's close now. Maybe ten minutes.

Christina paces because she's nervous. If all goes according to plan this morning the old man will deliver a violent and theatrical response to Joe Nola's art; which will provide her with a much-needed climactic scene for her television film. But in doing so it might damage beyond repair her relationship with her subject, Joe Nola.

What relationship is that, exactly? Here lies the source of her tension. It seems to Christina that two futures lie before her: one, a life with Joe, in which their teasing companionship deepens into a tender and lasting love; the other, a career as a maker of acclaimed arts documentaries. The trouble is, the one precludes the other. Joe Nola can be her subject or her lover, but not both.

So the minutes tick by, and the car rolls ever closer, and Christina, pacing, unaware of the cold, puzzles over this latest fork in her destiny.

How ambitious am I? How successful do I want to be?

The answer is: it all depends. If her work is to be her life, then let it be the best, let it bring her fame and fortune. But if there's a chance of love ...

Why does it have to be a choice? Why not both? Because life's a bitch. Because no one gets everything. Because love leads to babies and then you're gone. She's seen her friends disappear into motherhood, that alien land where she can't follow them until she too is a mother. A mother! Thirty-one years old and a few years' grace still, but how long does it take to meet the right man? And how long before you know each other well enough to make promises that bind you for the rest of your life? Two years? Five? It's almost too late already to start from scratch with a perfect stranger. Your future partner, your husband, had better be close at hand right now. He'd better be someone you know and have probably known for a while. For example, Joe.

The man himself now emerges from the gallery, driven from the modernist warmth by the need for a cigarette. He comes over to her side, his slender fingers expertly at work on a roll-up.

'How's Leni Riefenstahl this morning?'

'How's the impish-dissonant-sublime?'

This is a reference to one art critic's summary of his work.

'Shouldn't the old man be here by now?'

'Any minute.'

She's told Joe about Armitage's visit. Also Bill Lennox, the gallery director. But she hasn't told them what she expects to ensue.

'Guess what?' Joe lights his roll-up, cupping his hand against the wind. 'I'm actually looking forward to seeing the old bugger.'

'I don't think he'll like the show.'

'No, of course not. He'll hate it. I don't care. I owe him anyway. He was the first person who ever made me believe I had something.'

Christ, the old man's his father-figure. And he's going to smash his work with a hammer.

'He's quite an angry old man, you know.'

'Great. Good for him. "Do not go gentle into that good night."'

'What?'

'Dylan Thomas.'

Christina realizes with sudden clarity that she's going to have to prepare Joe for what's coming.

'The thing is,' she says, 'he really hates modern art. What if he were to go berserk in the gallery?'

'Rage is a legitimate response. Actually it's more or less traditional these days.'

'What if he were to start hitting out with a hammer?'

'A hammer! Has he got a hammer?'

This precise, not to say concrete, question has in fact occurred to Christina. As a film maker she prides herself on her planning, on her attention to detail. Which is why she has taken the precaution of packing a hammer in her work bag.

'He might have.'

Joe gives her his impish-dissonant-sublime look.

299

'Darling one. Are we by any chance sprinkling a little *very* into the *verité*?'

Christina can maintain her innocence no longer. She has willed her own exposure, from the moment she uttered the word 'hammer'.

'It's all his own idea. Though just in case.'

She opens her bag and lets him have a peek. Joe is entranced.

'An actual hammer! Art criticism *à la outrance*. What a mensch! You'll film the act, of course?'

Sweet relief floods through Christina. The two paths of her bifurcated future rejoin. One high road now, heading into the sunset.

'But what about your installation?'

'I offer it as a sacrifice.'

'Seriously? You don't mind?'

'I don't give one little itty-bitty fuckity-fuck. *Vita longa, ars brevis*.'

'You are so sickeningly educated, Joe.'

'You can thank the Jesuits for that. Belvedere College, Alma Mater of James Joyce, Terry Wogan, and me.'

'If he really does it it'll make my film.'

'Anything to further your career, gorgeous. And of course, mine. Our fates are entwined.'

Such a wicked smile as he says this.

'I adore you too, Joe.'

And she does. But the words have no purchase on reality. Impossible to know what he really feels.

'We'd better alert Bill Lennox,' says Joe.

'No way!' says Christina. 'He'll never let us.'

'Leave him to me,' says Joe.

They catch Bill Lennox in his office furtively watching an episode of *Entourage* on his iPhone.

'Doesn't anyone knock any more?' he says irritably.

'No porn in office hours, Bill,' says Joe.

'It's not porn. It's contemporary culture. Go away.'

Joe outlines the plan for the morning's entertainment. Bill Lennox laughs a lot and then says, 'You don't expect me to go along with this, do you? It's an open invitation to every fruitcake in town.'

'That's just it,' says Joe. 'It's not an open invitation. It's a closed invitation. It's a scheduled art event. We can write the press release now. Artists Joe Nola and Anthony Armitage collaborate in an act of creation-slash-destruction et cetera et cetera.'

Lennox stares at him.

'Are you serious?'

'So help me God.'

'What if someone gets hurt?'

'He's over eighty, Bill. It's a hammer, not a Kalashnikov.'

'I'd have to bring in extra security.'

'Bring in the SAS if you want. Just tell them to stay cool.'

301

'And you're going to have to sign something for me, Joe. I'm not having one of your what-little-me? acts afterwards.'

'You know your trouble, Bill? You're a fucking bureaucrat. Show some fucking cojones. This'll have the punters queuing round the block.'

In the lift back up to the lobby Christina is awestruck.

'Joe, you were magnificent.'

'Just doing my job,' says Joe. 'All in a day's work for Artistman.'

Christina briefs the film crew in the café. Two South Bank security men show up and stand around in the lobby looking conspicuous. Christina's phone rings. The car is arriving.

She takes the lift to the ground floor and hurries out through the gloomy car park to the open space behind the Royal Festival Hall. A light rain has started to fall. She waits under the concrete overpass beside an immense skip, watching the great wheel of the London Eye, trying and failing to see it actually turning.

A black Mercedes turns the corner from Belvedere Road. She can see the muffled figure of Anthony Armitage in the back. The Mercedes comes to a stop in the middle of the road. Christina goes out into the drizzle to tell the driver to go on into the Hayward car park. It's the kind of rain that totally screws your hair, but what can you do?

The barrier rises. The Mercedes pulls to a stop just past the rank of parked motorbikes. The rear door opens and

Anthony Armitage gets out of the car very slowly. He's wearing a navy blue felt overcoat like an over-long donkey jacket, and a black Homburg hat. He looks older and frailer than she remembers. As he straightens up, reaching for the car door to steady himself, his eyes look round with an uncomprehending and fearful gaze. He's not wearing his glasses.

'Where am I?'

'This is the Hayward Gallery car park.'

He stares at the receding parking bays punctuated by concrete pillars. The ghosts of dimly lit cars. Then he fumbles in a pocket and pulls out a card.

'For you,' he says, pressing it into Christina's hand. 'Come to my show.'

Christina puts the card into her bag without looking at it. She steers him into the bowels of the car park.

'There's a lift.'

He enters the steel box with reluctance. He appears to be overwhelmed by his surroundings. He has closed his eyes.

'Are you all right? We'll be there in a minute.'

The lift doors open into the gallery lobby. Seeing it now through his eyes Christina is struck by the joylessness of the space. No grandeur, no colour, no wit. Even the crowd gathered round the entrance to the display rooms are sombre in appearance, clad mostly in greys and blacks.

The old man stands staring at the name of the show: BREAK OUT.

'Break out,' he says, forming the words slowly, like a child learning to read.

She offers to take his coat, get him a coffee. He shakes his head.

'All I need is a piss. Bloody bladder.'

She leads him to the men's lavatory. By the doorway she whispers, 'Do you have a hammer?'

'A what?'

She takes the hammer from her bag and slips it into his overcoat pocket. It takes him a moment to realize what she's done. Then a smile creases his much-creased face.

'Pinoncelli,' he murmurs.

Christina gives the cameraman a discreet sign to turn over as Anthony Armitage emerges from the toilet. She guides him to the gallery where Joe Nola's installation is on display. The room is packed. Word has spread. The old man, unaware that he is the exhibit they have come to see, pauses before the panel of explanatory text.

'*Break Fast.*' He reads out the heading. 'I can manage that. The rest is too small.'

'Do you want me to read it for you?'

'I think you'd better.'

So she reads it aloud to him while the soundman holds his furry blimp in the air between them.

'My work explores the tension between self-slash-other—'

'What what what?'

'Self-slash-other.'

'What does that mean?'

'You know the slash sign? The diagonal line you put between words to mean either-or?'

'Either self or other.'

'Exactly.'

'Go on.'

'The tension between self-slash-other in the medium of memory. Nostalgia is private-slash-shared—'

'Either private or shared.'

'Art is the slash that separates-slash-joins you-slash-me.'

'Either separates or joins either you or me.'

'The artist-as-child is made universal by brand magic, by in this instance the sacrament of Kellogg's Cornflakes.'

She waits for his gloss, but he says nothing. He seems to be listening attentively. She goes on to the end.

'The table an altar, the meal a Mass. True art is the priesthood of all believers.'

She falls silent.

'Is that it?' he says.

'That's it.'

'Deep, isn't it? Challenging. Makes you think.'

Christina's heart sinks. She wants anger, not irony. But he hasn't seen the exhibit yet.

'Joe was brought up a Roman Catholic, you know,' says Anthony Armitage. 'A flying start for an artist.'

The crowd parts before him. This should be a giveaway but he seems not to notice, cocooned in his long dark overcoat. He moves slowly towards the platform on which stands Joe Nola's work of art. Joe himself, Christina notes, has appeared in the doorway to watch.

The cameraman crouches before the old man, under instruction to capture his earliest responses to the installation. But the old man seems to have no response. He looks at the fully-laid breakfast table with an expressionless gaze, registering but not judging.

Christina closes in, realizing the response will have to be provoked. Aware also that she has promised a show, and her audience waits.

'What do you think?' she says.

'Joe arranged this? Joe Nolan?'

'Yes.'

'He was good, you know. He had talent.'

He sounds a little confused.

'You taught him at art college, didn't you?'

'Yes. I did. He was good. What I mean is, he could see. He could use his eyes.'

'What sort of work was he doing then?'

'Oh, this was long ago. He was my student. I taught Life Drawing. Joe Nolan was the best student I ever had.'

Joe has crept forward, keeping among the crowd. But there's a hush in the gallery. Everyone can hear.

'And what do you think of his work now?'

'Now?'

He gazes at the breakfast table and gives a very slight shake of his head. His hand reaches for the overcoat pocket where the hammer is stowed. Christina stiffens. Everyone has seen the movement. Everyone is motionless, anticipating the act.

Christina catches the mood of the crowd like a vibration in the air, like the smell of blood: they are willing the act. They want the work of art to be destroyed. They want the hammer to smash into the sacred space. They want to overthrow the god.

I want it too. Even though this is Joe's creation, I crave destruction.

Her eyes, flicking to all sides, meet Bill Lennox's eyes, and she sees it there too. He craves destruction.

How has this happened? When did we all start to hate art?

But now the old man is turning away from the exhibit, away from the camera. He looks down at the floor. Reaches up one hand to rub at his eyes. When he looks up again, Christina sees the smear of tears.

He's standing there in silence, weeping.

Only the cameraman moves, crabbing round and in, the black lens of his camera sucking up the old man's pain and grief. Well, there's a response. Not as dramatic as a blow with a hammer, but powerful for all that. Maybe more powerful. Only, like the art itself, the weeping man requires a panel of explanatory text.

Christina dares to ask.

'Can you tell me why?' Her voice soft, respectful of his all-too-visible emotion.

He shakes his head. She persists: it's her job.

'What is it you're feeling?'

'Loss,' he says. 'Loss.'

Joe Nola himself now comes forward. Unasked he takes Anthony Armitage's hand in his and holds it.

'Remember me? I'm Joe.'

The old man gazes at him through tear-blurred eyes.

'Joe, yes. Come to my show, Joe. I'd like you to be there.'

He withdraws his hand from Joe's, feels in his coat pocket, pulls out the hammer. For a moment he looks at it, uncomprehending. Then he holds it out to Joe.

'Here,' he says.

He starts shuffling towards the exit.

Christina is about to stop him, to get him to exchange at least a few more words with his former student, when Joe takes hold of her arm.

'Leave him alone. Let him go.'

'But he's hardly said a word.'

'He gave me this.' He holds up the hammer. 'One hammer is worth a thousand words.'

Anthony Armitage makes his slow way out through the gallery rooms to the lobby. Christina remains rooted to the spot. Before her gaze, before the shining eyes of the gallery staff and the security men, filmed by the crew from Sky

Arts, Joe Nola proceeds to destroy his own installation. The hammer falls on plates and bowls, on milk jug and marmalade jar, on the toast-rack and on the packet of Kellogg's Cornflakes. As he strikes he shouts over and over, 'Loss! Loss!'

When the breakfast things are all broken he attacks the table itself, splitting its planks, slowly forcing it to its knees.

Then suddenly exhausted, his passion spent, he stops striking and lets the hammer fall to the floor. The spectators look down, ashamed to meet each other's eyes.

'Cut,' says Joe.

28

On Tuesday morning, Belinda and Laura meet at the station in good time for the London train.

'I have to have a cup of tea,' announces Belinda. 'I can't survive another minute without caffeine.'

The station buffet stands on the broad triangular island between the London and Brighton lines. The licensee writes poetry. His poems are blu-tacked to the glass doors. Belinda and Laura pause before entering to read the latest poem, 'A River through Lewes'.

Where the river meets the bend gently meandering along
All your troubles seem to disappear in front of your eyes
The pure energy is worth sitting and being at one with nature.

The clock on the supermarket wall reminds you of
the time

Or just that time disappears ...

'I adore Vic's poems,' says Belinda. 'Don't you adore
them, Laura?'

'I think they're just about the best railway buffet poems
I know,' says Laura.

'Don't be a snotty cow. I love Vic.'

Vic is sitting at one of his own tables, composing his
latest poem. He rises as they come in.

'La-a-a-dies,' he sings in a rich baritone. Round his solid
form he wears a long black apron. 'Off to town for Christmas
sho-o-opping?'

He sings it like recitative in an opera.

'Oh, Vic,' says Belinda. 'Make us one of your nice cups
of tea. I'm so miserable.'

The clock in the buffet shows that they have three
minutes before their train, but it's set by tradition five
minutes fast. Belinda and Laura sit at one of the little
round tables beside the framed sepia-toned photographs
of Lewes station in bygone days. Vic goes behind the
counter, which is decorated with a painting of a jolly
green train bouncing off its wheels in its eagerness to please.
Overhead an indoor trellis is festooned with ivy and
twinkling white Christmas lights.

'I could write an opera, you know,' says Vic, pouring

their tea from a shiny stainless steel teapot. 'I could write about anything. I hear music in the air. I don't mean in my head. In the air. It's all round me.'

He brings them over their cups of tea, bursting into song again as he comes. 'When the teapot is empt-ee-ee I can make you a cup of coff-ee-ee.'

'They should have you at Glyndebourne, Vic.'

'You think you're joking. There's a fellow comes in here, he's big at Glyndebourne, he said to me, Vic, write it down. Write your opera.'

More customers come in, and Vic returns to his counter. Laura hasn't had a chance to catch up with Belinda since their lunch on Friday.

'What's all this about being miserable?'

'Oh, God, Laura. It's a nightmare. Tom's been having an affair.'

She gives Laura a rapid rundown on the headline facts, impatient to revert to her own feelings. She is in a state of confusion that interests her to the exclusion of everything else.

'The thing is, it's opened my eyes. I feel like I've been such a fool. Apparently this sort of thing's going on all the time. I mean, I'm not stupid, I know there's a lot of it about. But Tom! If Tom's got a secret life, then who hasn't? Only me, as far as I can see.'

'And me,' says Laura.

'Henry's bound to be poking some little telly dolly.'

'I suppose he might,' says Laura doubtfully.

'They're bastards, Laura. Take it from me.'

The train is already full when it pulls in to Lewes station. There are people standing in the bays by the doors. This adds to Belinda's sense of outrage.

'I'm not standing all the way to London,' she says. 'Just because they live in Eastbourne and get on earlier than us doesn't mean they have a right to a seat. I've paid the same as them.'

A man is talking loudly on his mobile in an Australian accent. 'You'll never go broke by making money, eh? Keep reading that Donald Trump book, eh?'

'There was a time,' says Belinda, 'when gentlemen gave up their seats to ladies.'

'You have to be pregnant,' says Laura. 'Or disabled.'

'Well, I am disabled. I've got an adulterous husband. That's a disability.'

'Not so loud,' says Laura, going pink. 'Everyone'll hear.'

'I don't care.'

Belinda has discovered against all expectations that there is relief in full disclosure. What hurts is trying to keep up appearances.

'There's bound to be someone we know in the carriage,' says Laura.

'No way,' says Belinda. 'They're all from Eastbourne. I don't know anyone from Eastbourne. All they do in

Eastbourne is sit on their bottoms.' She glares round the carriage. 'And have affairs, I expect. Look at that one. You can just tell he's cheating on his wife.'

The Australian has finished his call.

'Why don't you shut it, love?' he says mildly.

At Plumpton most of the men get out. It turns out there's a race meeting on. Belinda and Laura rush for the empty seats and sit there laughing like children.

'So where do you want to go?' says Laura. 'I have to do John Lewis at some point.'

'Selfridges,' says Belinda. 'They've got a better caff.'

'I'm totally stuck on what to get for Jack. Why are boys so difficult?'

'That's nothing. What am I supposed to give Tom for Christmas? A chastity belt?'

'I don't think there are chastity belts for men.'

'How about a pair of Spanx? His tummy could do with holding in. I'd like to see him get a stiffy in Spanx.'

Laura bursts out laughing.

'You don't think you're just a tad manic, do you, Belinda?'

'Probably. I don't know what I am, to be honest. It's like all the old rules have been torn up.' She drops her voice for the first time since they met at the station ticket window. 'Guess what I'm doing on the way home?'

'What?'

'Meeting up with Kenny.'

'Oh my God, Belinda! Where?'

'He's working at Gatwick. We're meeting at the Hilton.'

'My God!'

'I'm so excited. I'm seventeen again.'

In the taxi which Belinda insists on taking to Oxford Street – 'Let the fucker pay' – they get into conversation with the taxi driver. He's frustrated by the slow-moving traffic.

'This congestion charge, it's a joke,' he says. 'Look at it. It's a joke.'

'You know what jams up the streets,' says Belinda.

'I've got an idea or two,' says the taxi driver.

'Infidelity,' says Belinda. 'All the men going out to poke their mistresses.'

'You reckon?' says the taxi driver, intrigued. 'That's a new one on me.'

'They should have an infidelity charge,' says Belinda. 'That'd clear the streets in no time.'

When Laura rejoins Belinda an hour or so later, in the Food Hall at Selfridges, she's hauling two heavy carrier bags, the proceeds of a tiring but successful afternoon. Belinda has bought nothing.

'I can't concentrate,' she wails. 'I can't make decisions. I think I might be having a breakdown.'

'You're over-excited about Kenny.'

'Well, yes. That too.'

They queue up to be served at the Brass Rail.

'One ninety-five for a cup of tea!' Belinda is outraged. 'How can you have the nerve to charge prices like that?'

The young man behind the counter grins.

'Captive market, isn't it?' he says.

Laura carries their tray to the bar in the middle, where there are red leather stools on chrome stalks.

'Are you okay here? I love to swivel.'

Belinda is looking round.

'Every single person here is female,' she says in disgust. 'Where are their men? What are they doing? As if I didn't know.' She peers inside the white china teapot. 'One tea bag. So stingy.'

Laura displays her purchases.

'This is for Carrie. They're speakers for her iPod.'

Belinda puzzles over the large box.

'How are you going to get that into her stocking?'

'Stocking? This isn't for her stocking. This is her present from Henry and me. The stuff in her stocking is from Father Christmas.'

'But you are Father Christmas.'

'Yes, I know. But stocking presents are little things like felt-tip pens and hairbands and tangerines.'

'Christ, my kids would leave home if they got felt-tip pens and hairbands in their stockings.'

'Do you give them their big presents in their stockings?'

'Yes, of course. Everyone does.'

'No, they don't. They give them their big presents after lunch.'

'Are you seriously telling me that you make your children wait all morning on Christmas Day before they get their presents?'

'Yes. But they have their little presents, from Father Christmas. In their stockings when they wake.'

'That is sadistic.'

'But Belinda, you must see it.' Laura feels herself getting agitated, which is ridiculous. 'Your way makes no sense. If Father Christmas gives them all their presents, what do you give them?'

'My children aren't stupid. They know it's us giving them the presents.'

'Have they always known? From when they were tiny? Didn't they ever believe in Father Christmas?'

'Of course they did. Until Alex told Chloe it was all a story, when she was seven.'

'So up to the age of seven Chloe thought her mum and dad never gave her anything for Christmas? She never had that lovely feeling that her mum and dad had been thinking about what she'd like most in the world because you loved her so much? She thought it was all the kindness of a bearded stranger who gives presents to absolutely everyone?'

'For God's sake, Laura. It's not a big deal.'

'You're wrong. You're terribly wrong. Father Christmas

gives little presents. His elves make them, in their work-shops. Elves don't make iPod speakers.'

'Well, it looks like they're getting nothing from anyone this Christmas. Father Christmas has been porking his lady elves, and Mother Christmas has lost the plot.'

She looks down at her hands. She's been tugging at the rings on her right hand with the fingers of her left hand.

'Oh, God,' she says. Suddenly she sounds heartbroken.

'I'm really sorry,' says Laura. She wants to help, but she doesn't know how. 'I think you're just going to have to tough this one out.'

'Yes, I know.'

'He says he wants to stay, doesn't he?'

'Yes.'

'And you want him to stay?'

'I suppose so.'

'So maybe it'll kind of settle down after a while.'

'That's what he thinks. But it'll never be the same again. It wasn't broken before. It's broken now.'

From somewhere deep in the Food Hall the store music starts to play Christmas carols. All round them is seasonal cheer. The glitter of tinsel, the gleam of decorator's snow.

'It's a rotten time to do this to me,' says Belinda. 'When all the world's playing happy families.'

'But at least he doesn't want to leave you.'

'Yes. I know. I should be grateful, but I'm not. What I really want is for him to stay and for me to go.'

'Then do it,' says Laura. 'Go.'

Belinda looks up in surprise.

'You're not meant to say that.'

'If you really want to leave Tom, then do it. Alex and Chloe are old enough to cope.'

'Oh. Do you think I should?'

'I don't know, Belinda. You'd have to work out where you'd live. How much money you'd have.'

Belinda looks frightened. 'I'm no good on my own.'

'So run off with Kenny.'

'Laura! You're so bad! Why are you saying this?'

'Well,' says Laura slowly. 'Life's never going to be perfect. All you can do is choose between the options you've got. None of them gives you everything. So you take a good long look and you make your choice and you go with it.'

Belinda fixes Laura with her limpid blue eyes.

'Can I tell you what I'm really thinking?' she says.

'I know what you're thinking.'

'What am I thinking?'

'You're thinking, Maybe Kenny's the one. Maybe when we meet we'll both know it. Maybe true passion will come back into my life. Maybe my life's about to change for ever.'

'Yes,' she says, lips trembling, hardly breathing. 'How did you know?'

'Because it's what we all think,' says Laura.

'Even you?'

'Even me. I had my chance. A few years back.'

She can see him now, the boyfriend who came back into her life. The sudden intoxicating view of how everything could be different.

'Did you go for it?' says Belinda, eyes bright. 'Did you, Laura? Did you?'

'No.'

'Do you wish you had?'

'We did have one kiss,' says Laura, smiling at the memory. 'But it turned out that was enough.'

29

Alan has determined that today is the day he gets back to work on his screenplay. First he clears his emails. Then he reads through his notes. Then he reads, or rather skips, through the most recent draft. Then he goes and has a pee. Then he makes himself a mug of coffee. Then, back in front of his computer screen he sets up a new Final Draft document and fills in the title page: *SHEPHERD by Alan Strachan, Third Revision, December 16, 2008*.

Then the phone rings.

It's Jane Langridge.

'Alan. I'm in LA. It's the middle of the night here, but I couldn't wait to call you. I've been with Nancy at the studio all day. They're all buzzing about *Shepherd* over here. Your ears must be burning.'

'That's good to hear.'

'The thing is this, Alan. Do you follow the numbers?'

'The numbers?'

'I'll give you the headlines. Dramas are tanking. *Frost/Nixon*, *The Reader*, *Doubt*, all dead on arrival. The recession is changing the mood music. People want to be cheered up. And guess what looks like being the big winner over Christmas? *Marley and Me*.'

'*Marley and Me*?'

'It's a movie about a dog. A *dog*, Alan. Fox are tracking a final BO of over two hundred million.'

And it's a movie about a dog.

'So have you started on the next pass yet, Alan?'

'Just about to.'

'Fabulous. Hold the front page. Breaking news. Got a pencil?'

'Yes, Jane. I have a pencil.'

'Our movie is going to take your brilliant idea and run with it. It was you who made us love the dog, Alan. Now we want you to go all the way. Follow your heart. Put the dog at the heart of the picture.'

'At the heart of the picture.'

'That's what Nancy wants. A story about a dog who goes into the world of investment banking and beats the pros at their own game.'

'The dog becomes a banker?'

'You got it. The dog makes a fortune. No one can believe it's the dog, of course. They all think the shepherd's doing it.'

'So does the dog talk?'

'Good question. The jury's still out on that. What I want you to do is punch out a treatment for the new approach. Work out the best way to go. Maybe the dog talks. Maybe it works the keyboard with its nose. Your call.'

'A treatment.'

'Sure. We don't want you wasting your valuable time on another full draft. And change the title. It's not about the shepherd any more, it's about the dog. What's the dog called?'

'Maggie.'

'No, that's no good. Has to be a boy dog. Get it a new name. And Alan – make the story funny. Loveable and funny. That's where the market is now. Call the dog Harvey. No, that was the rabbit, wasn't it? You'll think of something.'

Then she's gone.

Alan sits in his little study staring at the screen, breathing slow controlled breaths. A treatment: that means no money, or very little. He should ring his agent. She'll tell him not to touch it. But what happens then? They get another writer. Better to hang on in.

A talking dog who becomes an investment banker. That's insane, isn't it?

As ever after contact with the movie world he feels that he's slipped into a parallel universe. His own judgement is no longer to be trusted. His perception of reality is faulty.

I can't do this. I can't I can't I can't—

He becomes aware of dull thuds from the top floor. The plumber building the new bathroom. The plumber who plays the violin. All day he does sound constructive work, and in the evening he makes music. That's perfect, isn't it? No one says to him, I've changed my mind, rebuild this bathroom as a battleship. His world has a simple solidity to it, a respect for craftsmanship, a beginning and an end. What am I doing in this windless ocean of dreams, this Sargasso Sea where all my talent lies becalmed?

He hears light footsteps past his door on the stairs. Liz is out at work. Of course! Alice is home.

He jumps up at once and follows her to her room.

'Sorry,' she says as he looks round the door. 'I didn't mean to disturb you.'

'You didn't. I've just had my producer on the phone from LA. I need someone to tell me I'm not going mad. It's you or the plumber.'

She's sitting at her little desk in front of her laptop. One glance tells him she's writing a story. Just the shape of the text on the screen. But now she shuts the lid and gives him a sweet grin.

'Let's hear it, then.'

He tells her, making it so funny in the telling that she rocks with laughter.

'Are they all mad?' he says, feeling much better. 'Or am I?'

'Of course they're mad.'

'But what if they're right? Suppose they get someone to write their dog banker story and it makes a fortune?'

'Listen,' she says. 'It's all very simple. Can you write this story they want?'

'No. How? What do I know about talking dogs? I wouldn't know where to begin.'

'There you are, then. You have to pull out. They've changed the terms of the contract, not you. They have to pay you for what you've done so far.'

Alan looks at her in awe.

'You are so together, Alice.'

'If only.'

Cas appears at the door. By some sixth sense he has intuited that Alan has left his keyboard.

'Can I go on your computer, Dad?'

'Only for a moment, Cas. I'll be back at work in five minutes.'

'Okay.'

He scampers off down the stairs.

'Though Christ knows what work,' he says.

'Write a play,' says Alice.

'What about?'

'About how people get together. I'd come and see that.'

'Like, a love story?'

'Yes. A story about someone who loves someone, and – surprise ending – he loves her back.'

'Oh, Alice.'

325

'I'm not being bitter or anything. I'd just really like to know how it's done.'

'Who would the main characters be?'

She meets his smiling gaze with another wry grin. We understand each other, he thinks, Alice and me. Always have.

'Okay,' she says. 'She's a quiet girl, clever, reads too much, not pretty but not a fright or anything. He's a sweet boy, nothing special, but he's funny and he knows what she's talking about, which in her experience is seriously rare. They get on really well together so long as they're just friends, but she wants more, she wants to have a proper boyfriend, and she wouldn't mind if it was him. Only there's a twist. He fancies someone else. A girl who's sexy and gorgeous and everything she isn't.'

'But the idea is that they end up together.'

'That's the general idea. But how?'

'Well,' says Alan, playing along with the game. 'Maybe he goes after the sexy girl and she rejects him in some humiliating way and he realizes he really loves the plain girl best.'

'Would you believe that?'

'No, not really.'

'So how does the plain girl ever get a boyfriend?'

'Alice. Darling. You're not plain.'

She shakes her head, a glisten of tears in her eyes.

'No,' she says, 'no. Stick with the story. This is a story about a plain girl.'

'When you love someone they stop being plain.'

'Yes. Fine.' She's almost angry now. 'So how does that happen?'

Alan doesn't answer.

'See? No happy ending. It's a tragedy.'

But Alan is thinking. He wants to be as honest as he knows how.

'I'll tell you a different version of the story,' he says. He speaks slowly, frowning, piecing together the ideas as they form. 'This is from the boy's point of view, but I don't see why it shouldn't be much the same for girls. To start with the boy wants a girlfriend so that he can be like everyone else. So of course he wants the kind of girlfriend the other boys want. He wants her to be beautiful. But then as he gets older he starts to find out how tough life is. There turn out to be far more compromises than he thought. The right job doesn't come along, so he goes for a half-right job. The right girl doesn't come along, so he starts seeing a half-right girl. He doesn't care so much any more about what other boys think. He wants someone he can get along with. Someone he can be himself with. Someone who'll be good to him and not expect him to be perfect. He spends time with her, and she makes him happy. The more she makes him happy, the more he loves her. The more he loves her, the more beautiful she gets. Then one day he wakes up and realizes that every little detail about her has become beautiful to him. Because she's the one he loves. Because she makes him happy. So he ends up with a beautiful girl after all.'

Alice's eyes shine as she listens.

'Is that it?'

'That's it.'

'Oh, boy. Some story.'

'Would you believe it?'

'How long does all this take?'

'A few years.'

'Is there any way of speeding things up? Like, show him a video reconstruction of the next ten years of his life and say, Let's skip all that and get on with loving each other now?'

'If only.' A sudden thought pops into his head. 'That's how to rewrite *A Christmas Carol* for today, isn't it? Have Scrooge be shown the ghosts of girlfriends past – all his failed relationships – so that he gets so scared of his lonely future he gets on with it and asks his current girlfriend to marry him.'

'There you go. Write it.'

'Better than a sheepdog banker.'

Steps on the stairs. The plumber at the door in stockinged feet.

'I'll be off now, if that's okay.'

'Yes, of course,' says Alan.

'I'm going over to your sister. Fix her shower.'

'Oh, thank you. I hope it's not too much bother.'

'Just a pump needs replacing.'

He pads off down the stairs.

'Oh, God,' says Alan. 'Cas has been on the computer all this time. I hate those bloody computer games.'

'They won't hurt him.'

'He should be out in the woods playing with his little friends.'

'How about me? Should I be out in the woods playing with my little friends?'

'You were writing a story when I came in. I saw.'

'Just tinkering.'

'Can I see it?'

'Not yet.'

'What's it about?'

'It's about a boy like Cas. It's about finding out for the first time that there's unhappiness in the world.'

'Oh, Alice.'

'Don't worry. I'm okay. As much as anyone's ever okay.'

Alan finds it hard. She's so brave, so beautiful.

'You know,' he says, 'I want you to be happy far more than I want to be happy myself. I don't mind about life being hard for me. But I don't want it to be hard for you.'

'It's not so hard. Though sometimes I do wish it could be that tiny little bit easier.'

'Give me a hug, then.'

They hug.

'I'll go and boot Cas off the computer.'

Cas turns out not to be playing video games at all. He's on Google.

'I'm doing a secret,' he says.

'What sort of secret?' says Alan.

'Not telling.'

He's closed the screen windows he had open.

'Well,' says Alan, 'I need to get back to work.'

'That's okay. I've finished.'

He scoops some sheets of paper from the printer tray. For a moment Alan is amazed that a child of six can search Google and print out the results. But then he thinks, it's not exactly difficult.

'Cas, I really ought to know what you've been looking at. There's bad stuff on the Internet.'

'Trains,' says Cas.

'Trains? What for?'

'I like trains.'

With that he runs off to his room, clutching his print-outs. Alan wonders if he's found out yet about unhappiness in the world. It seems unlikely. He still believes firmly in Father Christmas.

30

All the time that Matt Early is working on the shower pump he's aware of Meg's movements in the other parts of the flat. The conversion of the Victorian rooms has been shoddily done, the divider walls are poorly insulated, the door frames poorly fitted. The sounds of the television come through clearly from the lounge. Then after the television is switched off he hears the gush of the kettle being filled in the little kitchen, then the hiss as it boils, then the tinkle of music from a radio.

In a little while the job will be done. He will gather up his tools, exchange a few brief words with Meg, and leave. In those short minutes he must somehow establish a means of seeing her again. How? This is a problem more insuperable than any he has ever encountered. It seems to Matt to be a literal impossibility. Even given the slight connection formed between them on his last visit, when she had wept in his presence, he can see no way forward.

In a well-run universe, where true feelings are truly expressed, he would say to her, 'I like you, and I'd like to know you better.' He would suggest they share a pot of tea, or go for a walk on the Downs, or some such safe and innocent pastime. It would be nothing grand, and might lead to nothing, but it might just as easily be a beginning to everything. And yet it could not be done. He might want it with all his heart, and she might welcome it, but it was not going to happen.

In his practical way he puzzles over why this should be so, as he tightens the bolts on the refitted pump. If he wants a pint of milk he goes into a shop and asks for it. A perfect stranger takes his money and gives him the carton. How is it different if he were to ask Meg to join him on a walk?

The answer is brutally plain. You ask for a pint of milk and that's it, no other hopes are concealed beneath the request. Ask a young woman to walk out with you and you might as well be saying, Do you love me? Will you marry me? Shall we set up house together and have children?

Well, maybe not quite that far; but the first move contains all that is to come, or all that will not come, which is even more daunting. Lifelong joy or lifelong loneliness lie tightly twined in those few brief words. The burden is too great, the risk too terrible. Matt knows he dare not make the move.

It's a bit late to expect the girls to come knocking on your door.

His mother's words haunt him. We'll see, he says to himself. We'll see about that.

The pipe work sealed once more, he opens the water valves and tests the system. The pump starts up with a slight shudder. The water streams out of the shower. He checks that the thermostat is performing as it should, turning up the setting until the water scalds his hand and then down again. Then he shuts off the shower and cleans up the grease marks he has left.

He's aware as he packs away his tools that he's moving slowly. What am I waiting for? Nothing is going to happen unless I make it happen. There's no war on any more.

Matt envies his granddad, who met the love of his life in a bombed-out building in the Blitz. He pulled her out of a hole in the ground and carried her in his arms down a flaming street, or so he said. So of course they fell in love and were married.

I could carry Meg in my arms across a universe in flames. But I can't speak a few simple words.

They manage things better in other countries. Your parents make a match for you, with someone you've never met. They let you meet, and if you're not totally turned off you say, Okay, why not? The love comes later. Anyone can love anyone, really, if they try.

So why do I know that Meg is the one for me?

Because of the way she looked when she was crying. No, I knew earlier than that. Truth to tell I knew before I even saw her. I knew from the sound of her voice. Can't say how or why. She just sounded right.

He can delay no more. He opens the bathroom door and joins her in the lounge. She's sitting on the sofa with her eyes closed listening to the radio. A Brahms trio.

Her eyes jump open as she hears him come in. She reaches out and switches off the radio.

'All done,' he says.

'Oh, that's wonderful. Thank you so much.' She gets up, avoiding his gaze, and looks round for her handbag. 'How much do I owe you?'

'Well, the pump was £109. It's a very straightforward job. I quoted you £150, didn't I?'

'That doesn't seem enough. Are you sure?'

'Yes, that'll be fine.'

She writes him out a cheque. Her hand is shaking. Her face is very pale. In a moment she'll tear out the cheque and give it to him, and he'll pick up his tools and his shoes and go. Then the greatest test his life has yet offered him will have come and gone and he will have failed.

'There,' she says.

The sound of the cheque being torn from its stub fills the universe.

'I'm so grateful,' she says.

He takes the cheque and pushes it unseen into a pocket.

He picks up his tools with one hand, his shoes with the other. Four steps between where he stands now, by the little white coffee table, and the door.

'Any time,' he says. 'You've got my number.'

One step. There's a humming sound in his ears. He feels flushed, short of breath. Maybe I'll faint, and she'll have to revive me. But of course he's not going to faint.

A second step. Time moving slowly.

Dithering in the doorway like my dad. But not in the doorway yet.

She goes ahead of him, opens the door for him, can't wait for him to go. Or a kindness, seeing that both his hands are full.

Someone has left a window open in the stairwell. A gust of cold air rushes in to the centrally heated flat. It picks up some papers resting on a music stand in the corner and flutters them onto the floor by his feet.

He puts down his shoes to pick up the papers. Sheet music. Handel.

'Are you a musician?' he says.

'Oh, no,' she says. 'I just sing in a local choir.'

'I play the violin.'

'Do you?'

She looks at him with startled eyes.

'I've played Handel. His Violin Sonata in A major.'

'I didn't know Handel wrote violin sonatas.'

'Oh, yes. All the composers who write for the voice

write for the violin too. It's the closest instrument to the voice. The sound is made in the same way, really. A violin has a part called the voice box. It's different for every instrument. There's a tiny part in a violin called the sound post, it goes just under the right-hand foot of the bridge, its position makes all the difference to the instrument's tone. Move it as little as a quarter of a millimetre and it changes everything.'

He knows he should stop talking but he can't. She's gazing at him wide-eyed.

'There's a special tool called a sound-post-setter which slips in through the F-holes, the sound holes, and goes round the corner to grasp the sound post and lets you move it. There are special dedicated tools for everything to do with making violins. I have a spoon gouge made by J. Spiller that I found in an antique shop, a junk shop really, I only paid a fiver for it, and it's the best you can get. I was so happy when I took it home.'

He stops as abruptly as he started, and finds he's standing in the open doorway, his eyes on the floor, breathing rapidly. His cheeks are hot and his back is cold in the wind.

I'm a nutter, he thinks. What on earth do I think I'm doing?

'Do you make violins?' she says.

'Restore,' he says. 'I restore old violins.'

'That's amazing,' she says. 'I had no idea.'

'No,' he says, still looking down.

'Why?' she says. Wonder in her voice.

'It's just something I do,' he says. 'I have a shed out the back, where I keep all my tools. I like to go out there and work.'

He looks up then and finds her eyes fixed on him with such an intense gaze, as if she truly wants to understand him, that he says, 'I could show you, if you like.'

'Your shed?'

'The violins. The tools.'

As he says it he hears himself and drops his eyes again. The violins, the tools: why would she want to see all that?

'Would you?' she says. 'I'd love to see how you work on the violins.'

'I've got about forty instruments. Some in pieces.'

'Forty violins!'

He's breathing deeply now. He feels suddenly buoyant, like a balloon. He wants to soar.

'You could come over tomorrow evening.'

There: the dangerous words are out. No flash of lightning. No end of the world.

'I'd really like that,' she says.

He has asked her to come and see his violins. She has said yes. The first highest most unclimbable wall has tumbled before them. Now it can all begin.

He tells her where to come. They agree a time: seven o'clock tomorrow evening. He picks up his shoes and his tools and leaves her flat.

Outside there's an icy wind blowing across the car park. Matt Early smiles at the wind, he hugs the wind, the beautiful wind that blew the sheets of music to his feet. This late afternoon December wind is his blitz, his miracle, his matchmaker. Meg knows nothing of how close he came to leaving her without a word. Maybe one day in years to come, sitting side by side in a house they share together, listening to the roaring of a south-westerly outside, he'll tell her why she must always be grateful to the wind. She'll say, Oh, but we would have sorted things out one way or another. But he knows this isn't true. It takes some outside agency to get things started. An accident, a break in the pattern.

My God! I told her about the sound-post-setter! She must think I'm insane.

He drives home smiling to himself.

31

As the train pulls in to Gatwick Belinda becomes ever more silent. It's not nerves, or fear; she's focusing her energy. Already her mind is reaching forward to the coming encounter. What she has been calling to herself 'a bit of a laugh' has grown into an event of significance, a test of something that matters to her very much.

Have I still got it? Or am I old now?

'Good luck,' says Laura. 'Don't do anything I wouldn't do. Not that there's much I wouldn't do. In fact, I can't think of a single thing.'

'I wouldn't go camping,' says Belinda.

'Yes, you're right. There are limits.'

They smile at each other. The doors go pip-pip-pip.

'Hey ho,' says Belinda. 'Away we go.'

She gives Laura a last wave as she crosses the platform to the escalator. At the top a short blank passage leads to automatic doors. They open before her, as if controlled by her will, ushering her into a space that seems no longer to be located within her everyday world. Above the check-in desks the flight destinations cast their magic spell: Orlando, Agadir, Faro, Kos. Distant gleams of sunshine and sensuality, the sheer otherness of the names flickers in this brightly lit and thronging hall. A ceaseless stream of passengers with trolleys or hauling wheeled suitcases flows across her path. People in an airport are no more beautiful than elsewhere, but they have about them an aura of soiled glamour that suits Belinda's mood. Their lives are in flux. No social expectations bind these hurrying forms. They come from everywhere, go to everywhere, free from memory or obligation. The arrivals hall shivers with rootlessness.

Belinda looks for signs to the Hilton hotel and finds none. At the information desk she's told to head for the coach station, where there will be signs. She joins the stream of arriving passengers, her own lack of luggage marking her out as an alien among aliens, and rides the travelator past a long red Virgin advertisement. The travelator moves too slowly. She starts walking on it, carried forward by her own power and by the motion of the conveyor beneath her. This makes her think of the greater motion that propels her, the spinning of the earth. And the planet's orbit round the sun. Everything is in motion. Everything on the point of departure.

Caution. You are reaching the end of the conveyor.

Yeah, right. Slow down. I'm not jetting away for a holiday

romance. Not seventeen any more. Kenny'll take one look and send for the cocoa.

But what if …

All those years ago, the rumour shared in girly whispers among her group of friends. Jimmy Kennaway has a really big one. Like, Oh boy! That is big!

The coach station is down one level. She descends the long ramp in a stream of screeching trolleys. Here at last she finds a sign to the Hilton, discreetly tucked beneath the arrows pointing to the Short Stay Car Parks and the Pick-up Point. That could be quite funny if she stopped to think about it, but she's not stopping and she's not thinking. On past the Orange Car Park. Turn left into the final approach: a wide white windowless walkway that rises gently towards the hotel entrance.

It seems to Belinda that her flight has now begun. This is take-off. With each step she's leaving her former life behind. Somewhere below her now, rapidly dwindling from sight, is the land where Tom had his fling. Now it's my turn.

Do I really mean that?

Hey, no one's listening. It's just me here. Who do I think I'm fooling? I'm a bad girl out to have some fun.

Christ, that takes me back. I was a bad girl once. Those were the days.

At the end of the walkway she finds herself passing through a Costa coffee bar. A cluster of men, all wearing suits, all with their ties removed, are talking to each other in low voices. Beyond the bar the hotel lobby proper opens up, an atrium of sorts, though without the grandeur the term implies. On three sides of a long rectangle rise open corridors of hotel rooms. Above, vaults of grey and grubby glass.

For the first time it strikes Belinda that she's not sure exactly where she and Kenny are to meet.

She cruises the lobby looking for him. Or rather, since she has no idea what he looks like these days, looking for a man who looks like he's looking for her. One or two of them glance up as she goes by, but then look away again.

Then she recalls that she's to ask for him. She goes to the concierge's desk. A screen on the wall is running Sky News. British banks admit losses in the Madoff fraud.

'I wonder if you have a message for me. I'm Belinda Redknapp.'

A shiny-faced concierge consults a screen concealed before her at waist level, as if casting her gaze down in respectful modesty. Yes, there is a message. Mr Kennaway is in Room 1229. She dials the room and speaks into an unseen microphone, now looking a little to Belinda's left and into the distance.

On the TV there's a picture of a house in Dorset with a giant Christmas tree that comes out through the roof. How did they do that? You wouldn't cut a hole in your roof for a Christmas tree, would you?

'Miss Redknapp is in the lobby, sir. Certainly, sir.'

The concierge turns to Belinda with a smile that glistens with hostility.

'Through Costa's. Take a left. Room 1229.'

She looks down once more at her concealed screen. Belinda is dismissed.

What's her problem? What does she think I am, a hooker or something?

This possible misunderstanding rather boosts Belinda's self-esteem. As she walks back through the coffee bar she catches sight of herself in a glass divider screen. I could pass for forty in a dim light.

The promised corridor opens directly off the café. It stretches away into the distance, offering door after door as if reflected in parallel mirrors, identical and infinite. The carpet is ginger and cream, the doors pale blond veneer. She can feel her heart beating. The truth is she loves hotels, even corporate clones like this one. Their rooms offer anonymity and privacy, which is odd when you think how close they are one to another. How do they soundproof them? Behind any of these doors anything could be happening, and no one else would know. But it's not hard to guess. What do you find behind every door? A room with a big wide bed. No wonder hotels are sexy.

Now she has reached Room 1229. She stands before it, preparing herself. The first look will tell all. He'll open the door, he'll see her, and ... What? Will his face register

343

a momentary flicker of disappointment? She wishes now she'd sent him a picture of herself as she is today. But how could she? That would have been too open an admission that they are meeting for a date. And anyway, he's not stupid. He knows she's over fifty. Even if she's still seventeen inside.

So am I really going to do this?

Do what? It's only a catch-up with an old friend.

She knocks on the door.

'Belinda?' A deep voice from within.

'Yes.'

'Door's open. Come on in.'

She opens the door. She comes on in.

The room is in semi-darkness, the curtains drawn over the tall windows. A blond-wood desk. A flat-screen TV. The only light comes from a lamp with a boxy cream-coloured shade standing on the far bedside table.

The bed almost fills the room. The bedspread is dark blue. The pillows white. And lying on the bed, stark naked, is a man with a bald head and an erection. And, Oh boy! That is big!

'Surprise, surprise!' he says.

Yes, it's a surprise.

'Making up for lost time,' he says.

She stands motionless, the door still open behind her. She knows she should turn and leave, at once, but for the moment shock has frozen her to the spot.

'Shut the door,' says Kenny. 'Hell of a draught.'

She shuts the door. She's in the room with a naked middle-aged man in a state of arousal, and she's shut the door. I must be mad, she thinks. But what are you supposed to do in these circumstances?

She realizes she must speak. Whatever she says now must lay the groundwork for her exit. Dinner waiting to be cooked, Chloe waiting to be fed, Tom waiting …

'Hello, Kenny,' she says.

She hears herself with surprise. There seems to be a disconnect between what she wants to do and what she actually does. Who's in charge here?

'Hello, sunshine,' he says. 'Come and be friendly.'

He pats the side of the bed. His voice is a soft blur in her mind. He wants to be friendly. The habit of a lifetime prompts her to respond with answering friendliness. Already it's too late to say, What are you doing there? She had just the one chance and she missed it. Perhaps she should have screamed. But why? She's not a Victorian spinster.

On one point Belinda is crystal clear. This naked stranger does not excite her. His well-advertised desire does not arouse in her an answering desire.

Yet here she is, crossing the room like a sleepwalker, sitting down by him on the side of the bed, all to be friendly. She is held in the iron grip of politeness.

'You know what's so bloody wonderful about growing older?' he says. 'You don't have to pretend any more.'

'No,' says Belinda, pretending.

'You have no idea how much I've been looking forward to this,' he says. 'I swear, I've been hard for days.'

He pats his enormous cock with a broad hairy hand.

'That's nice,' says Belinda.

She has no idea why she's saying these trite and point-less things, except that they seem to come naturally. Like when some friend does her hair in a new way that makes her look like a dead lesbian and you say, 'Love the hair.' It's just the way the world works.

Kenny puts an arm round her waist.

'One of my lifetime regrets,' he says. 'That you never got to meet Matey down here.'

Matey. Oh, God.

He holds his cock in his hand and wags it at her, speaking as he does so in a growly mock-Cockney voice.

'Wotcher, Belinda. I'm Matey.'

'Hello, Matey,' she answers helplessly.

'Shake 'ands, sweetheart,' says Matey.

Kenny takes her hand and places it on his cock. The cock feels warm and hard against her palm. In order not to look at it she looks at Kenny's face, and because he's smiling, she smiles.

Up to now she has avoided taking in the details of his appearance. The very first glance told her the Kenny she has treasured down the years has gone. Now in his place she sees a slack-jawed face, flushed cheeks, hairs growing out of both nostrils, one discoloured tooth. And that smile.

Her hand is moving up and down his cock.

When did I start doing this? Why am I doing it?

Somehow the situation requires it. When you have your hand on a man's erect penis, you stroke it. What else are you there for? It's a matter of common etiquette. To do anything else would be embarrassing to all concerned.

'My golly, Kenny,' she says. 'This certainly is a surprise.'

'Isn't it just?' he says, beaming away. Then in his Matey voice, 'Give us a kiss, darling! Give us a kiss!'

At the same time he gives her thigh a squeeze with the hand wrapped round her waist.

Belinda makes a kissy sound with her lips, hoping by this to show friendliness but not enthusiasm. Matey is unimpressed.

'What you doing, darling? Blowing bubbles?'

'No hurry,' says Belinda.

At once she regrets it. Her primary aim is to leave this room as soon as is decently possible.

'Damn right,' says Kenny. 'After thirty-four years I reckon we're entitled to take our time.'

'My God!' says Belinda. 'Is it really thirty-four years?'

She wants to get a conversation going, talk about the old days. Then with a bit of luck Matey will lose interest.

'Who cares?' says Kenny. 'You're here now, and I'm here, and Matey's here. I vote we get snuggly.'

'I was thinking we might do some catching up first,' says Belinda.

Why am I saying *first*? When did we agree that we were going to fuck? She looks back in her mind and realizes that she signalled her willingness the moment she closed the room door behind her. Even earlier, maybe. As long ago as early this morning, when she chose her underwear for the day with such care.

But I'm not willing. I don't want to do this. I owe Kenny nothing. He has no power over me. So why am I going to do it?

Because he's set the agenda from the start. Because he's friendly and means no harm. Because his giant erection is flattering, in its way. I mean, the guy's making an effort.

'Okay with me,' says Kenny. 'Let's check with Matey. You want to do some talky-talky, Matey?'

He holds his cock and makes it wiggle about in Belinda's hand.

'Bloody rubbish!' he says in his Matey voice. 'Get yer kit off!'

Then in his own voice, 'Now, now, Matey. Show respect for the ladies.'

'Show us yer tits!' says Matey.

'Sorry about this,' Kenny says to Belinda. 'Matey's not very sophisticated. But he's a good lad at heart.'

'Good at me job,' cried Matey. 'Satisfaction guaranteed or yer money back.'

'He's right there,' says Kenny.

'Satis-fuck-tion!' cries Matey. 'Satis-fuck-tion!'

'You're a comedian, Matey,' says Kenny.

It's a well-rehearsed act, presumably performed many times before. Belinda wants to laugh, both at Kenny and with him, but she also wants to maintain some last vestige of distance.

'I can see you two have done this before,' she says.

'Oh, yes,' says Kenny. 'But this is the gala performance.'

'I don't know that we should,' she says.

Kenny gives her a look that's puzzled and sweet at the same time. 'I've been waiting so long, gorgeous. Now you're here, it's a dream come true.'

'Is it, Kenny?'

This is the point of no return. Now is her last chance to make her excuses and leave. But what can she say? That he's grown old? That his humour isn't to her taste? That she doesn't find him attractive? He's crass and he has no understanding of her, but he wants her so much, which is a gift of a kind. And the plain fact of the matter is she finds she hasn't got it in her to disappoint him. His expression of desire has set the terms of their encounter. The appropriate response on her part can only be to satisfy his desire. For any other course of action she must generate what amounts to a counter-desire, she must show anger or disgust, she must hurt and humiliate him. Does he deserve that?

You make your bed, you have to lie on it.

'So how about you get your kit off?' he says.

'I'll undress in the bathroom,' she says.

The light in the bathroom is brutal. She avoids looking at herself in the mirror as she undresses. The pretty bra and knickers come off too. Kenny has ordained that they cut to the action. Naked among the white tiles Belinda feels herself shivering.

Hey, it won't take long. It's not like I haven't done it before.

'Kenny,' she calls through the closed door. 'Turn out the light.'

'Whatever you say, sunshine.'

The lamp clicks off in the bedroom. The bathroom light switch is on the outside of the door. She opens the door a crack and feels for it.

'Don't I get a look?'

She opens the bathroom door so that he can see her naked but in silhouette. She stands tall to lift her breasts, and pulls her tummy muscles in. Then she finds the light switch and plunges them into darkness.

As she lies down on the bed beside him he says, 'We've got all the time in the world, gorgeous. I took a little blue pill. Matey's good for hours.'

32

No one notices Cas leave the house, which is the way he wants it. It's Wednesday morning and his mum is out at work. Alan is in his study, Alice is in her room, and the man building the new bathroom is at the top of the house. Cas has not asked if it's okay to go out because then they'll want to know where he's going, and he means it to be a surprise.

Cas is going to visit his half-father Guy in London.

He's been planning the journey for days. He's wearing his camouflage coat, which is warm and waterproof and zips up to his chin. He's going to go by train. He's copied down Guy's address and phone number from the computer. Guy lives at 19 Windsor Street N1. Cas knows Guy will be pleased to see him, but more than that he'll be amazed that Cas has come all by himself. That's really what Cas is doing it for, that look of amazement on Guy's face. He's taking Roboguy with him in a Tesco carrier bag. He wants to show Guy the dance he can now make Roboguy do.

The station is close to where they live. He finds it without difficulty and goes through the swing doors into the ticket office. There's a long queue for tickets. Cas thinks that as a child he doesn't need a ticket, but just in case he's brought some money with him. He borrowed the money from his mum's purse. He has a ten pound note.

Into the ticket office comes a chattering laughing swarm of children accompanied by several adults. The children are older than Cas, but not much. There must be twenty of them at least. Cas watches them, wondering if they have to have tickets. One of them, a stocky girl in a pink tracksuit, sees him staring at her and puts her tongue out at him.

The grown-ups with them start to herd the children through the side gate. The station man holds the gate open for them. He doesn't ask to see any tickets. So Cas knows he's right and he doesn't need a ticket. He follows the children through the gate, and down the steps to the platform.

He doesn't need his ten pounds after all. He's pleased about that. He can put it back in Mum's purse and she'll never know.

There turn out to be several platforms. The crowd of children line up on the platform by the café. They want to go into the café but the grown-ups won't let them. They have to wait for the train to come.

Cas goes into the café because he's travelling on his own

and has no grown-up to stop him. He thinks he might spend some of his ten pounds there. He examines the cakes on display in the glass case on the counter. There's flapjacks and there's chocolate brownies. Behind the counter a man in a black apron is pouring tea and singing to himself. Cas likes brownies best, but only if they're gooey inside. Some brownies are dry inside, like ordinary cake. It's much the same with flapjacks. You don't want the hard kind, and you don't want the dusty kind. You want the chewy kind. These ones are all wrapped in clear plastic wrappings, and kept under a glass lid, so you can't even squeeze one to find out.

A train comes roaring into the platform.

'Does that train go to London?' Cas says to the man with the teapot.

'Certainly does, young man.'

Cas hurries outside and sees the herd of children getting onto the train. They must all be going to London too. No surprise there. That's where people go on trains.

He gets into the same carriage as them, but doesn't sit too close, because he doesn't like the girl in the pink tracksuit. His seat has a fold-down table in front. He folds it down and it makes a screamy noise. Hastily he folds it up again.

The train leaves the station. Outside the window the fields are grey and the winter trees are bare. For a while he can see the river where there are sometimes swans, but today there are no swans. A crowd of birds flies across the sky. Probably they're migrating. Cas holds the Tesco bag with Roboguy in it close to his chest and thinks about how surprised Guy will be when he sees him. 'You came all on your own?' he'll say. 'That's amazing.'

The train stops at a station, but you can easily tell it's not London because outside is all fields and white fences. London is all houses. Also the other children aren't getting off. They're making a lot of noise, kicking each other and laughing. Cas wonders what they're going to do in London. Go Christmas shopping, maybe. People do that in London.

Just the name itself excites Cas. London. You can tell from the name how big it is. Cas has never been there before. Mum goes there just about every day. Alan goes there. Alice lives there. Guy lives there. It's where everything important happens.

Guy's street, Windsor Street, is the same name the Queen has. It's the Queen's last name like Cas's last name is Strachan, though Alice's last name is Dickinson, like Mum's. It could have been Caulder, which is Guy's last name, since he's her dad. If Guy was Cas's dad he'd have called himself Cas Caulder. He asked Alice once if she'd rather be Alice Caulder but she said no.

He wants to pull the fold-out table down again so he can stand Roboguy on it and make him dance but he doesn't like the screamy noise the table makes. He feels hungry.

He wishes he'd bought a flapjack. When you're really hungry you don't care if it's chewy or not.

Outside the window there are buildings now. Big buildings. Now there's a big car park. It's huge.

The children are being made to get up and put their backpacks on. It must be London. Some of them are jumping up and down. They're excited. So Cas gets up. He's excited too.

The train stops and they all get out. Cas gets out too. He wishes he'd brought his backpack, it's annoying carrying the Tesco bag, it bangs against his knees. He follows the children down steps, along an underground tunnel, into a ticket hall. And then they all go out into the cold air of a street.

London is very big and strange. There are lots of taxis, and a road beyond where cars pass all the time, nose to tail. A bus is waiting for the children. They all get in, with their grown-ups, and the bus drives away.

Cas stands by the taxis and looks around. There are lots of ways to go. He wonders which way goes to Windsor Street. He wants to do it all himself so that Guy will be amazed, but it's more confusing than he expected. People keep pushing past him. Cars drive up, car doors open and close, cars go hurrying away. There's a flower shop and a sandwich shop and across the road a place that sells cars. He's got Guy's phone number, he can always call him. But that would spoil the surprise.

He decides to ask the lady in the flower shop.

'Please, do you know the way to Windsor Street?'

The lady has very thin hair, you can see her head skin through it. She's wrapping up some flowers for a man.

'Windsor Street? Can't say I do, dear.'

The man knows.

'It's off the Wivelsfield Road, isn't it? You go down Sussex Road into Wivelsfield Road, take the first – no, the second right, which is Edward Road, then you take a left into – Lord, I'll forget my own name next! What's it called? Vale Road. Left into Vale Road. The next left is Windsor Close.'

His flowers are ready and paid for. The lady is unimpressed.

'How's the little lad supposed to remember all that?'

'Windsor Close. You nearly had me there. Who needs SatNav, eh?'

He leaves the shop. The lady frowns down at Cas.

'It's a long way,' she says. 'Can't someone come and fetch you?'

'It's where my dad lives,' says Cas. 'My half-dad.'

'I should get him to come and fetch you.'

'It's supposed to be a surprise.'

The lady looks at Cas, squeezing her lips together, making the ends of her mouth go down.

'You got a phone number for your dad?'

'Yes.'

'Why don't I call him and tell him you're at the station?'

'But then it won't be a surprise.'

'Even so, love. You shouldn't be walking all the way down the Wivelsfield Road by yourself. And I can't leave the shop to come with you.'

'Well,' says Cas, 'I suppose at least I've come this far all on my own.'

He gives the lady Guy's phone number.

'What's your name, pet?'

'Cas.'

She calls the number. Cas listens intently but can only hear her end of the conversation.

'Hello?' she says. 'I've got a little lad here called Cas. He wants you to pick him up from the station.'

She listens to the voice on the phone. Cas doesn't like it that Guy is talking to the lady and not to him.

'There's only the one station,' the lady says to the phone.

Cas pulls at the lady's arm.

'Let me speak to him.'

The lady gives him the phone.

'Hello?' says Cas. 'Is that Guy?'

'Caspar,' says Guy's voice. 'What's going on? Where are you?'

'I've come to see you,' says Cas. 'I've got Roboguy. I can make him do a dance. I've come all by myself.'

'Where are you, Cas?'

'I'm in London. At the station.'

'Which station?'

'You know,' says Cas. 'The one the train goes to.'

'Let me have a word with that woman again.'

Cas gives the lady back the phone. The lady looks flustered.

'He's only a little lad,' she says. 'He's got himself into a muddle. He's in the flower shop by the taxi rank. Betty's Blooms. I'm Betty. He's in Haywards Heath.'

33

Alice has vowed to herself she will finish her short story before Christmas. She's started stories many times before but has never finished them. Something happens between the first rush of excitement when the story idea forms in her head, and the actual tapping of sentences onto the screen. It's like cresting a hill on a bicycle: the surge of speed at the start of the descent, so effortless, so purely powerful, then slower and slower until she rolls to the inevitable stand-still, all impetus spent. And there ahead, another hill to climb.

She thinks of Alan, pushing himself on, writing a screen-play he no longer believes in. How do you do it?

This is what it comes down to: I can only do things I want to do.

She feels ashamed of herself, but the shame fails to prod her into action. She stares at her laptop screen and she knows with absolute certainty that she will never finish her story. The impulse has gone. She's lost interest.

What is this fickle interest that lands now here, now there, and always moves on? Its will is stronger than her own. She has become its slave. How do other people, normal people, ever manage to do anything they don't feel like doing?

Partly it's the thing about being alone. You need other people to push you along. You need other people to talk it over with, someone to tell how useless you are, someone who says, Hey, you're not alone. But who? She doesn't want to interrupt Alan in his work, and her mother is out.

I could call Jack.

She dismisses the thought with a laugh. Jack wants Chloe to call him, not her. But then it strikes her that he may need someone to share his problems with as much as she does. The great thing about her and Jack is they know nothing's going to happen between them, which makes everything so much easier. It's like having a gay friend.

She needs a pretext for calling him, even so. She could tell him something about Chloe. Chloe remains the unlikely link between them.

So first she calls Chloe.

Chloe picks up right away. She's on a train.

'I expect I'll go into a tunnel any minute. Any more action your end? Has Jack called you?'

'Of course he hasn't called me. It's you he wants.'

'Tell him, no chance. Tell him I'm in love.'

'Are you?'

'Cra-a-azy in love. I'm so, so, so crazy about this man.'

'What man?'

'He's an older man. That's all I'm saying. Alice, find yourself a grown-up. Don't waste your time with boys.'

'Jesus, Chloe. You don't hang about. When did this happen?'

'I met him at the weekend. I'm on my way to him now. We're going to celebrate our hundredth-hour anniversary together this evening.'

'Wow! So who is he?'

'Total secret, babe. I could tell you but I'd have to kill you. Here it comes. Here comes the tunnel. Bye-eee!'

Chloe is swallowed up by the tunnel. Alice remains, alone in her silent room. The drama of Chloe's love life shines a cold bright light on her own passivity.

Why don't I go crazy over some man? Young, old, who cares?

Jack can forget his fantasy.

She catches the bitterness in her thought and is ashamed. Even so, she should tell him, shouldn't she? Every moment he spends pining for Chloe is a wasted moment. At least until Chloe's current passion has run its course.

She calls Jack. He's at home, alone in his room like her.

'It's about Chloe. I thought you should know. She's got some other guy.'

'Yes, I know. She's got a boyfriend in Exeter.'

'No, this is a new other guy. An older man.'

Jack goes quiet.

'It's all very new. She met him at the weekend.'

'When she wasn't meeting me.'

'Something like that.'

'Oh, hell.'

He sounds so miserable.

'I'm sorry,' Alice says.

'Back to staring at the wall.'

'Come over here. Stare at my wall.'

'Okay.'

As easy as that. No burden of expectation. They like each other's company. Why not?

Alice makes no attempt to go back to her story now. In her heart she knows she'll never complete it. But the space around her has stopped oppressing her. She's no longer becalmed. She's waiting. Jack's coming round.

She hears the steady pad-pad-pad of the builder passing shoeless up the stairs. She thinks maybe she'll go and talk to Cas. Then she thinks she'll make herself a cup of coffee. But in the end what she does is play some music and sit by the window looking out over the street and wait for Jack.

Cas sat by the window all day, waiting for Guy. When was that? Saturday. Could be five minutes ago, could be a century.

The odd thing is, waiting is okay. Alice doesn't feel impatient. She feels happier than she's been all morning. Nothing is happening, but in a little while something will happen. Jack will come. That brings with it no great change in her life. Nothing of any significance will improve. But for now the passing minutes have taken on a direction, and so she is released from passivity. It's like being on a train, gazing out of the window at the world going by.

Down in the street cars crawl past, jolting over the bumps placed on the road to slow them down. It's called traffic calming. An odd name, given that what it does is make the cars bounce up and down. Now a car has decided to pull into a parking space and all the others have to wait while it attempts the manoeuvre. Jack will have to park somewhere, most likely in the Priory car park. The parking tickets there are for half an hour, an hour, or two hours. Which one will he get?

Chloe's known her older man for a hundred hours, almost. Idly, Alice does the sums in her head. That's four twenty-fours and a few left over, and today is Wednesday. She must have met him on Saturday, after she came round to plot Operation Jack.

A man comes down the street carrying a Christmas tree sleeved in orange netting, its branches flattened to its trunk. Alan says he's going to get a Christmas tree but he keeps forgetting. Mum says she's been sick of Christmas since September, because of all the Christmas-themed articles she has to write. A day on a turkey farm. How we secretly love round-robin Christmas letters.

She listens to the music, the song is all about love gone wrong, about what you don't have, what's there for a moment and then it's gone, an electric frustration. Why can't anyone make it work?

Then there he is, coming up the street, hands in his pockets, head down, not knowing she sees him. Oh, Jack. She runs down the stairs and has the door open before he rings the bell.

They settle in the kitchen. They huddle round the kettle like hunters round the fire. She forages for biscuits and finds Rich Tea. Cas must have finished the cookies.

'Actually they're the best for dunking,' Jack says.

He smiles at her. His voice is soft, defeated.

'So who's this older man of Chloe's?' he says.

'She won't tell me. He's a secret. I expect he's married.'

'Oh, well.'

He dunks with care, balancing the biscuit as he carries it from the mug to his mouth.

'At least you've had a real love affair,' says Alice. 'Being broken-hearted is quite glamorous, really.'

'I'd rather be loved back.'

'Try option three. Not having anyone in the first place.'

'I've been there too.'

'I'm still there. It's like those board games where you have to throw a six to get started. Everyone else is off and running, but I'm still on the edge of the board trying to throw a bloody six.'

She watches him dunking. He leaves his biscuit in far longer than she does hers, but it never breaks.

'How do you do that?'

'Years of practice,' he says. 'Nerves of steel.'

'Mine falls off.'

'Keep it vertical as you take it out. Turning it horizontal subjects it to too much stress.'

She tries it his way.

'Hey! It works!'

'Don't tell everyone.'

'It's so soggy.'

'Melts in the mouth, right?'

For a few moments Alice concentrates on perfecting her dunking technique. As she does so she ponders the enigma of Chloe. How is it that someone as clever and interesting as Jack cares about someone as obvious as Chloe?

'So what is it about Chloe?' she says.

'What's what about Chloe?'

'Why do boys go for her? Why do you go for her?'

'Oh.' He looks uncomfortable. 'I don't know, really.'

'I mean, I know she's pretty and everything. But I mean, how does that work? Why does being pretty matter so much?'

'Christ, Alice, I've no idea. Maybe it's evolution.'

'But how? Why should our genes care about prettiness?

It's not as if it's got anything to do with survival, or fertility, or the things genes care about.'

'I suppose it's like flowers attracting bees.'

'Bees go to the boring flowers too.'

'Do they?'

'Animals don't only go for the pretty ones. If you're a dog any bitch will do so long as she's on heat.'

Jack blinks at that.

'Well, sorry. But it's true.'

'Even so,' says Jack. 'We're not dogs. Or bees. It's all much more complicated.'

'So tell me. Maybe I can learn something. God knows, I need to.'

Jack frowns, and dunks, and thinks.

'You're right,' he says. 'It is all very odd. I'm actually not all that interested in Chloe, but I really want … It's something physical.'

'Yes, Jack. It's called sex. But why her?'

Jack tries to work it out. She can see him interrogating his own responses.

'When you look at Chloe,' he says, 'you get this feeling she'd be good to kiss.' He looks up, suddenly concerned. 'Do you really want to hear this?'

'Yes, I absolutely do. Go on.'

'You feel like she wants to be kissed. And cuddled. You feel like she wants it.'

'How does she make you feel that?'

'It's how she looks at you. How her body is. I don't know. She just really makes you feel like – like – you know.'

'I can guess.'

He grins at her little ruefully.

'But how?' Alice persists. 'Just by being pretty?'

'Not exactly. More because she's ...'

Once again he runs out of words.

'Because she's up for it?'

'Maybe.'

'But it can't be that, Jack. If it was then any girl could get any boy just by being easy. And you know it doesn't work like that.'

'No. No.' He's still puzzling it out. 'I think it's about how Chloe makes you feel about yourself. You don't feel useless with Chloe. You feel quite good, actually. Like you're quite a guy.'

'Aha!'

'Aha what?'

'I bet that's it. I hadn't thought of that. She makes you feel manly. She's all girly-girly sexy, and that makes you feel manly. Boys like that, don't they? They worry a lot about how manly they are.'

'Do they?'

'You tell me.'

'Well, I do, it's true.'

'And you've got to feel manly to do it. I mean, you've

got to, haven't you? Or it doesn't work. So the more girly the girl is the more manly the boy feels, and that makes him want to do it with her.'

Jack doesn't deny this.

'I'll tell you what,' he says. 'You do really want to feel wanted. Not just because you're a nice guy. You want to feel physically wanted. Actually you can't really believe that would ever happen. But it's what you want.'

'Oh, Jack.'

'Am I talking bollocks?'

'No. It's just so exactly how a girl feels, too. Oh, God. Why does it all have to be so difficult?'

'There's something else, too. Something a bit rubbish.'

'Come on, then. We might as well go all the way.'

'You want your friends to fancy your girlfriend.'

'Why wouldn't you? What's so rubbish about that?'

'It's just that you want it quite a lot.'

'And that's all about looks.'

'Pretty much.'

'Though here's a question. Suppose there was a girl who was okay-looking, not gorgeous, not a dog. Suppose all your friends fancied her. Would that make you fancy her too?'

Jack nods slowly.

'I suppose Hannah was like that,' he says. 'She wasn't gorgeous.'

'She wasn't gorgeous but you fell in love with her.'

'She was beautiful. She wasn't gorgeous, but she was beautiful.'

Alice gazes at Jack in an awed silence.

'What?' he says.

'You loved her, so she became beautiful.'

A statement not a question.

'Yes.'

'Oh my God. So it's true.'

The phone rings, making them both jump.

'It's okay,' Alice says. 'Alan'll pick it up.'

'What's true?' says Jack.

'Oh, all that Keats stuff. You know. Beauty is truth and truth beauty. I bet Fanny Brawne wasn't gorgeous.'

Footsteps hammer down the stairs. Alan appears, looking panicky.

'Cas has run off!' he says. 'That was Guy on the phone. Cas called him. He's at Haywards Heath station.'

'What!'

'I'm going to jump on the next train.'

'But how? I don't understand.'

'Stay here, in case I miss them. Guy's on his way to Haywards Heath from London. Christ, Alice. He must have been gone for hours!'

Alan leaves at a run, pelting up Friars Walk to the station.

Alice is confused and frightened.

'What's he doing in Haywards Heath?'

Sudden panic overwhelms her. Anyone could take him.

He'd go with anyone. Please be safe, little Cas. What are you doing? Why didn't you tell me? I'd have come with you. Please be safe, darling.

Jack takes in the situation and speaks quietly, calmly.

'He's phoned Guy, so he's all right. Guy's on his way to pick him up. He'll be home in an hour.'

'I shouldn't have neglected him. It's all my fault. I'm so selfish. All I think about is my own stupid miseries. What's he doing in Haywards Heath?'

'Where does Guy live?'

'In London.'

'There you are. He was going to London. Like Dick Whittington. He probably took a red spotted handkerchief.'

'Oh, Cas. Oh, my darling little brother.'

She's starting to cry.

'He's having a wonderful adventure. He'll be just fine.'

'But Jack,' says Alice, now weeping freely, 'he's in Haywards Heath!'

She bursts into violent sobs. He takes her in his arms, as if she's a frightened child just woken from a bad dream. He rocks her gently in his arms.

'He's fine,' he murmurs. 'Cas is fine. He's having an adventure.'

She clings to him, her face on his shoulder, her tears wetting his T-shirt. Slowly her sobbing ceases. She starts to hiccup. She dries her eyes with her sleeve.

'Thank you,' she says.

The hiccups won't stop. She holds her breath and the trapped hiccup makes her chest jump.

'Are you okay now?' says Jack. 'I feel like I'm in the way. This is family stuff. I should go.'

'Please don't go. Not yet. Stay with me till they get back.'

Neither of them has any idea how long that will be. Jack has the sensible idea of looking up the train times. Alan will have caught the 12.19 that gets to Haywards Heath at 12.35. The first train back leaves Haywards Heath at 12.50 and gets to Lewes at 13.07. That leaves at least three-quarters of an hour before they can be home.

'I'll go crazy,' says Alice. 'I can't stand it.'

At least the hiccups have stopped.

'Let's watch a DVD,' says Jack.

'Watch a DVD? What are you talking about?'

'Come on. Where do you keep your DVDs?'

He goes into the living room and finds a mess of DVDs all round the television. He gets down on his knees and pushes them about.

'Here we are,' he says. '*Fawlty Towers*. Perfect.'

So they sit and watch *Fawlty Towers*, Alice with both the house cordless phone and her own mobile on her lap. She means to think about Cas all the time but when you're watching a screen you find it takes over your mind, and soon she's laughing and squirming as she always does at *Fawlty Towers*.

The phone rings. It's Alan. They've got Cas and they're on their way back, all three of them. Cas is fine.

Alice feels a deep flood of gratitude wash through her. For Cas being safe. For Jack being with her. For being able to laugh. She curls up on the sofa like a child, hugging her knees tight.

'I'm happy now. Remind me if I ever complain again. There is such a thing as happiness.'

They watch the rest of the episode, and half the next, until the wanderer returns.

Cas comes bouncing in through the door with a cheerful, 'Hello! I'm back!'

Alice seizes him in her arms and smothers him with kisses.

'Cas, darling, darling, darling! What a bad, bad boy!'

'I went to London,' says Cas. He's entirely unrepentant. All the attention has gone to his head. 'All by myself!'

'How am I going to tell Liz?' says Alan, following behind. 'She'll crucify me.'

'Don't tell her,' says Guy, coming in after Alan.

Jack makes himself useful. 'Tea? Coffee?'

'You don't have a beer, do you?' says Guy.

Jack finds a beer in the fridge. Cas is hungry and asks for Coco Pops. Alice sees to it.

'Not that you deserve it,' she says.

'We've given him the talking-to,' says Alan. 'Haven't we, Cas? You won't run off like that again.'

'No,' says Cas. 'I did it for a surprise.'

'Yes, well, we were all surprised.'

'Surprise isn't the half of it,' says Guy. 'I was in the middle of a client meeting.' He checks his watch. 'And I've got a date in town at six twenty-five.'

'What are you?' says Alan. 'A dentist?'

'It's an anniversary.'

'Guy, you have to see Roboguy dance,' says Cas, mouth brown with chocolate milk.

'Okay, buddy, but move it along. I have to be getting back.'

Cas jumps up to fetch his robot from the Tesco bag. Guy catches Alice's eye.

'This is my reward,' he says. 'They say no good deed ever goes unpunished.'

'What do you mean?' says Alice. It annoys her the way Guy has paid her no attention as usual.

'I bring Cas a present and my whole life gets turned upside down.'

Cas has Roboguy on the kitchen table now.

'Watch this.'

He makes the robot caper round the table. The sight is utterly ludicrous. Everyone laughs. At the end of the dance the robot and Cas bow together. Everyone claps.

'I'm off now, little buddy.'

Alice is wondering what Guy means by saying his whole life has been turned upside down. He has a date in town. An anniversary.

373

Then she gets it.

Guy is leaving. He makes his goodbyes. Shakes Cas by the hand.

'I'll walk up to the station with you,' says Alice.

Anger is building within her. She waits until they're out of earshot of the house.

'You and Chloe,' she says.

'What?'

'You're having a thing with Chloe.'

'So?'

No attempt to deny it. His usual smiling blue-eyed self.

'She's my age. It's disgusting. How can you do that? How can you?'

'She's grown up, Alice, and it's none of your fucking business, okay?'

Despite the swear word he speaks without rancour, with a kind of friendly reasonableness. Alice feels herself shaking with rage.

'You're sick!' she says. 'You're a sick old pervert! She's my friend, of course it's my fucking business! What the fuck do you think you're doing, waltzing into my house and getting off with my friends?'

'Ask your friend, don't ask me. She came on to me like a bloody heat-seeking missile.'

'So? Are you helpless? Couldn't you protect yourself?'

'Frankly, I don't see the problem here. We're talking about two consenting adults—'

'You're my father!'

They've reached the station forecourt. Taxis are lined up, their drivers chatting in a small cluster.

'What's that got to do with anything?'

'You're my father!' she screams.

She starts hitting him, more like pushes than blows. The taxi drivers look on. He doesn't resist.

'Steady,' he says. 'Steady.'

She runs out of anger. She starts to cry.

'You've got to let me have a life, babe,' he says.

'Yes. Okay. Have your fucking life.'

She turns and leaves him there. She walks fast, still crying, not looking back. She half expects him to come after her but he doesn't. So fine. He's got a date.

She means to sort herself out before she goes back into the house but Jack is outside in the street. He sees her tears.

'I didn't want to go without saying goodbye,' he says.

No point in pretending. Alice realizes she wants someone else to know.

'You know what the bastard's doing, don't you?'

'What?'

'He's fucking Chloe. He's Chloe's older man. My father.'

Jack looks down and says nothing.

'How can he do that? He wasn't even sorry. He's so sick he can't see anything wrong with it.'

'No. I suppose he wouldn't.'

'But you can, can't you, Jack?'

'I can see what's wrong with it for me. What's wrong is I wish it was me, not him.' Then, after a pause, 'And I can see what's wrong with it for you. You wish it was you, not Chloe.'

Like a slap in the face. She stares at him.

'Are you saying I want my father to fuck me?'

'No. You want him to love you.'

Alice feels her legs go weak beneath her. She slips down until she's sitting on the pavement, her back to the house wall. The flagstones are winter-cold. Her hands have gone cold too.

He's right. Of course he's right. All childishly obvious when you think about it. That's what your dad is for, to tell you how pretty you look, to be proud of you, to make you feel like you're the girl the boys desire. Guy was always a rubbish dad. But then, it was never his idea in the first place.

She pulls out her phone, calls his mobile. He'll be on the train somewhere. Probably near Haywards Heath.

'Dad,' she says. 'Sorry.'

'Oh, sweetheart. I feel terrible.'

'No, I was wrong. You know what it is? I was jealous of Chloe. That's all. It's not incest or anything, don't worry. I just sometimes wish so much I was your girl.'

Silence on the other end. Then:

'You are my girl, babe.'

'Okay. Thanks.'

She knows he doesn't mean it. But at least he said it. Then his faraway voice on the phone.

'Listen, sweetheart. This isn't the moment, et cetera. But if I've not been up to much as a dad it's not because I don't love you. I have a whole mountain of guilt about Liz and you, to tell the truth. Maybe one day I'll get out from under it. Then I'll really show you how much I love you.'

'Oh, Dad. Please. Don't.' She's crying again.

'Sweetheart? Tunnel coming up. Don't give up on me. You're my girl. My only girl.'

And he's gone into his tunnel. But it's enough. It's good.

She looks up. There's Jack, hopping from foot to foot, getting cold.

'Jack,' she says. 'You're amazing.'

'Am I?' He sounds surprised.

'Can I bottle you and keep you in the cupboard for emergencies?'

'Aren't you cold? I'm frozen.'

'Yes. I can't feel my fingers any more.'

'So we should get out of this wind.'

They go back into the house. Alan and Cas are sitting at the kitchen table looking for names for dogs. Alan has printed out a list from the Internet of top dogs' names as compiled by an American pet insurance company. Max is number one, followed by Buddy.

'Wuffles,' proposes Cas.

'Too wuffly,' says Alan.

'Gruffles.'

'It's got to be friendly but strong,' says Alan. 'He's the hero of the movie.'

'Superwuffles,' says Alice.

Jack looks at the printout. He's affronted to find his own name comes at number twenty on the list.

'Jack's not a dog's name.'

'I can't call him Rocky,' says Alan. 'That's been done.'

'Snuffles,' says Cas.

'Cody? Rusty? Murphy?'

'Murphy's good,' says Jack. 'Shades of Beckett.'

'I don't think I want shades of Beckett. This is a talking sheepdog who turns out to be a financial wizard.'

'Oh, okay,' says Jack. 'Call him Rockefeller.'

Alan is startled.

'That's genius!' he says. 'Rockefeller! I'd go and see a movie called *Rockefeller*. Jack, you have christened a new franchise. I expect to be at work on *Rockefeller 7* while in my old folks' home.'

'See,' says Alice to Jack. 'I told you you're amazing.'

34

Anthony Armitage lays down his brush and takes a step back from the easel. He gazes on the painting with intense concentration for a few moments. Then he gives a slow shrug of his shoulders and turns away, as if disowning it. He fumbles round in a shadowy corner of the room, pouring himself a whisky into a handleless mug. He takes a drink of the whisky and looks back once more at the painting, this time with a gaze of fear and loathing.

'Fucked up again,' he says.

Carrie, sitting patiently in the chair by the window, does not take this performance too seriously. In the four sittings she's endured, such displays of high emotion have been commonplace. His relationship to his own work is that of a lover. He adores the canvas, and lavishes it with his obsessive attention. He pleads with it, and is wounded by its indifference. He spurns it, and rejects it, and sits in a corner and sulks.

This time, however, there is a new development. He

379

starts to pack away his tubes of paint and his brushes. He says nothing to her. This too she has become used to. In a sense she has ceased to exist for him, her reality transferred to the canvas.

'Have you stopped?' she says.

'Can't do any more,' he replies. 'I'm finished.'

He doesn't say, It's finished. He says, I'm finished. He sounds infinitely weary.

'So can I see it now?'

'If you like. See it. Take it away. Burn it.'

He pours himself more whisky.

Carrie gets up and goes to look at the painting: the portrait of her, who the artist has called beautiful.

The girl in the painting is not her, and is not beautiful.

'But that's not me,' she exclaims in surprise.

'There you are,' he says. 'Missed again.'

'Who is it?'

'Does it matter? I suppose I've wasted a few hours of your time. Sorry about that. But you're young. You're rich in time. You can afford it.'

Carrie goes on gazing at the portrait. She can see that in certain external details it does represent her. There's the navy blue top that he first saw her in, that he insisted she wore to every sitting. The hair is pulled back into a scruffy ponytail, as hers is. The chair, though only roughly sketched, is the chair in which she has been sitting; the window beside her is oddly bright in what is otherwise a muted dark-toned canvas, but it is recognizably the same window. But the girl at the centre of it all – a woman, not a girl – is so old, so sad, and so … so something else, something unknown that she can't quite define. It looks distantly like the face she sees in a mirror, but like a self that has been aged and harrowed. And the eyes! The eyes are shining with what could be tears and could be a wild abandoned anger. Yes, of course: that's what it is. The woman in the portrait is consumed with anger. She's defeated, pale with the loss, but she's angry.

Carrie looks from the painting to the old man and back again. He's painted himself, she thinks. He's put all his own feelings into my face.

'It's you,' she says. 'It's not me, it's you.'

'That's how it works,' he says. 'Didn't you know?'

'No. I don't understand.'

'All great artists do it. Even shit artists like me do it. You paint what you see and what you feel. I can see you but I can't feel what you feel, I can only feel what I feel. So I latch on to the little clues I get from your face that take me to my own feelings. Perfectly simple, really.'

'But then it's not me and it's not you.'

'It's a portrait, child. It's what was once called art.'

'But who's it a portrait of?'

'I don't know. Does it matter? It's a portrait of suffering humanity. One in a long, long line.'

Carrie looks at it again. She stops trying to see how it

resembles her. She looks at it as if it's nothing to do with her. That's when she sees how magnificent it is. That bleak stripped-down angry face is shockingly powerful.

'Well, whoever it is, it's wonderful,' she says.

'It's shit.'

'Don't say that! Why do you say that?'

'It's not got close. I thought I might get there. One last shot. But I've missed it. Missed again.'

'Missed what?'

'Oh, Christ, you know. It. How it is.'

The odd thing is that Carrie does know. She knows what he means by *it* even though she couldn't explain it. But she also knows he's wrong.

'You haven't missed it,' she says. 'You've got it. It's here.'

She looks at the painting again. It's so raw it hurts.

Of course it's me, she thinks then.

That's scary. But not all bad. The woman in the painting isn't beautiful but she's no victim. She's not feeling sorry for herself. She's trying to hold it back, but she's bursting out with her own power. Look at those eyes!

'You like it?' he says. 'Have it.'

'I don't know whether I like it or not,' she says. 'It scares me.'

'Scares me too.'

'You kept on telling me I was beautiful. She's not beautiful.'

'What!' He roars out his astonished, outraged refutation.

'Not beautiful! She burns with beauty! She's the eternal breaker of hearts!'

So Carrie looks again. Every time she looks the portrait has changed. This time the woman in the portrait has become beautiful. It's just not the kind of beauty that anything in Carrie's life has prepared her for. That haunted face is neither pretty nor glamorous. It's mesmerizing. Her power lies in her refusal to please. She stares out of the canvas, challenging you, defying you to want her to be other than she is. Yes, I'm unhappy, she says. Yes, I'm in pain. So what? I'm alive and I'm who I am and you can all go fuck yourselves.

That's one hell of a way to be beautiful.

'Can I really have it?'

'Take it.'

He's been watching her closely, she now realizes. Tracking the changes in her response to the painting.

'You don't want it for your show?'

'I'd rather you had it.'

Now he's smiling at her.

'You're not just beautiful,' he says. 'You have innocent eyes. I didn't think I'd ever find such a thing again.'

'I don't think I want to have innocent eyes.'

'Yes, you do. For you the joy of seeing all things freshmade. We live in an age of visual debauchery. The eyes are glutted and dulled by a ceaseless barrage of images. Seeing so much, so often, they see nothing. A world gone blind.

So no one believes what they see any more. They wait to be told.' He mimics imaginary voices in a comic pleading whine. 'What am I seeing? Is it good? Do I admire it? How much is it worth? Will it make me look smart if I hang it on my wall?'

He points a paint-stained finger at her.

'But you – you see with your own eyes. Thank you. Thank you. In our end is our beginning.'

He takes another pull from his mug.

'So what do I do?' she says. 'Just carry it home like that?'

'Just carry it home. Frighten the family.'

She laughs.

'Why can't I come to your show? I'd really like to.'

'My show is for the professionals. You, thank God, are not a professional. But you can have a preview if you want.'

'I'd really like that.'

He creaks to his feet.

'Remember the crockery smashing?' he says.

'Yes.'

'He smashed up his own art.'

'Who did?'

'Joe. The boy who made it.'

He points to a newspaper on the table. It's folded open to a picture of the Hayward Gallery: a heap of broken fragments, a crowd standing round. ARTIST DESTROYS OWN INSTALLATION, says the headline.

'I don't understand.'

'He smashed it up, and they're still coming to see it. Even more than before. Sharp as a tack, that boy.'

'Why would anyone want to see a smashed-up table?'

'Ghouls,' says the old man. 'They feed on pain, and destruction, and death.'

'Well, I don't.'

'Come on, then. We've lost the daylight now. We'll have to take a torch.'

He picks up his torch and shuffles laboriously out to the barn. Carrie follows, thinking how awkwardly he walks. As if just walking hurts. The outside world is bitterly cold.

He leaves the barn door open. Inside the barn it's as cold as outside. For a moment he stands there with her, not switching on the torch, letting her sense the space. She can make out the shapes of the paintings on the walls, and the beams and rafters that frame the barn roof, and the old armchair she helped to bring out.

'Twilight,' he says. 'Between light and dark. Good for seeing.'

She sits in the armchair.

'So you'll sit here, won't you?' she says. 'Like a king on a throne.'

'Like a king on a throne, yes.'

'And they'll all look at your paintings and tell you how wonderful they are.'

'No doubt the usual lies will be told.'

He turns on his torch and lights up one of the paintings.

The face of his one-time wife, Nell. Then the circle of light moves on to another painting. The face of an ugly laughing man. In this way he shows his works to Carrie like magic lantern slides.

She finds her view of his painting has changed. The process of looking and re-looking at her own portrait has sensitized her gaze. She is deeply moved. Everything he paints seems to her to reveal men and women in a new light: more real, more truthful, and above all, more beautiful. Painting after painting, his life's work, passes before her eyes.

She speaks this simple discovery aloud.

'You make everyone look beautiful.'

He says nothing. She can't see his face in the twilight.

'This is what you've been doing all your life.'

'Yes,' he says. He coughs a little as he speaks. 'How to waste a life, eh?'

'No,' she says. 'This is just great. Your life's been great.'

Poor words, she knows, but her own life so far has supplied her with too few words. Something else she never knew till now.

'It's not been a bad life,' he says. 'But then you get old.'

'Yes,' she says. 'Bummer.'

'Remember that, child.' He coughs again, a series of little choky sounds. 'I can take all the rest of the shit. The failure, the hypocrisy, the self-doubt, the posturing of fools. But in the end it's getting old that fucks you. No escaping that one.'

They go back into the cottage. He lights a lamp, and by its glow he searches out a plastic bag to put the portrait in, so she can carry it home.

'Is it worth a lot?' she says.

'Millions,' he says.

'It's the best present anyone's ever given me.'

He gives his dismissive shrug.

'Paint's still wet,' he says.

'I'll come back after your show's finished,' she says. 'Help you get the chair back into the house. I know the show'll be a huge success. You'll be so proud. So will I.'

'The show doesn't matter,' he says. 'I'm glad you like the portrait. It's not what I wanted it to be, but then, nothing ever is.'

She goes out into the cold once more, clutching the canvas in its plastic bag. One look back to wave. He's standing in the doorway, framed by the triangle of lamplight, his hair awry, one hand raised as if in blessing. She sees the scene as he might paint it, noting the way the low angle of the light turns the uneven plasterwork of the wall behind him into a moonscape of mountains and craters. And the way his face is dark but his white hair and beard have an aureole of amber light. And his shadow falling onto the overgrown path to the gate.

'Bye,' she calls, and plunges into the darkness of the coach road that leads home.

35

Third time up to London in three days which is kind of insane but Chloe can't keep away. Guy isn't exactly complaining. What the hell. It's Christmas, isn't it? Santa Claus brings gifts for all the little boys and girls who've been good, and as for the ones who've been bad, they have to have something to pass the time. Chloe's new toy is Guy, or maybe she's his new toy, who's counting?

She tip-taps down Oxford Street in her high heels as she's done for the last three days and the crowds on the pavement don't bother her. She looks through them and they part before her, in her Ralph Lauren blazer and her short flirty skirt and black tights. Guy says no jeans. Actually he says no tights as well but this is December and it's fucking freezing so give me a break. Not that she has to do as he asks about her dress, but here's the slightly creepy truth, she wants to. She loves the way he tells her what to look like when she meets him. She loves the way he orders her to be more sparing with her lipgloss, her eyeshadow, her perfume. 'You're not a tart, Chloe. If you were a tart I'd be paying you.' Not that any of it comes out as orders, more like idle remarks, let drop with that twist of a smile of his that says, Oh, really?

Chloe adores him. She worships him. She'll do whatever he asks of her and only wishes he'd ask for more. She wants her body to make him wild with desire because then she too, like a flame lit by a flame, burns with a passion she's never felt before. She shouts during sex, which is a first. She says things like, 'I want to be your slave.' It's all so ridiculously primitive but hey, it works. Don't knock it.

So she arrives at the corner of Rathbone Place and Percy Street. Here there is an iron staircase that leads down to a basement bar beneath a newsagent. The bar is called Bourne and Hollingsworth. He took her here for a drink on their second date, all of twenty-four hours ago. Her plan is so to arrange matters that he fucks her once every twenty-four hours. That way he won't have the desire or the energy to fuck anyone else.

The bar is a small square room with a parquet floor and floral wallpaper. A few tables covered in white tablecloths line two of the walls. The wooden upright chairs are all different, as if recovered from skips. There are candles in teacups on the tables. The fireplace is full of empty bottles of Mumm champagne. All this is a conscious ironic retro look, designed to call to mind perhaps a 1950s tea room, though the crowd who gather here do not drink tea.

Chloe heads for the corner table where she and Guy sat yesterday and orders herself the same drink he bought her yesterday, a cocktail called Re-bourne. She has a little time to herself before Guy joins her. They are here to celebrate their hundredth-hour anniversary, which they have agreed will occur at 6.25 p.m.

He'll be late, of course. He was there before her on their first date, but has since made clear that was exceptional. I'll be there when I can, he says. Expect me when you see me.

So he has other concerns that take priority over seeing her. This too thrills Chloe. It makes her crave his presence and value every minute. How does he get away with it? He's a good-looking man but there are plenty of others who are more her style. You wouldn't accuse Guy of being cool. He dresses like James Stewart in some black-and-white movie, only without the tie. She'd thought of buying him a tie for Christmas, but in the end she's bought him a key ring with an enamel cupcake on a chain. God knows why. It was cheap and the cupcake looked indulgent.

Her cocktail comes and she starts drinking it, sharp and zingy and big on the gin. Her phone shivers. It's Hal.

'Hi, Hal,' she says, unable to keep the impatience from her voice. 'Can't talk right now.'

He wants to know what she wants for Christmas. What's she supposed to say to that? Everything. Anything. Don't make me do the work of pleasing myself. Be like Guy. He gives me nothing.

'You okay?' says Hal. 'You sound weird.'

'I'm in a basement bar, okay?'

'Why? Who are you with?'

'I'm with whoever I fucking feel like being with, Hal. Don't hassle me like this. I don't like it. Now I've got to go. Look after yourself.'

She ends the call dead on 6.25 p.m., but no sign of Guy coming down the iron steps from the street. She wouldn't mind a quick pee but she doesn't want Guy to show up and find her not there.

I'm hooked on this man. He's my drug of choice. Fuck knows why. He's a selfish bastard who only ever does what the fuck he likes, and right now what he likes to do is me.

There's the liberation. Chloe feels set free, floating, flying. She has no responsibility for anything. She's the object of his delight. His desire for her is like a warm wind. Hal wants her too, but his is a needy grasping want, he drags her down until all she can do is push him away. No need to push Guy away. Let him out of your sight for a minute and he's gone. All the advantages of having an affair with a married man and it isn't even adultery.

Then there's the sex. Maybe that's all there is to it in the end, but that's okay. It's enough to be going on with. Never like this before. Never before the electric shock of command. Takes an older man to know how to do it. She does everything he asks, and the more she does, the more turned on she gets.

He's late. The bastard is late. My beautiful bastard.

She gets out the key ring with the cupcake and puts it on the white tablecloth before her. Some other people in the bar now, two boys and two girls, all skinny jeans and tiny tops, you can hardly tell them apart. Whose idea was this place? The flowery wallpaper and the teacups and the boy-girls drinking bourbon and tequila.

The bar is a long hatch in the wall, its counter decorated with a vase of lilies. On the street side there's a high wide window through which you can see the hard diagonal of the iron staircase. What kind of flowers are they on the wallpaper? White, cabbagey, bigger than roses. The teacup has flowers on it too. She looks underneath and it's Lady's Slipper, Royal Stafford Ware. What was all that about men drinking champagne out of a lady's slipper?

Suddenly he's there. He's dropping down beside her, giving her a peck on the cheek, ordering himself an Asahi beer.

'Sorry,' he says. 'Nightmare day. Something came up and I lost half the day and I still haven't caught up.'

'Poor baby,' she says, gently mocking. She puts one hand lightly on his thigh. He looks away.

'I can't stay long,' he says. 'I'm going to have to pull an all-nighter.'

'No time for little me?'

'Sorry, babe.'

She strokes his thigh, letting her hand creep round to his crotch.

'I'm sure you can spare half an hour.'

'Not tonight,' he says. 'One beer and I'm gone.'

Chloe withdraws her hand. She doesn't understand. He's not connecting with her the way he has done on their previous dates. He's not even looking at her. Something is wrong.

His beer comes. He drinks from the bottle.

'So did you get any Christmas shopping done?' he says.

'No.' What's this, small talk? 'I've decided to give Christmas a miss this year.'

'Oh? Why's that?'

'Does it matter? Do you care about Christmas?'

'Not really. Not my scene.'

Do you care about me?

'What is your scene, Guy?'

'I don't think I have a scene,' he says. 'In the great drama of life I haven't been assigned a role. I look on from the wings.'

What the fuck's that all about?

'What is it?' she says. 'What's got to you?'

'You don't want to know,' he says.

'Maybe I can help.'

'No, babe. You can't help.' He looks at her at last, but it's a look she's not seen before. It turns her cold inside. 'We had some fun, right? Let's leave it at that.'

'What do you mean, leave it at that?'

'Quit while we're ahead.'

'Quit?'

This makes no sense to her. Is she being dumped?

'What's the problem? You like being with me, don't you?'

'You know I do. But I'm the wrong guy for you, babe. I'm too old and too selfish.'

'So maybe I like selfish old men. That's up to me, isn't it?'

She feels herself trembling. Why is he doing this? Has he met someone else?

'No,' he says. 'It's up to me, too. It takes two.'

'Have you found someone else?'

'Someone else? Christ, no. When would I have the time?'

'Have you got bored with me?'

'No, of course not.'

'So why talk about ending it? I'm not asking for any more than you want to give, am I? I don't care if all you want is sex. That's fine with me. It's great sex. Bring it on.'

He looks at her with that faraway look that so frightens her.

'I'm wrong for you, Chloe. You know it.'

'I do not know it! Don't tell me what's right and wrong for me. I don't want to be protected. I want to be fucked.'

'You want a lover.'

'So be my lover.'

'That's the thing. I'm not a lover. I don't do love.'

'I don't care.'

'You will.'

'Don't keep saying that!'

She wants to scream, to hit him. She wants to burst into tears. The foursome at the other table are listening openly. Everything has turned horrible.

'What do I have to do to make you believe me?'

'Not care about what I'm saying,' he says.

There's the trap. If all she wants is sex, why not let him go? The world's full of boys only too ready to oblige.

But I don't want love. He's wrong about that. I don't want love, I want him. That's not love.

'Of course I care,' she says. 'I want to see you again.'

'I think we shouldn't do that.'

'Not see each other again? Why?'

It comes out of her as a howl of pain. What happened to making no demands? Turns out it's easy not to be needy when he's all over you. Then his hands go back in his pockets and the needs shoot up like weeds. Like bindweed. Christ, I'd bind him to me if I could.

Oh my beautiful lover don't leave me.

'I'm no good for you, Chloe. And that means the more time I spend with you, the more damage I do. And I don't want to do any more damage than I have to.'

'What damage? There isn't any damage. You teach me, you make me grow up, you give me pleasure. That's not damage. I should know, shouldn't I? Where's the damage?'

'That's just the way it looks to me, okay?'

Now she's actually for-real crying. The whole pity-me tears thing. It's humiliating. She doesn't want to. All it does is make him think he's right. Her mind is saying, Fine, if you want out then, *sayonara*, honey. Her mind is saying, Look at me, I'm dancing. But her heart is blubbing its eyes out.

The boy-girls are watching and smirking and whispering to each other. The bar has become hateful, with its faux-cosy décor and its tea-lights. Unable to bear it a moment longer, she jumps up, grabs her coat, and heads for the stairs. He can come if he wants.

Out in the ice-cold air of the street she stamps her high-heeled feet to keep warm and waits for him to follow her. Which he does. She takes his hands and gazes at him with moist and wounded eyes.

'So you don't want to see me again? Is that it?'

'That's it,' he says. His voice is gentle, but there's no apology, no possibility of appeal.

'This is so stupid. You know that.'

'I should never have let it happen in the first place.'

'You? What about me? You don't control the fucking master switch. I'm in this too.'

But he does control the master switch. Her heart is breaking. How is that possible? A selfish bastard, and her heart is breaking.

'We had a bit of fun together. Don't hate me for that.'

Don't love me for that. That's the message.

Summoning the very last of her failing strength, Chloe puts on a smile. Go down guns blazing.

'Okay, big boy. Call me if you change your mind. But I may not answer.'

She gives him a kiss on the cheek and she walks away. She walks as fast as she can because it's cold and she doesn't want to look back. But then at last she does look back. He's already gone.

So that's it.

Now she lets herself cry. She walks back down Oxford Street weeping helplessly, raging helplessly, wounded as she's never been before, hurting for love.

But I never asked for anything. It's not like I wanted to marry him, for fuck's sake.

She remembers the Christmas present she got him, the cupcake on the key ring. She forgot to pick it up. It'll still be on the white tablecloth in the bar.

I bought him a ring.

Oh, fuck. Of course I love him. Of course I want to stay with him for ever. That's what love is, right? So what if there's some damage along the way. I want the love, I'll take the damage. There's no one else. Only you. What am I supposed to do now?

The lights of Oxford Street hurt her eyes with their cold cheer. Crowds block the lonely pavements. People bunch at street crossings and surge forward again, meshing without contact. She walks on the kerb. She doesn't want to be one of them, the lumpy bodies with their sightless eyes.

I'm young. I want to live. You love or you die. Hold me in your arms, I'm not asking for too much. Only life.

36

A road of tidy red-brick semis, fitfully illuminated by street lamps. Cars parked nose to tail along the kerb. Lit windows restless with the jumpy glow of television screens.

Meg drives slowly, looking for house numbers on gates and doors, failing to find or to read a single one. Then she sees the red pick-up that the plumber drives, and so locates his house, Number 45.

Strange to be paying a social call on her plumber, but life has become strange. Or gone back to the way it was: exile once more. The day she learned her brother was leaving their shared room. The night when there came no answering whisper to her whisper.

Grateful for the chance to be somewhere new, to get out of her flat. Two nights sleepless in the bed where once—

Her mind has learned to flinch. Turn away from that memory. Closer than a memory: the pain with her every moment of the day, cold as winter air. And waiting beyond the pain the deeper darkness, a night sky of fear without end.

Alone for ever. Alone for ever.

Not too proud then to accept the plumber's invitation. No, no pride. At work she keeps her eyes averted, not wanting to see the pity in their eyes. She takes her lunch alone.

There is no one in all the world who needs me.

She finds a space at last where she can park, some way from Matt's house. Out on the pavement she pulls her coat tight round her, a dark red knee-length wool coat from Hobbs. She bought it the day Tom said they might go to Paris, she thinks of it as her smart coat. And here she is, wearing it to call on a plumber who lives on the Neville estate.

But the thought of Matt Early is comforting to her. His quietness and tidiness in doing his work; his modesty, the way he looks down at the ground, his soft-spoken voice; his air of authenticity, that he is what he is; and lastly a quality in him she guesses at, but which she is sure he possesses, which she wants to call goodness. Meg hungers for goodness. All the pain she feels over Tom has turned inwards and is lacerating her with self-punishment. She blames herself entirely. She allowed herself to believe a lie, and it's the lie that hurts far more than the sexual transgression. She allowed herself to believe that Tom wanted her – no call to use the word 'love', no place for the word 'love' – when all he wanted was 'it'. She feels tarnished by the lie, dirtied by it. She has no one she can tell. Nor does she want to tell. She has no appetite for wails of female solidarity, Oh men are all the same, men are only ever after one thing. She entered on the affair with her eyes open, she was not deceived by Tom. She was deceived by herself.

A little low gate leads into a paved path across a neatly maintained front garden. Curtains drawn in the lit front room. A front door with a panel of frosted glass. She rings the bell.

Matt is a good man, and he plays the violin. In his presence she will be clean again. He has sought her company, and she is grateful. All here is ordinary, all is decent.

The door opens and there he is, blinking a little, as if roused from sleep. The sounds of a television. She can tell from his face that he had not been sure she would come, and is a little amazed to see her.

'Come in, come in,' he says. 'So you found us all right?'

'Yes. No problem.'

'My mother is watching TV. She doesn't get about so well. I have to look after her a bit.'

He leads Meg into the lounge. Here a small red-haired woman is sitting in a large armchair with a rug over her lap and a supper tray on the table by her side, watching *Emmerdale*. She turns her eyes from the screen to give Meg a look of close appraisal.

'Mum, this is Meg. She's come to see my violins.'

'Nice to meet you, I'm sure,' says Mrs Early. 'So you like violins?'

'I like music,' says Meg.

'Music, is it?' says Mrs Early, as if she isn't fooled for one moment by Meg's fabrications.

'We'll leave you to your TV,' says Matt, beckoning Meg to follow him.

'Yes, I expect you will,' says Mrs Early.

Matt goes through the kitchen and out the back door. Meg follows.

'Best to leave her alone,' he says apologetically. 'She's not used to company.'

'Does she have health problems?' says Meg. Something about the rug puts her in mind of patients in hospitals.

'She's got a spot of arthritis. But she's got too much time and not enough to do, if you really want to know.'

He crosses the back garden to a large shed. He takes out a key and unlocks the door.

'Best to keep your coat on. I've got an electric radiator out here, but I don't keep the place all that warm.'

He switches on lights. The shed is big and crowded, but in a neat and orderly way. Every inch of wall space has its shelf or rack or hook, holding instruments, tools, and materials for the making of violins. The violins themselves lie on pegs, row upon row, reaching up to the ceiling.

'Heavens!' exclaims Meg. 'How many violins did you say you have?'

'About forty,' says Matt. 'But most of them are waiting to be restored.'

'Can some of them be played?'

'One or two.'

He takes one down from the rack, and reaches for a bow.

'This one's my favourite because it's the first one I ever restored. I bought it for five pounds. I've kept it ever since.'

He runs the bow over the strings, his head cocked to one side to hold the violin in place. The strings sing.

'The end block and the end ribs were out of alignment. I re-bushed the peg holes and fitted new pegs.'

He plays a few soft sweet notes.

'I was ten years old.'

Meg is captivated. Matt has become lighter and surer, he smiles as he handles the violin. He knows exactly what to do, she thinks. He has perfect touch.

'That is so incredible,' she says. 'You were only a boy!'

'I grew up with fiddles. My dad played the fiddle. Just for his own pleasure, nothing special. But he'd play at barn dances and the like. Mum used to say she was a fiddle widow.'

'Your dad's dead, then?'

'Yes. Dad left us, oh, ten years ago now.'

He plays a light tune on the violin, one she recognizes but can't name.

'What's that?'

'Bobby Shafto.'

'So do you play at barn dances?'

'No, I don't do any of that.'

He says it as if it's self-evident that such a venture is beyond his capabilities.

'Mostly I just pick up damaged instruments and work on them.'

He puts away the violin he's been playing and shows her examples of his work.

'Like this one here. The front has split. That's the most common damage you get. I take the front off and reglue it, then varnish and polish. You'd never know it had been broken. See this? It's a Jesse Dennis, made in the 1820s. I picked it up at a car boot sale in Brighton, I gave him £40 cash for it, only a year or so ago. By the time I'm done with it that'll be a valuable instrument.'

'Will you sell it?'

'Most likely send it up to Bonham's for auction.'

Meg looks round the shed and pictures Matt at work here evening after evening, all on his own. There's a kettle, a water keg, a radio, an electric heater. A kitchen chair. A stack of newspapers. It's a little world in here.

'You must miss your dad,' she says.

'Yes.'

He's looking down at the floor. Without a word, without any special expression on his face, she can still pick up how much he misses his father. There's a delicacy about him that she respects.

An electric bell buzzes sharply, two buzzes.

'That's Mum,' he says.

'Does it mean she wants you?'

'Yes.'

He makes no move to leave the shed. Instead he takes down another of his violins, rests it on his shoulder, and starts to tune the strings.

'Don't mind about me. If you need to go to her.'

'She can wait.'

He completes the tuning.

'This is Handel.'

He launches into a skipping, leaping tune that turns teasing and lyrical as he plays on. He plays with a slight frown on his face, swaying his body to the movements of his bow-arm. The sound is powerful, rich, inspirational. Listening to it Meg feels that even she, defiled as she is, can be cleansed and redeemed.

When Matt plays the violin he is no longer a big slow awkward man, lumbering through her flat in his socks. He becomes sure and graceful. The music flows from him as if it's the pure expression of his spirit.

The bell rings again. He stops playing.

'She won't let me alone,' he says. 'I'd better go to her. You stay here. I won't be long.'

He leaves her in the shed.

Meg sits on the only chair and waits for his return. As she waits she thinks about him, and how easy she finds it to be with him. It's because he's so unassertive, maybe. You don't have to be any kind of person with him to feel you're … what?

To feel he approves of you. To feel he likes you.

So do I want him to like me?

All at once she confronts the obvious simple fact that has been present throughout, the fact that more than any other makes her feel at ease in his company: Matt is courting her.

She doesn't know how else to express it. She could say: he loves me and wants me to love him; but the claim is too great. This is a tentative process. A courtship. Extraordinary as it seems, she is quite sure she's right. It's not so much what he says or does as the feeling he gives her about herself. He makes her feel approved.

This changes everything. Ridiculously she finds she now feels nervous. What is there to be afraid of? And yet when he returns to the shed she knows she'll blush and not be able to look him in the eye. She's never been able to flirt. The thought that some form of modest flirting might be appropriate paralyses her.

What she needs now is to be in his company while other things are going on. Alone together is frightening. She fears her own social incompetence, she knows that under pressure she'll freeze up. Better to be with him among other people.

So I want to be with him, then?

Oh, yes. Oh, yes. No doubt about that. This good man's

admiration and respect is what she craves. His strong arm can pull her up out of the pit into which she has fallen. How wonderful, how providential, that he should enter her life on the same day that Tom left it.

Still not back from seeing to his old mother. Maybe she's had a fall. Maybe it's an emergency and Matt can't leave her until an ambulance comes. Better to join them in the house. At least that way they won't be alone together.

Odd how now that I think of him that way I don't want to be alone with him.

She turns off the electric heater and finds the light switch, turning off the lights as she pulls the shed door shut behind her. The glow from the kitchen window throws a long beam across the garden, guiding her to the back door. The door is ajar.

As she comes close she hears raised voices from within. Matt is shouting at his mother.

'You don't know anything!' he's shouting. 'I'm not listening to you because you don't know anything!'

'What's she doing out in that shed with you?' says Mrs Early, her voice shrill and undaunted. 'She's no better than she should be.'

'Just shut up! I'm not listening to this!'

'I know her type. She can see what a big fool you are. She'll get what she wants out of you, no trouble. I'm only trying to warn you, Matthew. Women like her eat big fools like you for dinner.'

'I'm not listening. I'm going back to my shed.'

Meg, listening, backs away from the door. She doesn't want to be alone with Matt. She doesn't want to be anywhere with Matt. His mother has seen what he doesn't see: she's no better than she should be. Women see that sort of thing. She saw it right away. She saw the signs all over her body, the body she had given so wantonly to Tom even though he cared nothing for her. She could smell her desperation.

Matt comes out, shaking with anger, and finds Meg in the back garden, shaking too, with the cold.

'I have to go,' she says quickly.

'No!'

It comes out like a cry of anguish.

'Thank you so much.'

She hurries into the kitchen. He comes after her.

'Let me give you something. A cup of tea.'

'No, really. I have to go now.'

She can think of no excuse, and sees she needs none. The look of agony on his face tells her he understands. She heard his mother's taunts.

'You mustn't pay any attention to her,' he says to her. 'She's not all there.'

But she's sharp enough to know trash when she sees it.

'It's not that,' says Meg.

Impossible to say what it is. Impossible to say, I'm dirty and you're clean.

'I can hear every word,' says Mrs Early from the lounge.

'You keep out of this,' says Matt.

'I have to go,' says Meg, moving towards the lounge.

Matt reaches out and seizes hold of her wrist. Meg stops still. For a moment, in silence, they stand looking at each other. Matt's face pleads with her, his pain unconcealed. But he can't speak, because his mother can hear every word. And anyway, what is there to say? So the moment passes and he releases his hold on her. He drops his head, looking down at the floor.

'Don't go,' he says.

'Sorry,' says Meg.

She goes through the lounge, not looking at Mrs Early, to the front door. She opens it herself.

'Can I call you?' he says.

'If you want,' she says.

She goes quickly down the path to the gate. She glances back at Matt and sees him standing there, half in, half out. He lifts one hand in a silent gesture of farewell. Meg goes out onto the street where her car is parked.

As she drives away she looks again and there he still is, frozen in the bright doorway, watching her go.

37

Above the line of the Downs, low in the sky, there rises an irregular band of night-dark cloud, like the battlements of a castle. Above this lies a narrow strip of empty sky, which is a pale and almost colourless blue. Higher still, dominating the landscape, an immense canopy of quilted cloud moves majestically westward, a rippled blanket of dove grey and slate grey and black.

Tom Redknapp, up before the rest of the family, sits alone at the kitchen table with a mug of coffee warming his hands and watches the pre-dawn sky. He has not turned on the lights in the kitchen. The giant sweep of clouds across the land suits his present fatalistic mood. He feels himself to be in the grip of events beyond his power to control. Somehow, without having ever intended to do harm, he has brought misery to the two women he most wants to please. And as a result he himself has lost everything. No doubt this is a right and proper punishment, but it still makes no sense to him. It feels more like a whim of the gods, not the stern Christian God so much as the cantankerous deities of Greek legend, who in the course of quarrelling among themselves wreak havoc on random human lives.

This makes him think of a summer long ago when the family went on holiday to Greece. The olive groves below Delphi, like a grey-green inland sea. The tumble-down columns of Olympia lying like park benches among the weeds. Most of all the heat. Belinda wore a wide-brimmed hat, the brim a fine lattice through which the sun cast a pattern of bright speckles on her sweet face. Not a ruins person, Belinda, but she bore it for his sake, knowing he had wanted to go for so long. Ancient history for him, a villa with a pool for her and the children, that was the deal. Though truth to tell he wasn't sorry himself when they came to rest on the island. He finds he's forgotten the name of the island, though he remembers the pool, with its view over the Aegean. And he remembers their bedroom.

It's all about trust in the end. Marriage too is a deal, you don't leave me and I won't leave you. It's the assurance you both need to dare to build a home together and to have children, because that home, those children, will be for ever after hostages. Lose them and lose all.

The colours are changing in the sky. The high heavy mass of cloud is now edged with pink, its ribs glowing pink, the shadows between them still a deep grey. The band of clear sky is widening and becoming more blue. A plane crosses, trailing a tail of vapour. The high cloud, the roof of the world, continues to deepen in colour as he watches, the pink darkening to rose. All this so slowly that no change is visible, nothing but the little plane moving, and yet the whole world is being reborn before his eyes.

Now a single cloud the shape of a French loaf sails across the blue band of sky.

Everything changes. All the time. I grow older. The children leave home. Nothing is for ever. A marriage grows, a marriage changes. Is that so terrible?

Don't take this away from me.

He means his home, his memories, their love, their history, everything they've built together. Isn't this little world of theirs in which they've invested so much, isn't it too substantial, too founded and rooted to be overthrown by so small a thing as a passing office affair?

Except it wasn't small, was it? Not so much a passing affair as an earthquake. A lifetime's longing made flesh. Desire in action.

Oh, Meg. I never meant to hurt you. You who've given me the most intense joy of my life.

Only sex, they say. Only sex. Jesus, if they only knew.

Santorini, that was the name of the island. The children still small enough then to be in bed before dinner, though you never quite knew when one of them would reappear saying they couldn't sleep. Usually they were well down by nine. The rooms had no air-conditioning, so they slept under a sheet. By the morning the sheets were kicked off and lay in a white tangle on the floor.

He remembers those warm nights. Belinda naked on the bed beside him in the moonlight.

Sunrise coming. The rim of cloud on the horizon now shining gold. The sky above deep blue. The high cloud roof turning a muddy mauve, its ribs and hollows gone. The French loaf stretching, fragmenting, forming a long broken stripe of cloud that catches the unseen sun and glows, dazzles.

There are forces at work in the world that are beyond my power to control. I can't soften Belinda's anger or heal her wounds. What's done is done. All I can do is tell her again the simple truth.

I still love you as much as ever.

Here comes the sun. The high canopy of cloud burns away. All colour drains from the sky. Only this blinding dominating light that floods the universe.

Dazzled, Tom turns his head away from the window and finds the kitchen raked with brilliance. His coffee mug throws a long sharp-edged shadow over the table. Wine glasses glitter on the sideboard. Hanging copper pans glow with fire. The far wall is luminous with sunshine: this winter dawn in Sussex as radiant as high noon over the Aegean.

Belinda comes down to breakfast fully dressed, and finds

Tom sitting in the kitchen in his bathrobe. They've hardly talked since the weekend. It's like they've come to this agreement to act as if nothing's happened. Tom's been doing long hours at work, she's hardly seen him. And what is there to say that hasn't already been said?

I could tell him about Kenny.

She almost laughs aloud. She spent all day yesterday not thinking about Kenny. The very thought of telling Tom makes her feel dizzy with shame.

Then there he is in his stripy bathrobe looking all lost and alone. It's quite touching in its way. Or it would be if he wasn't such a tosser.

'How long have you been down here?'

'I've been watching the sky,' he says. 'I saw the whole dawn.'

'Nice for you.' But that sounds mean. 'How was it?'

'I don't think I've ever watched all of a dawn before. It makes you feel, oh, you know. Close to eternity.'

She pads about the sun-filled kitchen putting on the kettle, getting out bread for toast, reaching down the honey. Close to eternity. That's not the way he talks usually. But once again she feels touched.

'Do you want some coffee?' She sees he has a mug. 'Some more coffee?'

'No,' he says. 'I should get dressed.'

But he doesn't move. He's watching her. It's like he's waiting for her to tell him about Kenny. Which is ridiculous because he knows nothing, and doesn't need to know.

'I did something so stupid,' she says.

I don't believe this. I'm going to tell him. Why am I doing this? This is not a good idea.

But on she goes, quite unable to stop herself.

'Did I ever tell you about Kenny?'

'Kenny who?'

'A boy I knew a million years ago. When I was seventeen. Anyway, we got back in touch the other day.'

She's watching herself, fascinated, horrified.

Just how much am I going to tell? I'm a runaway train. Hold on to your seat belts. Adopt the brace position.

'He asked me to meet up with him. At the Gatwick Hilton. So I did.'

'The Gatwick Hilton? That's a crap hotel.'

'Oh, Tom.'

She almost laughs. He's offended because she did it in a crap hotel.

'Anyway, there he was. Lying on the bed.'

'In the Gatwick Hilton? Why?'

Slow off the mark, Tom. But you'll get there.

'He thought it was a date.'

'When was this?'

'Tuesday.'

'Tuesday!'

She's watching his face. He's putting it together, working

415

out what it all means. Slide over the details, for Christ's sake. Don't say too much.

'How do you know he thought it was a date?'

Because of the details. One of them, at least.

'Remember I was just so pissed off with you. Which I still am. For being such a fucking fucker.'

'Yes.' He concedes the point. 'I've not forgotten.'

'So I go into the room, and there he is, lying on the bed.'

'In the Gatwick Hilton.'

She starts laughing, without knowing why. Except that it's hilarious. And horrible. Tom starts laughing too, and he certainly doesn't know why. He's laughing because she's laughing.

'He's lying on the bed,' he prompts.

'And he's naked.'

'Naked!'

'And he's got this great big hard-on.'

'This great big—!'

Tom explodes with laughter.

'He's naked and he's bald and I hardly even recognize him,' says Belinda, 'and he's lying there with his dick in the air on this bed in the Gatwick Hilton and he says, "Surprise, surprise!"'

She can't go on. She's laughing too much.

'He actually said that? "Surprise, surprise"?'

She nods, tears of laughter streaming down her cheeks.

'He called it Matey.'

'Matey? No! He couldn't have!'

'I swear to you. He'd taken some Viagra. He said, "Matey's good for hours."'

Tom rocks back and forth hugging his knees with laughter. They're laughing together like they laughed in the old days, and somehow everything feels right again. Except he doesn't know the rest of it.

'Oh, Tom,' she says. 'I'm such a fool.'

'So what happened?'

'I don't want to tell you. You'll divorce me.'

'Makes a change from you divorcing me.'

'It's a really tricky situation, you know? I mean, you don't want to be rude.' She laughs again, hearing herself. 'I mean, like, impolite.'

'What on earth had you said to him?'

'Oh, God, I don't know. I suppose I had flirted with him in our emails. I just wanted to get back at you for being—'

'A fucking fucker. Yes, I remember.'

'But I never said anything about sex. I mean, you don't, do you? You don't say in an email, Get ready so we can do it the minute I walk in the door.'

'Knickers off ready when I come home.'

'What?'

'It spells Norwich. You were supposed to put it on the back of the envelope when writing to your girlfriend.'

'Norwich?'

'Don't worry about it,' he says. 'Go on. What did you do?'

'It's all right for you,' she says. 'You're a man. You can always blame Matey. But if you're a woman you can go ahead even if you don't want to. It happens all the time, actually.'

He's looking at her with such a sweet smile.

'So you went ahead.'

'Oh, Tom.' She feels terrible. 'I couldn't work out how not to. It just seemed so – well, so impolite.'

'Come here.'

She comes to him. He takes her in his arms.

'You're a very generous lady. And always polite.'

She feels his arms round her, softly stroking her, and she bends down and gives him a little kiss. It's going to be all right after all. He doesn't mind. Actually, he's quite turned on.

'So you did it.'

'I'm sorry, Tom. I'm so sorry. I'm such a fool. It wasn't any fun at all. I just shut my eyes and let him get on with it.'

'Not even a tiny bit of fun?'

'Not really. He's such a jerk. The only good bit …'

She stops. Don't say it.

'What was the only good bit?'

This confessional urge, it's out of control. He's stroking her bum and she's telling him stuff he seriously doesn't need to know.

'Well, this great big hard-on. You know, it does a girl good to feel like she's wanted.'

'Yes. I can see that.'

'Though I suppose it was only the little blue pill.'

'No, it was you. You're gorgeous.'

'Don't you mind?'

'I'd mind if I thought you were going to go off with him.'

'Oh, Tom.'

She kisses him again, this time for longer. As their lips touch she feels such a surge of love for him that it makes her giddy. She slips her hand down inside his bathrobe.

'This doesn't make us quits,' she says.

'No.'

'You started it. And yours went on longer.'

'That's true.'

She has her hand on his cock. It's getting hard.

'So you're far worse than me. And you had more fun.'

'Yes.'

'But I'm not going to do any better, at my age. And I've got used to you. And I need a husband to pay the bills.'

Now his cock is really hard. She wants to fuck him there and then. How has this happened? There's something so familiar about his cock. It does a man good to feel like he's wanted.

Then comes the sound of sleepy footsteps down the stairs.

★

Chloe's not usually up early but she's hardly slept all night and she feels like hell. She's wearing what she calls her pyjamas but are actually a tiny pair of shorts and a T-shirt. As she comes into the kitchen it's so bright she has to shut her eyes.

Her mother comes over to her while she's standing there, blinking, wishing she'd had more sleep, and she gives her this great big hug. Chloe feels her warm arms round her and oh Christ she wants so much to be loved, so of course the next thing you know she's sobbing her heart out.

'Darling. Sweetheart. What is it?'

'Nothing. I'm fine. It's nothing.'

She cries and cries in her mother's arms.

'Boyfriend trouble?'

She nods.

'Which one this time? I can't keep up.'

'Just some man. Just another bloody man.'

'Oh, a man. I know about them.'

'Why does it have to be so hard, Mum?'

'I don't know, darling. It just is.'

Chloe wipes her eyes and blinks some more in the bright sunlight. What happened to winter? Her mother gets her some juice from the fridge. They all sit at the kitchen table just like a real family. Which maybe they are after all.

'Could be worse,' says her father. 'At least we're not dead.'

'I'd rather be dead,' says Chloe.

'Life isn't boring. Things keep on happening.'

'Too bloody much, thank you very much.'

Her mother starts laughing for no reason.

'What's the joke?'

'Us,' she says.

'I don't see what's so funny.'

'Oh, you know. The way we always want what we haven't got and don't want what we have got until it's taken away from us. You'd think we were still five years old.'

'That's what wanting something is,' says Chloe. 'If you've got it, how can you want it?'

'Ah,' says her father. 'That's the trick.'

'That's the tricky trick,' says her mother.

They both start to laugh. Chloe looks from one to the other, both laughing at nothing at all, and she feels like laughing herself. No reason. But it is a mess, isn't it? You only really ever love the one who doesn't love you back. Like, who arranged that?

Her father gets up.

'Better get dressed, I suppose,' he says.

He goes upstairs.

A moment or two later her mother gets up too.

'There's something I have to talk to Tom about,' she says.

She goes upstairs too.

Chloe's left alone in the sun-filled kitchen. She realizes she's hungry. The Weetabix is all finished which pisses her off until she remembers it was she who finished it. So she has Sugar Puffs, making a high hill in the bowl. She thinks of Guy saying, 'I don't do love.' She thinks of the key ring she got for him. She starts to cry again.

What are you supposed to do? You meet someone who makes you feel things you've never felt before and he tells you to fuck off but where do you go? It's like someone says, Hey, here's the promised land, take a peek, just enough to know where you're living is crap. Then they shut the door and you're on the outside.

Don't expect too much, they say. Don't ask for the moon. But what if the moon's the only thing you want? It's not like you can control what you want. You can't say, Oh, goody, I've got this spoon. I'll want this spoon. No, you want what you want.

So fuck him. He's gone. I'll find someone else. And when I've found him I'll make him love me so much he'll never leave me, but if he does I'll kill him.

Got that? And don't tell me you don't do love. You do love or I kill you. You, my future lover, who's going to make everything be all right.

Or my past lover. That happens too. You go chasing round picking up strangers, waiting for lightning to strike, and all the time your true lover is someone you've known for ever.

Maybe it's Hal. She thinks of him then, sitting cross-legged on the floor with his brooding eyes and his guitar, pinging away at the strings. He asked her to send him a picture of her and she never did.

She fetches her phone. She can't let him see her face all blotchy with crying so she pulls off her T-shirt and takes a picture of her tits in the dazzling morning sunshine. Then she sends it.

My little Christmas present, boyo. Just so you don't forget me.

38

It's Joe Nola who insists that they go to Anthony Armitage's show. 'Of course we're going,' he says. 'He came to mine.' Joe can't drive, so now Christina's being the car service down to Sussex. Which at least gives them some time together on their own.

Suppose you have a friend and you want him to be more than a friend. For example, you've been working together for weeks, now you're sparking off each other, you know what he's going to say before he says it. And suppose the more you know him the more you see that beneath the jokey mannerisms there's a grave and thoughtful dreamer, wiser than his years, quietly in search of a more meaningful life. Then what's not to love? And loving him, you watch his ever-mobile mouth and sometimes you fall into his serene gaze, still as well water, and you ache for his touch. You lie alone in bed at night speaking his name, 'Joe! Joe!', while your hands move over your own skin. Well, there comes a time when something has to give.

So it's ten in the morning and he climbs into your car folding his lean body like a poolside lounger and he's wearing a stupid beanie hat but on him it looks divine. Do you tell him now? Later? Never?

The girl is not supposed to propose, and what is this but a proposal? If you don't ask you don't get. Christina is worn out with anticipation. Two hours in a Fiat Bravo, a definition of intimacy if ever there was one. If not now, when?

Also, Joe has changed. He's become quieter. Christina knows that she has been the catalyst for this change. It was she who brought Anthony Armitage to Joe's show. It was the old man's visit which triggered Joe's act of artistic auto-destruction, with its ensuing explosion of publicity. The video of Joe smashing his installation has been posted on YouTube. Since then Joe has been in hiding.

'Do you realize you've had over ten thousand hits?' she says as they head south. 'You're up there with the shoe thrower.'

'Right,' he says. He's looking out of the car window. The new muted Joe.

'So isn't that great? Or isn't it?'

She wants to know how he feels about everything that's happened. She wants to know how he feels about her.

'Doesn't mean much,' he says.

'Only that now everyone's heard of you. Only that you'll be able to double your prices.'

'Right,' he says.

You'd think he'd be on top of the world, but he isn't. It's like he's decided to back off from his own life for a while. Christina isn't stupid. She can guess what's going on.

'Okay,' she says, 'so it's all a game. So it's all a stunt. Who cares? Art has to have visibility, right? All that's happened is you've gained some visibility. The work itself remains.'

'Tell you the truth,' he says, 'I'm tired of it all.'

'Of the stunt?'

'No. All of it.'

'Like, you're tired of life?'

He doesn't answer. They're working their way through stop-start traffic somewhere in south London, Streatham, Norbury. Traffic lights every few hundred yards. Let him pick the topic of conversation. In his own time.

'You know this film you're making?' he says.

'Yes.'

'You know what would make it radical?'

'What?'

'If it told the truth.'

'Which truth is that, Joe?'

'How everything I do is a waste of time. How I've wasted my talent, if I ever had any. How it's all a scam.'

'Is that what you think?'

'It's what I know.'

Christina's first thought is, What does this mean for my film? Does this sink the whole enterprise? Or does it make it a historic turning point in the public debate about contemporary art? Then she thinks, What does this mean for us? For the *us* that doesn't yet exist.

'This is because of Armitage, isn't it?'

'Not really. It's been there from the beginning.'

'Thinking it's all a scam?'

'The old bugger would never get a show at the Hayward. Is what I do better than what he does?'

'That's the way it goes, Joe.'

'Today it is. Once it was about the work. But we've lost that.'

'Now you're turning into Anthony Armitage.'

'Come on. You know it as well as I do. He's right. Of course he's right. The minute I saw him looking at my work, the minute I saw his face, I knew he was seeing what was really there. Did you hear what he said?'

Christina has heard it a hundred times, back and forth in the edit suite.

'"Loss." He said, "Loss."'

Joe laughs, but it's a laugh like he's hurting.

'Loss,' he says. 'Right. Loss. So I'm fucked. What do I do now?'

'Well,' says Christina, 'whatever it is, the world will be watching. You smashed up one kind of work. They'll want to know what's going to take its place.'

'Fucked if I know.'

'Plus I need an ending for my film.'

'You and your bloody film.'

'You and your bloody existential crisis.'

That makes him smile. They drive on. Then his thoughts find words again.

'Don't you ever feel that everything we do is parasitic? It's all so fucking referential and ironic. It only makes sense because way back people created real beautiful things. If Leonardo hadn't painted his *Last Supper* I could never have got away with that breakfast table.'

'So that makes me a parasite on parasites.'

'Yes, it does.'

'Thanks a lot.'

'Don't tell me you don't feel it too. We're all just pissing away whatever talent we might have on fairground rides.'

'Nothing wrong with fairground rides. They give pleasure to a lot of people.'

'Don't talk like that. You're better than that.'

'How do you know, Joe?'

'I've listened to you. I've watched you. You're good. You're worth more. You think your own thoughts. You're an original.'

Christina keeps her eyes on the road but this is good. This is the first time he's ever said anything serious about her.

'You too, Joe.'

'No. I've got nothing to show for it.'

'Yes, you have. When you took that hammer and started breaking up your own work you became an original work of art in action. You're living your art, Joe. Even here, talking to me about how it's all a scam. We use art to reach for kinds of truth, right? Isn't that what you're doing?'

'Truth. Oh, boy. Been a long time coming.'

But she can tell he's pleased by what she's saying. His tone isn't so bitter. So she thinks, what the hell. Now or never. What have I got to lose?

'Can we talk about something that isn't art?'

'Please. Anything.'

'What do you mean when you say I'm an original?'

He doesn't answer for a while. Then he says, 'You bought a hammer. Scary.'

'That doesn't sound good.'

'And you're funny.'

'Better.'

'And beautiful.'

'Really?'

'And you can drive.'

'I sound perfect. What's the snag?'

'There isn't a snag. Why does there have to be a snag?'

'Because if I'm so wonderful, why don't you fancy me?'

There. No more games. Jump right in. So much easier to have this sort of conversation when you're driving. Keep your eyes on the road.

'How do you know I don't?'

Not exactly an affirmation.

'I've fancied you from the start.' Make it sound like a girly crush. 'Why do you think I put up the idea of doing a film on you?'

'Okay-ay-ay.'

It's like he's testing the idea for strength, as if it might collapse under him.

'Don't worry, Joe. You sound so worried. You don't have to do anything about it.'

'No, it's not that. It's just that I'm not all that sure about myself. I mean, what if I'm gay?'

'Don't you know?'

'No, I don't. Everyone acts like it's either-or. You're gay or you're straight.'

'You can be bisexual. That's allowed.'

'Only in theory. In practice gay men hate bi's, and straight women think they can convert them. No one says, Fine, go and fuck that boy and then come back to me.'

'You have a point there.'

But the odd thing is she doesn't mind. She still wants him. More, if that's possible.

Maybe I think I can convert him.

No, it's not that. It's *liking* him. He's Joe, and if you go for him, you take what you get.

'Half a loaf is better than no bread,' she says.

That makes him laugh.

'A bi-loaf.'

'We could have fun together,' she says.

God bless the motor car. Only sitting side by side, locked in utter privacy but unable to look into each other's eyes, could she dare to talk to him this way.

'So,' she says, 'you're a scam artist and you're half gay and I still fancy you. It must be love.'

'Do you think so?'

'You have a vote too, Joe.'

'I'm just frightened of getting into something I'll want to get out of later. I'm frightened of having anyone rely on me. I'm unreliable.'

'You think I don't know that?'

'Shouldn't that be some kind of a warning sign?'

'Yes. Probably. These things aren't rational, you know? I mean, nothing lasts for ever. Living doesn't last for ever. What are we supposed to do? Not love anyone because they're mortal?'

'Well, you're right there,' he says.

'And anyway, what about those relationships that start out as lovers, then become friends who live together to the day they die? Like Vanessa Bell and Duncan Grant.'

'He was gay.'

'They were lovers. They had a child.'

He thinks about that.

431

'That's quite something,' he says. 'A love affair that outlasts the giving up on love.'

'But you have to start by being lovers.'

'Is that the rule?'

'Let's say it's the recognized procedure.'

They drive on in silence. Christina does nothing to break the silence. She's made her pitch. He buys it or he doesn't. But he has to be the next to speak.

Now they're turning off the Brighton road and heading for the Lewes bypass.

'I'm not feeling that great about myself right now,' he says.

So there it is. Christina feels her body stiffen, the way you do when you walk round the corner of a street into a cold wind. So it's not going to happen.

Why not, Joe? I'm good for you, I know it. What more do you want?

'Okay,' she says. Keep it neutral.

'I don't want to mess anyone about,' he says. 'I don't want to let anyone down.'

'How could you let me down?'

'You tell me.'

'You could die,' she says. 'That would let me down.'

'You're safe there, then. I'm not planning on dying any time soon.'

'So what are you planning?'

Give me a straight answer, Joe. I've offered myself to you on a fucking plate. Tick the box to show you've read and agreed the terms and conditions.

He looks at his watch.

'How much further?'

'Ten minutes.'

'Poor old sod. He'll be wetting himself. I hate to think of all those frauds and phonies chewing up his work. But I don't expect they'll bother to come.'

'Are these the same frauds and phonies who hail Joe Nola as one of the brightest talents on the art scene?'

'The very same.'

They're off the A27 now and driving through Edenfield.

'If ever I get married and have children,' says Christina, 'I'll buy a house here.'

'Why?'

'I don't know. I like the look of it.'

Their time of intimacy has come to an end for now. To be resumed on the drive back.

They lurch down the rutted coach road to America Cottage. The ancient Peugeot is pulled up on the stony ground by the garden wall. No other cars.

'That's his car,' says Christina. 'Looks like no one else has come.'

'We've come,' says Joe.

There's a sign by the gate with an arrow pointing to the barn. *To the show*.

Christina feels suddenly protective. In this mood Joe could do anything.

'If you hate it, you won't say so, will you?'

'He hated my show.'

'Even so.'

'Don't worry. I'm not going to smash it up. Look, no hammer.'

They follow the path round the side of the barn to its double doors. One of the doors stands half open. Joe pulls it open, scraping its bottom on the chalky earth.

Inside light falls through the single dusty window onto the board walls. Paintings hang all round, packed closely together, mostly portraits, some groups, some landscapes. In the middle of the earth-floored space stands a bulky armchair with its back to the door. The old man is sitting in the armchair, surrounded by his lifetime's work. By his side, on the ground, there is a bottle of whisky and a glass.

'Look at you,' says Joe affectionately. 'Pissed already, and the show hasn't even started.'

He goes round the armchair to confront the old man with his grinning face. Christina follows.

Anthony Armitage sits in his navy-blue overcoat slumped in the armchair with his eyes closed. One hand rests on his lap, holding an empty pill bottle.

'Oh, Jesus,' says Joe softly.

He takes the old man's wrist and feels for a pulse.

'He's cold. He must have been here all night.'

Christina is too shocked to speak.

'You should get your crew out here fast,' says Joe. 'This is a better show than anything I could ever put on.'

'Oh, Joe.'

'It's what the old bastard wanted.'

'Oh, Joe. It's horrible.'

'No, it isn't. It's magnificent.'

He starts circling the barn, gesturing at the paintings on the walls, moving fast, talking fast.

'These are good. These are the real thing. He knew that. You see what he's forced us to do? He's forced us to look at them. He's put on a show in the modern style. He's beaten us at our own game. It's fucking brilliant!'

His circle brings him back round to face the dead man in the armchair. He talks directly to him.

'Your work's good, you old sod! I've always known it was good. I was coming to tell you so. Here I am. I've come. So why the fuck didn't you wait for me?'

He's shouting now.

'Why didn't you wait for me?'

Christina has got her phone out.

'I'm calling the police.'

She goes out of the barn looking for a signal but can't find one. Her hands are shaking.

Am I responsible for this?

She goes back into the barn.

'Come on, Joe. We have to report this.'

'Does that phone of yours take pictures?'

'Yes.'

'Take pictures, then. Take lots. Before they come and mess it up. This is his show. Record it.'

'With him in the middle?'

'Yes. That's why he did it. Everyone has to see.'

So Christina takes pictures on her phone of the barn and the paintings on the walls and the old man dead in the middle of it all. Then they get back into her car and drive away.

They don't talk as they drive. Christina knows the moment has passed. Whatever there might have been between Joe and herself died with the old man. Hard to say exactly why.

In the end it was you who died on me, wasn't it, Joe? You let me down the only way I can't overcome.

I tried. What more can you do?

Meet someone new. Start again. Christ, it's so fucking tiring.

In Edenfield she pulls up by the village shop and tries her phone again. This time she has a signal. She calls the police and reports the death. She doesn't tell them about the pictures on her phone.

The police ask her to wait so they can take a statement. They'll be with her as soon as they can.

'I know someone here,' she says to Joe. 'My old boss.'

39

The decoration of the Christmas tree is a family ritual. The decorations themselves live in a motley assortment of cardboard boxes, the more fragile ones cushioned in tissue paper. The boxes come up from the dust and cobwebs of the cellar, another year gone by already. Laura finds herself thinking, How many more Christmases will we have together? The children growing up now.

Out come silver balls, feathered birds, painted tin figurines, glass pendants, papier mâché eggs, china baubles. Each one brings with it a memory, preserved as it were also in the tissue paper, of the time and the place where it was bought. The little blue-and-white china spheres from Amsterdam, the ruby-red teardrops from Venice. Laura and Carrie take the decorations out and lay them carefully on the living room table. Meanwhile Henry, as is traditional, unpacks and untangles the rope of Christmas tree lights. Jack is in charge of the tinsel.

437

The ritual calls for the tree to be dressed in a preordained sequence, to the sound of Ella Fitzgerald singing her Swinging Christmas songs. The Christmas tree lights go on first. Henry tests them.

'My God, they're actually working!'

Standing on a chair, he winds the dark green flex round and round the tree, while the others tug the little lights here and there to make sure they're evenly distributed.

'Off you go, Jack.'

Next comes the tinsel. Ella Fitzgerald sings 'Jingle Bells', and they all jig gently to the beat.

'Oh, there's the bird's nest,' cries Carrie, holding out the little basket of twigs with its tiny silver eggs. 'I love the bird's nest.'

Laura has found the cookie-dough man which Carrie made when she was seven.

'Here's Horace. I think he'll last another year.'

Henry stands back, frowning, checking the symmetry of the tree so far.

'Too much gold tinsel on the right, surely, Jack?'

'Where's the angel?' says Laura. 'We have to make sure she can fit on the top.'

'He,' says Henry. 'Or possibly it.'

Now it's time to hang the baubles. This job is reserved for Laura and Carrie. Carrie begins with the parrot and the carrot, two brightly-coloured pendants made of punched tin, which always hang near each other because they rhyme. Laura begins with the waxy artificial fruit.

Henry meanwhile sets to work on the overhead paper chains. Every year these fragile Chinese decorations threaten to disintegrate, and every year, with patience and Sellotape, they are nursed back into duty.

Ella Fitzgerald is singing 'Santa Claus is Coming to Town'.

'Look, Carrie,' says Jack. 'Your sequin ball. I remember you making that.'

'You're going to have to cut the top branch,' says Laura. 'The angel won't fit.'

The silver balls are going on now, the most common of all the decorations, but the most effective. The fine threads that hold the necks of the glass spheres are easily broken, and have to be slipped over the prickly branches with delicate care.

Henry gets the fold-out steps and the secateurs and climbs up to trim the topmost sprig.

Laura, watching, the angel in her hand, sees Jack and Carrie cooperating without argument, and wonders what has happened to improve their mood. Perhaps it's just the approach of Christmas.

Henry returns to his paper chains. Season after season the cords that hold them up become hopelessly knotted and have to be teased out. Henry regards this as a challenge, and is patient and determined. Today is the first day of his Christmas break, he's happy to be out of the frustrations and compromises of the cutting room for two weeks. He looks up and sees Laura watching him and smiles.

'What's the news on the Roddy crisis?' he says.

'Oh, Diana's sorted all that out. She says it came to her in a flash. What Roddy needed was a shed.'

Henry bursts out laughing.

'A shed! Brilliant!'

'Diana says it's all about men and sheds. Men have to have sheds where they go to play with their hobby. So Roddy's being given a shed at the bottom of the garden where he can go and look for God.'

'An actual shed?'

'Yes. You buy them ready-made, windows, doors, lights, everything. Diana says Roddy's thrilled to bits.'

The phone rings. Henry goes into the kitchen to get away from Ella Fitzgerald. Laura can hear exclamations of surprise, but not the words.

'Have yourself a merry little Christmas,' they all sing along.

Henry returns looking grave.

'Something rather extraordinary,' he says. 'Do you remember a researcher called Christina who worked for me once?'

'Not really. There've been so many.'

'She's in the village. She's been to see that artist who painted Carrie.'

'My old man?' says Carrie. 'The one in my house?'

'Yes,' says Henry. 'Bad news, sweetheart.'

Carrie puts down the glass bauble she's holding and looks at her father with an unblinking gaze.

'He's dead, isn't he?'

'Yes. It looks like he's taken an overdose. I'm sorry.'

Carrie says nothing. The Christmas music fills the silence.

'Christina's coming over here,' says Henry. 'She's the one who found him. She has to wait for the police.'

Selfishly, Laura feels annoyed. She doesn't want anyone coming over right now. This is their special family time.

Jack says to Carrie, 'How did you know?'

'I don't know,' says Carrie. 'I just did.'

She goes out into the hall.

'I don't understand what all this has to do with your researcher,' says Laura.

'She makes art films these days. She was visiting him. Look, I'm sorry, darling. I felt I had to offer.'

'Yes. Of course you did.'

She looks through the open doorway into the hall. Carrie's painting stands there, propped up on the hall table. Carrie is gazing at it.

Laura goes out and puts her arms round Carrie's thin body.

'I'm so sorry, darling.'

'He was brilliant, Mum. He was a genius.'

'I wish I liked his picture of you more.'

'That's because you're not looking at it properly.'

'Yes, I expect it is.'

The doorbell rings. Laura opens the door. There on the step is the director from the Hayward.

'It's you!' says Laura.

'The golliwog lady!' says Christina.

They both start to laugh.

Behind Christina is a slender boyish man in a wool hat. He's gazing past her, into the house, at the portrait of Carrie.

'Come in, come in,' says Laura. 'What a terrible business. We shouldn't be laughing.'

The music stops playing in the living room. Henry joins them in the hall.

'Christina,' he says. 'Small world.'

'Hello, Henry.'

She introduces her companion.

'This is Joe Nola. He's an artist. I'm making a film about him.'

The artist is standing in front of Carrie's portrait, transfixed.

'Jesus, Mary and Joseph,' he says. 'That is the real thing.'

'See,' says Carrie to her mother.

'He should have this one in his show,' says Joe. 'He never did anything better.'

'Did he have his show?' says Carrie.

'Oh, yes,' says Joe. 'He had his show all right.'

'Did the people come he wanted to come?'

'They came.'

'It wasn't because nobody liked his paintings,' Carrie says, meaning his death. 'He just hated getting old.'

'Is that a fact?' says Joe.

'He told me so.'

They all go into the kitchen and Laura puts on a kettle so they can have coffee while Christina and Joe wait for the police. Henry tells Laura that Christina has become a star television director.

'And to think I had her running round libraries for me.'

'Henry was wonderful,' says Christina. 'He was my first boss. It was him who showed me you could work in television and still take your subject seriously.'

'So what's happened to you since?' says Henry. 'You're too young to be married yet.'

'Not too young,' says Christina. 'Not married.'

'What's this about golliwogs?' says Joe.

Christina explains. Joe is charmed.

'That's exactly what I did it for,' he says. 'People are supposed to come along and add their memories.'

'Except now you've smashed it,' says Christina.

'So I have,' says Joe.

Jack says, 'I saw the old man smashing things in his garden.'

'Ah, well, then,' says Joe. 'He was way ahead of me.'

'What did he look like?' says Carrie. She means what did he look like dead.

'Like himself,' says Joe. 'Only, like he'd left.'

Laura thinks of Roddy saying, 'I've left.' Keep thyself as a stranger and a pilgrim upon the earth. And now he's sitting in a shed at the bottom of the garden looking for God.

'I want to go and see him,' says Carrie.

'No, darling,' says Henry.

'Why not? I won't touch anything.'

'No. Leave it to the police.'

'What's it got to do with the police?' For the first time since she heard the news Carrie has tears in her eyes. 'The police don't care. I was probably the last person he talked to. I don't suppose I mattered very much to him, but he mattered to me.'

'You mattered all right,' says Joe. 'The way he painted you.'

'Well, then,' says Carrie. She holds up her head high and proud.

'Tell you what,' says Joe. 'We can show you pictures of him. Christina recorded it all on her phone.'

Henry frowns, but Laura says, 'Why not? She's not a child any more.'

So Christina gets out her phone and shows them the pictures of the old man in his armchair with his paintings on the walls all round him. Carrie looks and looks.

'He looks happy enough, doesn't he?' says Joe.

'No,' says Carrie. 'He wasn't happy.'

Again, Laura remembers Roddy.

'Being happy isn't what matters most,' she says.

Carrie looks up at her mother in surprise.

'Right, Mum,' she says.

'I have to go out soon,' says Jack. 'Can we finish the tree?'

So they put the music on again and Joe and Christina help with hanging the remaining decorations. Ella Fitzgerald sings 'Rudolph the Red-Nosed Reindeer' and 'Frosty the Snowman' and 'White Christmas'.

'I suppose what with global warming and so on,' says Henry, 'we'll never have a white Christmas again.'

40

It's Jack's idea. Alice doesn't question it.

'Come and look at the sea.'

He hardly knows himself why he wants to do this in such a cold season, but it comes upon him as a plain need. He wants to be somewhere wide and empty and bleak, somewhere stripped of all pretension, somewhere elemental. He thinks at first he wants to be there alone, but then he thinks he'd like to be there with Alice.

'Come where?' says Alice on the phone.

'Seaford,' he says. 'Seaford beach.'

Not the picturesque meanders of Cuckmere Haven, nor the grand drum-roll of the Seven Sisters, but unlovely little-visited Seaford. Out of season in a seaside town that is forever out of season.

'It's special,' he says. 'You'll see.'

He drives her there in the early afternoon and they park close to the Martello tower and walk together along the concrete broadwalk between the road and the beach. A blustery wind blows clouds across a grey sky and makes their eyes water. Gulls wheel and bank overhead, screaming their harsh screams. There are others out on the beach, lone figures walking their dogs, but few and far apart. Behind them the high cliff of Seaford Head. Before them, far off, the dark line of Newhaven pier reaching into the sea.

They walk briskly, their coats wrapped tight, scarves muffling their necks to the chins. Jack says they must walk the length of the crescent beach without talking, so they can empty out. Alice obeys as if this is a religious requirement, at first amused, but after a while she feels herself emptying out. Because of the cold wind and the wide space and the not talking.

Then they come to a stop, and turn about.

'We can talk now,' Jack says.

'What are we to talk about?' says Alice.

This is Jack's game and only he knows the rules.

'Real things,' says Jack. 'Not fluff.'

'I've got no fluff left,' says Alice. 'It's all blown away.'

As they walk back, warmer now, moving more slowly, they look out over the immense sweep of beach, over the unbounded grey sea, to the racing sky. Here and there through breaks in the cloud shafts of cool white sunlight pour down onto the water.

'That's the light of heaven,' says Jack. 'When we came here when we were little the sky often did that. My dad said, "Look, there's the light of heaven shining down on earth."'

'Why did you come here?'

'My father loved Seaford. He said somebody had to. So I started loving it. And now I think it's beautiful.'

Alice is pleased.

'I said that.'

'I remember.'

They go onto the pebbles, crunching down the slopes and terraces of the beach to where the waves come hissing in to shore. Here they stand still for a while, feeling the world roll beneath their feet. Alice feels giddy and takes Jack's arm. Her arm lightly looped through his, they walk on over the shiny sea-washed pebbles, over the many colours, grey and cream, amber and ochre, blue and indigo and black. The pebbles give beneath their tread, making the walking strenuous. Jack feels Alice's wind-blown hair flick against his cheek.

There are two ships on the horizon, long low shapes against the white sky.

'Why is it that ships are always on the horizon?' Jack says. 'Why aren't they ever between the horizon and the shore?'

'I expect they are.'

'No. Look.'

She looks and it's true. They find a third, smaller, ship, also on the horizon.

'Horizons are odd,' says Alice. 'They're an end that isn't really an end at all. You never get to the horizon.'

'I don't want to get to the horizon. I don't want it to be any kind of an end. I want it to be infinity.'

'It is infinity.'

'Does that make you feel small?'

'Maybe. But I like to feel part of something much bigger than myself.'

'That's exactly how I feel,' says Jack. 'Exactly.'

'This is somewhere to come when you're feeling down, isn't it?' Alice says.

'Definitely.'

'No pushy happiness to make you feel worse.'

They crunch back up the beach, skidding down a little with each upwards step. There are benches all along the concrete broadwalk, each one donated in memory of someone or other. They sit down on a bench dedicated to the memory of Walter Clapham, 1916–2005, Writer and Bomber Command Veteran. Now they are no longer in motion the wind feels colder. They press against each other.

'No pushy happiness,' says Jack. 'That's good. I like it that you get it.'

'Takes two,' she says.

He glances at her. He sees her pale cheeks, the bold line of her nose. Dark hair blowing across white skin. Asking nothing, claiming nothing.

She's beautiful in her own way. He sees it now. Maybe everyone's beautiful if you can only find their beauty.

She looks back at him, grey eyes saying, So here we are.

'So here we are,' he says.

She leans in closer to him and he puts his arm round her. Now they're both looking out to sea. Out at the light of heaven shining down on earth.

'Jack,' she says. 'Tell me to be careful.'

'Be careful, Alice.'

He holds her tight, following the flight of the gulls.

'So what changed?' she says.

'I don't know,' he says.

'It was Cas running away to London. That's what I think.'

'And you saying Haywards Heath, and crying in my arms.'

'Was it?' Her eyes bright with happiness. 'Was it Haywards Heath? That is so stupid.'

'It's not like we don't know each other,' he says. 'I feel like I've known you for ever.'

'Since we were four.'

They sit contentedly side by side, there on the Bomber Command Veteran's bench, huddled close together, watching the immense sky.

'I'm glad we came here,' says Alice.

'You don't think it's too bleak?'

'I like it being bleak. It leaves room for us.'

This is exactly what Jack thinks.

'You say the things I think, only better.'

450

'So now I'll always love Seaford too, like your dad. Even though it's so unromantic. We should be sitting under swaying palms on a tropical island. Or in a café in Paris.'

'We can do that too.'

'But let's always come back to Seaford.'

So this is how it begins, thinks Jack. Out there over the sea is infinity. There doesn't have to be an end. What's begun can go on for ever.

She turns her face to smile at him and he's looking at her. He kisses her lightly on her cold cheek. She moves her face against his and kisses his mouth. They kiss until their lips are warm.

Neither of them has used the word love. Too soon for that. Still shy in each other's company. But he's saying it to himself, practising for when he says it aloud.

I could love you, Alice.

And she's saying it to herself, being careful, because it's only just beginning.

I could love you, Jack.

'But let's always come back to Scotland.'

Author's Note

All the Hopeful Lovers picks up some of the characters of my earlier novel, *The Secret Intensity of Everyday Life*, which was set in 2000, eight years earlier. Like the first novel, the action unfolds in real time, in real places; though the village of Edenfield is invented. For those who are interested to track the geography of my world, Edenfield is just east of Lewes on the A27, in the position occupied in reality by the hamlet of Beddingham.

All the characters are fictional, with one exception: Victor Elsey, the proprietor of the café on Lewes station, has kindly given me permission to feature him in a walk-on part. For the painter Anthony Armitage I have borrowed a little from the career of the late Michael Reynolds. For the details of plastic surgery I am indebted to Nick Parkhouse FRCS, who gave me generous amounts of his time, access to his clinic, and the benefits of his insights into his profession.